Michelle Major grew up in Ohio but dreamed of living
in the mountains. Soon after graduating with a degree
in journalism, she pointed her car west and settled in
Colorado. Her life and house are filled with one great
husband, two beautiful kids, a few furry pets and several
well-behaved reptiles. She's grateful to have found her
passion writing stories with happy endings. Michelle
loves to hear from her readers at michellemajor.com.

Discover more at millsandboon.co.uk

CONVENIENTLY WED TO THE PRINCE

NINA MILNE

FALLING FOR THE WRONG BROTHER

MICHELLE MAJOR

FSC
www.fsc.org

FSC C007454

This book is produced from independently certified FSC
paper to ensure responsible forest management.

For more information visit: www.harpercollins.co.uk/green

Printed and bound in Spain
by CPI, Barcelona

MILLS & BOON

First Published in Great Britain 2018
by Mills & Boon, an imprint of HarperCollinsPublishers,
1 London Bridge Street, London, SE1 9GF

Conveniently Wed to the Prince © 2018 Nina Milne
Falling for the Wrong Brother © 2018 Michelle Major

ISBN: 978-0-263-26526-2

0918

MIX
Paper from
responsible sources

CONVENIENTLY WED TO THE PRINCE

NINA MILNE

This book is for my lovely parents,
who made my childhood a happy place.

Thank you!

PROLOGUE

Eighteen months ago, Il Boschetto di Sole—a lemon grove situated in the mountains of Lycander

HOLLY ROMANO STARED at her reflection. The dress was ivory perfection, a bridal confection of froth and lace, beauty and elegance, and she loved it. Happiness bubbled inside her— this was the fairy tale she'd dreamed of, the happy-ever-after she'd vowed would be hers. She and Graham were about to embark on a marriage as unlike her parents' as possible—a partnership of mutual love.

Not for Holly the bitterness and constant recrimination— a union based on the drear of duty on her father's part and the daily misery of unrequited love on her mother's. Their marriage had eventually shattered, and in the final confetti shards of acrimony her mother had walked away and never come back. Leaving eight-year-old Holly behind without so much as a backward glance.

Holly pushed the images from her mind—she only wanted happy thoughts today, so she reminded herself of her father's love. A love she valued with all her heart be- cause, although he never spoke of it, she knew of his dis- appointment that Holly had not been the longed-for son. And yet he had never shown her anything but love. Unlike her mother, who had never got over the bitter let-down of her daughter's gender and had never shown Holly even an iota of affection, let alone love.

Enough. Happy thoughts, remember?

Such as her additional joy that her father wholeheartedly approved of his soon-to-be son-in-law. Graham Salani was the perfect addition to the Romano family—a man who worked the land and would be an asset to Il Boschetto di Sole, the lemon grove the Romano family had worked on for generations. For over a century the job of overseer had passed from father to son, until Holly had broken the chain. But now Graham would be the son her father had always wanted.

It was all perfect.

Holly smiled at her reflection and half turned as the door opened and her best friend Rosa came in. It took her a second to register that Rosa wasn't in her bridesmaid dress—which didn't make sense as the horse-drawn carriage was at the door, ready to convey them to the chapel.

'Rosa…?'

'Holly, I'm sorry. I can't go through with this. You need to know.' Rosa's face held compassion as she stepped forward.

'I don't understand.'

She didn't want to understand as impending knowledge threatened to make her implode. Suddenly the dress felt weighted, each pearl bead filled with lead, and the smile on her face froze into a rictus.

'What do I need to know?'

'Graham is having an affair.' Rosa stepped towards her, hand outstretched. 'He has been for the past year.'

'That's not true.'

It couldn't be. But why would Rosa lie? She was Graham's sister—Holly's best friend.

'Ask your father.'

The door opened and Thomas Romano entered. Holly forced herself to meet her father's eyes, saw the truth there and felt pain lance her.

'Holly, it is true. I am sorry.'

'Are you sure?'

'Yes. I have spoken with Graham myself. He claims it meant nothing, that he still loves you, still wants you to marry him.'

Holly tried to think, tried to cling to the crumbling, fading fairy tale.

'I can't do that.'

How could she possibly marry a man who had cheated on her? When she had spent years watching the ruins of a marriage brought down by infidelity? In thought and intent if not in deed. Holly closed her eyes. She had been such a fool—she hadn't had an inkling, not a clue. Humiliation flushed her skin, seeped into her very soul.

Her father stepped towards her, placed an arm around her. 'I am so sorry.'

She could hear the pain in his voice, the guilt.

'I had no idea.'

'I know you didn't.'

Graham didn't love her. The bleak thought spread through her system and she closed her eyes, braced herself. An image of the chapel, the carefully chosen flowers, the rows of people, family and friends happy in anticipation, flashed across her mind.

'We need to cancel the wedding.'

CHAPTER ONE

Present day, Notting Hill, London

STEFAN PETRELLI, EXILED Prince of Lycander, pushed his half-eaten breakfast across the cherrywood table in an abrupt movement.

It was a lesson to him not to open his post whilst eating—though, to be fair, he could hardly have anticipated *this* letter. Sprinkled with legalese, it summoned him to a meeting at the London law offices of Simpson, Wright and Gallagher for the reading of a will.

The will of Roberto Bianchi, Count of Lycander.

Lycander—the place of Stefan's birth, the backdrop of a childhood he'd rather forget. The place he'd consigned to oblivion when he'd left aged eighteen, with his father's curses echoing in his ears.

'If you leave Lycander you will not be coming back. I will take all your lands, your assets and privileges, and you will be an outcast.'

Just the mention of Lycander was sufficient to chase away his appetite and bring a scowl to his face—a grimace that deepened as he stared down at the document. The temptation to crumple it up and lob it into the recycling bin was childish at best, and at twenty-six he had thankfully long since left the horror of childhood behind.

What on earth could Roberto Bianchi have left him? And why? The Count had been his mother Eloise's godfather and guardian—the man who had allowed his ward to marry Stefan's father, Alphonse, for the status and privileges the marriage would bring.

What a disaster *that* had been. The union had been beyond miserable, and the ensuing divorce a medley of bitterness and humiliation with Stefan a hapless pawn. Alphonse might have been ruler of Lycander, but he had also been a first class, bona fide bastard, who had ground Eloise into the dust.

Enough. The memories of his childhood—the pain and misery of his father's *Toughen Stefan up and Make him a Prince* Regime, the enduring ache of missing his mother, whom he had only been allowed to see on infrequent occasions, his guilt at the growing realisation that his mother's plight was due to her love for *him* and the culminating pain of his mother's exile—could not be changed.

Alphonse was dead—had been for three years—and Eloise had died long before that, in dismal poverty. Stefan would never forgive himself for her death, and now Stefan's half-brother, Crown Prince Frederick, ruled Lycander.

Frederick. For a moment he dwelled on his older sibling. Alphonse had delighted in pitting his sons against each other, and as result there was little love lost between the brothers.

True, since he'd come to the throne Frederick had reached out to him—even offered to reinstate the lands, assets and rights Alphonse had stripped from him—but Stefan had refused. *Forget it. No way.* Stefan would never be beholden to a ruler of Lycander again and he would not return on his brother's sufferance.

He'd built his own life—left Lycander with an utter determination to succeed, to show his father, show Lycander, show the *world* what Stefan Petrelli was made of. Now he was worth millions. He had built up a global property and construction firm. Technically, he could afford to buy up most of Lycander. In reality, though, he couldn't purchase so much as an acre—his father had passed a decree that banned Stefan from buying land or property there.

Stefan shook his head to dislodge the bitter memories—that way lay nothing but misery. His life was good, and he'd long ago accepted that Lycander was closed to him, so there was no reason to get worked up over this letter. He'd go and see what bequest had been left to him and he'd donate it to his charitable foundation. *End of.*

Yet foreboding persisted in prickling his nerve-endings as instinct told him that it wouldn't be that easy.

Holly Romano tucked a tendril of blonde hair behind her ear and stared at the impressive exterior of the offices that housed Simpson, Wright and Gallagher, a firm of lawyers renowned for their circumspection, discretion and the size of the fees they charged their often celebrity clientele.

Last chance to bottle it, and her feet threatened to swivel her around and head her straight back to the tube station.

No. There was nothing to be afraid of. Roberto Bianchi had owned Il Boschetto di Sole. The Romano family had been employed by the Bianchis for generations and therefore Roberto had decided to leave Holly something. Hence the letter that had summoned her here to be told details of the bequest.

But it didn't make sense. Roberto Bianchi had been only a shadowy figure in Holly's life. In childhood he had seemed all-powerful as the owner of the place her family lived in and loved—a man known to be old-fashioned in his values, strict but fair, and a great believer in tradition. Owner of many vast lands and estates in Lycander, he had

had a soft spot for Il Boschetto di Sole—the crown jewel of his possessions.

As an employer he had been hands-off,. He had trusted her father completely. And although he'd shown a polite interest in Holly he had never singled her out in any way. Plus she'd had no contact with him in the past eighteen months, since her decision to leave Lycander for a while.

The aftermath of her wedding fiasco had been too much—the humiliation, the looks of either pity or censure, and the nagging knowledge that her father was disappointed. Not because he questioned her decision to cancel the wedding, but because it was his dream to see her happily married, to have the prospect of grandsons and the knowledge Romano traditions and legacies were secured.

There had also been her need to escape Graham. At first he had been contrite, in pursuit of reconciliation, but when she had declined to marry him his justifications had become cruel. Because he had never loved her. And eventually, at their last meeting, he had admitted it.

'I wooed you because I wanted promotion—wanted an in on the Romanos' wealth and position. I never loved you. You are so young, so inexperienced. And Bianca... she is all-woman.'

That had been the cruellest cut of all. Because somehow, especially when she had seen Bianca, a tiny bit of Holly hadn't blamed him. Bianca was not just beautiful, she seemed to radiate desirability, and seeing her had made Holly look back on her nights with Graham and cringe.

Even now, eighteen months later, standing on a London street with the autumn breeze blowing her hair any which way, a flush of humiliation threatened as she recalled what a fool she had made of herself with her expressions of love and devotion, her inept fumbling. And the whole time Graham would have been comparing her to Bianca, laughing his cotton socks off.

Come on, Holly. Focus on the here and now.

And right now she needed to walk through the revolving glass door.

Three minutes later she followed the receptionist into the office of Mr James Simpson. It was akin to stepping into the past. The atmosphere was nigh on Victorian. Heavy tomes lined three of the panelled walls, and a portrait hung above the huge mahogany desk of a jowly, bearded, whiskered man from a bygone era. And yet she noticed that atop the desk there was a sleek state-of-the-art computer that indicated the law firm had at least one foot firmly in the current century.

A pinstripe-suited man rose to greet her: thin, balding, with bright blue eyes that shone with innate shrewd intelligence.

Holly moved forward with a smile, and as she did so her attention snagged on the other occupant of the room—a man who stood by the window, fingers drumming his thigh in a staccato burst that exuded an edge of impatience.

He was not conventionally handsome, in the drop-dead gorgeous sense, although there was certainly nothing wrong with his looks. A shade under six feet tall, he had dark unruly hair with a hint of curl, a lean face, a nose that jutted with intent and intense dark grey eyes under strong brows that pulled together in a frown.

Unlike Holly, he hadn't deemed the occasion worthy of formal wear and was dressed in faded jeans and a thick blue and green checked shirt over a white T-shirt. His build was lean and lithe, and whilst he wasn't built like a power house he emitted strength, and an impression that he propelled his way through life fuelled by sheer force of personality.

The man behind the desk cleared his throat and heat tinged her cheeks as she realised she had stopped dead in her tracks to gawp. She further realised that the object of her gawping looked somewhat exasperated. An expression that morphed into something else as he returned her gaze, studied her face with a dawning of... Of what? Awareness? Arrest? Whatever it was, it sent a funny little fizz through her veins. Then his scowl deepened further, and quickly she turned away and resumed her progress towards the desk.

'Mr Simpson? I'm Holly Romano. Apologies for being a little late.' No need to explain the reason had been a sheer blue funk.

The lawyer looked at his watch, a courteous smile on his thin lips. 'Not a problem. I'm sure His Highness will agree.'

His Highness?

As her brain joined the dots and his identity dawned on her 'His Highness'—contrary to all probability—managed to look even grumpier as he pushed away from the wall.

'I don't use the title. Stefan is fine—or if you prefer to maintain formality go with Mr Petrelli.' A definitive edge tinged his tone and indicated that Stefan Petrelli felt strongly on the matter.

Stefan Petrelli. A wave of sheer animosity surprised her with its intensity as she surveyed the son of Eloise, onetime Crown Princess of Lycander. The very same Eloise whom her father had once loved, with a love that had infused her parents' marriage with bitterness and doomed it to joylessness.

As a child Holly had heard the name Eloise flung at her father in hatred time after time, until Eloise had haunted her dreams as the wicked witch of the Romano household, her shadowy ghostly presence a third person in her parents' marriage.

Of course she knew that this was not the fault of Stefan Petrelli, and furthermore Eloise was no longer a threat. The former Princess had died years before. Yet as she looked at him an instinctive visceral hostility still sparked. Her mother's words, screamed at her father, were still fresh in her head as they echoed down the tunnel of memories.

'Your precious Eloise with her son—something else she could have given you that I can't. That is what you want more than anything—a Stefan of your own.'

Those words had imbued her three-year-old self with an irrational jealousy of a boy she'd never met. Holly had wanted to be a boy so much she had ached with it. She had known how much both her parents had prayed for a boy, how bitterly disappointed they had been with a girl.

Her mother had never got over it, never forgiven her for her gender, and that knowledge was a bleak one that right now, rationally or not, added to the linger of a stupid jealousy of this man. It prompted her to duck down in a curtsey that she hoped conveyed irony. 'Your Highness,' she said, with deliberate emphasis.

His eyebrows rose and his eyes narrowed. 'Ms Romano,' he returned.

His deep voice ran over her skin, and before she could prevent it his hand had clasped hers to pull her up.

'You must have missed what I told Mr Simpson. I prefer not to use my title.'

Holly would have loved to have thought of a witty retort, but unfortunately her brain seemed unable to put together even a single syllable. Because her central nervous system seemed to have short-circuited as a result of his touch. Which was, of course, insane. Even with Graham this hadn't happened, so until now she would have pooh-

poohed the idea of sparks and electric shocks as ridiculous figments of an overwrought imagination.

And yet the best her vocal cords could eventually manage was, 'Okey-dokey.'

Okey-dokey? For real, Holly?

With an immense effort she tugged her hand free and hauled herself together. 'Right. Um… Now introductions are over perhaps we could…?'

'Get down to business,' James Simpson interpolated. 'Of course. Please have a seat, both of you.'

In truth it was a relief to sink onto the surprisingly comfortable straight-backed chair. *Focus.*

James Simpson cleared his throat. 'Thank you for coming. Count Roberto wrote his will with both of you in mind. As you may or may not know, the bulk of his vast estate has gone to a distant Bianchi cousin, who will also inherit the title. However, I wish to speak to you about Count Bianchi's wishes with regards to Il Boschetto di Sole—the lemon grove he loved so much and where he spent a lot of the later years of his life. Holly's family, the Romanos, have lived on the grove for many generations, working the land. And Crown Princess Eloise spent many happy times there before her marriage.'

Next to her Holly felt Stefan's body tense, almost as if that fact was news to him. She leant forward, her mind racing with curiosity.

James steepled his fingers together. 'In a nutshell, the terms of Roberto's will state that Il Boschetto di Sole will go to either one of you, dependent on which of you marries first and remains married for a year.'

Say what?

Holly blinked as her brain attempted to decode the words. Even as blind primitive instinct kicked in an image of the beauty of the land, the touch of the soil, the scent of lemons pervaded her brain. The Romanos had given heart and soul, blood and sweat to the land for generations. Stefan Petrelli had turned his back on Lycander. And yet if he married the grove would go to *him*, to Eloise's son. *No.*

Before she could speak, the dry voice of the lawyer continued.

'If neither of you has succeeded in meeting the criteria of the will in three years from this date Il Boschetto di Sole will go to the Crown—to Crown Prince Frederick of Lycander or whoever is then ruler.'

There was a silence, broken eventually by Stefan Petrelli. 'That is a somewhat unusual provision.'

Was that all he could say? '"Unusual"?' Holly echoed. 'It's *ridiculous*!'

The lawyer looked unmoved by her comment. 'The Count has left you each a letter, wherein I assume he explains his decision. Can I suggest a short break? Mr Petrelli, if you'd care to read your letter in the annexe room to your left. Ms Romano, you can remain here.'

Reaching into his desk drawer, he pulled out two envelopes sealed with the Bianchi crest.

Stefan accepted his document and strode towards the door indicated by the lawyer. James Simpson then handed Holly hers and she waited until he left the room before she tugged it open with impatient fingers.

Dear Holly

You are no doubt wondering if I have lost my mind. Rest assured I have not. Il Boschetto di Sole is dear to my old-fashioned heart, and I want it to continue as it has for generations as an independent business.

The Bianchi heir is not a man I approve of, but I have little choice but to leave a vast amount of my estates to him. However, the grove is unentailed, and as he has made it clear to me that he would sell it to a corporation I feel no compunction in leaving Il Boschetto di Sole elsewhere.

But where? I have no children of my own and it is time to find a new family. I wish for Il Boschetto di Sole to pass from father and mother to son or daughter, for tradition to continue. So of course my mind goes to the Romanos, who have given so much to the land over the years.

You may be wondering why I have not simply left the grove to your father. Why I have involved Prince Stefan. To be blunt, your father is getting on, and his good health is in question. Once he is no longer on this earth Il Boschetto di Sole would go to you, and I do not know if that is what you wish for.

You have chosen to live in London and make a life there. Now I need you to look into your heart. If you decide that you wish for ownership of Il Boschetto di Sole then I need some indication that this wish is real—that you are willing to settle down. If you have no wish for this I would not burden you.

Whatever you decide, I wish you well in life.

Yours with affection,

Roberto Bianchi

The letter was so typical of Count Roberto that Holly could almost hear his baritone voice speaking the words. He wanted the land he loved to go to someone who held his own values and shared his vision. He knew her father did, but he didn't know if Holly did or not. In truth, she wasn't sure herself. But she also knew that in this case it didn't matter. Her father loved Il Boschetto di Sole—it was the land of his heart—and to own it would give him pure, sheer joy. She loved her father, and therefore she would fight for Il Boschetto di Sole with all her might.

Simple.

Holly clenched her hands into fists and stared at the door to await the return of the exiled Prince of Lycander.

CHAPTER TWO

STEFAN SEATED HIMSELF in the small annexe room and glared down at the letter, distaste already curdling inside him. The whole thing was reminiscent of the manipulative ploys and stratagems his father had favoured. Alphonse had delighted in the pulling of strings and the resultant antics of those whom he controlled.

During the custody battle he had stripped Eloise of everything—material possessions and every last vestige of dignity—and relished her humiliation. He had smeared her name, branded her a harlot and a tramp, an unfit mother and a gold-digger. All because he had held the trump card at every negotiation. He'd had physical possession of Stefan, and under Lycandrian law, as ruler, he had the final say in court. So, under threat of never seeing her son again, Eloise had accepted whatever terms Alphonse offered, all through her love for Stefan.

She had given up everything, allowed herself to be vilified simply in order to be granted an occasional visit with her son at Alphonse's whim.

In the end even those had been taken from her. Alphonse had decided that the visits 'weakened' his son, and that his attachment to his mother was 'bad' for him. That he could never be tough enough, princely enough, whilst he still saw his mother. So he had rescinded her visitation rights and cast Eloise from Lycander.

Once in London Eloise had suffered a breakdown, followed by a mercifully short but terminal illness.

Guilt twisted his insides anew—he had failed her.

Enough. He would not walk that bleak memory-lined road now. Because the past could not be changed. Right now he needed to read this letter and figure out what to do about this unexpected curveball.

Distasteful and manipulative it might be, but it was an opportunity to win possession of some important land in Lycander in his own right. The idea brought him a surge of satisfaction—his father had not prohibited him from *inheriting* land. So this would allow him to return to Lycander on his terms. But it was more than that… The idea of owning a place his mother had loved touched him with a warmth he couldn't fully understand. Perhaps on Il Boschetto di Sole he could feel close to her again.

So all he needed to do was beat Holly Romano.

Holly Romano… Curiosity surfaced. The look she had cast him when she'd learned his identity had held more than a hint of animosity, and that had been before they'd heard the terms of the will. Perhaps she had simply suspected that they were destined to be cast as adversaries, but instinct told him it was more than that. There had been something personal in that look of deep dislike, and yet he was positive they had never met.

No way would he have forgotten. Her beauty was unquestionable—corn-blonde hair cascaded halfway down her back, eyes of cerulean blue shone under strong brows, and she had a retroussé nose, a generous mouth…and a body that Stefan suspected would haunt his dreams. *Whoa.* No need to go over the top. After all, he was no stranger to beautiful women—the combination of his royal status and his wealth made him a constant target for women on the catch, sure they could ensnare him into marriage.

Stefan had little or no compunction in disillusioning them.

Enough. Open the damn letter, Petrelli.

The handwriting was curved and loopy, but strong, Roberto Bianchi might have been ill but he had been firm of purpose.

Dear Stefan

I am sure you are surprised by the terms of my will. Let me explain.

Your mother was like a daughter to me. I was her godfather, and after her parents' death I became her guardian. As she grew up she spent a lot of her time at Il Boschetto di Sole and I believe she was happy there, on that beautiful, fragrant land.

It was a happiness that ceased very soon after her marriage to your father—a marriage I deeply regret I encouraged her to go through with.

In my—poor—defence I was dazzled by the idea of a royal alliance, and Alphonse could be charming when he chose. I believed he would care for your mother and that she would be able to do good as ruler of Lycander.

I also did not wish to encourage her relationship with Thomas Romano—a man of indifferent social status who was already engaged.

Stefan stopped reading as his mind assimilated that information. His mother and Thomas Romano had been an item. A pang of sorrow hit him. There was so much he didn't know about Eloise—so much he wished he could have had time to find out.

As you know, your parents' marriage was destined for disaster, and by the time I realised my mistake there was nothing I could do.

Your father forbade Eloise from seeing me, and not even my influence could change that. In the end he made it a part of the custody agreement that if Eloise saw me she would be denied even the very few visits she was allowed with you.

Stefan stopped reading as white-hot anger burned inside him. There had been no end to Alphonse's vindictiveness. Familiar guilt intensified within him. Eloise had given up so very much for him, and had had no redress in a court in a land where the ruler's word was law.

When Eloise left Lycander I was unable to find her—I promise you, I tried. I wish with all my heart she had contacted me—I believe and I hope she would have if illness hadn't overcome her.

If Eloise were alive I would leave Il Boschetto di Sole to her. Instead I have decided to give you, her son, a chance to own it. In this way I hope I can make up to you the wrong I did your mother. I want to give you the opportunity to return to Lycander as I believe your mother would have wished.

Eloise was happy at Il Boschetto di Sole, and I truly believe that if she is looking down it will give her peace to see you settled on the land she loved. Land you could pass on to your children, allowing the grove to continue as it has for generations—as an independent business that passes from father and mother to son or daughter.

If you wish this, then I wish you luck.
Yours sincerely,
Roberto Bianchi

Stefan let the letter fall onto his knees as he considered its contents. He hadn't set foot in Lycander for eight years. The idea of a return to his birthplace was an impossibility unless he accepted his brother's charity. But now he had an opportunity to return under his own steam, to own land in his own right, defy his father's edict and win the place his mother had loved—a place she would have wanted him to have.

He closed his eyes and could almost see her, her delicate face framed with dark hair, her gentle smile.

But what about the Romano claim?

Not his concern—*he* hadn't made this will. Roberto Bianchi had decided that the grove should go either to Holly Romano or himself. So be it. This was his way back to Lycander and he would take it. But he was damned if he'd jump to Roberto Bianchi's tune.

Holly watched as Stefan re-entered the room, his stride full of purpose as he faced the lawyer.

'I'll need a copy of the will to be sent to my lawyers asap.'

James Simpson rose from behind his desk. 'Not a problem. Can I ask why?'

'Because I plan to overturn the terms of the will.'

The lawyer shook his head and a small smile touched his thin lips. 'With all due respect, you can try but you will not succeed. Roberto Bianchi was no fool and neither am I. You will not be able to do it.'

'That remains to be seen,' Stefan said, a stubborn tilt to the square of his jaw. 'But in the meantime perhaps it would be better for you to tell us any other provisions the Count saw fit to insert.'

'No matter what the outcome, Thomas Romano retains the right to live in the house he currently occupies until his death, and an amount of three times his current annual salary will be paid to him every year, regardless of his job status.'

Holly frowned. 'So in other words the new owner can sack him but he will still have to pay him and he can keep his house?'

She could see that sounded fair enough, but she knew that her father would dwindle away if his job was taken from him—if he had to watch someone else manage Il Boschetto di Sole. Especially Stefan Petrelli—the son of the woman he had once loved, the woman who had rejected him and broken his heart.

'Correct.' James Simpson inclined his head. 'There are no other provisions.'

Stefan leant forward. 'In that case I would appreciate a chance to speak with Ms Romano in private.'

Suspicion sparked—perhaps Stefan Petrelli thought he could buy her off? But alongside her wariness was a flicker of anticipation at the idea of being alone with him. How stupid was *that*? Hard to believe her hormones hadn't caught up with the message—this man was the enemy. Although perhaps it didn't have to be like that. Perhaps she could persuade him to cede his claim. After all, he hadn't set foot in Lycander in years—why on earth did he even *want* Il Boschetto di Sole?

'Agreed.'

The lawyer inclined his head. 'There is a meeting room down the hall.'

Minutes later they were in a room full of gleaming chrome and glass, where modern art splashed bright white walls and vast windows overlooked the City and proclaimed that Simpson, Wright and Gallagher were undoubtedly prime players in the world of law.

'So,' Stefan said. 'This isn't what I was expecting when I woke up this morning.'

'That's an understatement.'

His gaze assessed her. 'Surely this can't be a surprise to you? You knew Roberto Bianchi, and it sounds like the Romanos have been an integral part of Il Boschetto di Sole for centuries.'

'Roberto Bianchi was a man who believed in duty above all else. I thought he would leave his estate intact. Turns out he couldn't bear the thought of the grove being sucked up by a corporation.'

'Why?'

Holly stared at him. He looked genuinely bemused. 'Because to Count Roberto Il Boschetto di Sole truly was a place of sunshine—he loved it, heart and soul. As my father does.' She gave a heartbeat of hesitation. 'As I do.'

Something flashed across his eyes—something she couldn't fathom. But whatever it was it hardened his expression.

'Yet you live and work in London?'

'How do you know where I work or live? Did you check me out?'

'I checked out your public profiles. That is the point of them—they are *public*.'

'Yes. But…' Though really there were no 'buts'—he was correct, and yet irrationally she was still outraged.

'I did a basic social media search—you work for Lamberts Marketing, as part of their admin team. That doesn't sound like someone whose heart and soul are linked to a lemon grove in Lycander.'

'It's temporary. I thought working for a marketing company for a short time would give me some useful insights and skills which will be transferrable to Il Boschetto di Sole. My plan is to return in six months.'

Yes, she loved London, but she had always known it was a short-term stay. Her father would be devastated if she decided not to return to Lycander, to her life on Il Boschetto di Sole. She was a Romano, and that was where she belonged. Of course he wouldn't force her return—but he needed her.

Ever since her mother had left Holly had vowed she would look after him—especially since he'd been diagnosed with a long-term heart condition. There was no immediate danger, and provided he looked after himself he should be fine. But that wasn't his forte. He was a workaholic and the extent of his cooking ability was to dial for a take away.

Guilt panged anew—she shouldn't have left in the first place. The least she could have done for the man who had brought her up singlehandedly from the age of eight was not abandon him. But she visited regularly, checked up nearly daily, and she would be home soon.

Stefan stepped a little closer to her—not into her space, but close enough that for a stupid moment she caught a whiff of his scent, a citrus woodsy smell that sent her absurdly dizzy.

For a second his body tensed, and she would have sworn he caught his breath, and then he frowned—as though he'd lost track of the conversational thread just as she had.

Focus.

'I'd like to discuss a deal,' he said eventually, as the frown deepened into what she was coming to think of as his trademark scowl. 'What will it take for you to walk away from this? I understand that you are worried about your father—but I would guarantee that his job is safe, that nothing will change for him. If anything, he would have more autonomy to do as he wishes with the grove. And you can name your price—what do you want?'

Holly's eyes narrowed. 'I don't want anything.'

'You don't even want to think about it?' Disbelief tinged each syllable.

'Nope.'

'Why not?' The question was genuine, but lined with an edge—this was a man used to getting his own way.

'Because the Romanos have toiled on that land for generations—now we have a chance to own the land in our own right. Nothing is worth more than that. *Nothing.* Surely you see that?'

'No, I don't. It is just soil and fruit and land—the same as any other on Lycander. Take the money and buy another lemon grove—a new one that can belong to the Romanos from the start.'

His tone implied that he genuinely believed this to be a viable solution. 'It doesn't work like that. We have a history with Il Boschetto di Sole—a connection, a bond. *You* don't.'

His frown deepened but he remained silent; it was impossible to tell his thoughts.

'So why don't you take your own advice? You have more than enough money to buy a score of lemon groves. Why do you want *this* one?'

'That's my business,' he said. 'The point is I am willing to pay you well over the market price. I suggest you think carefully about my offer. Because I am also willing to fight it out, and if I win then you will have nothing. No money and no guarantee that your father will keep his job.'

For a second her blood chilled and anger soared. 'So if you win you would take his job from him?'

'Perhaps. If I win the grove it will be mine to do with as I wish.'

For a second a small doubt trickled through her—what if she lost and was left with nothing? But this wasn't about money; this was about the land of her father's heart. This was her opportunity to give her father something infinitely precious, and she had no intention of rolling over and conceding.

'No deal. If you want a fight, bring it on. This meeting is over.'

Before she could head around the immense table he moved to intercept her. 'Where are you going? To marry the first man you find?'

'Perhaps I am. Or perhaps I already have a boyfriend ready and eager to walk me to the altar.'

As if. Post-Graham she had decided to eschew boyfriends and to run away screaming from any altar in sight.

'Equally, I'm sure there will be women queuing round the block to marry *you.*'

He gusted out a sigh, looking less than enamoured at the thought. 'For a start, I'm pretty sure it's not that easy to just get married—there will be plenty of red tape and bureaucracy to get through. Secondly, I have a better idea than instant matrimony, even if it were possible. Let's call a truce on the race to the altar whilst my lawyers look at the will and see if this whole marriage stipulation can be overturned. There has to be a better way to settle this.'

'No argument here—that makes sense.' Caution kicked in. 'In theory…' Because it could be a trick—why should she believe anything Stefan Petrelli said? 'But what's to stop you from marrying someone during our 'truce' as a back-up plan?'

Call her cynical, but she had little doubt that a millionaire prince could find a way to obliterate all red tape and bureaucracy.

'The fact that even the thought of marriage makes me come out in hives.'

'Hives may be a worthwhile price to pay for Il Boschetto di Sole.'

'Point taken. In truth there is nothing to stop either of us reneging on a truce—and it would be foolish for either of us to trust the other.' Rubbing the back of his neck, he looked at her. 'The lawyers will work fast—that's what I pay them for. We're probably only talking twenty-four hours—two days, tops. We'll need to stick together until they get back to us.'

Stick together. The words resonated in the echoey confines of the meeting room, pinged into the sudden silence, bounced off the chrome and glass and writhed into images that brought heat to her cheeks.

Something sparked in his grey eyes, calling to her to close the gap between them and plaster herself to his chest.

'No way.' The words fell from her lips with vehemence, though whether it was directed at herself or him she wasn't sure.

In truth, he looked a little poleaxed himself, and in that instant Holly wondered if this attraction could be mutual.

Then, as if with an effort, he shrugged. 'What's the alternative? Seems to me it's a good idea to spend one weekend together in the hope that we can avoid a year of marriage.'

Deep breath, Holly. His words held reason, and no way would she actually succumb to this insane attraction— she'd steered clear of the opposite sex for eighteen months now, without regret. Yet the whole idea of sticking to Stefan Petrelli caused her lungs to constrict. *Go figure.*

'How would it work?'

'I suggest a hotel. Neutral ground. We can get a suite. Two bedrooms and a living area.'

Had there been undue emphasis on the word 'two'? A glance at his expression showed tension in his jaw— clearly he wasn't overly keen on the logistics of them sticking together either. But she couldn't come up with an alternative—couldn't risk him heading to the altar, and definitely couldn't trust him. And this was doable. A suite. Separate bedrooms.

So… 'That could work.'

'What are your plans for the weekend? We can do our best to incorporate them.'

'Nothing I can't reschedule.'

In fact her plans had been to work, chill out and continue her exploration of London—maybe meet up with a colleague for a quick drink or to catch a film. But such a programme made her sound like a complete Billy-no-mates. In truth she had kept herself to herself in London, because she'd figured there was no point getting too settled in a life she knew to be strictly temporary.

'I do have some work to do, but I can do that anywhere with internet. What about you?'

'I've got some meetings, but like you I should be able to reschedule. Though I do have one site visit I can't postpone. I suggest we go there first, then find a hotel and swing by our respective houses for some clothes.'

'Works for me.'

It would all be fine.

One weekend—how hard could it be?

CHAPTER THREE

STEFAN FIDGETED IN the incredibly comfortable Tudor-style seat that blended into the discreetly lavish décor of the Knightsbridge hotel. Gold fabrics adorned the lounge furniture, contrasting with the deep red of the thick curtains, and the walls were hung with paintings that depicted the Tudor era—Henry VIII in all his glory, surrounded by miniatures of all his wives.

The irony was not lost on Stefan—his own father was reminiscent of that monarch of centuries ago. Cruel, greedy, and with a propensity to get through wives. Alphonse's tally had been four.

Stefan tugged his gaze from the jewelled pomp of Henry, fidgeted again, drummed his fingers on the ornamental desk, then realised he was doing so and gritted his teeth. What was *wrong* with him?

Don't kid yourself.

He'd already identified the problem—he was distracted by the sheer proximity of Holly Romano. Had been all day. To be fair, it wasn't her fault. Earlier, at his suggestion, she'd remained in the car whilst he conducted the site visit; now they were in the hotel and for the most part she was absorbed in her work. Her focus on the computer screen nearly absolute.

Nearly.

But every so often her gaze flickered to him and he'd hear a small intake of breath, glimpse the crossing and uncrossing of long, slender jean-clad legs and he'd know that Holly was every bit as aware of him as he was of her.

Dammit!

Attraction—mutual or otherwise—had no place here. Misplaced allure could *not* muddy the waters. He wanted Il Boschetto di Sole.

An afternoon of fact-finding had elicited the news that the lemon grove wasn't just lucrative—a fact that meant nothing to him—but was also strategically important. Its produce was renowned. It generated a significant amount of employment and a large chunk of tax revenue for the crown.

Ownership of Il Boschetto di Sole would bring him influence in Lycander—give him back something that his father had taken from him and that his brother would grant only as a favour. For it to come from a place his mother had loved would add a poignancy that mattered more than he wanted to acknowledge. Perhaps there he could feel closer to her—less guilty, less tormented by the memory of his betrayal.

He could even move her urn of ashes from the anonymous London cemetery where her funeral service had taken place. For years he had done his best, made regular pilgrimage, laid flowers. He had had an expensive plaque made, donated money for a remembrance garden. But if he owned the grove he would be able to scatter her ashes in a place she had loved, a place where she could be at peace.

His gaze drifted to Holly Romano again. He wanted to come to a fair deal with her, despite her vehement repudiation of the idea. His father had never cared about fairness, simply about winning, crushing his opponent—Stefan had vowed never to be like that. Any deal he made would be a fair one. Yes, he'd win, but he'd do it fair and square and where possible he'd treat his adversary with respect.

He pushed thoughts of Alphonse from his mind, allowed himself instead to study Holly's face. There was a small wrinkle to her brow as she surveyed the screen in front of her, her blonde head tilted to one side, the glorious curtain of golden hair piled over one shoulder. Every so often she'd raise her hand to push a tendril behind her ear, only for it to fall loose once more. There came that insidious tug of desire again—one he needed to dampen down.

As if sensing his scrutiny, she looked up.

Good one, Petrelli. Caught staring like an adolescent. 'Just wondering what you're working on. Admin isn't usually so absorbing.'

There was a hesitation, and then she spun the screen round to show him. 'It's no big deal. One of the managers at work has offered to mentor me and she's given me an assignment.' She gave a hitch of her slender shoulders. 'It's just some research—no big deal.'

Only clearly it was—the repetition, her failed attempt to appear casual indicated that.

'Maybe you should consider asking to move out of admin and into a marketing role.'

'No point. I'm going back home in a few months.'

Then why bother to be mentored? he wondered.

As if in answer to his unspoken question she turned to face him, her arms folded. 'I want to learn as much as I can whilst I'm here, to maximise how I can help when I get back.'

It made sense, and yet he intuited it was more than that. Perhaps he should file it away as potentially useful information. Perhaps he should make a push to find something he could bring to the negotiating table.

'Fair enough.' A glance outside showed the autumn

dusk had settled in, which meant… 'I'm ready for dinner—what about you?'

'Um… I didn't realise it was so late. I'm quite happy to grab a sandwich in my room. I bet Room Service is pretty spectacular here.'

'I'm sure it is, but I've heard the restaurant is incredible.'

Blue eyes surveyed him for a moment. 'So you're suggesting we go and have dinner together in the restaurant?'

'Sure. Why not? The reviews are fantastic.'

'And you're still hoping to convince me to cut a deal and cede my claim.'

'Yes.'

'It won't work.' There was steel in her voice.

'That doesn't mean I shouldn't try. Hell, don't you want to convince me to do the same?'

'Well, yes, but…'

'Then we may as well pitch over a Michelin-starred meal, don't you think?'

She chewed her bottom lip, blue eyes bright with suspicion, and then her tummy gave a less than discreet growl. She rolled her eyes, but her lips turned up in a sudden smile.

'See? Your stomach is voting with me.'

'Guess my brain is outvoted, then,' she muttered, and she rose from the chair. 'I'll be five minutes.'

True to her word she emerged just a few moments later. She'd changed back into the charcoal skirt she'd worn earlier, topped now by a crimson blouse. Her hair was swept up in an artlessly elegant arrangement, with tendrils free to frame her face.

In that moment he wished with a strangely fierce yearn that this was a date—a casual, easy, get-to-know-you-dinner with the possibility of their attraction progressing.

But it wasn't and it couldn't be. This was a fact-finding mission.

Suddenly his father's words echoed in his ears with a discordant buzz.

'Information is power, Stefan. Once you know what makes someone tick you can work out how to turn that tick to a tock.'

That was what he needed to focus on—gaining information. Not to penalise her but so that he could work out a fair deal.

Resolutely turning his gaze away from her, he made for the door. But as they headed down plush carpeted corridors and polished wooden stairs it was difficult to remain resolute. Somehow the glimpse of her hand as it slid down the gleaming oak banister, the elusive drift of her scent, the way she smoothed down her skirt all combined to add to the desire that tugged in his gut.

She paused on the threshold of the buzzing restaurant, a look of slight dismay on her face. 'I don't think I'm exactly dressed for this.'

'You look…' *Beautiful. Gorgeous.* Way better than any of the women sitting in white cushioned chairs braided with gold, around circular tables illuminated by candles atop them and chandeliers above. 'Fine,' he settled on.

Smooth, Petrelli, very smooth.

But oddly enough it seemed to do the trick. She looked up at him and a small smile tugged her lips upwards. 'Thank you. I know clothes shouldn't matter, but I am feeling a little inadequate in the designer department.'

'I'm hardly up to standard either,' he pointed out. 'I'm channelling the lumberjack look—the whole jeans and checked shirt image.'

The maître d' approached, a slightly pained expression on his face until he realised who Stefan was and his expression morphed to ingratiating. 'Mr Petrelli. This way, please.'

'People are wondering why we've been allowed in,' Holly whispered. 'They're all looking at us.'

'Let them look. In a minute George here will have discreetly spread the word as to who I am and that should do it. Royal entrepreneurial millionaire status transcends dress code. Especially when accompanied by a mystery guest.'

'Dressed from the High Street.' Her tone sounded panicked. 'Oh, God. They won't call the press or anything, will they?'

'Not if they know what's good for them.'

She glanced over the menu at him. 'You don't like publicity, do you?'

In fact he loathed it—because no matter what he did, how many millions he'd made, whatever point he tried to get across, the press all wanted to talk about Lycander and he didn't. *Period.*

'Nope. So I think we're safe. Let's choose.'

After a moment of careful perusal he leant back.

'Hmm… What do you think? The duck sounds amazing—especially with the crushed pink peppercorns—but I'm not sure about adding cilantro in as well. But it could work. The starters look good too—though, again, I'm still not sure about fusion recipes.'

A small gurgle of laughter interrupted him and he glanced across at her.

'What?'

'I didn't have you down as a food buff. The lumberjack look didn't make me think gourmet.'

'I'm a man of many surprises.'

In truth, food was important to him—a result of his childhood. Alphonse's toughening up regime had meant rationed food, and the clichéd bread and water diet had been a regular feature. His stomach panged in sudden memory of the gnaw of hunger, the doughy texture of the bread on his tongue as he tried to savour each nibble. He'd summoned up imaginary feasts, used his mind to conjure a cacophony of tastes and smells and textures. Vowed that one day he'd make those banquets real.

Whoa. Time to turn the memory tap off. Clearly his repressed memory banks had sprung a leak—one he intended to dam up right now.

The arrival of the waiter was a welcome distraction, and once they'd both ordered he focused on Holly. Her cerulean eyes were fringed by impossibly long dark lashes that contrasted with the corn-gold of her hair.

'And do you cook? Or just appreciate others' cooking?' she asked.

'I can cook, but I'm not an expert. When I have time I enjoy it. What about you?'

Holly grimaced. 'I can cook too, but I'm not inspired at all. I am a strict by-the-recipe girl. I wish I enjoyed it more, but I've always found it quite stressful.' Discomfort creased her forehead for a second, as if she regretted the words, and she looked down. 'Anyway, today I don't need to cook.'

For a stupid moment he wanted to probe, wanted to question the reason for that sudden flitting of sadness across her face.

Focus on the goal here, Petrelli.

He leant forward. 'If you accept my offer of a deal you could eat out every day. You need never touch a saucepan again.'

'Nice try, but no thanks. I'll soldier on. Truly, Stefan, nothing you offer me can top the idea of presenting Il Boschetto di Sole to my father.'

'That's the plan?'

'Yup.'

'You'll sign it over lock, stock and barrel?'

'Yup.'

'But that's nuts. Why hand over control?' The very idea gave him a sense of queasiness.

'Because it's the right thing to do.'

'If Roberto Bianchi had wanted your father to have the grove he'd have left it to him.'

Something that looked remarkably like guilt crossed her face as she shook her head. 'My father has given his life to Il Boschetto di Sole—I could never ask him to work for me. I respect him too much. If the Romanos are to own the grove then it will be done properly. Traditionally.'

'Pah!' The noise he'd emitted hopefully conveyed his feelings. 'Tradition? You will hand over control because of *tradition*?'

'What is so wrong with that? Just because you have decided to turn your back on tradition it doesn't mean that's the right thing to do.'

His turn to hide the physical impact he felt at her words—at the knowledge that Holly, like the rest of Lycander, had judged him and found him wanting.

No doubt she believed the propaganda and lies Alphonse had spread and Stefan hadn't refuted. Because in truth he'd welcomed it all. To him it had put him in the same camp as his mother, had made the guilt at his failure a little less.

'So you believe that just because something is traditional it is right?'

'I didn't say that. But I believe history and tradition are important.'

'History is a great thing to learn from, but it doesn't have to be repeated. It is progress that is important—and if you don't change you can't progress. What if the inventor of the wheel had decided not to bother because *traditionally* people travelled by foot or on horseback? What about appalling traditions like slavery?'

'So do you believe monarchy is an appalling or outdated tradition? Do you believe Lycander should be a democracy?'

'I believe that is a debatable point. I do not believe that just because there has been a monarch for centuries there needs to be one for the next century. My point is that if the crown headed my way I would refuse it. Not on democratic principles but for personal reasons. I don't want to rule and I wouldn't change my whole life for the sake of tradition. Or duty.'

'So if Frederick had decided not to take the throne you would have refused it?'

'Yup.'

Stefan had no doubt of that. In truth he'd been surprised that Frederick had agreed. Their older half-brother Axel, Lycander's 'Golden Prince', had been destined to rule, and from all accounts would have made a great ruler.

As a child Stefan hadn't known Axel well—he had been at boarding school, a distant figure, though he had always shown Stefan kindness when he'd seen him. Enough so that when Axel had died in a tragic car accident Stefan had felt grief and would have attended the funeral if his father had let him. But Alphonse had refused to allow Stefan to set foot on Lycandrian soil.

Axel's death had left Frederick next in line and his brother had stepped up. *More fool him.*

'My younger brothers would be welcome to it.'

'You'd have handed over the Lycandrian crown to one of the "Truly Terrible Twins"?'

An image of his half-brothers splashed on the front page of the tabloids crossed his mind. Emerson and Barrett rarely set foot in Lycander, but their exploits sold any number of scurrilous rags.

'Yes,' he stated—though even he could hear that his voice lacked total conviction.

Holly surveyed him through narrowed eyes. 'Forget tradition. What about duty? Wouldn't you have felt a *duty* to rule? A duty to your country?'

'Nope. I think Frederick's a first-class nutcase to take it on. I have one life, Holly, and I intend to live it for myself.' Exactly as he so wished his mother had done. 'I don't see anything wrong with that as long as I don't hurt anyone.'

She leaned across the table and her blue eyes sparkled, her face animated by the discourse. 'You could argue that by not taking the throne Frederick would have been hurting a whole country.'

Stefan surveyed her across the table and she nodded for emphasis, her lips parted in a small 'hah' of triumph at the point she'd made, and his gaze snagged on her mouth. Hard to remember the last time a date had sparked this level of discussion, had been happy to flat-out contradict him. Not that Holly *was* a date...

As the silence stretched a fraction too long her lips tipped in a small smirk. 'No answer to that?'

'Actually, I do. I just got distracted.'

For a moment confusion replaced the smirk. 'By wh—?' And then she realised, and a small flush climbed her cheekbones.

Now the silence shimmered. Her eyes dropped, skimmed over his chest, and then she rallied.

'Good excuse, Mr Petrelli, but I'm not buying it. You have no answer.'

For a moment he couldn't even remember the question. *Think. They had been talking about Frederick.* What might have happened if he had refused the throne...

'I have an answer. It could be that Emerson or Barrett would turn into a great ruler. Or Lycander would become a successful democracy.'

'And you would be fine with that?'

'Sure. It doesn't mean I don't care about Lycander—I'm just not willing to give up my whole life for it, for the sake of tradition or because I "should". One life. One chance.'

His mother's life had been so short, so tragic, because of the decisions she'd made—decisions triggered by duty and love.

'Don't you agree?'

'No. Sometimes you have to do what you "should" do because it is the *right* thing to do. And that is more important than what you *want* to do.'

Stefan frowned, suspecting that she was speaking in specific terms rather than general. 'So what are your dreams? Your plans for life. Let's say you win Il Boschetto di Sole and give it to your father—what then?'

'Then I will help him—work the land, have kids…' Her voice was even; the animation had vanished.

'And if you don't win?'

'I *will* win.'

He raised an eyebrow. 'Humour me. It's a hypothetical question.'

'I don't know… I would have to see what my father wished to do—whether he wanted to stay on at Il Boschetto di Sole, what your plans for the grove would be.'

'OK. So let's say your father decides to retire, live out the rest of his life peacefully in his home or elsewhere in Lycander.' A memory of her utter focus on her work earlier came to him. 'What about marketing? Would you like to give that a go? Build a career?'

There was a flash in her blue eyes; he blinked and it was gone.

'My career is on Il Boschetto di Sole.'

'What is your job there?'

'I've helped out with most things, but I was working in admin before…before I came to London.'

'Tell me about what you were working on earlier today. In the suite.'

A hesitation and then a shrug. A pause as the waiter arrived with their starters. She thanked him, speared a king prawn and then started to speak.

'Lamberts have a pretty major client in the publishing field and they're looking to rebrand their crime line. I've been working on that.'

Her voice started out matter-of-fact, but as she talked her features lit up and her gestures were expressive of the sheer enthusiasm the project had ignited in her.

'I've helped put a survey together—you know, a sort of list of twenty questions about what makes a reader choose a new book or author, what sort of cover would inspire them to give something a try… Blood and gore versus a good-looking protagonist. Also, do people prefer series or stand-alones? We'll need to analyse all the data and come up with some options and then get reader opinion across a broad spectrum. Because we also want to attract readers who don't usually read that genre. Then we need some social media, some—'

She broke off.

'Oh, God. How long have I been talking for? You should have stopped me before you went comatose with boredom.'

'Impossible.'

'To stop me?'

Her stricken look made him smile. 'No! I meant it would have been impossible for me to have been bored. When you speak of this project you light up with sheer passion.'

The word caused him to pause, conjuring up other types

of passion, and he wondered if her thoughts had gone the same way.

Unable to stop himself, he reached out, gently stroked her cheek. 'You are flushed with enthusiasm…your eyes are alight, your whole body is engaged.'

Stop right there. Move your hand away.

Yet that was nigh on impossible. The softness of her skin, her small gasp, the way her teeth had caught her under lip as her eyes widened… All he wanted to do was kiss her.

Cool it, Petrelli.

Failing finding a handy waiter with an ice bucket, he was going to have to find some inner ice.

Leaning back, he forced his voice into objective mode. 'Sounds to me as though what you want to do is pursue a career in marketing. Not take up a job on Il Boschetto di Sole.'

She blinked, as if his words had broken a spell, and her lips pressed together and her eyes narrowed as she shook her head. Shook it hard enough that tendrils of hair fell loose from her strategically messy bun.

'That is not for me. I couldn't do what you did. Walk away from my duty to pursue a career.'

Her words served as effectively as an ice bucket could have and he couldn't hold back an instinctive sound of denial. 'That's not exactly how it went down.'

'So how *did* it go down? As I remember it, you decided to renounce Lycander and your royal duties to live your own life—away from a country you felt you had no allegiance to. But you were happy to accept a severance hand-out from Alphonse to help set you up in the property business.'

Gall twisted his insides that she should believe that.

'Alphonse gave me nothing.'

And Stefan wouldn't have taken it if he had tried.

'I ended up in property because it was the only job I could find.'

He could still taste the bitter tang of grief, fear and desperation. He'd arrived in London buoyed up by a sense of freedom and relief that he'd finally escaped his father, determined to find out what had happened to his mother. His discoveries had caused a cold anger to burn inside him alongside a raging inferno of guilt.

His mother had suffered a serious mental breakdown. The staff at the hostel that had taken her in had had no idea of her identity, but to Stefan's eternal gratitude they had looked after her. Though Eloise had never really recovered, relapsing and lurching from periods of depression to episodes of relative calm until illness had overtaken her.

In his anger and grief he had started his search for a job under an assumed name, changed his surname by deed poll and got himself new documentation, determined to prove himself without any reference to his royal status.

It hadn't been easy. And he would be grateful for ever to the small independent estate agent who'd taken pity on him. His need for commission had honed his hitherto non-existent sales skills and negotiating had come naturally to him.

'Luckily I was a natural and it piqued my interest.'

Holly tipped her head to one side. 'But how did you go from that job to a multibillion-pound business?'

Was that suspicion in her voice? The idea that she still believed Alphonse had funded him shouldn't matter but it did.

'I worked hard and I saved hard. I worked multiple jobs, I persuaded a bank to take a chance on me, I studied the market and invested in properties until I had a diverse portfolio. Some properties I bought, did up and sold, others I rented out. Once my portfolio became big enough I set up a company. It all spiralled from there.'

And when it had he had resumed his own identity, wanting the world to know what he had made of himself.

'You make it sound easy.'

'It wasn't. Point is, though, I did it on my own.'

Holly was silent for a moment, almost absentmindedly forking up some Udon noodles. 'So what about today? That site we visited? It looked like it was in a pretty poor area.'

'It is. We're building social housing. Projects like that are taken on by a separate arm of my business. The problem with the housing market is the huge differential in regional properties, and overall houses are becoming unaffordable—which is wrong. Equally, there is insufficient social housing and the system can backfire, or people are expected to live in unsafe, horrible conditions and not have a lot of redress. I work to try and prevent that. I plough a proportion of the company's profits back into building more houses, better houses. More affordable houses. Both for young people to buy and people who can't afford to buy to rent at reasonable prices. And for those who haven't the money to afford the most basic of rent. The amount of homelessness in rich countries is criminal and—'

He broke off.

'Sorry. It's a bit of a pet peeve I have. No need to bore you with it.' But it was a subject that he felt strongly about. His mother had spent periods of time homeless, too ill after her breakdown to figure out the benefits system.

'I'm not bored either,' Holly said softly. 'I think your commitment to put money into the system, to help people, is fantastic. Your enthusiasm lights up your face.'

She lifted her hand in a mirror gesture of his earlier one and touched his cheek, and his heart pounded his ribcage.

'I admire that. As well as your phenomenal success. I feel bad that I believed Alphonse funded it.'

'It's OK.' He knew the whole of Lycander believed the

same; his father's propaganda machine had churned out fictional anti-Stefan stories with scurrilous precision.

'But why don't you set the record straight?'

Her hand dropped to cover his; she stroked her thumb across the back and his body stilled as desire pooled in his gut.

'There is no point. For a start, who would believe me? Plus, at the end of the day I did walk away from Lycander.'

'Then why do you want Il Boschetto di Sole? You own properties throughout Europe. Why do you want one Lycandrian lemon grove if you have no love for Lycander at all?'

An image of his birthplace suddenly hit him—the roll of verdant fields, the swoop and soar and dip of the hills, the spires and turrets of the architecture of the city, the scent of lemon and blossom and spices borne on a breeze…

Whoa. It was a beautiful place but he owed it nothing. Rather it was the other way round. His father had taken away what was rightfully his and this was a way to redress the balance. A way to take his mother's ashes to their final resting place. *That* was what was important. This visceral reaction to Holly needed to be doused, and this emotional conversation with its undertones of attraction needed to cease.

'I'm a businessman, Holly. Why would I pass up the chance to add this to my portfolio?'

Her hand flew from his as if burnt, and he realised the words had come out with a harshness he hadn't intended. But it didn't matter. He and Holly Romano were adversaries, not potential bed-mates.

Her eyes hardened, as if she had caught the same thought. 'Good question. And now, seeing as the point of this dinner is to pitch to each other, do you mind if I go first?'

Stefan nodded. 'Go ahead.'

CHAPTER FOUR

HOLLY WAITED AS their main courses arrived, smiling up at the waiter, relieved at the time-out as her mind and body struggled to come to terms with the conversation. Her cheek still tingled from his touch and her fingers still held the roughness of his five o'clock shadow, the strength and breadth of his hand under hers.

This whole dinner had been a mistake, but somehow she had to try and salvage it. Though she suspected it was a doomed pitch, because she had nothing to offer. The only thing she could sell was the moral high ground, launching an appeal to his better, altruistic self. And whilst he clearly *had* one she didn't think it would come to the table on this issue.

So here went nothing.

'I understand you don't believe in tradition, but I hope you believe in fairness. I believe the Romano claim is stronger than yours. We have a true connection with Il Boschetto di Sole and we already fulfil one of Roberto Bianchi's wishes. For the grove to be a family affair, handed on from generation to generation.'

A pause showed her that he looked unmoved, his expression neutral as he listened.

'Also, you have no real financial incentive to pursue this—if you truly wish for land in Lycander you can afford to buy it. I know your father passed a law that made that difficult but surely your brother would rescind that decree?'

His dark eyebrows jerked upwards. 'And what do you base *that* opinion on? I didn't realise you had an inside track to the Crown Prince.'

A flush touched her cheek as she realised he was right; she had no idea of the relationship between the brothers but it obviously wasn't a close one.

'Are you saying he won't?'

'No. I am saying I don't wish to ask him.' His face was shuttered now, his lips set in a grim line, his eyes shadowed. 'This is my opportunity to own land in Lycander. Lucrative, strategic land—the equivalent to what I lost. You can't change my mind on this, I accept you have a case, but I'll fight you all the way.'

'Even if your lawyers can't find a loophole and you have to get married?' Perhaps she was clutching at straws, but she had to try. 'You said the thought of marriage makes you break out in hives. Imagine what actually going through with it would do to you? Surely you'd rather ask Frederick to grant you a land licence?'

Forget shutters. This time the metaphorical equivalent of a metal grille slammed down on his expression.

'Nope. If I have to get married for a year I'll suck it up.'

'But it's more complicated than that.'

'How so?'

'What about children?'

'What *about* them?'

Holly sighed. 'As I've already mentioned, Roberto Bianchi wanted Il Boschetto di Sole to pass from generation to generation—from father to son, or mother to daughter. That means that technically you'd need a son or daughter to pass it on to.'

He placed his fork down with a clatter. 'Without disrespect, Holly, Count Roberto is dead, and he certainly cannot dictate whether or not I choose to have children.'

'No, but surely you want to respect his wishes?'

'Why? I think the whole will is nuts—that's why I am trying to overturn it.'

'And I agree with that. But I don't think we can ignore what he wanted long-term. He truly *loved* Il Boschetto di Sole.'

'And I hope it brought him happiness in his lifetime. Now he is gone, and I will not alter my entire life to accommodate him. I certainly won't bring children into this world solely to be heir to a lemon grove. That would hardly be fair to them *or* me.'

She couldn't help but flinch, and hastily reached out for her wine glass in an attempt to cover it up. After all that was exactly why her parents had wanted a child so desperately—only they hadn't just wanted a child. They'd wanted a son.

His forehead creased in curiosity as he leaned over to top up her wine glass. 'Would you do it?'

'No. Not only for that!'

And yet she found her gaze skittering away from his. Her whole life her father had impressed upon her the importance of marriage and children, the need for a Romano heir to carry on tradition.

'Yes, I wanted to get married and have a family, but not only for the sake of Il Boschetto di Sole. I wanted it for *me*.'

The whole package: to love and be loved, to experience family life as it should be. With two loving parents offering unconditional love, untinged by disappointment.

One of those detestable eyebrows rose. '*Wanted?* Past tense?'

Holly speared a lightly roasted cherry tomato with unnecessary force. '*Want*. That is what I want.'

'So what happens if your children don't want to run a lemon grove? If they have other dreams or ambitions? What if they want to become a pilot or a doctor or a surfer?'

'Then of course they can.' And if he raised that bloody eyebrow again, so help her, she'd figure out a way to shave it off.

'But what about tradition and duty then? Surely if it's right for *you* to follow the path of duty it is right for them too?'

'I *want* to follow that path. I hope my children will want to as well, but if they don't I won't force them to.' Could she sound *any* lamer? Time to change tack. 'Anyway, at least I'll have a shot at fulfilling Roberto's wishes. Are you saying you have *no* plans to have children?'

'Got it in one. I have no intention of getting married if I can avoid it, or entering into any form of long-term relationship, and I won't risk my child being torn between two parents. It is as simple as that.'

His tone was flat, but for a second Holly had a glimpse of the younger Stefan, who had been torn between two parents. The custody battle, whilst one-sided, had been long and drawn-out, though the outcome had never been in doubt. An outcome that Alphonse had, of course, claimed to be better for Stefan—after all, Eloise had been condemned as an unfit mother, an unfaithful wife who had only married Alphonse for his money.

Holly had believed every word—after all, Eloise had already ruined her parents' marriage.

But... 'Some parents manage to negotiate a fair agreement.'

'That's not a risk I'm willing to take. I will not bring a

child into this world unless I can guarantee a happy childhood. As I can't, I won't.'

'You could opt for single parenthood. Adopt?'

He shook his head. 'Not for me. There are plenty of couples out there who want to adopt and can offer way more than I can. So, no. If the lawyers can't get us out of this I'll get married for a year. I'll do what it takes to win. Or my offer still stands. I'll buy you out here and now. You can start afresh—start a whole new Romano tradition if that's what floats your boat. That way you have a guaranteed win. Or you fight it out and risk ending up with nothing.'

The waiter returned, removed their empty plates and placed the dessert menu in front of them with discreet fluid movements, giving her a moment to let his deep chocolate tones run over her skin. Doubts swirled. Stefan Petrelli wanted Il Boschetto di Sole and she knew one way or another he would go all-out to get it.

She could end up with nothing. And yet... 'My father loves Il Boschetto di Sole—for him it would be unthinkable to give up the opportunity to own it.'

'What about you?'

Stefan held her gaze and she resisted the urge to wriggle on her seat.

'Is it unthinkable for you?'

Don't look away.

'Absolutely,' she stated.

There was no way she could let her father down over this—no way she could hand it over to Stefan. That was unthinkable.

So... 'No deal, Stefan. I too will fight and I will go all-out to win.'

'Then here's to a fair fight.'

The clink of glass against glass felt momentous, and then their mutual challenge seemed to swirl and change, morph into something else—an awareness and a mad, stupid urge to move around the table and kiss him.

Without meaning to she moistened her lips, and his grey eyes darkened with a veritable storm of desire.

Get a grip.

Yet she couldn't seem to break the spell. Any minute now she was going to do something inexplicably stupid.

Pushing her chair back with as much dignity as she could muster, she forced herself to smile. 'Just need the loo,' she said and, resisting the urge to run, she forced her feet to walk towards the door.

Stefan breathed out a deep breath he hadn't even been aware he'd been holding and tried to ignore the fact that his pulse-rate seemed to have upped a notch or three. This reaction to Holly was nuts. All he could hope was that his lawyers came through soon and this enforced proximity would come to a close.

Goodness only knew what it was about her… Yes, she was stunning, but it was more than that. There was something vulnerable about her, and that was exactly why he should be extra-wary. Thanks to the will Holly was on the opposite side of enemy lines, so any knight in shining armour urge needed to be tamped down. In truth, vulnerability did not usually appeal to him; he was no knight and well he knew it.

He took a few surreptitious deep breaths and kept his expression neutral as she walked back to the table, sat down and took up her knife and fork almost as if they were weaponry.

'So,' she said. 'Now the plan is to fight it out what happens next?'

'The truce holds until my lawyers call and then, depending on what they say, all bets are off. No loophole and we race to the nearest altar with whoever will marry us. If there *is* a loophole we fight it out in the courts.'

His mind whirred, looking for another option, because in truth neither of those appealed.

'Hard to know what to wish for.'

'The no marriage option has my vote.'

'But if it ends up in the courts it will come down to who has a better case. And how on earth can any judge decide that? It could drag on for years, and if it does Il Boschetto di Sole will end up with Crown Prince Frederick by default.'

Stefan's mouth hardened; there was no way on this earth he would let that happen.

He looked at her. 'So you'd prefer to duel it out through marriage?'

'I wouldn't call it a preference, exactly.' Her expression was suddenly unreadable. 'But maybe it would be easier?'

Stefan shook his head. 'It would be an equally big mess. For starters, let's say I find a bride before you find a groom. That still doesn't mean I win. I have to stay married for a year. What do I do if six months in she decides to divorce me, or threatens to divorce me?'

Not happening. He would not put himself in anyone's power. Ever again. As a child he'd been in his father's control. As an adult he controlled his own life, and the best way to maintain that control was not to cede it to anyone else. Physically or emotionally.

'Hmm…' She took a contemplative sip of wine, rubbed the tip of her nose in consideration. 'Or I could marry someone and stay married. Then I win and *then* he divorces me and demands half of Il Boschetto di Sole.'

Stefan watched her brooding expression and had a funny feeling she wasn't talking about a mythical person here.

'Or, even worse,' he offered, 'what if I marry someone and at the end of the year she wants to stay married and refuses to divorce me?'

Holly considered that for a moment and narrowed her eyes. 'What if it happens the other way round? She wants a divorce and you want to stay married?'

'Not happening.' Not on any planet, in any universe.

'Arrogant, much?'

'It's not arrogance. Most women in my experience are keen on the starry-eyed, happy-ever-after scenario. They must be overwhelmed by my good looks and rugged charm. Or could it be my bank balance and royal status?'

'Cynical, much?'

'Realistic, plenty.' Not one of the women he'd been with in the past years had been unaffected by his status.

'And that doesn't bother you?' Curiosity tinged her voice. 'That women want to be with you because of your assets—?' She broke off, a tinge of pink climbing her cheekbones as he raised his brows. 'Your *material* assets is what I meant. It *must* bother you.'

'Why? It makes it easier; we both make our terms clear at the outset. I always explain there will be no wedding bells ringing, that any relationship has no long-term future but I am happy to be generous in the interim and hopefully we'll have fun.'

'So, to sum you up: Stefan Petrelli—excellent taste but short shelf-life and no long-term nourishment.'

'I can see why you're in marketing.' A sudden need to defend his position overcame him. 'I've had no complaints so far. I'm upfront, and I'm excellent boyfriend material. In fact next time I'm in the market for a girlfriend I'll give you a call to represent me.'

'No can do. I'm not sure I approve of the product.'

'Ha-ha!' Though he was pretty sure she wasn't joking.

She tipped her head to one side. 'So at the beginning of a relationship you tell a woman there can be no future in it but they all date you anyway?' Her tone indicated pure bafflement.

'Not all. Some women decline to take it beyond the first date, and I'm good with that. Others are happy with what's on offer.'

'So for you every relationship is a deal?'

'Yes. That makes sense to me.' And he wasn't about to apologise for it. 'There's no point starting a relationship if you both want completely different things. That's a sure-fire path to hurt and angst.'

A shadow crossed her face. 'Maybe you're right.' A quick shake of her head and she pushed her plate away, rested her elbows on the table and propped her chin in her hands. She watched him with evident fascination. 'So then what happens? You both set out your terms and then what?'

Aware of a slight sense of defensiveness, he continued. 'We go on another date and take things from there…'

'Take things *where*? If you both know there's no future, there is no destination.'

'That doesn't mean we can't enjoy the journey. Because it's not the future that is important. It's the here and now.'

Stefan had spent all his childhood focused on the future because his present had sucked. It had then turned out that the future he'd pictured hadn't panned out either. So now he figured it was all about optimising the present.

'If you spend all your time homing in on the future you never actually enjoy the here and now.'

'So if the two of you keep on enjoying the "here and now", why curtail that enjoyment? You may as well keep going on into the future.'

'Never happened. I guess I like variety.' Even *he* cringed as he said it, but better to see the distaste that glinted in her eyes than pretend anything different. 'And so do the women I spend time with. I do my best to get involved with women with the same outlook as me. For the record, sometimes *she* ends it first—she opts to move on. Maybe to someone who has an interest in being seen, making headlines. Someone who wants to take extended holidays in the latest celeb hotspot.'

'So essentially you use each other and then trade in for a different model?'

'It works for me.'

He would never risk the idea that a woman's expectations might change, so it was always better to end it early so no one got hurt.

'On your terms?'

'On *agreed* terms. All we want is a good physical connection and some conversational sparkle over the dinner table every so often.'

'Define "every so often".'

'Once a week…once a fortnight. Depends on work commitments—hers and mine.'

There was a moment of silence—an instant during which Holly's eyes widened and looked almost dreamy, as if she were contemplating the whole idea. His heart-rate quickened and once again a wish that this *was* a date, that this conversation wasn't theoretical, pulsed through him. The urge to reach out, to take her hand, pull her up from the table and take her upstairs nearly overwhelmed him, and as her gaze met his he could feel his legs tense to propel him off his seat.

Whoa. Easy, Petrelli.

He didn't even know what her relationship criteria were. Whilst he'd been leaking information like a sieve he had no idea of *her* status.

'So what about you?'

'What *about* me?'

'What's your relationship slogan?'

'Holly Romano: uninterested, unavailable and un… something else. I'm on a relationship break.'

'Why?'

'Complicated break-up.'

He had the feeling she'd used that line before, perhaps to deflect unwanted attention, and the shadows in her eyes showed the truth of her words. Bleak shadows, like storm clouds on a summer's day. And there was a slump to her shoulders that betokened weariness. Only for an instant, though, and then her body straightened and she met his gaze.

'But if your lawyers don't find a loophole I'll get over it. *Fast.* Because, like it or not, we'll both have to contemplate matrimony. With or without romance.'

Picking up the bottle of wine, he topped up their glasses. 'Yes, we will.'

A germ of an idea niggled at the back of his brain, but before he could grasp it his phone buzzed. A glance down showed his lawyer's name. He looked around the still crowded restaurant and picked up.

'John. I'll call you back in five.'

Holly's eyes looked a question.

'Lawyer.' He rose to his feet. 'Guess we'll have to skip dessert. I'd rather talk to him in private, so let's head upstairs.'

CHAPTER FIVE

ONCE IN THE lounge area of their suite, Holly perched on the edge of a brocaded chair and watched as Stefan pulled his phone out of his pocket and pushed a button. Nerves sashayed through her as he paced the room with lithe strides. But her edginess wasn't only down to trepidation about his lawyer's verdict; her whole body was in a tizz.

There had been a moment—hell, way too many moments—over dinner, when she'd wanted nothing more than to be like one of the women he'd described. A woman happy to pursue the here and now and take advantage of the promise of a physical connection with him.

Ridiculous. And of all the men for her hormones to zone in on Stefan Petrelli was the most unsuitable—on a plethora of levels. She focused on the conversation.

'It's Stefan.'

He listened for a moment and his expression clouded, lips set in a line.

'You're sure?'

Another moment and he hung up, dropped the phone in his pocket and turned to face her.

Holly leant forward. 'There's no loophole, is there?'

'Not even a pinhead-sized one. James Simpson did a sterling job.'

'So we'll have to get married. Undertake that race to the altar.'

Holly clenched her hands as realisation washed over her. What an idiot she'd been. Instead of dining with Stefan Petrelli, getting her knickers in a knot over a Michelin-starred meal, she should have been shut up her room for-mulating a back-up plan. A marriage plan.

Chill.

It wasn't as if Stefan had been out there searching for a bride. That was the whole point of them staying together this weekend.

'Yes.'

The tightness of the syllable, the drumming of his fin-gers on his thigh, the increased speed of his stride all con-veyed his dissatisfaction with the idea.

Holly got to her feet. 'Right. I'd better get going, then. The truce is over. The stick-together phase is finished.'

Yet her feet seemed reluctant to move—or rather, for reasons she couldn't fathom, they wanted to move towards Stefan rather than away. *Get a grip*. Talk about getting it wrong. Stefan was now officially the enemy.

'So I guess this is it.'

There was no guesswork involved. This was over. Next time she saw Stefan it would be in a court of law, once one of them had succeeded in marrying. So this was their last few minutes together.

Get a grip faster, Holly.

She'd only met the man this morning. What did she want? A greeting card moment?

Damn it. She knew exactly what she wanted and this was her only chance to get it.

Without allowing common sense to intervene, she let her hormones propel her forward. She was so close to him now that the merest sliver of air separated them. His scent assailed her, her whole body tingled, and her tummy felt weighted with a pool of heat. The scowl had vanished from his expression and his grey eyes gleamed in the moonlight. Molten desire sparked in their depths as he closed the tiny gap between them.

'I know this is mad,' she whispered. 'But as we won't be seeing each other again would you mind…kissing me?'

'Not a problem,' he growled instantly.

Sweet Lord—she couldn't have imagined a kiss such as this. His lips were firm, and she could taste a tang of wine, a hint of lemon… And then nothing mattered except the vortex of sheer sensation that flooded her every sense.

Desire mounted, and her calf muscles stretched as she went on tiptoe and twined her arms around his neck to pull him closer, pressed her body against his in a delicious wriggle of pleasure. She heard his groan, felt the heat of his large hands against the small of her back.

It was a kiss that might have gone on for ever, but eventually he gently pulled away. For a moment she stood, swayed, the only sound the mingle of their ragged breathing. Slowly reality intruded—the red and gold décor, the darkness outside illuminated by the London streetlights and the brightness of the moon.

Think. Speak. Move.

The directions seemed to be blocked. Her synapses were clearly misfiring…all signals from her brain were fuzzed by the aftershock of the kiss.

Do something.

Finally the order made its way through and she took a shaky step backwards, regained control of her vocal cords. 'Right. I'll be on my way, then.'

'No. Wait.'

To her irritation he had pulled himself together way

faster than she had and now stood there eyeing her with a gleam of something she couldn't interpret.

'There is no need for me to wait.' To her relief, annoyance had served to dispel the effect of their lip-lock. 'I *need* to go and locate a groom.'

'Do you have anyone in mind?'

There was an edge to his voice. His grey eyes held a speculative nuance and she wondered if he was trying to probe her for information in the hope of using it against her.

'I have options,' she said, and kept her voice noncommittal even as she reviewed said options.

Her father had suggested he speak with one of the Il Boschetto di Sole employees, but the idea left Holly cold. Graham still worked on the grove—and the thought of marrying *another* Il Boschetto di Sole employee, even in name only, felt foolhardy. An employee might well hold out hopes of becoming a co-owner, of remaining married to her. Come to that, *anyone* she married might think the same.

She ran her London colleagues through her mind— whittled them down to three possibilities. But she could hardly call them up and propose. Plus, she barely knew them—how could she trust any of them to stick to an agreement? Il Boschetto di Sole was a huge asset—an immensely lucrative business.

'But no one specific?' he persisted.

'I'm not a fool. I wouldn't tell you if I had. Do *you* have a bride lined up?'

Now his lips quirked up in a smile that left her both baffled and suspicious. 'I'm not sure. Let's just say I have an idea.'

Which put him ahead of the game—seeing as his tone

indicated that *his* idea was a good one and hers sucked. 'Bully for you. Now, I really need to go.'

'Give me five minutes. I need to make a phone call to my lawyers. I may have a way out of this. Promise me you won't go until I've talked to them.'

Holly hesitated. 'A way out that your hotshot lawyers haven't already thought of?'

'They don't call me The Negotiator for nothing.'

'I didn't know they called you The Negotiator at all.'

'I'll be five minutes. Tops.'

'OK. I'll pack slowly.'

In fact he was marginally longer than the allotted time, and she had her suitcase packed and was at the door before he emerged from his bedroom. To her irritation her tummy did a little flip-flop—he looked gorgeous, and his smile held a vestige of triumph as he walked towards her and gestured to the sofa.

'You may want to sit.'

'I'm good here. Right by the door.'

Warning bells began to peal in her head; his smile was too self-assured for her liking. *Dammit.* Maybe he'd discovered a legal way to grant him victory.

'Just say it, Stefan.'

'Marry me.'

Holly stared at him as her brain scrambled to comprehend the words, tried to work out the trick, the punchline. Because there had to be one.

'Is this your idea of a joke? It's either that or you've gone loop-the-loop bananas.'

'No joke. I'm not entirely sure on the bananas front, but it makes sense.'

'On planet bananas, maybe.'

'Hear me out. If we marry each other we effectively

cancel out the competitive element of the will because we *both* fulfil the marriage criteria.'

The thought arrested her and she moved further into the room, studied his face more closely. 'But we'd have to stay married for a year.'

'Correct.'

'What would happen at the end of the year?'

'We would co-own Il Boschetto di Sole. Yesterday neither of us thought we'd own even an acre, so why not settle for fifty-fifty?'

'Split it?'

'Yes. Why not? This way guarantees us half each—I realise we'd need to figure out a fair way to actually divide the land, but I would be happy to do that up-front.'

Suspicion tugged at her as she searched for an ulterior motive. Was this some way to trick her out of everything? But instinct told her Stefan Petrelli didn't work like that.

Get real, Holly.

Had she learnt nothing? Her instinct when it came to men and their motives was hardly stellar.

'I don't get it. Why are you happy to do this?'

'A guaranteed fifty percent works for me. This way it also means I don't end up with a wife who will try to manipulate me. We would both be equally invested in the marriage and the subsequent divorce. This works. For *both* of us. If we have to marry, it makes sense to marry each other.'

Logic dictated that he was correct. Her brain computed the facts. She knew that her father would be more than content with ownership of any percentage of Il Boschetto di Sole. Plus she had to marry *someone*—way better to marry someone who wouldn't have power over her. But as she looked at him her tummy clenched at the mere thought of marrying him. She would be signing up to a year under the same roof as a man her hormones had targeted as the equivalent of the Holy Grail.

Grow up and suck it up.

This made sense—guaranteed her father ownership of the land he loved.

'This could work.' Deep breath. 'But we'd need to work out the rules. The practicalities.' Another deep breath. 'This would be a marriage of convenience.'

To her annoyance, she could hear the hint of a question in her tone.

Clearly so could he.

His eyebrow rose. 'Unless you have something else in mind?'

'No!' Though a small voice piped up asking *Why not?* This man was sex on legs, and they were attracted to each other. They would be sharing a roof for a year—didn't it make sense to take advantage?

Yet every instinct warned her that it was a bad idea. Stefan had freely admitted his only commitment was to a relationship carousel and she had no wish to climb aboard. What would happen when his need for variety came into play? If…*when*…she wasn't woman enough? She could almost taste the humiliation.

'This would be a strictly business arrangement.'

'Agreed. I make it a general rule not to mix business and pleasure. So, subject to working out the details, do we have a deal?'

'We have a deal.'

Without thought Holly held out her hand, and with only a fractional hesitation he stepped forward and took it.

Mistake. As she stared down at their clasped hands sensation shot through her and her body rewound to their kiss, imagined the heat of his hand on her back.

Quickly she tugged her hand free. 'I'm headed to bed.

I'll see you in the morning and we can iron out the details.' With that, she grabbed her suitcase and forced herself to walk rather than sprint for her bedroom.

Stefan stared at the closed door for a long moment. Was this marriage idea lunacy or genius? Best to go with the latter. This gained him land in Lycander and a place to scatter his mother's ashes. It also gave him control of the situation. The only issue was the thorny one of attraction—one that needed to be uprooted.

Holly did not fulfil his relationship criteria. She wanted a family, a relationship that held more than just the physical, and he couldn't offer that. If he couldn't pay he shouldn't play—and he shouldn't even have considered the idea that their marriage might be anything other than strictly business. He'd still been under the spell of that kiss. From now on in he'd make sure to keep his distance, and he was pretty damn sure Holly would do the same.

His phone buzzed and surprise shot through him as he saw the caller's identity. Take the call or decline the call? In the end curiosity won out.

He sank into the armchair and put the phone to his ear. 'Hi, Marcus. What can I do for you?'

Marcus Alriksson was Chief Advisor and one of the most influential men in Lycander—a man who was close to Prince Frederick, and a man who worked behind the scenes to help shape Lycander's future.

'Stefan. We need to talk. Any chance of setting up a video call?'

Hell, why not? It would be a relief to have his thoughts distracted from Holly.

'Sure.'

Minutes later Stefan faced Marcus, keeping his body deliberately relaxed as he studied the dark-haired man on the screen. The Chief Advisor gave nothing away, but his dark blue eyes studied Stefan with equal interest.

'So, Marcus, what can I do for you?'

'I want to discuss the situation with Il Boschetto di Sole. Will you be pursuing your claim?'

'Yes.'

'Good.'

Stefan raised his eyebrows. 'I'm flattered, Marcus. I didn't know you cared.'

'I *do* care. More to the point, Frederick cares. You and he could be friends. You choose not to be.'

That was not an avenue he wanted to go down. He didn't want to be friends with his half-brother—didn't want to be anything. He wanted to maintain a simple indifference.

Liar.

Deep down he still craved an older brother who'd fight his corner. Once Frederick had done that. Then he'd withdrawn. Stefan knew why—because Frederick had blamed his younger brother for Eloise's departure. Worst of all, Frederick had been right to condemn him.

All too aware of the other man's scrutiny, he dispelled the memories. Now was not the time.

'Is that what this is about? A call to friendship?'

'I want to discuss a deal.'

'What sort of deal?'

'I'll get to that, but first some background. Have you heard of an organisation called DFL?'

Stefan frowned in thought. 'It stands for Democracy for Lycander, right?'

'Correct. It is growing in prominence and support.' Marcus's expression matched his grim tone, and his dark eyebrows slashed in a frown. 'But I *will* take it down.'

Stefan emitted a snort. 'People are entitled to their opinions. *Everyone* can't agree with the idea of a monarchy.

Months ago you told me Frederick wanted to allow free-dom of opinion, planned to be less tyrannical than our fa-ther. Yet you want to "take it down"?'

'People *are* entitled to their opinions. But I have a per-sonal dislike for those people who choose to express said opinions through violence and racism.'

Marcus pressed a button on his screen and turned it round for Stefan to see.

Stefan perused the site, quickly assimilating sufficient information to realise that Democracy for Lycander was an organisation of the type that turned his stomach: a group that incited racism and violence under the guise of free-dom and democracy.

'OK. I take your point and I hope you nail them. But I'm not sure what this has to do with *me*.'

'Times have been hard recently. Frederick is doing his best to reverse the injustices perpetrated by your father but he needs time. Under Alphonse, housing, hospitals, education— every system—was allowed to fall into disrepair and the people are restless. The storm last year caused further dam-age to property, land and livelihoods. Frederick is still not trusted by everyone—is still judged as the Playboy Prince, despite the fact he is now married with a son.'

Stefan shrugged, tried to block off the unwanted pang of emotion. He'd meant what he said to Holly over dinner— this was not his problem. He owed Frederick nothing… owed Lycander even less.

'I'm still not sure where I come in.'

'If you plan to pursue your claim to Il Boschetto di Sole then I assume you're getting married?'

No surprise that Marcus Alriksson knew the terms of the Bianchi will—perhaps the only shocker was how long it had taken him to make contact.

'Yup.'

'Good. Then I have a deal to offer you.'

Not interested. Stefan bit the words back. Marcus wasn't a fool. He wouldn't have come to the table unless he was sure he had something concrete to offer.

'I'm listening.'

'Your marriage could be an opportunity for you and Frederick to mend fences.'

Stefan snorted. 'Don't play me for a fool. You don't give a damn about a touching Petrelli reunion—this is *politics*.'

'Partly. As I explained, Frederick could do with some support and the people could do with some positivity. You could provide both. The return of the exiled Prince... If you come back to support your brother it would show solidarity, and your acceptance and approval would boost Frederick's popularity. Especially if you gild that return with a wedding.'

'I'm not even sure I *do* accept and approve of Frederick and his policies.'

'Then come and see for yourself. Frederick and Sunita are in India at the moment. Come to Lycander—have a look. Then make a judgement call.'

'And if I approve? What do I get from this deal?'

'I want to use your marriage to bring you back into the family. Whether we like it or not there will be media coverage of your marriage, and there will be a lot of speculation about the will.' Marcus's face suddenly relaxed into a smile that seemed to transform it. 'My wife April...' Now his voice glowed with pride. 'She is a reporter and she assures me this is celebrity news gold. It will be played out as brother versus brother. Your story will be latched on to and revisited and I'm guessing you won't like that.'

'No, I won't. But I don't think there's a damn thing you can do about it.'

'I can provide you with a suitable bride and I can help orchestrate the publicity around your wedding.'

'I can do that myself. Hell, I could have a private ceremony on a secluded island and hide out there for a year. I get that you want to big up the marriage—make it a public spectacle for Lycander—and that you want the whole reunion and brotherly support. What do I get in return?'

'In return Frederick will restore your lands and titles, *and...*' He paused as if for an imaginary drum roll '...we'll give your mother recognition. Set the record straight once and for all—set up a foundation in her name. Whatever you want.'

Stefan's heart pounded in his ribcage.

Don't show emotion. Maintain a poker face.

But there was little point in faking either. He knew that many people believed the worst of his mother—thought her departure from Lycander had been an abandonment of her son and saw her through the tainted veil of rigged history—and he loathed it. This was a chance to vindicate her memory and he'd take it.

'Deal. But only if Frederick is on the level.' If his brother was simply a 'mini-me' of Alphonse, there was no way Stefan would play nice. 'I'll need to judge that.'

'Understood. The bride I have in mind is Lady Mary Fairweather. The licence is sorted and the helicopter is ready to go. You can be in Lycander in two hours.'

Stefan rose. 'Not so fast. I've already got a fiancée. I'm marrying Holly Romano.'

It gave him some satisfaction to see the surprise on Marcus's face.

Before he could react, Stefan finished, 'We'll talk again tomorrow.'

CHAPTER SIX

STEFAN RUBBED A hand over his face and tried to tell himself that two hours' sleep was sufficient. He pushed open the door to the living area of the hotel suite and came to a halt on the threshold. Holly stood by the window, her blonde hair tousled and shower damp, clad simply in jeans and a thick cable knit navy jumper, bare feet peeping out.

Desire tugged in his gut even as he recognised the supreme irony of the situation. This was his fiancée and she was completely off-limits. There could be no repeat of that kiss, no more allowing their attraction to haze and shimmer the air between them. For a start Holly did not share his relationship values, and secondly they now had a deal—one in which the stakes were now even higher.

For him it wasn't only Il Boschetto di Sole to be won. He could have all that Alphonse had taken from him in a deal that did not leave him beholden. And, even more importantly, he could win public recognition for his mother; set the rumours and falsehoods to rest once and for all.

But to do that he and Holly would have to play their marriage out in the public eye—something he needed to know she was on board with. It also meant they could not risk any complications, and giving in to their attraction would rate way up there on the 'complicated' scoreboard.

'Good morning.'

She turned from the window, her eyes full of caution. 'Good morning.' She gestured outside. 'Look at all those people out there…going about their normal business whilst *my* world has been upended.'

He moved closer, tried to block out the tantalising scent of freshly washed hair, the tang of citrus and an underlying scent that urged him to pull her into his arms and to hell with the consequences. But life didn't work like that. Actions had consequences, and once you'd acted you couldn't take that act back. Lord knew, *he* knew that.

So instead he stood beside her, careful not to touch, and looked outside at the scurrying figures. 'You'll find that a lot of those people will be experiencing their own upheavals and worries. But I agree—yesterday was a humdinger of a life-changer. But it is only temporary. One year and then you can have your life back. And half of Il Boschetto di Sole.'

One year. Three hundred and sixty-five days. Fifty-two weeks. God knew how many hours.

'And life doesn't have to change *that* much,' she added hopefully. 'I've thought about it. I know we have to live under the same roof, but if we can find a big enough roof we don't have to actually *see* each other much. We could even get somewhere with separate kitchens, or work out a rota or…'

'I get it—and I appreciate the amount of thought you've put into it.' Obscurely, a frisson of hurt touched him, even though he knew he should applaud her plan. It wasn't as if he wanted to act out happy coupledom. 'That sounds good, but before we settle down to wedded bliss there's the actual wedding to think about.'

'Yes. But that's not so complicated, is it? We'll give twenty-eight days' notice and then we can do a quick register office ceremony. Simple.'

'It's a little more complex than that.'

Go easy here. Clearly Holly's ideas for the wedding were a long way from the public spectacle now on the cards.

Suspicion narrowed her eyes. 'Complex *how*?'

'How about we discuss this over breakfast? And coffee?'

Coward.

'Fine.' Her forehead creased. 'Though I have the distinct impression that you hope food and drink will soften me up.'

'Busted.'

She sighed. 'Dinner does feel like a lifetime ago, and I *am* hungry. But do you mind if we go someplace else? Perhaps we could grab a takeaway coffee and walk for a while? I'd appreciate a chance to clear my head.'

'Works for me.' A chance to move, to expend some energy—perhaps the fresh air would blow away the cobwebs of intrigue. 'Any preference as to where?'

'I thought we could go to the Chelsea Physic Garden,' she suggested. 'It's not far from here. Every Sunday since I've got here I've explored somewhere in London. To begin with I did all the usual tourist places—you know, Big Ben and St Paul's Cathedral, which is awe-inspiring. I went to watch the Changing of the Guards too.'

Her smile was bright and contagious, and for an instant he could picture her, eyes wide, intent on watching the traditional ceremony.

She shook her head. 'Sorry—I must sound so gauche. It's my first time away from Lycander and I decided to...'

'Make the most of it?'

'Explore as much as I could. But I've also discovered lots of amazing quirky places, and the Physic Garden is one of them.'

So five minutes later they headed across the marble lobby, through the sleek glass revolving doors and out onto the cold but sunny autumn street. Russet leaves fluttered past in the breeze and the sun shone down from a cloudless sky.

They walked briskly. Holly made no attempt to make conversation and yet the silence felt comfortable rather than awkward. For him it was a much-needed buffer until they sat down to negotiate exactly how their marriage would work.

Fifteen minutes and a café stop brought them to the gardens, with bacon and avocado sandwiches and take-away coffees in hand. As they wended their way through he looked around, feeling a sense of tranquillity and awe at the number of different plants on show and their medicinal properties.

'We'll walk through the rock garden, if you like?' Holly offered. 'It's the oldest rock garden in the world, partly made with stones from the Tower of London and also Icelandic lava that was brought over here in 1772.'

Her face was animated as she spoke, and for an instant he wished that they could simply wander around and explore this place she clearly loved. That there was no agenda.

'Once we get through here, and then go round a bit, there is a secluded part where we can sit.'

Different scents wafted through the air, and soon they arrived at a pretty walled area and settled onto a bench.

Once seated, he unwrapped his sandwich and turned to face her. He waited until she'd taken her first appreciative bite and figured it was as good a time as any.

'So the wedding—there's been a change of plan. I've decided to go public with our engagement.'

She stilled, her sandwich halfway to her mouth.

'This is a good time for the exiled Prince to return to Lycander—I want to use our wedding as a publicity stunt to smooth that return.'

Lowering the sandwich, she opted for a gulp of coffee. 'When exactly did you decide that? You didn't mention any return over dinner. Or when you "proposed".' She tilted her head to one side, her blonde hair rippling in the breeze as she studied his expression, her blue eyes now wary, as if in search of a trap.

'I spoke with Marcus Alriksson last night. Lycander's—'

'Chief Advisor. I know who Marcus Alriksson is.'

'And we agreed that this is an optimum moment for my return.'

'Because Crown Prince Frederick could do with some family support,' Holly agreed, and suddenly there was that smile again. 'I *knew* you couldn't be as indifferent about Lycander as you made out yesterday.'

For a daft second Stefan wished he deserved the approval that radiated from her—but he didn't, and he wouldn't let her cast him in family-man mode, nor as a knight in shining armour.

'That is not my motivation. Marcus and I have made a deal. If he can convince me that Frederick is genuine about reform in Lycander then, yes, I will offer my support—in return for the lands my father took from me. No land, no support, no return.'

Careful here. He had no intention of sharing *all* the details of the deal he'd made, and he didn't want to bring up Eloise.

He forced himself to hold Holly's gaze, saw the flash of disappointment and steeled himself not to give a damn. He owed Frederick nothing. The whole point of severing family ties was the fact that they no longer existed—couldn't be used to push or pull.

'But my motivation is beside the point. The point is that it does change the parameters of our marriage. The wedding will now be a grand spectacle, acted out on the global stage, and our marriage will be under public scrutiny. In order to be able to offer Frederick support I need the Lycandrian public to accept me—and you would be a key player in that. I would want you to be in charge of "branding" us as well, of course, as being part of that brand. I will pay you a generous salary for that.'

That was the bunch of carrots. Now for the stick…

'However, if this is too much for you take on board, I understand. We can abandon our marriage plan and go back to the marriage race. But I think it's fair to tell you that Marcus has a bride lined up for me.'

There was silence as she thought, her hands cupped tightly around her coffee cup. He realised he was holding his breath, his whole body tense as he awaited her decision. *Relax.* Worst-case scenario: he'd marry Marcus's choice of bride. Not his preferred option, but not the end of the world either.

Turning, she looked at him. 'I accept your offer—but I have an additional condition.'

'What?'

'If you don't have children I would like you to leave your share of Il Boschetto di Sole to me or my children. That way one day the land will be reunited. It seems fair to me. You are asking for my help to win more land for yourself—this way my family will gain something in the future. Something important.' Her gaze didn't leave his. 'Of course you can refuse. Marry whoever Marcus has chosen. But I think you have a better chance of pulling off a "branding" exercise with me. Otherwise, I guarantee all the publicity will be about the "marriage race".'

Annoyance warred with admiration. It turned out Holly

had a talent for negotiation too. Her request was unusual, but reasonable.

'Agreed.' No point prolonging negotiations. 'So we have a new deal?'

'Yes.'

This time she nodded her head, kept her hands firmly around her cup. 'But I'll be up-front. I *do* think you have a better chance with me, but this wedding won't be an easy sell. People will realise we are getting married through legal necessity. We certainly can't pretend it's a love match. Especially when we plan to start divorce proceedings in a year.'

'You'll need to find some positive spin.'

'Ha-ha! I'm not sure an army of washing machines could provide enough spin.'

Placing the coffee down, she tugged a serviette from her bag, a pen from her pocket and began to scribble.

'The terms of the will are bound to be published, so any story we come up with needs to acknowledge the legal necessity of our marriage. But we need to incorporate some sort of "feel-good" factor into it.'

For a few minutes she stared into space and he watched her, seeing the intense concentration on her face, the faint crease on her brow, hearing the click-click of the pen as she fiddled with it. Her blonde hair gleamed in the autumn sunlight, gold flecks seemed to shimmer in the light breeze. His gaze snagged on her lips and a sudden rush of memory hit him. The taste of her lips, the warmth of her response…

'Stefan! Earth to Stefan!'

'Sorry.'

Get with it, Petrelli.

'How about this? When I came to London a year ago I was intrigued by you—the exiled Prince of my country—so I called you up and asked to meet you. We hit it off and started a relationship. A low-key relationship, because that suited both of us. Perhaps Roberto Bianchi found out—we'll never know. Anyway, when we came to know the terms of the will we really did not want to fight—we even wondered if he'd been hoping we'd marry each other and that's what we decided to do. It could be that it won't work, and we both know that, but in that case we will each own half the grove.'

Stefan looked at her appreciatively. 'I like it. That has a definite ring of authenticity and, whilst we *are* fibbing, it isn't so great a fib as all that. Hell, it could even have happened like that.'

For a second his imagination ran with the idea. Their meeting, the tug of attraction… Only in this version it was an attraction that had no barriers, an attraction that could be fulfilled…

Whoa. Rein it in.

The silence twanged. Her cheeks flushed and then she let out a sigh. 'I think we need to role-play it.'

'Huh?' Given where his imagination had been heading, he couldn't hold back the note of shock.

'No!' Her flush deepened; pink climbed the angles of her cheekbones. 'I don't mean every detail. *Obviously.* I mean we're going to be questioned closely on this. How did we meet? Where was it? What were we wearing? How did we feel? I assume part of this gig will involve press interviews and appearances on TV. So I think we need to have a practice run. I know it feels stupid, but I think it's important.'

Stefan shrugged. 'OK. Here and now?'

'Sure. Why not?' Holly looked around, checked there was no one to see them, no one close enough to overhear them. 'So… I've written to you, asking to meet with you. Why do you agree, given that you are known to have little interest in Lycander?'

'You sent a photo?'

'No!'

'Joking! I'm *joking*.'

'Well, I'm not laughing.'

But he wasn't fooled. There was smile in her eyes—he could see it. 'Inside you are. But, OK, fair enough. I can see why this is a good idea. But let's back up a step. What did you say in your letter?'

'Hmm… Let's work backwards—what would have persuaded you to meet me? How about if I'd asked for help? For Lycander? Extolled Frederick's virtues?'

'I'd have told you to take a hike. Preferably a long way away.'

'All right. Let's say that's what you did and I took umbrage and demanded an apology. I turned up at your offices, sweet-talked my way past the front desk and…'

'You'd never have got past my PA.'

She glared at him. 'OK. I lingered behind a potted plant until she left to make a cup of coffee—or maybe she was on holiday, so it was a temp and…'

'You got into my office and I was so intrigued by your initiative I agreed to listen.'

'Perfect. We got talking and decided to continue the conversation over dinner.'

'Italian. I think we had spaghetti marinara and fettucine Alfredo.'

Dammit, he could almost taste the tangy tomato sauce, smell the oregano, picture her forking up the spaghetti with a twirl, her laugh when she ended up with a spot of sauce on the tip of her nose.

'And then a tiramisu to share, with coffee and a liqueur.'

There was a silence, and he was suddenly intensely aware of how close Holly was. Somehow during their conversation they had moved closer to each other, caught up in the replay. Now the animation had slipped from her face, left her wide-eyed, lips slightly parted. One hand rose to tuck a tendril of hair behind her ear.

She looked exactly as she would have looked on that mythical first date.

'And then this…' he said and, moving across he turned to face her, cupped her face in his hand and kissed her.

Imagination and reality fused. The surrounding scents of the garden combined with the idea that this was really a date. The kiss was sweet, and yet underlain with a passion that heated up as she gave a small moan against his mouth. In response he deepened the kiss, felt the pull of desire, the caress of her fingers on the nape of his neck.

He had no idea how long they kissed until the real world intruded in the shape of a terrier. The small dog bounded up to them and started barking, leaping up, desperate for the remains of Holly's abandoned bacon sandwich.

They pulled apart. His expression was no doubt as dazed as hers, and her lips were swollen, her hair dishevelled. The dog, uncaring, continued to target the bacon, and within minutes its owner had hurried up, hand in hand with a toddler.

The little girl beamed at them. 'Hello!'

Stefan pulled himself together. 'Hello. Is this your dog?'

'Yes. He's called Teddy.'

'What a lovely name.' Holly leaned down and patted the dog, which promptly rolled over and presented his tummy.

'He likes you.'

'I like him too.'

'Come on, Lily. Come on, Teddy.' The woman grinned at them. 'Sorry for the interruption!'

'No problem,' Holly managed.

Once the trio had receded into the depths of the gardens she put her head in her hands. 'I am *beyond* embarrassed.'

'The exiled Prince of Lycander and his fiancée—caught necking like a couple of teenagers.'

'On a bench over a bacon and avocado butty!'

Suddenly Holly began to giggle and, unable to help himself, Stefan chuckled. Within minutes they both couldn't stop laughing. As soon as his laughter nearly subsided he would catch her eye and he'd be off again. In truth, he couldn't remember the last time he'd laughed so freely.

Eventually they leant back, breathless, and Holly shook her head. 'I'm exhausted!'

Stefan glanced at his watch. 'And we've still got loads to do if we're going to catch a plane tomorrow morning.'

'Tomorrow morning?'

'Yup. We're headed to Lycander first thing.'

The words were a reminder of what this was all about. The reason for their role-play was to create an illusion, to enable him to keep his deal with Marcus.

'There's no point hanging about—especially as I want to pre-empt any publicity about the will.'

The private jet was already booked. Marcus had offered the use of a royal helicopter, but Stefan had been resolute in his refusal. Until he sussed out whether Frederick was on the level he would accept nothing from the monarchy.

'I can't just pack up and go at such short notice. I have a job and...'

'I am sure Lamberts will understand—especially given the publicity potential. If they kick up a fuss negotiate. Say you'll use them to help with the wedding.'

All trace of laughter had disappeared from her eyes now. 'Is *everything* a deal to you?'

He rose to his feet. 'Everything in life is a deal. You'd do well to remember that.'

CHAPTER SEVEN

THE FOLLOWING MORNING Holly unclicked her seat belt as the jet cleaved its way through the clouds. The whole idea that she was aboard a private jet seemed surreal; in fact the whole situation seemed to personify the idea of a waking dream.

The past day they had been caught up in a whirl of arrangements—conference calls with Marcus Alriksson, packing, planning, plotting... Oddly, the most real event had been their time in the Physic Garden. Great—how messed up was her head when that role play felt real?

A glance at Stefan and her breath caught in her throat. Damn the man for the way he affected her hormones. Their kiss was still seared on her brain—just the thought of it was enough to tingle her lips, send a shimmer of desire over her skin. But it was a dead-end desire and she knew it—it was imperative that she focus on reality. Actual cold, hard facts.

This marriage was to be undertaken for legal reasons and the wedding itself was to be a publicity stunt—a means for the exiled Prince to stage a return.

A sudden sense of empathy surfaced in her. If this was surreal to *her*...

Tucking a tendril of hair behind her ear, she looked

away from the window and towards him. 'How are you feeling?'

'Fine.'

'Hang on…' Reaching out, she prodded his chest and a fizz jolted through her, demonstrating that their attraction was still alive and kick-boxing.

'What are you doing?'

'A check to see if you're made of granite or some strange alien substance. Because, assuming you are flesh and blood, you *must* be feeling something other than "fine". You haven't been to Lycander in eight years…you're about to be reunited with your brother…you—'

'I'm *fine*. It's just a place like any other.'

But his gaze couldn't quite hold hers, and for a tell-tale second his eyes scooted to the window, as if to gauge their direction, estimate the time that remained until they got there.

She shook her head. 'I don't believe you can be fine.'

'You can believe what you want.' He ran a hand over his face. 'Sorry. I didn't mean to snap, but how about we change the subject? Go through the plan of action?'

'Distraction therapy?'

'Whatever.' But his tone belied the word, held a hint of a smile. 'Let's just do it.'

'OK.' Holly ticked the points off on her fingers. 'First up, a meet-and-greet and a joint press interview with general questions.'

Stefan nodded. 'Marcus will be there, and his wife April. She'll take us off to coach us for the television interview.'

'What about Frederick?'

'He and Sunita are on a trip to India—they have an educational charitable foundation out there. I told Marcus I'd rather postpone the touching reunion scene until I've had a chance to look around…see if I want to support him.'

Holly glanced at him, caught the note of bitterness. 'You must be nervous about seeing him again?'

'Nope. He's just a person.'

'It doesn't work like that. Lycander isn't "just a place". It's the place where you were born, part of your royal heritage, and so it's part of you. Frederick is your *brother*. You grew up with him.'

Wistfulness touched her. If only *she* had had a brother her whole life would have been different. Her whole family's life would have been different. Perhaps her parents' marriage would have blossomed instead of withering; perhaps her mother would have loved her…bonded with her.

'That has to mean something.'

'Not necessarily anything good.'

His tone was flat, dismissive, and yet she sensed an underlying hurt. 'I don't buy the whole flesh-and-blood bond.'

'It's not about that. You spent time together—you shared a family life. That bonds you…gives you something to build on.'

Or it should. Sadness touched her that it hadn't worked that way for her—that her mother had been unable to find it in her to love her. Had been able to walk away and leave her behind without a backward glance in the quest for a life of her own.

Perhaps Stefan would agree that her mother had done the right thing? One life. One chance. Every man or woman for themselves. But at least he had specified that the mantra only worked as long as no one got hurt. Holly *had* been hurt, with a searing pain that had banded her chest daily in the immediate aftermath, with the realisation that she would never win her mother's love. Even now sometimes she would catch herself studying her reflection, wondering what it was about her that was so damn unlovable.

Stop, Holly. This wasn't about her.

'I just think that you should give Frederick a chance.'

'That is exactly what I *am* doing,' he said evenly. 'Marcus has arranged various visits and meetings with government officials. I'll be doing some of my own spot-visits as well. If Frederick is on the level I will uphold my end of the deal.'

In theory he was right. But she could sense his resistance to the idea that this could be more than a deal—sensed too that it was time to leave the subject.

'Right. I'm going to go and change.'

'You look fine to me.'

Holly glanced down at her outfit. 'I'm in jeans and a T-shirt,' she pointed out. 'I don't want Lycander's first impression of me as their exiled Prince's fiancée to be that I couldn't be bothered to dress up a bit.' She eyed him. 'And neither do you.'

It was his turn to look down. 'What's wrong with it? I'm still channelling the lumberjack look.' His smile was still drop-dead gorgeous, but his chin jutted with stubbornness. 'I am not going to play the *part* of a prince. I *am* one—whether the people like it or not.'

'So you're going for the accept-me-as-you-see-me approach?'

'Yes. I asked you to sell my brand—this is it. Jeans, T-shirt and shirt.'

Holly studied his expression, knew there was some undercurrent there that she didn't understand. 'Actually you asked me to *create* our brand.'

'Tom-ay-to, tom-ah-to.' He waved a hand in dismissal.

Royal dismissal, no doubt, that brooked no argument. Well, *tough*.

'You are asking me to help you win the support of the Lycandrian people. You must know that feelings are mixed about you in Lycander?'

'The people who hate me will hate me whatever I do or say.'

Why was he being so stubborn about this? He wasn't an idiot. What was his problem with playing the part of a prince? After all he had *chosen* to make this return from exile.

'What you wear is your choice. I can't strip you down and dress you in—'

Oh, hell. Had she really just said that?

'You could try,' he offered, and his voice was like molten chocolate.

'I'll pass, thank you.' Her attempt to keep her voice ice-cold was marred by a slight tremble she couldn't mask. 'The point is…'

What *was* the point? Oh, yes…

Narrowing her eyes, she erased the vision of a naked Stefan and snapped her fingers in an *aha* movement. 'When you went for that estate agent interview all those years ago, what did you wear?'

'A suit.'

'Why?'

'Because I needed to show respect. I needed to project the right image because I was the seeker, the supplicant.'

'Well, like it or not, that's what you are now. Not with the people who will hate you regardless, but the people who are willing to give you a chance. Show them that you care what they think—give them a good first impression. Once they get to know you then you can go lumberjack whenever you want. This isn't about proving you're a prince—it's about showing them what sort of prince you *are*.'

His jaw clenched and she sensed her words had hit home, though she didn't know why.

Then he shook his head. 'Point taken. But I didn't pack a suit.'

'Lucky for you, I did. Or rather I got Marcus to sort one out. It's in the back.'

There was a pause and she braced herself, then he huffed out a sigh. 'You're *good*. I'll be back in five.'

'Me too.' No point in Stefan looking the part if she didn't too.

Holly grabbed her case and headed towards the bathroom. Half an hour later she surveyed herself with satisfaction. She loved the outfit she'd chosen for her debut appearance as the exiled Prince's fiancée. Not too over the top, she'd blended designer with High Street. A pretty floral dress, with a matching cardigan over the top.

Right. Time to rock and roll.

As she re-entered the seating area her feet ground to a halt. The man was gorgeous in his uniform of checked shirt and jeans, but *this*…this was something else. The grey of the suit echoed his eyes, seeming to enhance their intensity, and the snowy shirt was unbuttoned to reveal the strong column of his throat. All she could think about was the encased power of his body, the shape of his hands, the unruly black curl on the curve of his neck…

Oh, God.

She swallowed the whimper that threatened to emerge. 'I approve.' Wholeheartedly.

The pilot's voice came over the intercom, announcing their imminent landing, and she hauled in a breath. For a moment their gazes held and she saw the sudden skitter of vulnerability in his.

No matter what he said, his nerves must be making their presence felt. Soon enough he'd set foot on Lycandrian soil for the first time in nigh on a decade. What had happened between him and Alphonse? Why hadn't he returned for his father's funeral or his brother's wedding? How was he feeling?

No doubt if she asked he'd say 'fine'. So there was no point.

Instead she stepped forward, placed her hands on the wall of his chest, feeling the pounding of his heart through the silky shirt material. She stood on tiptoe and gently brushed her lips against his. Stepped back and smiled.

He tipped her face up gently, the touch of his fingers against her chin soft and sensuous, and then he lowered his lips to hers, gently brushed them with his own. The sensation was so sweet, so tender, that she closed her eyes.

The plane jolted onto the runway, lurching enough to bring her to her senses even as his arms steadied her, ensuring she had her balance before he released her.

Then he held out his hand. 'Let's do this.'

CHAPTER EIGHT

As THEY DESCENDED onto the tarmac the smell hit Stefan with an intensity he hadn't expected. Lemons and citrus blossoms mingled with the tang of fuel, floating towards him on a breeze that had a lightness found nowhere else in the world. Familiarity hit him, and his head whirled with a miasma of repressed memories.

For an instant he froze—couldn't move, couldn't breathe—his gut lurched and he set his defence barriers at maximum in an attempt to quell the tumble of emotions that swirled inside him.

Images of his younger self—the iniquities and bleakness of his formative years, the anger and the pain and the dull ache of grief. The determination that the moment he could escape his father's control he would turn his back on being a prince.

And now he was back. Perhaps this had been a mistake.

A pressure on his hand tugged him back to reality. Holly's warm clasp offered comfort and gave him the impetus to move forward. Hell—he'd be damned if he'd show weakness. The exiled Prince would return in style.

A glance down at Holly strengthened that resolve, caused the fake rictus on his lips to morph into a genuine smile. He was back for a reason—to regain his rights, and most of all to vindicate his mother, set the record straight.

He'd walked away from Lycander with nothing—he sure as hell could walk back in now. Stand tall in his mother's memory.

Scanning the crowd, he spotted Marcus at the back of a line of press, a vibrant redhead by his side, and then questions flooded the air.

'Stefan, how does it feel to be back?'

'When are you meeting Frederick?'

'Holly, how did the two of you meet?'

'When is the wedding? What about the will?'

'Why have you come back?'

The barrage pumped his adrenaline as he worded his answers, strove for balance, aware that each answer needed to be closed against misinterpretation and twist.

'Overwhelming…in a good way… As soon as possible, but I'd like our first meeting to be in private…'

Holly's turn, and she didn't even flinch.

'I moved to London for a couple of years and curiosity overcame me—I wanted to know more about the exiled Prince, and once I got to know him better I wanted to bring him home.'

Holly again.

'I'm sure you've all heard rumours about Count Roberto's will and its connection with us—we will explain it, but in an official interview.'

Marcus stepped forward. 'Time to break it up now, guys. I promise you'll have a chance to ask more questions in the next few days. Contact my office for the official schedule, if you haven't already.'

'Hold on,' Stefan interrupted. 'I think there was one more question. Someone asked why I've come back, and I'd like to answer that. I've come back because Lycander is part of my heritage. It's the place where I was born and where I grew up—it is the place that helped make me who I am today.'

With that, and with Holly's hand still firmly clasped in his, he followed Marcus and April towards a dark chauffeured car.

Once inside the spacious interior, Marcus leant forward. 'Did you mean that last answer?'

'Does it matter?'

'No. I was just curious.' The Chief Advisor sat back. Turning, he looked at his wife and smiled, his whole face transformed with warmth. 'April will take you to your hotel now.'

'Yup. Ostensibly I'm doing an interview for my old magazine,' April explained. 'But I'll also be coaching you, checking you can pull this off.'

Stefan glanced at Holly, relieved that she had gone through their story in such detail. 'Sounds like a plan.'

Within minutes the car pulled up and Marcus nodded. 'This is my stop. I'll see you both tomorrow, for the first round of official visits.'

Soon the car pulled up again, outside a charming hotel-front, and Stefan inwardly applauded Marcus's choice—expensive without being in-your-face luxurious, just the right backdrop for a younger brother who didn't wish to upstage Lycander's ruler. The hotel had an olde-worlde charm—it was a converted chateau, complete with ancient stone walls, a paved courtyard and iron balconies.

They all climbed out, and there loomed the might of the palace in the middle distance. More memories crowded in—flash images of times he would rather forget. The enforced physical regime, the pain as he forced his trembling muscles into yet another push-up, another hoist of weights. Knowing if he missed his target by even a single rep there would be no food. And, worse, that it would be even longer until he saw his mother again.

His father's voice.

'You'll thank me for this one day, Stefan. You'll be a tougher man than me, a better prince. Tough enough so you won't fall prey to the stupidity of love. It never lasts. It never lives up to what you expect it to be. And it makes you weak. Look at your mother. Her life is miserable because she won't give you up. I would have given her wealth, prestige, but she wouldn't take it. Look at you—you show your weakness by your refusal to give her up. Your love for each other gives me the power, gives me the control.'

His father's words seemed to float towards him on the breeze, echoing in his ears, and he realised that April was staring at him. But before the red-haired woman could say anything Holly had launched into a series of questions about the forthcoming interviews and photographs, about whether April would be covering the wedding.

They were questions that politeness forced April to respond to, giving him time to recover. This had to stop; he would *not* let his father control him from the grave.

'OK. Follow me,' April said. 'Franco will bring in your luggage. I've booked a room where we can chat in private and set it up to look like your television interview will.'

Minutes later they were ensconced in a meeting room. April sat herself on a comfortable leather chair and gestured for them to sit on a small sofa.

Stefan glanced at the seat—it didn't look as if there was any choice but for them to sit up close and personal. Trying for nonchalance, he lowered himself onto the red velvet fabric and waited whilst Holly manoeuvred herself next to him. Under April's expectant gaze Holly shifted closer to him, the warmth of her thigh pressed against his, and he willed his body not to tense.

'Right,' April said briskly. 'I know the truth, but I'd like you both to act as though I don't. As if you are on camera.' Green eyes studied them critically. 'You need to look more relaxed at being so close.'

Easier said than done.

'Show you're comfortable together and that you get reassurance from each other. Like you did when you arrived.'

Stefan blinked as an alarm bell rang in his head; he *hadn't* been acting when he'd descended from that plane into Lycander's heat-laden breeze. *No biggie.* He'd have clutched anyone's hand for reassurance when he'd been so stupidly stricken by memories.

'Let's get started,' he suggested.

April ran them through their first meeting and nodded her approval at the end. 'Good. Now, the next complicated question you'll need to field is: what happens in a year? Is this wedding just a legal necessity?'

Holly leant forward. 'We wouldn't have got married now if it weren't for the will, because it's so early in our relationship.'

'But you went to London a year ago—many would say that is a long time.'

Stefan shook his head. 'Marriage is way too important to rush into until you're sure. My father had four wives and he married each of them within weeks of meeting them. I'd like to think I've learnt from his mistakes.'

'Fair enough.' April nodded. 'But that still hasn't answered the question. What happens in a year?'

Holly intervened. 'Neither of us can predict the future; all we can do is wait and see and assess our relationship then. But...'

'Obviously we want a happy ending,' Stefan finished for her.

'That works,' April said. 'But you need to look at each

other when you say that. Look as if the happy ending you're picturing is riding off into the sunset together—not waving farewell in the divorce court.'

Holly exhaled a small sigh and Stefan felt a pang of guilt that he had asked her to do this—go on air and fake a relationship. Without thought he reached out and covered her hand with his.

'Good idea,' April said with approval.

He tried to look as though it was all part of the role-play, reminding himself that Holly stood to gain from this too. Guilt did not have to come into play.

'So, next big question,' April continued. 'Are you in love? Holly, you go first.'

The silence went on too long. 'We're…um…certainly headed that way…'

'No, no, *no*!' April said. 'That is not going to work. You try, Stefan. Are you in love?'

Stefan met the green eyes. 'Absolutely,' he stated, but even he could hear the false bonhomie.

The green eyes closed. 'OK. That is going to fool no one. To be blunt, it's pants, and you are going to have to practise. Given the circumstances, you *will* be asked that question or a variant.'

'Fine, we'll work on it.' Stefan shifted on the chair. 'Now, can we please move on to some easier questions?'

April met his gaze. 'I'm not sure there *are* many easy questions. For example, you will be asked why you left Lycander. About your relationship with your father.'

Stefan could feel moisture sheen his neck. 'Then I'll decline to answer. I'll confirm what everyone knows: we parted on bad terms.'

No way would he bare his soul or the memories of his childhood for the media to grab hold of. He didn't even like sharing memories with himself—had locked them away deep inside. And that was where they would stay.

'And your mother?'

'I'll tell the truth about her. That she was a good, loving woman who didn't deserve the type of divorce that was meted out to her. But I won't be drawn into a big discussion.'

Next to him he sensed Holly's withdrawal, a movement of discomfort as if she were about to say something.

April frowned, glanced across at both of them. 'Is there a problem with that?'

'Of course not.' Holly's voice sounded sure, but he could still sense her tension.

'Good.' April closed her notebook with a snap and smiled. 'You need to work on being more lovey-dovey and then I reckon you can pull it off. As a reporter, I don't usually condone lies, but I have learnt that sometimes there are shades of grey and I think what you are trying to do here is a good thing for Lycander. But it *is* risky. So please be careful. People will be watching you; they will be looking for evidence of a break-up or a fake-up. There will be a huge amount of interest in you both and you will be subject to intense and invasive scrutiny. People will do *anything* to get information, because information is valuable. So stay in character.' April rose. 'I'll be in touch for another practice session before the television interview.'

'We'll look forward to it.' He made no attempt to hide the irony but April took no umbrage, merely smiled at him.

'I'll let Marcus know how it went.'

Stefan nodded. 'I'll see you out.'

Holly watched as Stefan and April exited the meeting room and exhaled a long breath. She felt as if she'd run a marathon. Her whole body ached from the conflicting signals she'd sent it for the past two hours. Pretending to be attracted to a man she was desperately attracted to but didn't want to be at all attracted to—the conundrum was testing her hormones to the limit.

She looked up as he re-entered the room. 'I've asked the kitchens to rustle us up a picnic supper and bring it to our room,' he said.

To her surprise her stomach gave a small gurgle, and it occurred to her that she was hungry. 'That sounds brilliant.' She looked at him. 'You are very good at providing meals.'

The idea was a novelty. Ever since her mother had left Holly had taken on the role of cook, desperately wanting to look after her father, and the correct meals had become even more important when her father's heart condition had been diagnosed.

'Food is way too important to miss,' Stefan said.

'No arguments here.'

They made their way up the stairs to their suite, and Holly halted on the threshold. The suite was an exquisite mixture of contemporary comfort and historic detail. The stone walls of the lounge boasted a medieval fireplace, ornate gilded mirrors and beautifully woven tapestries. Latticed windows showed a view of the mountains in the distance and the hustle and bustle of the city below. The furniture was the last word in simple luxury—warm wood, and a sofa and armchairs that beckoned you to sink into their comfort.

So she kicked off her heels and did exactly that, just as someone knocked on the door.

Stefan let a waiter in and the young man pushed in a trolley laden with sandwiches, mini-pastries, slices of quiche, miniature pies and bowls of salad in a kaleidoscope of greens and reds.

Once the repast was arranged the waiter withdrew. Stefan seated himself opposite her and they both served themselves.

'This place is utterly incredible,' Holly said. 'Just the sort of place I imagined princesses living in when I was a little girl.'

'Is that what you wanted to be when you grew up?'

'It was one of many scenarios. I also wanted to be an award-winning actress, a famous pop star, a ballerina, an astronaut and a prize-winning scientist. The key elements in all these scenarios was that I'd win prizes... Oh, and for some reason I also always imagined myself arriving to pick up my prize in a pink limo!'

Perhaps that had been her own personal assertion that she was a girl and everyone would just have to lump it.

'What about you? What did you imagine yourself being when you grew up? I mean, you were already a prince.'

Stefan's face tightened and a shadow crossed his eyes. She knew her words had twanged a memory, and not a good one. But then he shrugged,

'I was never a real prince; that's why I left my kingdom as soon as I could. But I'm back now, and if we're going to pull this off we have some more work to do.'

Her tummy plummeted as she wondered if he was going to suggest they practise being 'lovey-dovey.' Not a good plan—not here and now, with her body already seesawing after the forced proximity of their interview.

'I think we need to get to know more about each other,' she said. 'The kind of facts you learn over time. So how about we do twenty questions? I'll go first. Favourite colour: pink.'

One eyebrow rose and his lips quirked with a small hint of amusement. She had little doubt that he knew exactly why she was rushing into a fact-finding mission.

'Dark blue. Favourite film genre: Action.'

'I'll watch anything. Ditto with books.'

'Anything sci-fi.'

Forty minutes later he stretched. 'That was a good session—and now I'm ready to hit the sack. Unless, of course, you want to practise anything else?'

'Nope.' As far as she was concerned the whole lovey-dovey issue could wait. 'I'm ready for bed too.'

In one synchronised movement they both looked around.

In one synchronised syllable they both cursed. 'Damn.'

There was only one interconnecting door.

Stefan walked over to it and pushed it open to reveal one bedroom. *Well, duh.* Of *course* they only had one bedroom. They were meant to be in a relationship.

'Um… I'm happy to take the sofa and you can have the bedroom.' Even as she made the offer she knew it was foolish—knew what he'd say, knew he would be right.

On cue: 'Too risky. Given what April said, I'm sure the hotel staff will practically have a forensics team in here tomorrow. The last thing we need is a story on how we didn't share a bed.'

'So what are we going to do?' Her voice emerged as a panic-engendered squeak.

Stefan frowned. 'You're completely safe, Holly. I won't try anything on.'

That was the least of her worries—she was more concerned with what *she* might do. 'I know that.'

'So what's the problem?'

Yet for all his nonchalance a tiny bead of perspiration dotted his temple and she could see that his jaw was clenched. Maybe he was as spooked as she was.

'The problem is…' *I'm scared I'll jump you in my sleep.* 'I don't want us to get carried away by mistake.'

'We won't.' Now his voice was firm, all sign of strain gone. 'We both agreed this is a business arrangement, a marriage of convenience. That is the point of it—convenience. So adding any form of intimacy into the mix would be foolish, and I'm not a fool. We're both adults. Let's act like that. We are hardly going to succumb to pangs of lust like adolescents. The bed is huge—plenty of room for both of us to sleep in.'

Stefan seemed totally capable of letting his brain rule his pants and she should be pleased about that. His words all made perfect sense and yet hurt pinged inside her, each syllable a pin-prick of irrational pain. If he were truly attracted to her wouldn't it be hard for him to be so logical, so rational and in control?

Graham's words still echoed in her brain: *'Not woman enough…' 'Inexperienced…'* Maybe she wasn't woman enough for Stefan either—maybe he thought she was behaving like an adolescent. Maybe she'd got those kisses all wrong. Maybe what had been dynamite for her had been a damp squib for him.

'You're right.' No, no, *no*! That sounded colourless and flat, as if she didn't really believe he was right. 'It would be stupid to muddy the water when the whole point of this is to make it clean and fair. Entering into a physical relationship with each other would be messy—and I'm not a big believer in your type of sex anyway.'

'*My* type of sex? What the hell is that supposed to mean?'

His anger flashed now, but Holly didn't care. If he could sit there so calm and unbothered by the idea of spending a whole night next to each other then she might as well throw diplomacy out of the window.

'The kind that has no emotional context. It's negotiated physical sex. That's too clinical for me.' A part of Holly reeled at the sheer idiocy of this statement. But the principle was sound.

'I've had no complaints.' There was an edge of frost in his voice now.

'That's because you go for the sort of woman who is on the same page as you. I'm not.'

That at least was true. Stefan Petrelli liked variety—swapped his women out at regular intervals. That was not for her.

'In which case sharing a bed with me shouldn't pose a problem.' The frost had dropped a few degrees to ice now. 'I'm turning in. Would you like to use the bathroom first?'

'Yes, please.'

Perhaps a cold shower would help. She felt hot and bothered, mixed up, deflated, angry, relieved… Every emotion in the lexicon swirled inside her. Hell—they weren't even married yet.

Fifteen minutes later she was safely under the duvet on her side of the king-sized four-poster bed, flanked by a barricade of pillows, clad in flannel pyjamas buttoned to the top, eyes tightly shut as she simulated sleep.

The bathroom door opened and closed, then a few minutes later opened again. A scent of sandalwood, a burst of steam and she sensed him by the bed. Then there was a shift of the duvet, a depression of the bed.

Holly wriggled closer to the edge of the bed and waited for dawn.

CHAPTER NINE

HOLLY OPENED HER EYES, her synapses slowly firing into life. Warm. Safe. Comfortable. *Mmm...* Her cheek seemed to be pillowed on soft cotton underlain by a hard wall of muscle. Her leg was looped over—

Her synapses quickened and her brain began putting sums together...

Oh, hell!

So much for the barricade—somehow she had cleared that in a sleep-ridden assault and she was now plastered all over Stefan. Stefan, who—thank God—was dressed in boxers and a T-shirt. Probably because he didn't own any pyjamas...which meant he usually slept naked.

Suppressing the urge to leap up with a scream, she tried very, very slowly to disentangle herself.

Too late.

His arm tightened around her and then his body stilled. Clearly he went from asleep to awake far more quickly than she did, and his eyes opened to meet hers, his expression a mix of ruefulness and question.

Panic lent her speed and now she *did* move, rolling away in a scramble devoid of dignity and hampered by the row of stupid, *useless* pillows.

'Sorry. No idea how that happened. Sorry. I'm going to have a shower.'

A shower went some way to restoring her equilibrium—perhaps one day in about a hundred years she would even be able to laugh at the whole incident.

Poking her head round the bathroom door, she felt relief wash over her that Stefan was nowhere to be seen. *Chill.* It was imperative that she focused on the day and their trip to Il Boschetto di Sole. The thought brought a semblance of calm, a reminder that all this was worth it because it would enable her to give her father his dream.

She took a deep breath and went into the living area, just as the door opened and Stefan entered.

Goodbye, equilibrium. His hair was shower-damp, its curl more pronounced. He was dressed in a tracksuit and T-shirt and her gaze snagged on his forearms, their muscular definition, the smattering of hair.

'I went to the hotel gym—showered there.'

'Good plan.'

Silence resumed, and then he grinned. 'About earlier...'

'I'd rather not talk about it.' After all her protestations of being uninterested in his type of sex she'd made an utter idiot of herself.

'Don't worry about it. It's no biggie.'

'That's not how it felt to me.' Oh, God, had she *said* that? The innuendo was not what she had meant at all. The blush threatened to burn her up. 'I mean...'

Now his grin widened. 'It's OK. I know what you mean, but I'll take the compliment anyway.'

'Please could we just agree to forget the entire incident?'

But despite herself she could feel her lips twitch; somehow the sheer mortification had receded before the force of his smile.

'Deal.' There was a knock at the door and he moved towards it. 'I've ordered a room service breakfast—smoked salmon, scrambled eggs and pancakes—so we can talk in private. Hope that's OK?'

'Sounds good.'

Five minutes later she forked up a fluffy mouthful of egg and gave a small sound of appreciation.

'What do you want to talk about?'

'Well, we've talked about a whole lot of things, but we haven't talked about how we handle our actual presence on Il Boschetto di Sole.'

He studied her expression for a moment and she focused on maintaining neutrality.

'How does your father feel about it all? About our deal?'

'My father is honoured that the Romanos will own part of Il Boschetto di Sole.'

Holly remembered his face, and the awe that had touched it when she'd video-called him with the news. Once again a conflict of emotion swirled inside her—a happiness that she could give this to him, repay her father for the years of love, the years of bringing her up single-handedly. And a selfish underlying of sadness that any hope of a career away from Il Boschetto di Sole had receded further into the realm of impossibility.

'I will need you now more than ever before, Holly. Roberto Bianchi has given the Romanos a chance to create a dynasty of our own, entrusted us with the place he loved most. To pass on for generations to come.'

'Holly?'

Stefan's voice pulled her back to the present and she pushed away any thoughts of negativity. Until eighteen months ago she had been genuinely content to live her life on Il Boschetto di Sole, to live the fairy tale happy-ever-after with Graham, have children, fulfil her father's expectations. Once she returned to her home that same contentment would return.

And if it didn't she'd fake it—because she had no intention of letting her father down. Full stop.

Focus.

Stefan continued to look at her. 'Why do I get the feeling there's something you're not telling me? If I'm right you need to 'fess up. Because I do not want any surprises.'

Stefan was right. 'It's all a bit…complicated. My father is thrilled…*honoured* to be in line for part ownership. He believes the split is fair and that this marriage is an equitable solution. But I'm not sure how he feels about *you*.'

Her father had withdrawn behind an emotionless mask when she'd explained the marriage deal, that she and Stefan would come to visit him, that he would need to welcome Stefan as his son-in-law. He had agreed to play his part, but Holly had no idea how he felt about the idea of meeting Eloise's son.

'Why? Because he disapproves of me? Half of Lycander disapproves of me, so I can understand that.'

For a moment she was tempted to let him believe that, allow that to be her explanation as to why she was worried about this visit. But there was a bitter flavour to his words that she wanted to diffuse.

'It's more personal than that. It's because of Eloise.'

'My mother? Why?'

Now his voice was a growl, and she knew that this was a touchy subject. Hell, she could relate to that—her own mother was not a topic she wished to discuss. Come to that, she wasn't over-keen on talking about *his*.

'Our parents—my father and your mother—they were…involved.'

'Roberto mentioned that in my letter, but it was the first I'd heard of it.'

'Well, they were an item. My father loved her and she threw him over in favour of royalty.' Try as she might, she

couldn't keep the anger from her voice. 'Broke his heart.'
Thus doomed his marriage to her mother from the outset.
'In return for the crown jewels.'

Now anger zig-zagged in his grey eyes; his hands were
clenched and she could see the effort it took him to unfurl
his fingers. 'My mother was *not* a gold-digger.'

'Then why did she marry Alphonse?'

'According to Roberto Bianchi because Roberto persuaded her into it—he saw it as a grand alliance, believed
she would make a great princess, and he wanted to scotch
the romance between her and your father. Partly because
of their social disparity, partly because your father was
already engaged.'

'She didn't have to agree.'

'No, she didn't. But she didn't agree for the money or
the prestige. She wasn't like that.'

His tone brooked no argument and his eyes were shaded
with so much emotion that she stilled in her chair even as
her own emotions were in tumult inside her.

Part of her wanted to howl, *How do you know that?* But
she bit the words back. Stefan had the right to hold a rose-
coloured vision of his mother, but Holly had no wish to
share it. Her childhood had been blighted by Eloise; *she*
had been the reason for acrimony, slammed doors and
misery. So Holly had no wish to hear any defence of the
woman who had doomed her parents' marriage. The only
thing that might have salvaged it was a son. When that
hadn't happened the bitterness had continued for eight
years of Holly's life. Until Eloise had left Lycander; soon
after that her mother had walked out.

*'I know what you want to do, Thomas. You want to fol-
low her. You never got over a woman who rejected you,
treated you like the dirt beneath her designer shoes.'*

Her mother's voice had been full of weary venom and

Holly had put her hands over her ears in a familiar futile attempt to block it out.

'Go if you wish. But I will not be here when you come back, rejected again. I have had enough. We could have been happy if you could have returned my love.'

'I always told you, Angela, that our marriage would not be one of love; it would be one of duty.'

'And it could have been happy if you had been able to let go of her, given us a chance.'

'I could say the same to you.'

That had been her father's weary voice.

'Would you have loved me if I'd given you a son?'

'Perhaps I would have cared for you more if you could have shown love to our daughter.'

'What does she have that I don't? Why do you love her when you can't love me?'

'She is my daughter—my flesh and blood. How can I not love her? Her gender isn't her fault.'

Holly had pulled the blanket over her head then—variations of that conversation had been played out so many times. But that time there had been a different end: the next day her mother had packed her bags and gone. All because of Eloise.

Holly tore off a minute piece of croissant, glanced down at it, rolled it between her fingers and told herself that none of that was Stefan's fault. Or his business.

'Perhaps we need to focus on the here and now. I believe my father has complicated feelings about this marriage because of who you are, but he understands the role he needs to play and he has explained the will to the staff and workers and told them the same story we're telling the world. All we need to do today is reassure everyone that nothing will change—that their jobs are safe.'

Stefan studied her for a moment, then nodded tersely. 'Understood. Let's get this show on the road.'

The journey to Il Boschetto di Sole was achieved in silence—a silence that contained a spikiness that neither of them broached or breached. The memories evoked by mention of Eloise swirled in Holly's mind in an unsettling whirlwind, and worry surfaced about her father's state of mind and whether all this would impact his physical health.

The car slowed as they approached their destination. Further memories floated into its interior as she rolled the tinted window down so the fragrance of lemon could waft in. The familiarity of the scent soothed her, calling up images of the beauty of the lemon grove, reminding her of times tagging along at her father's heels, racing through the fields of trees, watching in fascination as the lemons were harvested, loving the tart hit of the juice.

But there had been other, less salubrious times. Despair at her mother's treatment of her counterbalanced by gratitude for her father's kindness. The fairy tale of falling in love with Graham and the pain of the betrayal that had followed. Somehow now only the pain felt real, because the happy times with Graham had been nothing but an illusion.

A glance at Stefan and she saw his look of concentration, the way his eyes were scanning the surroundings as though in search of something. Perhaps it was an attempt to picture his mother, the girl she'd once been, the young woman who had apparently spent happy times here. *Eloise.* His mother. Her nemesis.

Sudden guilt ran over her—she hadn't even given him a chance to talk about Eloise. Eloise had left Lycander when Stefan had been a child—whatever her shortcomings, that must have hit him hard. Lord knew she could sympathise with that.

Almost without meaning to she moved a little closer

to him. 'There are people here who will remember your mother,' she said softly. 'I'll make sure I introduce you. If you want.'

There was a pause. His grey eyes seemed to look into the distance, perhaps into the past, and then he nodded. 'Thank you. I'd like that. And Holly...?'

'Yes.'

Reaching out, he took her hand in his. 'About earlier. Whatever happened between your father and my mother all those years ago it sounds like your father ended up hurt, and I'm sorry for that. I truly believe my mother acted as she thought best, but I accept I can't know how it all went down.'

Neither could she. The realisation was ridiculously shocking. In truth, all she had was her own interpretation of her parents' viewpoints. Eloise could never put her side forward now.

The car arrived on the gravelled driveway and Holly saw that the entire staff had congregated to greet them. Embarrassment tinted her cheeks. 'Sorry... I wasn't expecting this.'

'No worries. It's good practice. In a few weeks we'll be on show for the world en route to the altar.'

'That makes me feel heaps better.'

'You'll be fine.' Stefan smiled, and all of a sudden, against all logic, she did feel better.

Franco opened the door and she climbed out, saw her father at the head of the group and ran forward.

'Papa.' Anxiety touched her—Thomas looked older than when she'd seen him a couple of months before. 'Are you taking your medicine?' She made sure she kept her voice low and the smile on her face.

'Of course. You must not worry. The past days have been very emotional, that is all. That the Romanos will own part of this… That you are marrying Prince Stefan… It is a lot to take in.'

'The marriage is for one year only, Papa. You do understand that?'

Worry began to seep in along with her sense of guilt. Thomas looked thinner, even his face was gaunter than a year before. She shouldn't have run to London. Since her mother had left she had looked after her father—made sure he ate, took the medication he needed to manage his heart condition. Provided he followed all advice the doctors were confident he could go on for many years. But had he been following the advice?

'Of course I do. Now, let us move on. Introduce me.'

Stefan moved forward, his hand held out, and the older man took it. 'Welcome, Your Highness,' he said, his voice full of dignity.

'Please call me Stefan. It is good to meet you, sir.'

'You too, Stefan.'

For a long moment grey eyes met blue, and Holly felt a jolt of something akin to her jealousy of years before. Was her father looking at Stefan and thinking of what might have been? That this was the son he might have had with Eloise? Was he wishing Holly away?

Stop. That way led madness.

'I thought you might like a tour.'

'Very much so.'

Thomas stepped back and smiled, though Holly could see the strain in his eyes. 'I think it would be fitting if Holly shows you round. Soon this land will belong to the two of you.'

'I told you, Papa. It will belong to *you*.'

'It will belong to our family.' He turned to Stefan. 'When you are done come and join me for a drink and I will answer any questions you may have. And of course feel free to ask anyone whatever you wish.'

With that he turned and headed towards the house. Holly submerged her anxiety, tried to quell the worries, suspecting that her father was overcome with emotion because the sight of Stefan had triggered memories of the past, of wandering round Il Boschetto di Sole with Eloise.

Later. She would speak with him later. Now it was all about Stefan and the creation of a good impression. Soon some of these employees would work for Stefan—men and women Holly had grown up with, people who had looked out for her and after her. Others she knew less well…a couple were new faces completely. But to a degree she held the responsibility for their well-being, and the idea was both scary and challenging.

She started the round of introductions, then stood back to allow the staff to assess Stefan, watching with mixed emotions as their wariness and in some cases suspicions thawed as they spoke with him. Stefan was courteous without being fawning, and best of all he seemed genuine.

When he spoke to each individual he listened and focused his attention on that person, which allowed Holly to observe *him*. The way he tipped his head very slightly to the left as he concentrated, the glint of the autumn sun on his dark hair, the strong curve of his jaw, the intensity of his gaze, the firm line of his mouth, the contained power of his body.

'I have a lot to learn,' he said, once he had spoken with everyone. 'But I'll do my best to be a willing pupil. I want to get to know Il Boschetto di Sole, to understand how it works.'

Once the employees had dispersed Holly looked at him in query. 'Did you mean that?'

'If I am going to own it then I accept the responsibilities that go with it. Now, how about that tour?'

Five minutes later Stefan followed Holly through a mosaic paved courtyard and up a steep flight of drystone stairs cut into the mountainside. He came to a standstill as he gazed out at the panorama of terraced areas that positively burst with lemon trees, the fruit so bright, the fragrance so intense that he felt dizzy.

'This is…incredible.'

For a strange instant the whole moment transcended time and he could almost picture his mother here, walking amongst the trees, inhaling the scent, lost in dreams of a happy future.

Next to him Holly too had stilled, perhaps reliving memories of her own childhood. Then she grinned up at him, as if pleased that he shared her appreciation of the vista.

'It's pretty cool, yes? This is the last couple of months of harvest; some people say the lemons are at their best earlier, but I reckon these are damned good. Come and try one.'

She wended her way through the trees, surveyed each and every one, finally decided on the lemon she wanted, reached up and plucked it. His eyes didn't waver from her, absorbed in the lithe grace with which she moved, the way her floral skirt caught the breeze, her unconscious poise and elegance as she turned and handed him the fruit.

'Just peel it and taste!'

The fruit was surprisingly easy to peel, the burst of scent tart and refreshing, and as he divided it into segments and popped one into his mouth he raised his brows in surprise. 'I thought it would be more bitter.'

Holly shook her head. 'It's what makes our lemons stand apart; their taste is unique—tart with a layer of sweetness.'

He handed over a segment to her, felt a sudden jolt as his fingers, sticky with juice, touched hers. He watched as she raised it to her mouth and rubbed it over her lips.

'And the texture is pretty amazing too; they stay firm for longer. That's why—'

His gaze snagged on the luscious softness of her parted lips and suddenly all his senses were heightened. The taste of the lemon lingered on his taste buds with exquisite sharpness, the trees took on an even more intense hue; the noise of a circling bird was preternaturally loud. Holly had broken off, her blue eyes had widened, and he forced himself to snap out of it. Before he did something foolish...like kiss her.

'Why what?'

'It doesn't matter.'

'Yes, it does.' Shaking away the tendrils of desire, he realised it *did* matter. 'Come on. I'm really interested.'

She shrugged, continued to walk through the tree-lined area. 'That's why I believe we should focus on a different aspect of the business.'

'Such as?'

'Well, at the moment we stock the majority of Lycandrian supermarkets and we have a pretty successful export market. All of which is great. But—'

Again she broke off and he came to a halt. 'Go on.'

'I want to make it more...*personal*. I'd like to install a factory. Make products with the lemons ourselves. We could make lemonade, cakes... There are Romano recipes going back generations. My grandmother made the best lemon cake in Europe! And there are other dishes as well—really amazing ones. Lemon chutneys and jams... And I'd like to do tours, have a museum. Honestly, the history of this place is amazing and the history of the lemons themselves is… It's really interesting. Did you know this lemon has taken hundreds of years to get like this? Originally it was a fraction of this size and inedible, bitter. Farmers were intrigued, though, and they crossed it with local oranges and eventually we ended up with this.'

'So why not do it? Take these ideas and run with them?' The enthusiasm in her voice lit her face.

Holly shook her head. 'The cost would be phenomenal; my father won't do it. I'm not sure he would want tourists here, or to be involved in making and selling products. To him all that matters is the production of the best lemons in Lycander.'

Stefan frowned. 'And he is to be commended for that. But in today's day and age you are right—other markets should be considered. You are the future of Il Boschetto di Sole and these ideas are good.'

'Maybe. But they need experience I don't have, even if I *could* persuade my father to implement them. You said it yourself—you didn't build your business overnight.'

'No, but I was starting from scratch. You already have a means of raising money. But I agree—you do need more experience first. So why not pursue the marketing idea? That would give you excellent additional experience on top of what you have already learnt. Why not ask Lamberts if they would train you?'

Holly shook her head. 'Because I don't think it would work. They've already offered me a trainee position for next year.'

'That's brilliant.' There was a silence and he frowned. 'Isn't it?'

'It's kind of them, but I refused.'

'Why?'

'For a start they're only offering it because of my new

elevated status as soon-to-be princess. For a second thing there's no point. My future is on Il Boschetto di Sole. My half of it.'

'If you believe you can do the job it doesn't matter *why* they're offering it. Plus, this job would help with your future plans for Il Boschetto di Sole.'

'I really don't think my father will buy the idea. Plus, I'd need more than a year's experience. Plus, I don't want to be based in London after our year.'

'OK. Then you could transfer to a PR company here. Even better.'

Holly sighed. 'Maybe I *will* do that one day. But not yet. My father wants me here...learning the ropes.'

There was something else. 'I'm missing something, aren't I?' he asked. 'I don't get why you can't do both. Have a job you love in marketing *and* learn the ropes. There's no rush. Why not have it all?'

'Because there are other things I want to do with my life as well.'

'Such as?

'Just let it go.' Holly's voice was low now, as they emerged from the shade of the grove.

'No.'

For a moment a warning bell pealed in his head. This was none of his business; there was no need for him to get involved in Holly's life choices. Yet he couldn't help it.

'I can see how much you want to pursue marketing, and use it to take Il Boschetto di Sole forward. I recognise that fire because I've felt it myself.' In his case it had been born of a determination to succeed, in whatever he undertook. For Holly it was a real passion, born of itself. *One life*. 'This is your life, Holly, take the risk. Go for it.'

'It's not that easy.'

The words ricocheted with an intensity that impacted him.

'It's no secret—you'll find out soon enough. My father is ill.'

'I am so sorry…'

Before he could say any more she waved a hand. 'It's OK. He has a long-term heart condition, managed with medication and a healthy lifestyle. But there is a chance he won't make old bones, and I want him to see his grandchildren. I want my children to have a shot at knowing their grandfather. Even more so now. I want my father to know the Romano dynasty will continue. I want him to see his grandchildren running around these lemon trees, watch the lemons grow.'

The words silenced him, because he could see her point, but… 'I understand that—I really do. But your father may live for years. And to have children you need…'

'A father for them. I know.' Her mouth took on a rueful twist.

'Also, having children doesn't preclude having a career.'

'I know that too. But I want to spend time with my father and I want to be here for my children. Full time.' The words vibrated with sincerity, even with love for these as yet unborn children. 'That doesn't mean I don't agree with women working—I do. But for me it's important to give my all to being a mother. I can always go for a career later on.'

She resumed walking, and as they emerged from the shade of the grove he could see an ancient stone chapel in the near distance.

Relief touched Holly's face as she pointed to the building. 'Now would be as good a time as any to show you the chapel. Then we can decide if we want the ceremony to take place there.'

The topic of her future was clearly closed.

CHAPTER TEN

As THEY APPROACHED the chapel Holly realised she had been so caught up in their conversation that she hadn't given a thought to the fact that this was her first visit to the chapel since her wedding fiasco. Not that she'd actually made it to the chapel then.

For a second her footsteps faltered. She wondered if perhaps she should have come here alone, to lay the ghosts of her nearly-wedding to rest. Yet somehow Stefan's presence made her feel better. His sheer solidity, his energy, reinforced the knowledge that it had been better to have the fairy tale shattered before the ceremony rather than after.

Graham had wanted to marry her for her family position, to have a job for life. Had never loved her. Their whole union would have been fake, built on foundations of quicksand.

As they approached the chapel an old familiar sensation of peace crept over her. The ancient stone walls… the arched door with its honeysuckle surround… It was a place she had come to countless times when life's complexities had overwhelmed her—when she'd been small and hurt by her mother's indifference, an indifference that had bordered on dislike. Somehow the pews had given her comfort, and she'd studied the stained-glass windows, marvelling that those red and green and blue sainted figures had looked down and seen centuries, hundreds of people coming in hope of solace.

'This is a beautiful place,' Stefan said softly as they entered, and she knew from the reverence in his tone that he could sense the history in the very air they breathed.

As she watched him walk around she felt a strange warmth that he shared her appreciation of this hallowed place.

'It's always been special to me. My go-to place when life throws a curve ball.'

'I get that, and I would understand if you don't want our wedding to take place here. If you want to wait for the real thing.'

'I'm not sure if I'll ever experience "the real thing". And somehow, because this marriage is for Il Boschetto di Sole, it feels right that we should do it here. This chapel must have seen countless marriages. Many of them will have been made for reasons of duty rather than love. Some of them will have been forced unions of misery and others will have been joyous.' As she'd thought *her* marriage would be. 'I think we should have the ceremony here. If you're good with that?'

'I'm fine with wherever we do it.'

'No doubt you'd prefer to have the ceremony in a boardroom, with an agenda and the deal written out carefully. *I, Stefan Petrelli, agree to marry you subject to the following terms and conditions.*'

Odd that she felt able to tease him, and his smile made her heart give a funny little dip.

Then his expression took on a serious hue. 'But really that is what marriage is—the ultimate deal between two people. You enter a pact to look after each other in sickness and in health. It's a deal. It's just a non-negotiable one that should last for life. Which is why I wouldn't enter it—I don't deal if I can't keep my side.'

'Does it bother you that we'll be standing here taking vows we know we won't keep?'

'No, because we both know that this is a one-year deal. It will be *With this ring I thee wed...for a year.*'

The phrase rolled off his tongue and she gave a sudden shiver. The enormity of those vows, even for a year, felt huge even as she reminded herself they weren't for real. They would be bound together for a year not by love but by legal necessity. Husband and wife. Any attempt to untie the knot before meant Il Boschetto di Sole would be forfeit.

'Is it bothering you?' he asked.

'A bit. I know we aren't lying to each other, but we are lying to all the people who will be watching.'

'Hah! Most of the guests won't give a rat's ar— bottom. And a large proportion of them will be laying bets on how long we'll last. Plus, how many people *really* believe the promises they make when they say their marriage vows? *Really* believe in the "ever after" bit of the happy-ever-after?'

'I'd like to think most of them do.'

'That is naïve. In today's age you would have to be an idiot not to consider the very big possibility that you'll end up divorced. Or that one of you will be unfaithful.'

Graham hadn't even waited to make his vow of fidelity before he'd broken it. 'Then why bother?'

'People figure it's a way of making some sort of commitment, but they know there's a get-out clause—they know they aren't really signing up for life. We've just agreed our get-out clause up-front. And I suppose some people get married because they want kids and see marriage as a natural precursor, the right thing to do.' He gestured around the chapel. 'For me, this wedding is the only one I will undertake. I know that. But you want the whole deal, and one day you might want to get married for real here.'

Holly shook her head. 'Right now it's hard to picture. I used to believe hook, line and sinker in the whole fairy tale. Now…not so much.'

'Because of the "complicated break-up"?'

'Yes.'

Holly hesitated. At some point they needed to discuss past relationships. Now seemed as good a time as any. No doubt the press would find out about Graham, and whilst she doubted it would feature in an interview, there might well be some coverage or commentary in the press.

'About that… It really was complicated. We were due to get married. Here, in fact. Then on my wedding day I found out he'd been cheating on me, so I cancelled the wedding.'

She looked down at the stone floor, traced a pattern with the toe of her foot. She didn't want to see pity or compassion in his eyes.

'That took guts,' he said at last. 'And in my opinion you did the right thing. If you tell me who he was I'll go and find him, bring him here and make him grovel.'

That surprised her enough that she looked up and met his gaze. She saw that his expression held nothing but a sympathy that didn't judge, mixed with an anger that she knew was directed at Graham.

'That's OK. I don't need him to grovel—it's over and done with. And, whilst I don't doubt your ability to make him grovel, you can't make him mean it.'

'I'd be happy to try.'

'It wouldn't be possible. In Graham's world he didn't do anything wrong.'

'How does he figure that?'

Holly hesitated. She'd never spoken to anyone about Graham's crass revelations. Yet here and now, with Stefan, she wanted to.

'The whole relationship was a con. Graham worked for my father and he saw a way to further his career. Marrying me would give him a direct line to the Romano wealth and prestige—a job on Il Boschetto di Sole for life, a house, prestige, social standing...yada-yada. He never loved me. I don't think he even liked me. But he pretended to and I fell for it. Hook, line and proverbial sinker. And the whole time he was sleeping with a "real" woman.'

'So what are you? An alien?'

All she could do was shrug and he shook his head.

'The man must be blind. Or stupid. Take my word for it. You *are* a real woman.' He leant forward, his expression intent and serious. 'You are beautiful and gorgeous and...hell, you are *all* woman.'

Shyness mingled with a desire to move forward and show him that he was a hundred percent right. To kiss him, hold him and...and then what? This was a business arrangement, and most importantly there was no future to this attraction except potential humiliation. This man liked variety.

But his words had warmed her, acted as a counter to Graham's betrayal, and for that she could say, 'Thank you. Really. I mean that.'

'No problem. I'm sorry you went through what he put you through.'

'On the plus side, I think I've learnt from it. It's shown me that love isn't the way forward for me.'

'Why? If you want love you shouldn't let one loser change your mind.'

'It's not that. Love made me blind.' And delusional. She should have learned from her parents' example;

love had warped their lives. Her father's love for Eloise had affected his whole life. As for her mother—she had loved her father with a love that had made her miserable, persevering for years in a doomed marriage in the hope that her husband would love her.

'It made me unable to see what sort of man Graham really is. I think I'd be better off in a marriage without love. Finding a good, decent man—a man who will love Il Boschetto di Sole, who has a love and understanding for the land, who is willing to make his life here. A man who wants children, who will make a good dad.'

Because that was more important than anything.

She broke off and narrowed her eyes at his expression, his raised brow. 'What?' she demanded. 'Am I amusing you?'

'No, but I think you're talking rubbish. This paragon of a man sounds boring, and the whole idea of a union like that would be soulless.'

'Soulless? Just because *you* need variety and a different woman every month it doesn't mean a good, decent man has to be boring or a union with him soulless.'

'Where would the spark be?'

'There would have to be an element of attraction, but that isn't the most important consideration.'

An element of attraction? Jeez. A sudden memory of their kisses filled her brain—and she banished them.

'Physical attraction doesn't guarantee a happy, stable relationship.'

'No, but I'm pretty sure it helps with the "happy" part of it.'

'You can have an enjoyable physical relationship without love. That's what *you* advocate, isn't it?'

'Sure, but only on a short-term basis.'

'Probably best if you stick to your relationship criteria and I'll stick to mine.' *And never the twain shall meet.*

'Fair enough. But don't go looking for this paragon on *my* watch.'

'Meaning?'

'Meaning don't forget that whilst we are married we will be on show. If you find a suitable man don't follow up until our divorce goes through.'

There was a hint of steel in his voice and she narrowed her eyes.

'And does the same go for you? Because *that* is something we haven't discussed.'

'Meaning?' His question echoed hers.

'Well, what *is* your relationship plan for this year? We've agreed this is a marriage of convenience, but I'd prefer it if you didn't see other women, no matter how discreetly.'

His expression solidified to ice. 'I have no intention of seeing other women. I'm not a fool either. It would hardly do my image any good. And even if I were guaranteed anonymity I wouldn't expose you to that sort of public humiliation. I'm not as unprincipled as you seem to think. Liking variety does *not* make me a cheat. Whilst we are married I'll be taking my vows seriously.'

For some reason the words seemed to ring through her brain, taking the whole situation from the realm of the surreal to cold, hard reality. *Vows.* They would be standing up and taking vows. In this very chapel. Looked down upon by the figures in the stained-glass windows, watched by a congregation seated on these pews. How on earth had all this happened?

Pull yourself together.

'Good. I'm glad that's sorted. Shall we go and meet with my father now?'

* * *

Stefan entered the cool confines of the Romano villa and wondered whether his mother had been a regular visitor or whether she and Thomas Romano had tried to fight their feelings for each other. There was so much Thomas could tell him, but he knew he couldn't ask.

Holly had made it clear that Eloise had hurt Thomas deeply, and he suspected the ramifications of that hurt had gone deeper than Holly had told him. In addition, Thomas was not a well man. So this visit needed to be polite but impersonal, kept to questions about Il Boschetto di Sole so that a fair split of the land could be devised.

He watched as Holly went forward to greet her father, saw the worry and the anxiety and the love in her blue eyes as she laid a hand on his arm, questioned him in a low voice.

Her father smiled, nodded and then moved forward to greet Stefan. 'Welcome to our home.'

'Thank you.'

He followed Thomas and Holly into a spacious kitchen. Though clean and sunlit it had an air of disuse, no smell of cooking lingered, and the surfaces were almost too pristine.

Holly glanced around and a small frown creased her forehead. 'Would you like a drink?' she offered. 'Tea?'

'That would be great.'

He noted that once she put the kettle on she went around and did a quiet check of all the cupboards. Her lips pressed together and her frown deepened.

Thomas Romano seemed oblivious to his daughter's actions, and instead focused on Stefan. 'So what do you think of Il Boschetto di Sole? I hope the staff were all helpful.'

'It is a truly beautiful place.' A place he knew his mother had loved...a place he would bring her ashes.

'Yes.' The older man sighed and then smiled. 'I understand from Holly that you wish to divide the estate between you?'

Holly approached the table, placed a tray with a teapot, delicate china cups and a plate of biscuits down. 'That is what Stefan wishes to discuss, Papa, but that need not be done today if you're tired.'

'I have already given the matter some thought.' Thomas turned his gaze to Stefan. 'I have looked at yields, at the economic and practical feasibility of where to draw the lines so that from a monetary viewpoint the split is as fair as can be. But there are other matters to consider. This place is a community, and I care about all the people who work here. Any split has to take their livelihoods into consideration.'

'Of course.' Stefan nodded. 'I understand that there are further considerations. I am sure there are places here that are meaningful to the Romanos.' He turned to Holly. 'I believe the chapel is important to you and I understand that—perhaps that should be included in your half? In return, I would like the Bianchi villa to be included in mine.'

The villa where his mother would have stayed.

Holly glanced at her father and Stefan pushed down a sensation of frustration. He did understand the idea of respect, but Holly was part of this too. Technically this was *her* decision to make.

'I have already included that in my proposal.' Thomas sipped his tea. 'I have also suggested giving you Forester's Glade. It's a place that your mother loved—Eloise said she found peace there, even when the decisions she had to make were hard.'

He grimaced suddenly and Holly leaned forward, her face twisted with worry.

'Papa?'

'I am fine, Holly.'

'No, you aren't. Have you been taking your medication?'

'Of course. I told you. I am *fine*.'

'I'll stay here tonight.'

'No.' Now Thomas's voice was authoritative. 'I do not want ill-founded rumours of my ill-health to circulate and I know how important it is that you and Stefan present as an engaged couple should.' He reached up and took Holly's hand. 'Truly. Holly, I am fine. But if it will make you feel better I will ask Jessica Alderney to come and stay.'

Holly twisted a tendril of hair around her finger. 'That *would* make me feel better. And I'll check in tomorrow.'

'Good. I will look forward to it. I have missed you; I am happy that soon you will be back here.' Thomas nodded to Stefan. 'Stefan, it was good to meet you. Please feel free to visit Il Boschetto di Sole any time. I look forward to your views on my proposal.'

'I am sure we can all come to an agreement.' Rising, he held out a hand, shook the older man's hand and turned to Holly. 'You ready?'

'Yes.' Not that she sounded sure, and her blue eyes were worried as they rested on her father.

'Go!' Thomas smiled as he made shooing motions with his hands. 'I will talk to you tomorrow.'

Holly moved over to kiss his cheek and then followed Stefan from the room.

As they headed to the car she stopped, turned to him. 'Would you like to go to Forester's Glade?'

He halted, touched at the question.

'It may be a while before you can head out here again.'

'I'd like that.'

Or at least he thought he would. The idea sent a skitter of emotion through him.

As if she sensed it, she slipped her hand into his. The gesture felt somehow right and he left it there, clasped firmly as they wended their way through another terrace of lemon trees, the fragrance as intense as earlier. Once through this they started to climb a set of steep winding stairs cut into the mountain face.

A glance at her face and he could see that anxiety still lingered in the troubled crease of her forehead. 'I think you're worrying too much about your father.'

'That's easy for you to say. I know my father. Before I went to London I made sure he took his medication, ate right and followed the doctor's orders. Now he's on his own I am not at all convinced he is doing any of that.'

'He looked OK to me.'

Holly shook her head. 'Nowhere near as good as he looked last time I saw him. I checked his cupboards and they are all full.'

'That's good, isn't it?'

'No—because they are full of unopened bags of pasta, unopened *everything*. I don't think he's cooked anything since I left. I think he's been getting take-aways and he's done a big clean-up before I arrived.'

'Surely that is his choice to make?'

'So you suggest that I sit back and allow him to jeopardise his health?'

Stefan considered her words. 'Pretty much, yes. Sure, you can advise him to take care, remind him, but other than that it is up to him. He's a grown man; he is also a man with huge responsibilities on the work front. I can't believe he is incapable of sticking to a healthy diet.'

'It's not incapability. It's habit. He's just used to someone doing it for him.'

'Then hire a housekeeper.'

'He doesn't want to do that. Says he prefers family

around him. Jessica Alderney is a friend—she's also a trained nurse and an excellent cook—but she isn't *family*.'

Stefan frowned. 'So you will live on Il Boschetto di Sole for life?'

Through duty. Do the right thing, marry her supposed paragon, have Romano heirs, look after her father. It was not his business—and who was to say she was wrong?

'You make it sound like a prison sentence. It isn't. *Look* at this place. Plus, my father is entitled to my support and my help. I love him and I have a vested interest in keeping him healthy.'

They came to the end of a small wooded copse and she stopped.

'OK. We're here. Forester's Glade—or Radura dei Guardaboschi.'

The view stopped his breath. The glade had an aura of magic, conifers, a babbling brook, meadow flowers, a waterfall.

'I always used to imagine sylvan nymphs lived here,' Holly said softly. 'My father used to bring me up here sometimes when I was small and I'd play for hours. Anyway, would you prefer if I left you on your own?'

'No. It's fine.'

Stefan hauled in a breath, inhaled the scent of the conifers overlaid by the meadow flowers, looked at the verdant greens mingled with the deep copper brown of the soil, the blue of the late afternoon sky. He wondered if his mother had come here to make the fateful decision to marry his father—whether she had done it because she had been pressured into it by her guardian, persuaded to do her duty because it was the 'right' thing to do.

In so doing she'd made a grave mistake. And he didn't want Holly to do the same. Before he could change his mind, he turned to her.

'My mother...' he began. 'I know you have doubts about her, and in truth I don't know the history between her and your father. What I *do* know, from what Roberto Bianchi said, is that he pushed her into marriage with my father for the sake of duty. Perhaps she stood right here and made the decision. And perhaps she figured it wouldn't be so bad. Maybe she was swayed by the idea of the pomp and glamour of being a princess. Perhaps she did want to rule—to be the mother of royalty. Perhaps she believed she was doing the best for your father. Roberto Bianchi would never have permitted them to marry. Maybe she did what she thought was right. Just like you are trying to do.'

As he talked they continued to walk through the glade. They came to a stop at the edge of a cliff and he sat down on a grassy tussock, waited as she settled beside him.

'There is a lot I don't know—will never know now—but what I do know is that her marriage was worse than miserable. All the possessions in the world didn't change that.'

He didn't look at her—didn't want to see her expression of dismissal or disbelief. He knew that many in Lycander did still believe that his mother had been at fault. Instead he focused on the horizon, on the feel of the grass under his fingers.

'She didn't complain, but I sensed her unhappiness, saw how my father treated her—he made no attempt to hide it. Perhaps their marriage was doomed because she didn't love him. Because she loved your father. Alphonse claimed to love her, but it seemed to me that he treated her like a plaything—a remote-controlled toy that *he* needed to control. If she didn't comply, made a mistake, it made him angry. I saw the bruises on her. I just didn't understand where they came from.'

He sensed Holly's movement, her shift closer to him.

Her body was close and so he continued, hoping against hope that she'd believe his words.

'So whatever her reasons for marrying him—doing her duty, doing what she felt to be right—it was a mistake. If she could have turned the clock back she wouldn't have made the same decision.'

'Maybe she would because she had you.'

The words cut him like a knife. 'No. I was the reason she was in my father's control—he had the power to take me away from her.'

He'd been the pawn that had ensured her compliance and in the end had brought her down. So it had all been for naught; she should have cut her losses long before.

'She loved you, Stefan. Be glad of that.'

Glad—how could he be glad when her loving him had cost her so much? *Enough.* This was not a conversation that he wanted or needed to have.

'Holly, just take heed. Live your life as you want to live it—you've got *one* shot. Don't waste it, or throw it away to do what is "right" for others.'

Holly sighed and he turned, saw the tears that sparkled on her eyelashes.

'What's wrong?'

'It's all so sad…'

A swipe of her eyes and then she shifted to face him, leant forward and kissed his cheek. The imprint of her lips was so sweet his heart ached.

'Thank you. For sharing.'

Warning bells clanged in his head. *Again.* A chaste kiss should not evoke an ache in his heart. Time to pull back— way, *way* back.

'You're welcome.'

A glance at his watch, a final look around the glade and he rose to his feet, stretched out a hand to pull her up.

He noted the feel of her fingers around his, the jolt it sent through his whole body.

Make that time to pull way, way, *way* back. This marriage was a business deal, and he had no intention of blowing it with an injudicious sharing of emotion.

CHAPTER ELEVEN

HOLLY OPENED HER EYES, relieved to see that this morning she was firmly on her side of the pillow barrier. A quick glance over showed that Stefan's side was empty, and she wondered if he'd even made it to bed. He had cited work the previous evening on their return from Il Boschetto di Sole, and remained glued to his laptop for the duration.

Part of her had welcomed the time to reflect, and part of her had wanted to hold him, to offer comfort after he'd given her that insight into his parents' marriage.

Guilt and mixed emotions had swirled inside her. She had grown up believing Eloise to be evil incarnate, the harbinger of all her parents' troubles. Now that picture no longer held good; the woman evoked by Stefan had been a victim just as much as anyone else. Another victim of love and duty. Could Stefan be right? That sometimes following the dutiful path wasn't the right way?

No! Her situation was a far cry from Eloise's. Her father loved her, and she wasn't in love with anyone else… The choice to look after her father was made from love, not duty, and she wanted a family. Yet doubt had unfurled a shoot, and she swung her legs out of bed, determined not to contemplate it or allow it to flourish.

Showered and dressed, she emerged into the living area, found him sitting again in front of the screen.

A continental breakfast was already spread on the table and he glanced up, gestured towards it. 'Help yourself.'

As she ate, he pushed the screen aside and came to join her. 'Have you looked at the itinerary for the day?'

'Of course.' She sensed the question was part rhetorical, part designed to indicate that today was all about business. 'We're visiting a nursery, a school and a community centre. Are you feeling OK?' Surely he must feel *some* trepidation about the day ahead; the idea of putting himself out there to many Lycandrians.

'Of course,' he returned. 'I'm looking forward to seeing if Frederick is making a difference.'

The statement had an edge to it, and she wasn't sure whether he hoped his brother was succeeding or failing.

The rest of breakfast was a silent affair, only today the silence didn't feel comfortable, and later, when they left the hotel, although he took her hand it felt false—she would swear she sensed reluctance in his fingers, knew it was done solely for the sake of their charade.

The car drove them through streets that spoke of the rich elite that Lycander was known for, filled with colonial mansions, freshly painted terracotta villas, but gradually, as they proceeded, the surroundings became dingier, evidence of poverty more and more apparent in graffiti and an air of dilapidation. Yet there were signs of change: construction under way, the hum of lorries transporting building materials, rows of newly built houses.

Still, the contrast between the glitz and glamour of Lycander's centre and its outskirts was stark indeed.

Franco pulled up in a narrow street outside a ramshackle building that, despite its lopsided air, did attempt a sense of cheer. The walls were painted bright yellow, and a sign jauntily proclaimed 'Ladybirds Nursery'. Yet Stefan's face looked grim as they emerged from the car, stepped forward to meet Marcus.

'Does this building comply with *any* building standards?'

'Yes.' Marcus's voice was even. 'I know it doesn't look like much, but it is safe—and, as you can see, the staff have made an effort to make it look welcoming. The children are also looking forward to showing you the garden at the back. Feel free to inspect every centimetre of it yourself. It *is* safe or I would not allow it to be open.'

Stefan relaxed slightly, and his smile was in place as the nursery leader came out with a group of young children to meet them. A small pigtailed girl approached Holly, curtsied, and handed her a posy of flowers

Holly went down on her haunches to thank her. 'Thank you, sweetheart. What's your name?'

'Sasha.'

'Well, Sasha, these are beautiful, and we are really looking forward to seeing your nursery.'

'I love it,' the little girl confided. 'My big sister is really jealous, because it wasn't here when she was little. The teachers are really nice, and we have lots of fun. And it means my mum can go and work. "So everyone wins," she says.' She gave a hop of excitement. 'And we get lunch here and it's really nice. Me and my best friend Tommy are going to show you and the Prince around the kitchens. Is it fun being a princess?'

'Well, I'm not quite a princess yet. But I think one of my favourite things will be meeting people like you!'

Sasha looked up at Stefan, then back to Holly. 'Is it OK if I ask him something?' she whispered.

'Of course it is.'

Stefan, who must have overheard the whispered words,

smiled down at her. 'Go right ahead—what do you want to know?'

'Are you like a prince from the fairy tales?'

Stefan smiled, but Holly caught sadness behind the smile.

'No, I don't think I am. But I want to be a good prince if I can. I want to help people.'

The words, though simple, were sincere, and Holly knew with gut-deep certainty that he meant them. That this wasn't all part of the charade.

'Now, Holly and I would love it if you'd show us round.'

Sasha slipped her hands into theirs and they entered the nursery. The converted house, though small, had been subdivided into four rooms, each one brightly painted, its walls covered with children's paintings and letters and numbers. Boxes stored toys that, though clearly second-hand, were serviceable and clean; the children were a mix of shy and confident, tall and small.

'We set up as a voluntary place after the major storm that hit last year,' the leader explained. 'It was somewhere parents could leave their children safely whilst they tried to cobble their lives together…rebuild their homes. But now the crown is funding this nursery and others—not completely, and we do still rely on donations, but we can afford to pay our staff something and the children get one good square meal a day. Now, I think these children desperately want to show you round.'

Even as Holly focused on the children, admired their work, laughed at their jokes and answered their questions as best she could, she was all the time oh, so aware of Stefan by her side—his stance, his relaxed air, the way he treated each child as an individual.

Once in the garden, the children proudly showed off the vegetable plots, as well as the sunflowers that stretched towards the sky with an optimism that seemed to reflect this nursery. Out of the corner of her eye she saw a little boy come forward, urged on by the pigtailed Sasha. But he pulled back and the two engaged in a spirited conversation.

Stefan had spotted it too and he headed towards them, looked down at the little boy, and Holly saw sudden compassion touch his eyes.

He leant down and spoke with them both. The words were too low for Holly to overhear, but she saw the little boy's face light up, then saw Sasha and the boy high-five.

Later, as they prepared to leave, Sasha bounded up and wrapped her arms around Stefan's legs. 'I think you're a very good prince. Better than a fairy tale one. And you *did* help.'

'What did you do?' Holly asked, once they were in the car en route to their next visit.

'It's no big deal.'

'It was to the little boy. I saw his face light up.'

'He and his brother were trapped in a building during the storm. A beam fell on his leg and now he can't play football any more. Both he and his brother are ardent football fans. Sasha wanted me to help cheer him up. All I did was say he and his brother could be the mascots at the next game of their favourite team.'

'That *is* a big deal. For those kids it's a huge deal.' Warmth touched her at what he had done.

'Yes, but maybe the house they were in wouldn't have collapsed if it had been built properly in the first place.'

'Which is why there is a whole new housing programme under way, and new standards and regulations are now being enforced.'

'My father has a lot to answer for.'

Anger darkened his face and she could sense him pull it under control, contain it.

'I think your brother is trying to do just that.'

He opened his mouth and then closed it again. She could almost see him make the decision to close the conversation down. To close her out.

He said politely, 'I'm sure you are right. Now, if you'll excuse me, I want to sort out this mascot issue.'

Two weeks later

Stefan glanced at Holly over breakfast, saw that she looked a little pale, with dark smudges under her eyes, and wondered if she too found it hard to sleep every night next to that damn barrier of pillows, knowing how close and yet so far she was from him. But, difficult though it had been, he'd stuck to his resolve—made sure he kept a physical and emotional distance from her when they weren't in the public eye.

Every day he held her hand, looped his arm round her waist, inhaled the strawberry scent of her shampoo, and every day his libido went into overdrive—only to be iced as soon as they entered their hotel room.

'Are you all right?' he asked. 'You look tired. I know this isn't what you signed up for, but you've been incredible.' She truly had, and guilt prodded him that he hadn't thanked her before. He had been so busy closing any connection down that he had failed to acknowledge her efforts.

'I *am* tired, but I've enjoyed every minute of it.'

He raised his eyebrow. 'Even the TV interview?'

'Fair point. *Not* the television interview. That terrified me and I'm still not sure we pulled it off.'

'We did OK.'

Hours of coaching from April had allowed them to put forward a pretty credible performance—perhaps the 'L' word had sounded a little forced, but Holly had laughed it off, blamed her falter on nerves and how hard it was to declare emotion in front of a global audience.

'Are you sure it's not all getting too much? Especially with the wedding plans as well?'

'It's not too much. Seeing all the problems Lycander faces, meeting the people affected by the floods, by the lack of public funding over the years, but also seeing how people cope in adverse conditions, how they pull together is…humbling. It's made me realise what a bubble I live in at Il Boschetto di Sole.' She hesitated. 'It has also made me realise what a great job Frederick is doing and how much there is left to do.'

'Yes.' Stefan refilled his coffee cup. 'He is.'

Like it or not, Holly was correct: his older brother *did* appear to be doing a sterling job and Stefan had no issue in supporting that. He had appeared with Frederick at some official events, and had indicated his willingness to continue to do so. But despite that the couple of attempts he and Frederick had made to spend 'brother time' together had been disastrous.

Not that he had any intent of discussing that with Holly. Not her problem, not her business. In truth, it didn't need to be a problem. Their deal had not included the establishment of a brotherly bond.

Aware of her scrutiny, he cleared his throat. 'Do you need any input on the wedding plans?'

Holly picked up the final flakes of her croissant with one finger as she considered the question. 'To be honest, Marcus and his department have done loads of the work. But there are a few things we need to figure out. For example, we need a song.'

'Huh?'

'The bride and groom start the dancing at the reception—take to the floor to whatever "their" tune is.'

'You pick.'

'Actually, I thought maybe we could put a different twist on it.' Holly hesitated. 'Did your mother have a favourite song?'

'She loved jazz—she had a whole collection.'

'Perfect. We'll have a jazz band. That will set the right tone as well. And it will be wonderful in a marquee. Wait till you see the marquee—it is amazing. Just right to house the very impressive guest list Marcus has come up with, and the perfect backdrop for the wedding of a younger, returning royal.'

'Excellent. You truly are doing a great job.'

'So are you,' she said softly. 'You've won the people over—showed them that you want to bring about change just as Frederick does.'

A twinge of discomfort touched him. 'I do agree that change is needed, and as part of my deal with Frederick I will support his position, but remember this is all part of the deal. I am here to win my lands back, to regain my right to visit Lycander. No more than that.'

Holly frowned. 'I don't buy that,' she said. 'I saw you with that little boy at that nursery, and since then I've seen you interact with hundreds of people. You *do* care; you just don't want to admit it.'

'Don't kid yourself, Holly—and don't give me attributes I don't possess. I care about these people, but it isn't my responsibility to create change in Lycander or to undo my father's wrongs. That is down to Frederick. Once this year is out I will be returning to London and my life.'

How had this conversation got personal? Rising, he hooked his jacket from the back of the armchair. 'I've got a meeting with Marcus. Gotta run. I'll swing by and pick you up later for the luncheon with the charity commission.'

She nodded and he headed for the door.

Holly watched as the door closed behind him, leant back in the armchair and closed her eyes.

Get real, Holly.

Stefan Petrelli was a businessman. She must not try and imbue him with attributes he didn't have; he'd made it clear from the start that duty was an irrelevance to him.

A knock at the door pulled her from her reverie and she rose to open it, stepping back in surprise at the identity of her visitor. Sunita. Frederick's wife. Exotic, beautiful. Ex-supermodel. Fashion designer. Mother of the heir to the throne, three-year-old Amil.

'I am sorry to turn up unannounced; if it's inconvenient please say.'

'No. Come in.'

Pulling the door open, she stepped back and Sunita swept in on a swirl of energy and vibrant colour. Her dark hair was pulled back in a sleek high ponytail and her vivid orange and red tunic top fell to mid-thigh over skinny jeans.

'I thought it would be good for us to meet unofficially. I also know how hard it is to arrange a royal wedding, so I've come to offer my help. Though I won't be offended if you refuse it.'

'No. Your advice would be great. Really useful.'

'OK. But before we begin can I ask you something? I know about the deal—I understand that this wedding wins you half of Il Boschetto di Sole—but are you sure you're happy playing the part you're playing? Because if you aren't we'll cancel it.'

'Just like that?'

'Yes. Frederick and Stefan may be princes, but that doesn't mean they get it all their way.'

Holly couldn't help but laugh. 'No. I'm good with this. Really.'

'Good. There is something else I'd like to know. Has Stefan said anything to you about how it is going with Frederick?'

'You know that proverb about getting blood from a stone…?'

'Hmm… I also know the one about peas in a pod. Sounds as if they are more alike than they would care to admit. Frederick is being similarly reticent, but as far as I can tell their private meetings are a disaster. Enough that I think Frederick may bail on them soon.' Sunita wrinkled her nose. 'The problem is getting them to let go of the past—all those old resentments and feuds that Alphonse fed and nurtured and encouraged.'

Holly frowned. Perhaps she should stop Sunita there… But, damn it, she wanted to know more than Stefan had told her. All he'd said was that his mother's marriage had been miserable—he'd clammed up about what had happened after.

'It was awful for both of them when Alphonse divorced Eloise. You see, Eloise was kind to Frederick—tried to be a good stepmum—but as part of the custody agreement Alphonse refused to let her see Frederick at all. Frederick had already lost his own mother, and losing Eloise really got to him. Alphonse used that to pit Frederick against Stefan. And so it went on.'

Sunita sighed.

'Now they can't get past it. Even the Amil factor didn't work. I asked them to keep an eye on him and after an hour I went back, expecting them all to be in a group hug. But instead I walked in to find Amil happily playing in a corner and the two brothers sitting in awkward silence.'

'Surely they can discuss Lycander?'

'You would think so. But Frederick doesn't want Stefan to think he's blowing his own horn.' Sunita grimaced. 'Anyway, I'm out of ideas.'

Holly's mind raced, imagining a young Stefan and a young Frederick, both of them hurting and having that hurt exploited by their father. The man who should have supported and nurtured and cared for them had instead manipulated them, set them against each other. Stefan had been right. Alphonse *did* have a lot to answer for.

'I think I may have an idea…' she said slowly.

'I'm listening. And then I promise we'll move on to wedding talk.'

CHAPTER TWELVE

THE WEDDING TALK progressed over the next few weeks to the wedding day, which dawned bright and clear with just a nip of chill in the air as a reminder that autumn was well under way.

Holly gazed at her reflection, knowing that Sunita's expert help had provided the finishing touches to an ensemble that would hold up to any and all media scrutiny. Anticipation panged in her tummy as she wondered what Stefan's reaction would be as she walked towards him.

As a real bride would have done, she had opted to move to Il Boschetto di Sole for the past few days—to prepare, to ensure the groom didn't so much as glimpse the dress. Though she sensed that Stefan, unlike a real groom, had welcomed her removal.

The door opened and her father entered. A scrutiny of his face satisfied her that he looked well; Jessica Alderney was still in residence, keeping a strict eye on him, and he already looked the better for it.

'You look beautiful.'

'Thank you.'

'And, Holly, I wish to thank you for this; you are doing a good thing for the Romano family—past, present and future. Of that I am proud, and you have my gratitude.'

The words warmed her soul, made it all worthwhile.

'Time to go.'

He held out his arm and she took it, tried to quell the butterflies that danced in her tummy.

She followed him from her childhood home, then paused on the threshold and blinked, nerves forgotten. There, in full glory, instead of the horse and carriage she'd been expecting, sat a pink limousine. 'Papa...?'

Thomas shrugged. 'Did you not order this?'

'No.'

It dawned on her that the only person who could have done this was Stefan. She gave a small chuckle and suddenly the whole ordeal ahead felt easier.

The afternoon took on a surreal quality as she climbed out of the limousine and smiled her well-practised smile at the selected photographers. Entering the chapel on her father's arm, she inhaled the scent of the fresh-cut flowers she'd chosen—a profusion of pink and white atop elegant stems.

The pews were filled with dignitaries and Il Boschetto di Sole staff. And out of the corner of her eye she spotted Sunita, bright and exotic in a golden *salwar kameez*, declaring her Indian heritage with pride, sitting next to Frederick, whose blond head glinted in the sunlight that shone through the stained glass. Amil looked adorable in a suit and bow tie.

Eyes forward and there Stefan stood—drop-dead, heartstoppingly gorgeous—in a tuxedo that moulded his form, emphasised the intensity of his presence, his lithe, muscular power and the deep grey of his eyes. The black hair was nearly tamed, but the hint of unruliness added to his allure.

This man would soon be her husband, and she walked towards him now, watched by the world.

Remember Sunita's advice. Stand tall. Picture happy scenarios.

Il Boschetto di Sole in her father's hands. Stefan and Holly posing for the camera with a tiny dark-haired baby in Holly's arms. A girl. And they didn't give a damn... were engulfed in love for their daughter...

Whoa—hang on a second. What was *Stefan* doing in her happy picture? Idiot! Surely she wasn't stupid enough to delude herself that this was for real? Yet the vision was hard to shake...

At a gentle squeeze on her arm, Holly realised that she'd slowed down, that people were looking at her askance.

Come on, Holly. It had been a blip—nothing more. The important part of that happy scenario had been the baby. Stefan was merely an unwanted intruder, sneaked in by a brain that had been temporarily dazzled by this marriage fiction.

Reset button and resume walk.

She reached Stefan, kept the smile on her face, revelled in the appreciative look in his.

Fake, fake, fake.

This was a show for the public—a term of the deal he'd agreed with Marcus. The vows were a dream, the solemnity of the words underscoring her hypocrisy, and no amount of justification could quiet her conscience. All she could do was tell herself that she would make sure that some good came from this marriage—that it would benefit Lycander and give her father Il Boschetto di Sole.

'With this ring...'

Stefan slipped the ring over her finger, and as the simple gold band slid over her knuckle she felt panic war with disbelief. Fake or not, here and now, in this chapel, they had pledged their troth. And, even though she knew that the words did not bind them for ever, for the next twelve months they were joined as man and wife.

'You may kiss the bride.'

The words seemed to penetrate the dreamlike fog of the past half-hour and she raised trembling hands to lift her veil—though a part of her wanted to keep hidden. Stefan's hands helped her, pushed the veil back and then cupped her face. His clasp was firm and full of reassurance, his grey eyes full of appreciation and warmth.

Fake, fake, fake, her brain warned her.

But then his lips brushed hers and sweet sensations cascaded through her body until, in a mutual recall of their surroundings, they both stepped back. He took her hand in his and they made their way back down the aisle, through the arched stone door around which honeysuckle grew, permeating the air with its scent and outside into the graveyard.

History seeped into the air from the weathered gravestones and the stone walls and spire of the chapel itself—a place that had witnessed generations of happiness and heartache. Here she and Stefan, Prince and Princess of Lycander, greeted their well-wishers until they were whisked off for photos.

Her realisation that these photos would go down in Lycandrian history threatened to call on her panic, but somehow she kept the smile on her face, remembered all the coaching, placed her hand on his arm and looked up at him in a semblance of loving wife, absorbed in the way he looked at her.

Fake, fake, fake.

But her awareness of him was, oh, so real, and nigh on impossible to ignore with their enforced proximity. His nearness played havoc with her senses. Each and every one was on high alert, revelling in the idea that for a year they were husband and wife.

As the hours wore on, through the reception and the four-course dinner, her head whirled. Gleaming cutlery clinked, conversation flowed, and the sound of laughter mingled with the pop of champagne corks. Dish followed dish—exquisite artichoke hearts, melt-in-the-mouth medallions of wild boar, crispy potato *rosti* and simple buttered spinach. The marquee glowed, illuminated by the warm white glow of fairy lights.

Once the food was cleared away, the jazz band started to warm up and Holly looked at Stefan.

'Are you ready?' he asked.

'As I'll ever be.'

And so they went onto the dance floor, to the smooth strains of a saxophone and the deep velvet voice of the singer as he crooned out the words. She'd hoped that dancing to jazz wouldn't be as tactile as to any other music, but in fact it was worse. The sensual sway of their movements, the to and fro, the distance and the proximity, messed further with her head.

Was he equally affected? Every instinct told her that he was. Each time he pulled her into his body she could sense the heat rising in him, see the scorch of desire in his eyes as they focused solely on her. When his hands spanned her waist, circling the wide belt of satin, she felt lighter than air—and yet heavy desire pooled in her gut.

Finally the first dance came to an end and they moved off the dance floor. She kept a smile pinned to her lips even as her head whirled. He walked beside her, coiled taut, and she knew his body was as tense as her own.

'How long until we leave for our honeymoon?' he asked, his voice a rasp.

She gave a shaky laugh. A laugh that tapered off as the word 'honeymoon' permeated her desire-hazed brain.

'About the honeymoon…'

'Yes. We agreed on Paris—nice and clichéd, plenty of romantic social media opportunities.'

Desire faded into a background hum as she met his gaze a touch apprehensively. 'There may have been a slight change of plan.'

Now an eyebrow was raised. 'Define "slight".'

'Actually, do you think we could discuss it later? People are watching us now and we need to mingle.'

Coward.

Perhaps, but it would be foolhardy to spark a potential argument now.

There was a pause and then he nodded. 'OK. I'll look forward to my surprise destination.'

Three hours and much mingling later, they were once more in the back of the pink limousine. Stefan handed Holly a glass of pink champagne—her first of the whole day. His too, for that matter.

'To pink limos,' she said. 'I haven't had a chance to say thank you. It's fabulous.'

'I'm glad you like it. I gather it is not, however, taking us to the airport so we can catch a plane to Paris?'

'No...' Holly took a deep breath and apprehension returned to her blue eyes.

As the silence stretched he took the time to study her. She had changed out of her wedding dress into her 'going away outfit'. A simple cream linen dress. Her hair now hung loose in all its golden glory, and she still looked every bit as beautiful as she had when she'd walked down the aisle, a vision in ivory satin and lace.

'You're going to have to tell me some time,' he pointed out.

She took another sip of champagne—presumably for fortification. 'We aren't going anywhere. We're staying here.'

Stefan closed his eyes and then opened them again,

pinched the bridge of his nose and focused on keeping his voice calm. 'Why?'

'Because the past few weeks have all been about being in the public eye, being on show. I thought it might be nice to explore Lycander differently. I reckon it would look good to the public as well—fit well with the "returning prince" theme. What do you think?'

He thought she wasn't speaking the whole truth; there was something in the way her gaze had fluttered away from his for an instant.

'Wouldn't you like to go to Paris? Explore there.'

'One day I would, yes.'

Damn it. Maybe she didn't want to go there on a fake honeymoon; maybe she wanted to save Paris for when she could do the clichéd romance for real.

'But now you want to remain in Lycander?'

'Yes. I've realised that even though I have lived here all my life there are still so many places I haven't seen—and I think it will be fun.'

A study of her expression yielded nothing but apparent sincerity, and he did believe her. He recalled how she had described her exploration of London. But he suspected there was an additional ulterior motive, and wariness banded his chest at the idea he was being manipulated in some way.

Well, if he was then he'd never give something for nothing. He shrugged. 'OK. If that's what you want. We can find Lycander's equivalent of the Chelsea Physic Garden. But I want something in return.'

It was her turn to look suspicious, and her forehead creased as she sipped her drink and looked at him narrow-eyed over the rim of the glass. 'Like what?'

'Take the marketing role at Lamberts.'

'Jeez. Why can't you let that go? We've been through

it. There is no point—I will be taking up residence on Il Boschetto di Sole in a year.'

'I understand that; I am simply suggesting that this year you take the chance to do a job you enjoy—give it a try. It will be good experience that will help with Il Boschetto di Sole. One year. Where is the harm in that?'

Holly hesitated, twisting a tendril of hair around her finger. She considered his words and then suddenly she grinned. 'What the hell? You're right. Why not? I *can't* live on Il Boschetto di Sole during our marriage, and I *do* want to try marketing, and it *will* be good experience. I'll do it.'

'Good.' He raised his glass and a smile tilted his lips. 'To your new job.' And to his private hope that it would be the first step for Holly to veer from the path of tradition and duty. 'It's important to enjoy life—grab the good times whilst you can.'

This he knew.

And just like that the atmosphere in the limousine subtly changed. The air became charged with a shimmer of awareness—he'd swear he could almost see it—a pink glitter of desire. And he knew that really all their talk had simply been to put off an inevitable decision—a decision they had been headed for ever since he'd seen her walk down the aisle…ever since he'd lifted her veil and kissed her.

Holly stilled, her blue eyes wide as their gazes met and locked. Then slowly—so slowly, so tentatively—she shifted across the seat. The swish of her dress against the pink leather mesmerised him.

There was no need for words; instead he cupped her face in his hands and brushed his lips against hers, the movement so natural, so right, that he let out a small groan as her lips parted beneath his.

The kiss seemed timeless. It could have been seconds or it could have been hours before the limo glided to a halt.

By then he was gripped with a desire so deep he ached, and he felt her answering need in the press of her body against his, the tangle of her fingers in his hair.

As they emerged, hand in hand, he tugged her towards the revolving door of the hotel, through the lobby and towards the stairs. Once inside their suite they didn't—couldn't—wait. His jacket fell to the floor and her fingers fumbled with the buttons of his shirt, crept underneath the material, and as she touched his chest, he exhaled a pent-up breath.

The words of their vows rang through his head: 'With my body I thee worship.' And without further ado he scooped her up and carried her to the bedroom.

Holly opened her eyes, turned to look for Stefan and saw the empty bed. Her languorous happiness started to fade and for a moment she clung to it, allowed herself the memory of the previous night. Laughter, joy, passion, gentleness… The swoop and soar of desire and fulfilment.

Her face flushed and she suddenly wondered exactly how to face him. But she had to—she had plans for the day…plans she was determined to see through.

Swinging her legs out of bed, she felt gratitude that he had discreetly exited, saving her an undignified scramble for clothes. Far better to face him clothed. Unless, of course, he had left because he was worried she'd request a replay. What if she hadn't measured up? Hadn't been woman enough? No—that was foolish. Last night had been magical—she knew it.

Yet that certainty dipped as she entered the living area. He looked so gorgeous and yet so remote that for a crazy moment she wondered if she'd imagined the previous night.

'Hey…'

'Hey.'

Misgivings continued to smite her. There was a grim set to his mouth, and his lips strained up into a smile that did not match the cool glint in his eyes.

'We need to talk.'

'Sure.'

His fingers drummed against his thigh and she could sense his frustration.

'Last night... I'm sorry... It shouldn't have happened like that.'

The onset of hurt began to pool inside her tummy, and she focused on keeping all emotion from her face and her voice. 'How *should* it have happened?'

'I should have checked that it was really what you wanted.'

'I think it was pretty clear what I wanted.'

'I meant in the longer term. We decided that we didn't want this relationship to become physical. Last night it did—without either of us considering the consequences.'

'We used protection.'

'That isn't what I meant. I meant the consequences to our marriage of convenience, to our deal.'

'So you regret last night?' Damn it, she hoped that hadn't been a tremor in her voice.

'No, I don't. But I do regret that we didn't figure out the rules first. Now we need to decide what happens from here.'

What *did* she want? Right now her body still strummed in the aftermath of the previous hours, and it was telling her in no uncertain terms that it really *didn't* want to give up that sort of pleasure.

'You said to me that you believe relationships with a time limit work—relationships based around physical fulfilment and a bit of sparkle over the dinner table occasionally. We could do that.'

'And *you* said that that sort of relationship wasn't for you. I think you may have mentioned "clinical sex".'

'Yes… Well, it turns out I may have been wrong about that. Turns out clinical sex is right up my street.'

Her words pulled the glimpse of a smile from him before the grimness returned.

'This isn't *about* that, though. The point is this is not the type of relationship you want and I knew that. So last night should not have happened. You are looking for a real husband, a father for your children, and I am *not* that person.'

'I know that—and I knew that last night. If I hadn't wanted to go ahead I would have said so. You are right that I want a real marriage and a family, a man who shares my values and beliefs. You don't—and I get that. But right now you are in my life and we *do* have some sort of attraction thing going on.'

She hauled in a breath.

'So last night happened and I don't regret it. As you said, the question is where do we go from here?'

Stefan has a point! yelled a voice in the back of her head. *This is not what you want—imagine the humiliation when he tires of you.*

I may tire of him.

Yeah, right. Dream on.

Fine.

'I think we should have a very short-term relationship— just for the honeymoon. Once we get back to London we'll live separate lives for the year.'

He hesitated, searched her face as if he wished he could penetrate her very soul. 'You are sure that is what you want?'

'Yes.' This was under *her* control—*she* was putting the time limit on it. This way she couldn't get hurt and she would get to replay last night. Win-win, right? 'But only if you do.'

'Oh, I *definitely* do.'

Finally his face relaxed into a grin that curled her toes and sent a thrill of anticipation through her entire body.

'In fact, why don't I show you *exactly* how much I want this? Want *you*.'

Temptation beckoned, but she shook her head. 'No can do. I have a plan for the day. We need to get going.'

'Get going to where?'

'Xanos Island.'

The smile dropped from his lips but she soldiered on. 'Sunita mentioned it. She said it's an amazing little island, completely secluded, with sand, rocks, caves—the works. I've figured out the tides, a boat awaits us, and we have the most amazing picnic ever.'

'Did Sunita say anything else about it?'

'Yes.' There was no point lying about it. 'She said Eloise used to take you there.'

'So you figured it was a good place to go to?'

'Yes.'

Because she thought the best way for him to let go of the past might be to revisit the good bits of it. He might not have had many good bits, but it seemed clear that he and Eloise had shared a few happy years before the divorce and its horrors. More than that, so had he and Frederick, under Eloise's guidance.

'I thought you might like to revisit some of your good childhood memories. I know there may not be many of them, but that makes them all the more precious.' She hauled in breath. 'And it's not only for you—it's for me as well.'

'How so?'

'I told you that your mother broke my father's heart

when she married your father. But the repercussions went deeper than that. My mother loved my father and she couldn't deal with his relationship with Eloise. Couldn't deal with the fact that my father didn't really love *her*. So she hated your mother with real venom—and I was brought up to do the same. To me, your mother was the wicked witch incarnate and I never questioned that.'

It hadn't taken the young Holly long to figure out that the best way to win a crumb of her mother's attention, if not her affection, had been to insult Eloise.

'I'd like to make amends—go somewhere like Xanos Island and remember Eloise differently.'

Stefan met her gaze and then he nodded. 'Thank you. For feeling able to give her memory a chance. I truly don't believe she wanted to hurt anyone. And she wouldn't have wanted the fall-out to hurt *you*—I know first-hand how horrible it is to be a child caught in the web of your parents' destructive marriage. I'm sorry you went through that and so would she be.'

He rose.

'Xanos Island here we come.'

As the small red and white motorboat bobbed over the waves Stefan could picture his younger self, recall the sheer joy of being on a real boat, singing a sea shanty with the Captain and his mother joining in, the soft lilt of her voice helping him with the words.

But it hadn't only been the three of them singing—it had been Frederick as well. The memory, long buried, slipped into focus. His five-year-old self sitting on Frederick's lap, leaning over the side, safe in the knowledge that his older brother held him secure around the waist as he trailed his fingers in the water.

Enough. That had been then. Before the horror of the

divorce. Before Eloise's departure. Before his father's *'toughen Stefan up and make him a prince'* notions. Before the anger and the blame in his brother's eyes. Before the emotions he couldn't forget, followed by his brother's utter lack of support through his father's *'make Stefan a prince'* regime.

Hell, he was trying, but each meeting with Frederick was so damned awkward—there was a vibe of anger, of strain, that neither of them seemed able to circumvent. Not that it mattered. As long as they continued to pull off a public pretence of civility that was all that was needed. All that he'd signed up to.

The Captain steered the boat to a small harbour and Stefan followed Holly onto the wooden jetty, hauling the picnic basket with him, and soon they were crossing golden sands.

'It's magic,' Holly said as they came to a halt. 'It feels like it's a million miles from anywhere.'

The sea seemed impossibly blue and the waves lapped gently against the sands. Flecks of sunlight dotted the green fronds of the palm trees that dotted the beach.

'I think that's why my mother loved it here: the seclusion gave her peace. I remember the last time we came here…'

The scene was vivid. The present faded and Eloise seemed to shimmer in front of him, kneeling in the sand, making a reluctant Frederick apply sun lotion, helping build a sandcastle.

'Frederick ran off to explore the caves and I had a monster tantrum because my mother wouldn't let me go with him—said it was too dangerous. I lost it, but she didn't— she didn't even raise her voice.'

She never had… It had almost been as if she'd known their time together was limited.

'Instead she hugged me, told me that when I was older we'd explore the caves together. It never happened.' It was a promise she hadn't been able to keep. 'This is the first time I've been back since then.'

'Then let's go and explore now.'

'You sure?'

Holly raised her eyebrows. 'I'm twenty-four years old, and I was brought up on a lemon grove where I roamed wild. I'm pretty sure I can rock-climb.'

'Then let's go.'

As they clambered over rocks, discovered trickles of water and debated the difference between stalagtites and stalagmites, he watched Holly, saw the lithe, sure grace with which she moved, the impatient pushing away of tendrils of blonde hair as they escaped her ponytail so that vibrant corn-coloured curls bounced off her shoulder.

As if she sensed his scrutiny, she smiled at him. 'You OK?'

'Yes.'

Somehow Holly had taken a bittersweet memory and created a new, happy one to blend with it. And he hoped that somewhere, somehow, his mother could see this, would know that he'd finally explored the caves.

For heaven's sake, Petrelli. Get a grip.

'Let's go eat—I've gone from ravenous to desperate!'

Once back on the beach, they unpacked the food: mini-quiches, tabbouleh salad, pork pies, tiny sandwiches, cheese straws and succulent Lycandrian olives, black and green and glistening in oil. They heaped their plates, sat back in the warmth of the sun and ate.

She shifted closer to him, turned to face him. Almost as if she had read his mind, she said, 'If Eloise could see you she'd be proud of you.'

The words cut him, threatened to destroy the warmth of the day, and as if on cue the sun hid behind a passing cloud.

Stefan shook his head. 'I don't think so.' If he'd been stronger, toughened up faster, jumped through the hoops his father had set, he could have saved her. *That* would have been something to be proud of.

'Well, *I* do.'

'Even if she would it wouldn't change anything.'

Not a single one of his achievements could change his mother's life and how it had panned out.

'The misery of her marriage, the horror of the custody battle, the fact that her love for me meant she suffered whatever my father meted out, her exile from Lycander...'

'That wasn't your fault. None of it.'

'If she hadn't loved me her life would have been a whole lot easier. Without me her life would have been immeasurably better.'

If he had been stronger, better, more princely, then her life would have been easier too. But he'd failed—or so his father had said. He had come in one day and announced the end of the regime. It was over and Eloise was gone.

In that moment, as he'd seen the cruelty on his father's face, Stefan had vowed that he would never be a prince— that as soon as he could he would follow his mother into exile. When he'd learnt of her death, in his grief and anger, he'd renewed that vow.

'I'm sorry.' Holly hesitated, then reached out and clasped his hand. 'Truly sorry. All I can say is please try to remember that she loved you and treasure the memories you have. I know she did.'

Stefan frowned, sure that alongside the compassion in her voice there was a strange wistfulness. As if she had a paucity of similar memories.

As if aware of it, she shifted slightly, turned to face the

sea, choppier now, with white crests on the waves looping and rolling in the breeze, casting a salt scent towards the shore along with their spray.

She'd said her parents' marriage had been embittered, and she had hardly ever mentioned her mother.

'What happened with *your* parents?' He kept his voice gentle, non-intrusive.

'My mother left when I was eight—went to Australia.'

'That must have been tough. How did they sort out custody?'

'They didn't. She decided to make a clean break; I haven't seen her since.'

Now she turned to him.

'I know it's awful that your mother suffered, and it breaks my heart when I think about it. But I also know that you are so lucky that she loved you. Because you see my mother never did—never loved me. My parents wanted a boy. Desperately. After Eloise left, my father knew he needed to get married—needed Romano heirs. He was up-front with my mother, told that he didn't love her, that his heart belonged to Eloise, but that he'd do his best to make her happy. Maybe if they'd had a brood of children they would have been. But it didn't happen, and as time went by they became desperate. For a boy. When Eloise had you I think it tipped my mother over the edge—made her feel a complete failure. She did everything; she went to herbalists, soothsayers, every doctor she could think of. I think she would have sold her soul for a child—or rather for a boy. When I turned up they were devastated. I've heard people talking about it.'

Stefan scooted across the sand, moved as close to her as possible and hoped his proximity would offer some comfort. The idea of tiny baby Holly, left unloved, desperate for care and love, made his chest ache.

'My father hired a nurse…tried to persuade my mother to take an interest. But she didn't. I think she couldn't. It was as though the sight of me turned her stomach. It always did and there's nothing I can do to change that. My father was different; his disappointment has never fully faded, but he has always shown me love and kindness and I will be grateful for ever for that.'

It explained so much about why Holly was willing to do anything for her father. Gratitude, a desire to make up for his disappointment in her gender and of course love. Confirmation, perhaps, that love gave power; if you accepted love then you had to give something back.

Next to him, she gave a sudden tight smile. 'Don't look so gutted—it could have been worse. My mother never physically hurt me, and there were plenty of staff around— they all looked out for me. And my father was amazing.'

She glanced at her watch.

'The tide is turning and the boat will soon be back for us. We'd better go.'

'Wait.'

Turning, he pulled her into his arms, rested her head against his shoulder, felt the tickle of her hair against his chin. For a second she resisted, and then she relaxed. He rubbed her back, hoped he could soothe her childhood pain.

They sat like that for a while and then she pulled back, touched his cheek with one gentle finger. 'We really do need to go.'

He nodded, rose and held out his hand to pull her up from the sand.

As they packed up the remains of their picnic a small voice warned him to take care. Holly had been rebuffed all her life by the person who should have loved her most and she was vulnerable.

But not to *him*, he reassured himself. Holly knew he wasn't a long-term prospect and she didn't even want him to be one. She'd been more than clear on that. But he knew that in this honeymoon period he wanted to make her happy, give her some memories to treasure.

They had a week—and he wanted to make it count.

CHAPTER THIRTEEN

HOLLY WOKE WITH a feeling of well-being and opened her eyes sleepily, aware of warmth, security and Stefan's arm around her. Her brain kicked in and computed the day. Already in countdown mode, she was aware that their honeymoon period was tick-tick-ticking away. But it was OK. They still had a few days to go.

Relief trickled through her and she closed her eyes—just as the alarm shrilled out and her brain properly kicked into gear, dissipating the cloud of sleep. She sat up.

Stefan made a small noise of disapproval, reached up and pulled her back down. The sleepy caress of his hands down her back caused the now familiar jolt of desire. But today she couldn't act on it. Instead she placed a gentle hand on his chest, leaned over and nuzzled his neck and then sat up again.

His eyes opened in protest.

'We have to get up,' she explained. 'Today we have somewhere we need to be.'

'Where?' Now alertness had come into play, and his grey eyes watched her.

Holly bit her lip. Part of her wanted to tell him, but another part suspected he'd refuse to go. 'I'd rather not say.'

Now he too sat up, leant back against the wooden headboard, and a frown grooved his forehead. 'I'd rather you did.'

Holly shook her head and plumped for honesty. 'You may not go if I do.'

'And you want me to go?'

'Yes.'

A pause, and then he shrugged. 'Then we'll go.'

'Thank you.' She dropped a kiss on the top of his head and grinned at him. 'I'm going to get ready.'

'Lumberjack look or suit?'

'Lumberjack is fine, and there won't be any reporters. Or I hope not.'

Now she frowned. Despite promises from the press that they would respect their privacy, April had been correct. Stray reporters dogged their steps. Not many, to be fair, but enough that they had taken to sneaking out through the back door of the hotel en route to quirky corners of Lycander, where they wandered hand in hand, eating ice cream, or savoury crêpes, chatting or walking in silence. But even then every so often she'd been aware of the click of a camera, the sense of being followed.

'OK. Let's get this show on the road.'

Swinging her legs out of bed, she headed for the bathroom, trying to soothe the jangle of nerves, her anxiety that she was making a monumental mistake—a massive overstepping of the bounds of their marriage deal.

Stefan looked out of the window of the official car, watching as the prosperous vista dropped away and the houses became progressively more dingy, the vegetation more sparse and scrubby, the poverty more and more clear. He realised they were headed to the now familiar outskirts— back to the suburb they had first visited, where they had met Sasha.

The car glided to a stop near the nursery, and once again the sheer contrast between life here and in the af-

fluent city hit him anew. Roofless houses, patched over
with tin, smashed windows... And yet a community re-
sided here. Children were playing in the streets, looking
at the cars with rapt interest.

Cars in the plural... Another car from the royal fleet
was parked opposite.

The door opened and he watched with a sense of inevi-
tability as Frederick emerged, flanked by two security men
whom he waved away to a discreet distance.

The Crown Prince's expression mirrored his own—
surprise mixed with resignation—and a sense of solidarity sneaked up on Stefan. Seconds later Sunita also
stepped out, clad in a discreet dark blue dress. His sister-
in-law waved cheerily and Stefan lifted a hand in an attempt at enthusiasm.

'Why are we here?' he hissed out of the side of his
mouth.

Holly gave him a tentative smile, though her blue eyes
shaded apprehensively. 'You'll see. Come on.'

Compression banded his chest and the sense that he had
been manipulated fuzzed his brain as he considered his
options. He could ask Franco to turn the car and rev it out
of here. But wiser counsel prevailed—that would hardly
back up the impression of brothers reunited. Whilst there
were no reporters visible, he was pretty sure this meeting
could hardly be kept secret.

A glance at Frederick indicated that he'd come to much
the same conclusion, and he headed towards them as Stefan climbed out, no doubt propelled by a prod in the back
from Sunita.

'Stefan,' he said formally.

'Freddy.'

Stefan couldn't resist. His brother had hated being called
Freddy as a child, and the sense of being pushed into an

awkward position had clearly sent Stefan straight back to childhood. Any minute now he'd find a pram and start chucking toys.

To his surprise, Frederick's face split into an unexpected smile.

'No one's called me that since you left,' he said. 'And, for the record, this wasn't my idea. At a guess, it wasn't yours either.'

'Nope.' *Damn right.*

'Then we've been ambushed.' Frederick turned and smiled affably at his wife. 'Perhaps you want to enlighten us as to why we're here?'

'Actually, this is Holly's show. I am merely her assistant— or accomplice, depending on how you want to look at it. Holly, over to you.'

Holly's show. The words pulled the band tighter round his chest. Since his father, it had never been anyone's show but Stefan's own. Warning bells clanged as he focused on her, watched as she straightened up, pushed a tendril of hair behind her ear and divided her focus between Frederick and himself.

'This community has been hard-hit. It was already in trouble and the storm made things worse. What you both have in common is a desire to right the wrongs and injustices your father committed and help make Lycander a better place. I thought maybe you could work together on this specific community—use the ideas and strengths you both have. Frederick, I know how much you care about education. And, Stefan, I know of your belief in social housing. Together you could build houses…schools. I know you are doing that throughout Lycander, but perhaps this could be the one place that represents Stefan's return to Lycander. If that makes sense. What do you think?'

She held her ground in the silence that followed.

Frederick glanced at his wife and Stefan could sense some sort of silent communication in progress. He suspected Sunita was issuing an escape route veto. Well, she had that right. Holly didn't.

In reality escape wasn't possible—this community *did* need assistance and he could provide it. But, right or wrong, the whole scenario didn't sit well with him. Holly had pushed him onto the moral high ground—was pulling his strings, pushing his buttons. *Find the cliché and apply.*

So it might be. But these people in this community had been pushed into poverty and destitution by the policies his father had instigated. His father had pushed buttons and pulled strings to cause dissension and unhappiness. He knew Holly's motives were good, that her aim was to help sow accord and not discord, and to achieve help for this place and the people who lived in it. Yet he couldn't shake the warning buzz in his head, the shades of discomfort.

But that was for later. Here and now, this was a project he believed in.

'I'm in.' He turned to his brother. 'But don't feel you have to do this—I can handle it solo.'

Impossible to guess the thoughts that were going through Frederick's blond head, but his face lightened into a smile. 'Actually, I think this *should* be a joint enterprise. I know it's your honeymoon, but do you want to stick around here for a bit and have a look? Bounce some ideas.'

One deep breath and then Stefan nodded. 'Sure.'

In unison, Sunita and Holly stepped forward.

'Grand!' Sunita said. 'Holly and I will take one car and you boys can have the other. Have fun!'

Holly paced the hotel room, anxiety edging her nerves as she wondered how it was going—whether this project would bring the brothers together. She wondered if she'd misread Stefan's body language, the sense of irritation at her perceived interference. Yet she couldn't regret it.

Her phone buzzed and she snatched it up, tried not be disappointed at the identity of the caller.

'Hi, April.'

'Holly. That's a *great* write-up on you and Stefan. That should definitely nail it with regard to everyone buying into the two of you.'

Huh?

'I haven't heard of the reporter but it's a fair article—she did well.'

Still not with it, she held her phone in place with her shoulder and pulled her laptop towards her. Pulled up the article April was describing in happy detail.

Oh, hell.

'April, I'll call you back.'

Disconnecting, she sank onto the armchair and started to read.

Love for Real? The Verdict is In.

As all of Lycander knows, last week Prince Stefan tied the knot with Holly Romano, and amid a complicated backdrop of wills and lemons, the big question has been: Are they in love for real?

Well, let's take a look at some of the evidence.

Exhibit One: The official interview done by April Fotherington —aka wife of Chief Advisor Marcus Alriksson—accompanied by the first official photograph.

Analysis: A little posed, a little formal, expressions a little strained. But who can blame them? It's hard to pose officially.

Verdict: Are they in love? Possibly...maybe.

Exhibit Two: The televised interview.

*Analysis: They talked the talk, walked the walk...
until it came to the L question. Then they stumbled,
but made a quick recovery.*

Verdict: Are they in love? Maybe, baby.

Exhibit Three: The wedding.

*Analysis: Definitely looking hot—but who
wouldn't in a dress like that?*

Verdict: The jury is still out.

So I undertook a little casual surveillance...

*Please note that I made no attempt to breach the
privacy of the honeymoon suite itself, but I am guilty
of a bit of ducking and diving whilst I followed the
newlyweds around Lycander.*

And so to Exhibit Four:

Holly's heart hit her boots as she skimmed the photos.

Herself in the palace gardens, looking up at Stefan, a
smile on her lips and love in her eyes. *Jeez.* She looked as
if she thought he was the best thing since sliced granary.
Oh, and joy! There was a picture of them in a clinch. She
was literally hanging off his lips. But it wasn't only that
photo. The next was the killer. Her hand was on his T-shirt,
brushing off a speck of dirt, and the goddamn look in her
eyes was one of love.

She didn't need to read the verdict, but she did it anyway—just in case there was even a sliver of a possibility
that she'd got it wrong.

Verdict: One loved-up princess...

*So, the best of luck to our new royals. Life gave
them lemons and it looks like Princess Holly is going
to make lemonade!*

Panic strummed every single synapse—how had it happened? This reporter had got it *right*. Somewhere down the

line she'd fallen for Stefan. Fool that she was. He'd made it more than clear that he was no fairy tale prince and she'd been damned sure her fairy tale days were over. Yet somehow she'd done it again—fallen in love with a man who didn't love her back.

What to do? *What to do?*

For a start she had to make sure Stefan didn't so much as suspect the truth. If he saw this article she'd laugh it off, put it down to the light, her acting skills, sexual afterglow… anything but the truth.

Speak of the devil… She looked up as the door opened, braced herself, shut the laptop and rose to her feet.

'Hi. How did it go?' *Too breezy.*

'It went fine.'

His voice was even—not cold, but not warm, and the glint she'd become used to over the past days was gone. She'd been right—he was mad at her.

'Good—and I'm sorry.'

'For what?' He shrugged off his jacket and threw it over the back of an armchair.

'I know I forced your hand. I didn't think you'd go if I'd told you where we were going.'

Even as she focused on the words the truth whirled inside her head, made his coolness hurt more. *Love…* She *loved* him.

'It should have been my decision to make. I don't like being bulldozed or manipulated. But I do understand that you did it with the best intentions, and Frederick and I had a productive few hours. The community wins…brand Petrelli Princes wins.'

'That isn't why I organised it.'

'Then why *did* you?'

'Because I knew you and Frederick weren't bonding and I wanted to give you a chance to sort it out, to bring you closer together, to show you how much you have in common. I thought you could both let go of the past by doing something worthwhile together *now*. If you can let go of the past then you have a future.'

She could only pray that he didn't read the subtext she was seeing herself. Damn it, she wanted a future with this man. Wanted him to decide love was for him after all.

'The past makes us who we are,' he said. 'The past matters—you can't just let go of it. But you can learn from it.'

'But maybe sometimes the lessons we learn from it are wrong. Sunita told me that your father pitted you and Frederick against each other; it was Alphonse who fostered the dislike. You and Frederick can overcome that.'

His grey eyes darkened, and bleak shadows chased across them as he shook his head. 'If it were as easy as that perhaps we could. But it isn't. In any case, I don't want closeness with Frederick.'

'Why not?'

'That's not my way, Holly. I prefer to walk alone. I like the control it gives me to do what I want to do without answering to anyone else.'

The certainty in his voice was unassailable, and his words made her heart ache as she began to accept the futility of her love.

But maybe she could make him see reason.

'You can still have control and be close to others—you would still have choices.' *Deep breath.* 'I know how much seeing your mother suffer must have hurt you, and I know it must feel like it was your fault…that loving you resulted in hurt for her.'

'It didn't *feel* like that. That is what *happened*. Fact, not feeling.'

'But *all* love doesn't have to be like that. Your mother wouldn't want you to give up on closeness or love. I know that.'

'Then she would be wrong. She had one life, Holly. One life—and most of it was miserable because of her love for *me*. She was chained to an abusive man who used her love for me to humiliate her, to make her life hell. Her love for me gave my father power. Love gives power.'

Oh, God. As her brain joined the dots all she wanted to do was hold him, but as she moved towards him she saw him move imperceptibly backwards and she stopped.

'And your love for her…it gave your father power over *you*?'

'Yes.' His voice was flat. 'And he used that power. He made me pay dearly for every visit to my mother. He decided her love for me had weakened me, made me less "princely". So he devised a regime—a training programme. If I adhered to it, if I achieved my goals, I'd get time with my mother—as well as becoming a *real* prince, of course.'

The sneer, the bitterness, made her ache even as she was appalled at Alphonse's actions. It twisted her insides. The image of a young boy, desperately missing his mother, being put through such a regime made her feel ill.

'But even then he changed the rules. One day the regime was over. I'd failed and my mother was gone. Exiled.'

'But…*why*?' It seemed impossible to fathom how anyone could do that.

'He'd met his next wife. She wanted rid of Eloise. He wanted it to look as though she'd abandoned me and he was remarrying to give his children a "proper" mother. It worked for him. And love *still* gave him power—over both of us. My mother went without a fight because she was scared of what he might do to me. As for me, there was nothing I could do—I'd already failed her.'

'No!' The word was torn from her, and now she did move towards him—didn't care if he rejected her. She stepped into his space and put her arms around him. 'That's not true.'

But she could see exactly why his younger self had thought that—knew that deep down, despite his adult understanding, he still believed it. His body was hard, unyielding, no trace of the man she'd shared so much passion with, the man who had held her, whose arms she had woken up in these past three mornings.

'Just like it's not my fault that my mother didn't— couldn't—love me. That wasn't *my* failure. I was a child. So were you. You didn't fail your mother.'

She held her breath, and then hope deflated as he shrugged.

'Whether it's true or not isn't the point. I don't want closeness. Closeness leads to love. Love is not for me—I won't give anyone that power again. Hell, I don't want that power over anyone either.'

That told her. Any not yet formed idea of telling him of her love died before it could even take root. She could not, *would* not, repeat the past. He was right—the past was there to be learned from.

Her mother, her father, *his* mother, *his* father, had all been caught in the coils of unrequited love. It had caused bitterness and misery and she was damned if she would walk that path. Or do that to him. Because if he even so much as suspected she'd fallen for him he would be appalled, and she couldn't stand the humiliation of that.

She loved him—he didn't love her. She would not do what her mother had done: hang on for years, becoming progressively more bitter, hoping in perpetuity that he would miraculously change his mind and love her. The only path—the only *sensible* path—was to walk away. At speed, with as much dignity as possible.

Think.

She couldn't walk away from their marriage—ironically those vows *did* bind them for another few months—but she could change the terms of the deal. That was a language Stefan *did* understand. Because she couldn't have any sort of relationship with him—not now she knew she loved him.

'I don't agree,' she said simply. 'Love doesn't have to give abusive power. Look at Sunita and Frederick. Look at Marcus and April.'

'That is the choice they have made. It's not a choice I agree with.'

'And that's your right. Just like it's your right and choice not to engage with Frederick. But you're missing out. Yes, you won't get hurt, but you won't experience closeness either.' Another deep breath and she forced herself to continue. 'On that note, I think we need to cool it.'

His eyes registered shock, surprise and a fleeting emotion that looked like hurt, and for an instant she nearly changed her mind. But Stefan did not love her; he would never love her. Right now, she had to protect herself.

'Why?' he asked.

Another deep breath. 'There's an article about us.' Her gaze flicked to the laptop. 'It's on there, if you want to look.'

Bracing herself, she waited as he flipped the screen up, scanned the article. Then his grey eyes came up to study her.

Hold it together. She wouldn't, *couldn't* allow the humiliation of letting him know what a fool she had been.

'It made me realise that I *do* want the real thing one day—a real marriage with love. So what we are doing feels wrong to me. I want to call it a day now, instead of in a few days. No big deal, right?'

Stefan's expression was unreadable, though she could

see the tension in the jut of his jaw, the almost unnatural stillness of his body.

'No big deal,' he agreed, his voice without any discernible emotion.

No big deal. A hollow feeling of being bereft scooped her insides. She'd never feel his touch again, never hold him, never wake up in the crook of his arm, never walk hand in hand with him. *Never...* The word that rhymed with *for ever* and it meant the opposite. Her heartache deepened and her whole being scrambled to find some semblance of pride.

He must not suspect the truth.

CHAPTER FOURTEEN

STEFAN EYED HIS brother over the piles of reports that littered the table between them, tried to focus on the figures before him. Lord knew they were important. The community project had grown and developed over the past few days of discussion. Days when they had found common beliefs and causes, a mutual desire to help those less fortunate, to give something back.

Yet despite the importance of the documents on the table it took all his willpower to focus, to try and block the images of Holly that invaded his brain wherever he was.

It shouldn't matter—he shouldn't miss her so damn much. Shouldn't keep wanting to talk to her, tell her about the project. Shouldn't miss the warmth of her body next to his in the night. Shouldn't miss the sound of her laughter, the way she swirled a tendril of her hair, the tantalising *Holly*-ness of her.

Frederick closed the lid of his computer. 'I think we should finish up for today.' A hesitation and then, 'I know Holly is at Il Boschetto di Sole for a few days—I hope her father is OK?'

'He's fine.' His illness was a cover story to explain Holly's absence.

'Sunita's out for the evening. Would you like to come back

to the palace? Have a beer…spend some time with Amil. I know he'd like that.' Another pause. 'And so would I.'

Stefan opened his mouth, closed it again. He realised the idea appealed—that the idea of a return to the hotel where Holly's absence was like an actual physical pain didn't.

'That would be good. Thank you.'

Twenty minutes later he entered Frederick and Sunita's home, watching as Amil hurtled across the floor away from the nanny and into Frederick's outstretched arms with a cry of, 'Daddy!'

Stefan stood still, aware of a pang that smote him. A pang of what? Envy? Surely not—this was exactly what he *didn't* want.

Frederick thanked the nanny before she left and then grinned at his son. 'Today Uncle Stefan is here for your bath.'

Amil beamed at him and Stefan's heart gave a funny little twist. Twisted further as he ended up in the bathroom, sleeves rolled up, sitting by the tub where Amil sat, four rubber ducks bobbing in the water.

'Sing the song, Uncle Stefan.'

Stefan shook his head. 'I don't know it, Amil. I'm sorry.'

'Yes, you do. Eloise and I sang it to you in *your* bath,' Frederick said from the doorway, and started to hum.

The tune ricocheted around his brain…evoked a crystal-clear memory. Himself in the bath, surrounded by bubbles, a rubber duck in each hand, splashing in time as his mother and Frederick sang.

'"Five little ducks went swimming one day…"'

Soon he and Frederick were singing and Amil was splashing and moving the ducks around the bath. Finally Frederick called a halt, helped Amil out of the bath, wrapped him in a fluffy towel and carried him into the lounge.

'Help yourself to a drink whilst I put Amil to bed.'

'Uncle Stefan. Please read my book?'

Frederick hesitated, then glanced at Stefan with a rueful smile. 'Do you mind?'

'Not at all.'

And he meant it. So he read his nephew a book featuring a variety of farmyard animals and felt his heart tug again.

Later, when Amil was in bed, Frederick poured two glasses of deep red wine and heated up a casserole. He sat down opposite Stefan in the spacious kitchen as the scent of herbs filled the air. 'Can we talk?'

'Sure.' Though wariness touched him.

'I know the deal you made with Marcus. Support me and get your lands back. I went along with it because I knew you wouldn't accept the lands otherwise. But I have always been happy to restore them; they are yours by right. I want you to know that.'

Stefan shook his head. 'I don't work like that. Our father took my rights and my lands away—that was his right. I would like them back, but I have no wish to be beholden.'

'We're brothers. You wouldn't be beholden. It wouldn't give me any power over you. That's what you're worried about, isn't it? Giving anyone power over you. Me? Holly?'

Stefan froze. 'Holly has nothing to do with this.'

'Yes, she does. You made a deal with her too—a marriage deal. And now I think you care about her. Maybe even love her.'

'Of course I don't. I don't *do* love.' Inside him something twisted, turned, unlocked with a creak, opening a floodgate of panic.

His brother smiled. 'Famous last words, little brother. Sometimes love doesn't give you a choice.'

'There is *always* a choice.' And right now he chose to cut himself loose before it was too late to uproot love. Love that had already coiled around his heart, inserting insidious tendrils of weakness.

Whoa… *Love?* He *loved* Holly…? *Loved* her?

Frederick leant forward, his blue eyes arresting, his mien serious. 'This may be none of my business, but you are my brother. We shared a childhood…we shared an upbringing. I cared about your mother and I cared about you. But when Eloise left, when you still got to see her and I didn't, I was angry and I blamed you. Instead of becoming a better brother I switched off, insulated myself from all emotions and feelings, allowed our father to mess with my head. Like I know he messed with yours. I owe you an apology, Stefan; I didn't step up when I should have.'

Stefan could feel emotions long-buried begin to surface. The hurt he'd felt at losing Frederick's affection… the guilt of his belief that he'd deserved to lose it…their father's relentless pitting of brother against brother. But through it all he hadn't thought about how *Frederick* felt, how *he* was affected.

'Maybe it's time to put it behind us.'

He saw an image of Holly's face, heard an echo of her voice. *'If you can let go of the past then you can have a future.'*

'Go forward from here.'

'I'd like that.' Frederick took a breath. 'But there's something else I'd like to say. Our father messed with my head so much I didn't believe that I could be a good husband or father. Sunita and Amil showed me that I can—maybe Holly can show you the same. Don't let our father mess with your head from beyond the grave. If you love her, go for it—I promise you it will be worth it.'

Frederick paused and leant over and ruffled Stefan's hair. The gesture was ridiculously familiar.

'Lecture over, little bro, but if you need anything then let me know.'

Stefan stood up, unsure of what to say. He loved Holly—and now he had a choice as to what to do about it.

Holly looked up from her computer as her father knocked on the door, a look of concern on his face. 'Holly, Jessica has made dinner. It will be ready in half an hour—come eat something.'

'I'm sorry, Dad. I'm just not hungry. But you two go ahead.' Holly summoned up a smile. 'I'm glad it's working out with Jessica.'

'That is thanks to Stefan.' Thomas uttered the name with caution. 'It was he who spoke with me, persuaded me to talk to Jessica.'

'He did?' Holly looked up. She knew she shouldn't encourage the conversation—she was trying to forget Stefan—yet she wanted to know.

'Yes, he did. In fact my temporary son-in-law was quite vocal on the subject.'

'He was?' Holly tried to feel annoyed. Instead all she could summon was a picture of Stefan—the jut of his jaw, the intensity of his eyes, the gentle touch of his hand, his smile.

'Yes, and what he said made me think.'

Her father entered the room and sat down on the bed, just as he had when she was younger, studying for exams.

'I owe you an apology.'

'No. You don't.' Now she really *was* annoyed. 'And if Stefan told you that I hope you told him to get knotted.'

'He said nothing so discourteous and neither did I. What he *did* tell me about was about your job prospects at Lamberts. Something *you* hadn't told me.'

'Because it's not important.'

'Yes, Holly, it *is* important. You should have told me—but also I should have asked. Instead I assumed that you wanted what I wanted, that your wish was to live here with me, marry, settle down, have Romano heirs, and of course work here on Il Boschetto di Sole. I assumed all that and that was wrong.'

'No, Papa. It wasn't wrong. Our family has worked here for generations. I do want to work here—of course I do.'

'But it doesn't have to be *now*, Holly. You need time to spread your wings, see the world, travel. Yes, of course I want you to live here, settle down, but most of all I want you to be happy. I can look after Il Boschetto di Sole and I can also look after myself. That is *my* responsibility. I want to be here to see your children and I will do my best to do so. I am sure Jessica will help me do that.'

Holly stood up, moved over to her father and hugged him. 'Thank you.'

'Now, come and eat with us and tell us about the new job. I want to know all about it.'

Holly grinned at him, and for a moment her heart lightened. But before she could say anything more there was another knock on the door and Jessica popped her head round, looking flustered.

'We have a visitor.'

'Who?'

'Prince Stefan. I've put him in the lounge.'

Holly's heart jumped as her tummy went into freefall.

Her father rose to his feet and smiled. 'Go to him, Holly.'

'I can't. Tell him I'm not here—that I'm sick, have been beamed up by aliens... Anything!'

Her father shook his head. 'Do you love him?'

She flinched. 'Of course not. You know that this is a marriage of convenience.'

'Are you sure?'

Holly tried to hold his gaze, but couldn't.

'Love is nothing to be ashamed of,' her father said gently.

'I'm not ashamed.' Holly twisted her hands together, saw the love in her father's eyes and opted for the truth. 'But Stefan doesn't want my love. He doesn't want anyone's love. I was a fool to fall for him. All I want to do now is get over it.'

'Have you told him you love him?'

'No! And I'm not going to. There is no point in humiliating myself and making him feel bad. This is not his fault.' Unlike Graham, Stefan had not strung her along or pretended love—he'd been up-front. 'I don't want to be like you and my mother.'

Thomas closed his eyes for a moment, then opened them, reached out and touched her arm. 'Holly. Please do not let me and your mother's actions destroy your relationship or taint your attitude to love. Our mistakes, our issues, do not need to be yours. Stefan is not me, and you are not your mother. Give your love a chance.'

Holly looked at him and her own words to Stefan came back to her. *If you can let go of the past then you can have a future.* And his words, about the past being there to be learned from.

What if they were both right?

What if her father was right?

Maybe she *should* let go of her past and tell Stefan of her love. And if he rejected that love then she would learn from her parents and she would walk away, knowing she had done all she could to give love a chance.

'Thank you, Papa.' She dropped a kiss on his head and then, pulling up every reserve of courage, she headed for the lounge.

As she entered her heart pounded so hard it was a wonder her ribcage could cope. Her lungs certainly couldn't. Her breath caught in her throat as she saw him, standing by the mantelpiece, studying the array of photographs there, his whole body tense.

His fingers drummed his thigh as he turned to face her. 'Holly. We need to talk.'

What to say? What to say? And where to say it?

Not here. Somehow she wanted to be outside, under the sky, amongst the trees in the vast beauty of Il Boschetto di Sole.

'Shall we go outside?'

He nodded, and together they made their way to the front door and stepped out into the early evening, where the last rays of sunshine were giving way to the dusk. His proximity made her head whirl, and his familiar scent made her want to bury herself in his arms and burrow in.

Rather than that, she sought some form of conversation. 'So…um…how is it going with Frederick?'

'Good. We've come up with some pretty solid ideas that we're both excited about.'

'Good.'

Conversation dwindled after that as they walked through the garden of the villa and headed by tacit consent to the lemon groves, where the intense fragrance offered her the comfort of familiarity as they wended through the trees towards a bench. A breeze holding the first chill of the year blew and she gave a small shiver.

'Here.' He shrugged off the green and blue checked shirt that he wore over a deep blue T-shirt. Seeing his bare arms made her shiver with the sudden bittersweet ache of desire and the memory of being held. Perhaps she should refuse the shirt, but she couldn't. She wanted to feel the material that had touched his skin against hers.

'Thank you.'

They sat on the bench and she turned to him, knowing she needed to do it—take the plunge.

'I'm glad you're here. I need to talk to you. We left some things unsaid.'

The ghost of a smile touched his lips. 'Yes, we did. That's why I'm here too. To say…'

Goodbye? Had he discovered some legal loophole that would allow their marriage to be annulled?

'Could I go first? Please.' Before she bottled it.

For a moment she thought, almost hoped, he'd refuse, but then he nodded. 'Go ahead.'

After a deep breath she launched in. 'I wasn't fully truthful with you and I should have been. But before I say what I need to say I need you to know that this is not your fault.'

Come on, Holly.

'I love you.'

There—she'd said it. Admittedly whilst staring down at the slats of the wooden bench, but she'd said it.

She hurried on. 'I just wanted you to know. I don't want anything back…don't expect anything back. And please don't feel bad—I don't regret loving you.'

'Holly.' His voice sounded strangled. 'Look at me.'

She looked up, braced herself for pity, anger, sorrow, but instead saw a shell-shocked look of stunned disbelief succeeded by a dawning of joy, a light so bright, so happy, that her own heart gave a small cautious leap.

'I came here to tell you *I* love *you*.'

Happiness sparked, but she doused the joy, needed to know he meant it, that it was real and not an illusion.

'Don't say it because you feel sorry for me.'

'I would never do that. I do not feel sorry for you. I love you.'

'But just days ago you told me you didn't want love... didn't *do* love.'

'It turns out I knew absolutely nothing about love. I love you whether I want to or not, and it turns out I *do* want to.' He sounded almost bewildered. 'I love you and I want to shout it from the rooftops. I love the way you smile, I love the way you twirl your hair round your finger, I love your warmth, your generosity, your loyalty and how much you care. Loving you makes me a better person—a stronger person, not a weaker one. Maybe it does give you power over me, but I trust you not to abuse that power. I've been falling for you since the moment I laid eyes on you; and now you have made me the happiest man on this earth.'

Now he paused.

'As long as you're sure too. You're not mistaking love for duty? It's not for your father, or for Il Boschetto di Sole, or...?'

'No! This love is for real! I love you—I love how you bring out the best in me, make me strive and question and leave my comfort zone. You make me smile, you make me laugh, you make me feel safe, you encourage me and you make me so happy I can feel the happiness tingle through my whole body.'

He rose to his feet and pulled her up with him. He spanned her waist with his hands and twirled her round, and then he sank to one knee and took her hand in his.

'In this beautiful place—*our* beautiful place—will you, Holly Romano, stay married to me, Stefan Petrelli, for ever? To have and to hold, till death us do part?'

She beamed. 'Yes, I will.'

And as he stood and kissed her, she knew that they would fulfil each and every vow they had made with love and happiness. For ever.

EPILOGUE

STEFAN LOOKED OUT over Forester's Glade—Radura dei Guardaboschi.

'You OK?' Holly asked, slipping her hand into his.

'Yes. Really I am.'

They had just scattered his mother's ashes over the earth she had loved so much and a sense of peace enveloped him.

'I hope she is now at rest.'

Holly moved even closer to him, increased the pressure of her clasp. 'I wish I could have known her. I wish it could all have panned out differently.'

'Me too. But I know she would have been happy for me and I know she would have loved you. Not, of course, as much as I do, but she would have loved you.'

For a moment they looked out over the lush, verdant land, listening to the babble of the stream, the rush of the waterfall.

'I love you very much, Holly. And I am very proud of you. Especially for that award.'

'I'm pretty stoked myself.'

She'd won Global Marketing Trainee of the Year and she more than deserved it.

'But the wonderful thing is how much I love the work. And did you see my father's face when they handed me the prize?'

'I thought he'd burst, he was so proud.'

She nestled closer to him. 'I wouldn't have tried it if it wasn't for you.'

'Well, I wouldn't have such a great relationship with Frederick if it wasn't for you.'

His closeness with his older brother made him feel warm inside. He knew Frederick would always have his back and vice versa.

'I guess we work pretty well together, huh?'

'I guess we do.'

Turning, he pulled her into his arms and knew that this marriage deal was one that would last for ever—and it was the best deal he'd ever made.

* * * * *

FALLING FOR THE WRONG BROTHER

MICHELLE MAJOR

To Amy: thanks for being a fantastic friend
and co-mom. I couldn't do it without you! XO

Chapter One

Why did wedding dresses have to be so white?

The question flitted through Maggie Spencer's mind as she hurried down the tree-lined street in Stonecreek, Oregon, the town that had been her family's home and passion for over a hundred years. Away from the First Congregational Church, away from her family and friends and from her remorseful, apologetic and cheating fiancé.

Oh, yes. Far away from Trevor Stone.

Hurried might not be the right word. It was difficult to hurry wearing five pounds of satin and lace plus high heels that pinched her feet to the point that she was ready to lop off a baby toe just to ease the pain.

She refused to take off the shoes because the physical discomfort distracted her from the ache in her chest. Tears threatened each time she thought of the repercussions of running away from her wedding five minutes before the ceremony was scheduled to begin.

The clock in the tower overlooking the town square a few blocks away began to chime, echoing the rhythmic lurch in her stomach. The wedding was starting.

Without her.

She gathered bunches of fabric in her hands and draped the dress's train over one arm. Grammy had insisted on a dress with a train, mainly so Maggie's younger sister would have a reason to hold it, putting Morgan on display for the good people of Stonecreek.

"It worked for Pippa," Grammy had commented drily. "Morgan's backside is just as worthy of going viral if you ask me."

Although no one needed to ask Grammy's opinion because she was happy to offer it unsolicited.

A car drove past, honked once. It wasn't every day that a bride took a stroll in her wedding gown. Sweat trickled between Maggie's shoulder blades, despite the June breeze fluttering the blooms on the oak trees that canopied the street. Not a cloud marred the robin's-egg-blue sky, a stroke of good luck for the marriage, according to Maggie's grandmother.

So much for positive omens.

Maggie kept her gaze forward, sending out a silent prayer the honking driver was no one she knew. Then again, most everyone Maggie knew was waiting in the church. Close to three hundred people crammed into the pews to witness the two most powerful families in Stonecreek finally united by marriage.

Or not.

She picked up the pace, wincing as her heel caught on a crack in the pavement and her ankle rolled. She'd just righted herself when a hulking SUV pulled up next to her.

"I'm fine," she called, holding up a hand and keeping her eyes trained forward as she lifted her dress higher off the ground.

"You're going the wrong way, Maggie May," a voice said, the tone a deep timbre that sent shivers along her bare arms.

The fabric dropped from her hands as that voice ricocheted through her. The tip of one heel tangled in her wedding dress, and she tripped and fell hard to the pavement. She managed to get herself to all fours, tears pricking the backs of her eyes, as much from embarrassment as the sting to her palms and knees.

She focused on drawing in a few deep breaths, but the air escaped her lungs when a pair of scuffed cowboy boots moved into her line of sight.

"Need a hand?"

"I'm fine," she repeated, giving a little shake of her head. A thousand rattlesnakes could have her surrounded and she still wouldn't accept help from Griffin Stone.

Faking composure, Maggie started to stand, then yelped when her right ankle screamed in protest.

"You're hurt." Griffin wrapped his hands around her arms and lifted her to her feet like she weighed nothing.

Glancing up through her lashes, she saw that a decade away from Stonecreek had honed him into every inch an alpha male, rugged and broad-shouldered. His dark blond hair was longer, curling at the ends as it skimmed the collar of the crisp white dress shirt he wore under a suit jacket. She knew he was well over six feet—even in her heels he towered over her. A

few years older than she was, he'd been the cutest boy
in high school—and the wildest by far—but now his
looks were downright lethal.

"I twisted my ankle," she confirmed, shrugging
out of his grasp and trying not to put weight on her
right leg. "Stupid shoes. I still don't need your help."
She glared at him. "What are you doing here anyway?
Trevor said you weren't coming back for the wedding,
and you never RSVP'd."

He inclined his head and she felt more than saw
his smile, a slight softening around the corners of his
stormy green eyes. "Last-minute change of plans."

"You're late," she muttered, sweat beading on her
forehead as the pain in her ankle began to radiate up
her leg. She needed to get away from Griffin and take
off the stupid heels her bridesmaids had convinced
her to buy.

"Apparently, I'm not the only one." He took a step
forward, then reached around her to open the passenger-
side door on his vintage Land Cruiser. "You don't have
to like me, Maggie, but get in the car before you pass
out from the pain of whatever you did to your ankle."

She bit down on her lip to keep the tears at bay. Of
all the people to see her in this state, why did it have to
be Griffin? He'd been the star of every one of her foolish teenage fantasies. She hadn't even cared that bad-
boy Griffin Stone barely acknowledged her existence,
even though she and Trevor had been friends since
she'd thrown up on him their first day of kindergarten.

Griffin was three years older and a world apart from
Maggie. He'd made it clear in the sneering, searing
way he had that he thought her nothing more than a
silly, spoiled princess. Now she was a pathetic mess.

It grated on her nerves to have Griffin bear witness to the most humiliating moment of her life. Chances were good he'd eventually congratulate his younger brother for escaping a lifetime shackled to the darling of the Spencer family. That thought was equally irritating since her only sin had been trusting the wrong man.

She gingerly put her right foot on the ground, hoping the pain might have miraculously disappeared. Instead, a sharp stab of pain caused her to whimper, and she turned without a word and hobbled the few steps to the Land Cruiser.

To his credit, Griffin didn't say anything or try to help her. It was like he could sense that her composure was as thin as an eggshell and might splinter into a thousand pieces if he got too close. She hated feeling fragile, hated being hurt, hated Trevor and his litany of excuses.

Griffin shut the door when she finally managed to get herself up into the SUV and gather the dusty fabric of her wedding gown's train into the vehicle.

He'd left the Land Cruiser running, and Maggie was profoundly grateful for the cool air blowing from the vents. The strap of the heel cut into her flesh, but she didn't pull off the shoe. There was a decent chance she'd scream or throw up if she did, and neither was going to happen in front of Griffin.

"I'm guessing we aren't headed back to the church," he said as he pulled away from the curb.

"I bought Grammy's house a few years ago. She lived—"

"I know where your grandmother lived." Griffin's knuckles turned white gripping the steering wheel. "I grew up here."

She had the odd sense she'd hurt his feelings, although that would be far-fetched on a good day. Griffin had always made his derision for Stonecreek crystal clear, and he'd left them all behind the first chance he got. Still, she couldn't help being a champion for the town. It was in her blood. "The neighborhood has a lot of young families now. It's nice."

Griffin's response was a noncommittal grunt, and Maggie let out a sigh. She shouldn't be trying for small talk, not under the best of circumstances, and let alone when she was running away from her wedding to his younger brother.

Trevor had promised he'd stall as long as possible, so Maggie figured she had about thirty minutes until her family descended on the two-story Cape Cod–style house she'd purchased from her grandmother three years ago.

Grammy wasn't going to take the news well, no matter how justified Maggie was in walking away.

Another complication, because Maggie couldn't tell her grandmother the truth. She'd promised Trevor—

"What did he do?" Griffin asked suddenly, like he could read her mind.

"It wasn't Trevor." The words were sawdust in Maggie's throat. "He'll always be a friend, but we were never suited for marriage." She gave what she hoped was a bittersweet smile. "I'm just sorry it took me so long to realize it."

That was good. She sounded regretful but not angry. Surely, people would accept her explanation. Everyone knew Maggie Spencer wouldn't lie.

"Is he gay?" Griffin asked conversationally.

Maggie's eyes widened. "No. We had a healthy... I mean, we're both busy so it wasn't exactly... Just no."

"Another woman? A gambling addiction? Internet porn?"

"Why can't you believe I made the choice to walk away?"

"Because you always do what's expected, and a union between the Spencers and the Stones is something people around here have wanted for ages." He pulled up in front of her house and threw the Land Cruiser into Park. "You don't have the guts to defy them."

Too stunned to move as Griffin got out of the SUV, Maggie watched him walk around the front toward her side. It was like he'd clocked her with a sledgehammer. A man she hadn't seen for almost a decade—a man who'd never said a nice thing to her in all the years they'd known each other—had just summed up her life in one sentence, and it didn't reflect well on her.

Especially because it was true.

"You don't know me," she said through clenched teeth as he opened the door. She went to push past him, a challenge with her ankle, but it didn't matter. Griffin scooped her into his arms, ignoring her protests, and stalked toward the front door.

"Is it locked?"

"No," she muttered, "and put me down."

"Once we're inside."

He shifted his hold to reach for the doorknob, pulling her more tightly against his chest. She couldn't help but breathe in the scent of him, tempting and dark like every rebellious thought she'd ever had but never acted on.

His heat enveloped her and she fisted her hands in the lapels of his navy suit jacket. She had the unbidden urge to press her mouth to the suntanned skin of his throat and forced her gaze to remain fixed on his striped tie.

The house was quiet, and he set her gently on the sofa, then knelt down in front of her.

"What are you doing?"

"Checking your ankle." He pushed up the fabric of her gown, revealing her open-toe sandals with the delicate pearl detail across the straps. The shoes were elegant and glamorous and she needed them off her feet about as much as she needed to breathe.

Yet Griffin touching her was too much when she was in pain and emotionally vulnerable.

"I can handle it."

"Let me look." He undid the ankle strap, and she was amazed at how gentle his calloused hands were as they gripped her leg. "I was a combat medic during my time in the army."

The pain had lessened slightly, or maybe she'd become numb to it. "You wore your dress blues to your dad's funeral." It was the last time Griffin had been home to Stonecreek, although she doubted he considered the town his home any longer.

His broad shoulders stiffened, but he nodded.

"Are you out of the army now?"

Another slight nod.

She winced as he manipulated her ankle, rotating it gently to one side then the other. "Why did you leave?"

He glanced up at her, his gaze both guarded and intense. "Why didn't you marry my brother?"

"I already tol—"

"Trevor did something, Maggie." He lowered her foot to the floor and sat back as he studied her. "Tell me what it was."

"So you can rush off and slay my dragons?" she asked with a laugh, flipping her gown down over her knees. "Playing the part of hero doesn't suit you, Griffin."

Something flashed in his gaze, but it was gone before she could name it. "An understatement, especially coming from you." He stood and rubbed a hand across the back of his neck. "Your ankle should be fine when the swelling goes down, but you might want to rethink your heel height in the future."

She bent forward and undid the strap on her other shoe. "It was my wedding day. The shoes were special."

"It's a strange phenomenon," he said quietly, "the focus on the details surrounding a wedding. Seems to me the only important part is a man and woman committed to loving each other for the rest of their lives."

Emotion clogged her throat. "Yes, well… Trevor and I love each other. We've been friends forever. Everyone knows it."

Griffin raised a thick brow. "Then what are you doing here?"

A car door slammed, saving her from answering.

"My family," she whispered, glancing around wildly like she could find a place to hide. A ridiculous idea, because there was no hiding from what she'd done today. Not in Stonecreek.

"I'll go out the back, then circle around to get my car." Griffin was already moving toward the hallway leading to the kitchen. "No one is going to want me here for this."

I do, Maggie wanted to tell him, although she couldn't figure out why. Griffin was nothing to her.

"Are you staying in town long?" she blurted, using the arm of the sofa to lever herself to standing. She needed to be on her own two feet—or at least the one that wasn't screaming in pain—to face her grandmother.

Griffin looked over his shoulder, raking a hand through his already-tousled hair. The air between them sparked, his gaze going dark as Maggie sucked in a breath.

"Put some ice on that ankle," he said instead of answering, then disappeared down the hall.

A moment later the front door burst open and various members of her family flooded through.

"Are you okay?" her father asked, tugging at his black bow tie.

"Are you crazy?" Vivian Spencer, Maggie's grandmother, asked, pushing past her son. "You can't call off the wedding, Mary Margaret. It isn't done."

"She just did." Maggie's sister, Morgan, followed Grammy into the house, picked up a cardboard box from a wingback chair and then sat down.

"No sass from you," Vivian scolded, wagging a finger at Morgan.

Sixteen-year-old Morgan, the picture of teenage petulance, responded with an eye roll and a dismissive sigh. Grammy's eyes narrowed, although her angry gaze returned to Maggie.

"I'm sorry," Maggie said, looking at each of her family members.

Her fourteen-year-old brother, Ben, shrugged out of his rented tux jacket. "You should have seen how bad people were freaking out," he told her, his eyes going wide. "Trevor's mom looked like she wanted to shank someone."

"Definitely me," Maggie muttered.

"Jana Stone wasn't going to shank anyone," their father said. "Naturally, she's upset and confused." He glanced toward Maggie and then away. "We all are."

Ben didn't look convinced. "If someone handed her a rusty knife, she would have gutted Maggie like—"

"Not helping, Ben." Jim Spencer leveled a glare at his teenage son.

Undeterred by the gruesome talk, Vivian moved toward Maggie until they were inches apart. Grammy barely reached Maggie's chin and she'd proudly been a size-two petite for as long as anyone could remember. Her hair was teased into a silver pouf, and she wore a rose-hued coat and matching crepe dress that made her look like she took fashion advice from the Queen of England.

Her diminutive stature belied the fierceness of her spirit. Maggie's grandmother was more than the family matriarch. She was the backbone of the Spencer clan, still with a hand in actively managing most of the family's business holdings in town and the land they owned throughout the valley.

The Spencers, along with the Stones, had founded Stonecreek in the mid-1800s. It still grated on the nerves of various relatives, Grammy included, that the town had officially been named Stonecreek instead of the planned Spencerville.

The Stones claimed that founders Jonathan Spencer and Charles Stone flipped a coin for naming rights. According to Spencer family lore, Charles got Jonathan drunk, then sneaked out to file the town's name in the early-morning hours while his friend slept off a night of whiskey and women.

That spark lit the fuse on the Hatfield-and-McCoy-esque rivalry between the two families. The friction had ebbed and flowed over the decades until settling into a civil, if awkward, truce.

Recently, the animosity had heated up again. The Spencers had been the more successful family for years, owning most of the businesses in town, as well as much of the land in the surrounding area. But Griffin and Trevor's father took over the struggling family farm when the boys were still in diapers. Dave Stone began growing grapes in the volcanic soil and within a decade had turned the vineyard into one of the leading producers of pinot noir varietals in the lush Willamette Valley.

Suddenly, power shifted, and the rural farming family began to assert its muscle in ways the Spencers didn't appreciate. The power play was subtler these days, with deals over dinner and drinks more than fistfights at town meetings. It had been Vivian who'd pushed Maggie to view Trevor as something more than a platonic friend.

Both of them had gone away to college, then returned to Stonecreek to work with their respective families. It had been easy to ramp up the childhood friendship to a more intimate level.

They'd dated for three years, and Trevor had been at her side when she'd won her first mayoral election, becoming the youngest person to hold that office in the town's history.

If you asked her grandmother, it was the two families' combined support that had propelled Maggie, relatively inexperienced in politics, to victory in the election. But Trevor had made her feel like she'd won on her own merit, and remained quite possibly the only person in either of their families who believed it.

He'd proposed last Christmas. Of course, Maggie had said yes. So what if their relationship was more of a comfortable partnership than romantic or exciting? She didn't need excitement and believed Trevor felt the same. Oh, how wrong she'd been.

"You embarrassed me today," her grandmother said, pale blue eyes flaring with temper, "and brought shame to the Spencer name."

Maggie swallowed and purposely put weight on her right foot, focusing on the physical pain instead of the emotional sting of her grammy's words.

"Mom." Maggie's father let out an exasperated sigh. "Let her explain."

"Can you explain yourself, Mary Margaret?"

"I changed my mind," she whispered, her gaze trained on the corsage pinned just below the collar of her grandmother's dress. "Trevor and I realized we don't love each other in the way two people who are getting married should." She couldn't look Grammy in the eye as the half-truths spilled from her mouth.

Not complete lies. She went into the wedding with a bone-deep understanding that her marriage to Trevor had more to do with her family than any kind of grand passion. But she would have gone through with it if she hadn't walked in on him locked in a furtive embrace with the curvaceous date of one of his groomsmen.

"What did Trevor do?" Grammy demanded, much

like Griffin had earlier. Good thing Maggie wasn't a gambler because she clearly had no poker face.

"Nothing." She lied outright this time. She'd decided at the church that she'd rather be the bad guy in this scenario than the poor, duped and undesired fool. Trevor had agreed. He would have agreed to anything Maggie had asked. "I'm sorry, Grammy. I'll take back the gifts and write apology notes to each of the guests. I'll do whatever it takes to make this right."

Vivian held up a weathered hand, the manicured tips of her fingers trembling. "This cannot be undone, Mary Margaret." She turned to Maggie's father. "Take me home, Jim."

He glanced between his mother and older daughter. "Maybe Maggie doesn't want to be alone right—"

"She made her choice," Vivian said through clenched teeth. She waved a hand at both Morgan and Ben. "Let's go."

Morgan stood and placed a hand on her dad's sleeve. "I can stay with—"

"We're all going," Vivian insisted, walking toward the front door without a backward glance.

"It's fine," Maggie whispered when Morgan's delicate brows drew together. "I'll text you later, Mo."

Her father took a step toward her, but Maggie shook her head. "It's okay. Go. I'm fine."

He looked like he wanted to argue, but she forced a smile and motioned for him to follow Grammy. Right now she needed time alone.

"I love you," her dad whispered, then walked out behind Grammy and Morgan. Ben turned back to her with his hand on the doorknob.

"I wouldn't have let Mrs. Stone shank you," he said gravely.

Maggie managed a watery smile. "Thanks, buddy."

He nodded, shutting the door behind him. As soon as the latch clicked, Maggie's knees buckled. She collapsed to the hardwood floor with a sob, her life in pieces around her.

Chapter Two

Griffin pushed open the church doors and strode through, ignoring the gasps and stares of the small crowd still gathered near the front of the sanctuary.

His younger brother stood in the center aisle between the pews, talking to a woman Griffin didn't recognize, although she seemed vaguely familiar.

Growing up it felt like Griffin had known everyone in the close-knit community, and he'd chafed at both the expectations and scrutiny of being part of one of Stonecreek's founding families. How could he expect anonymity when the town bore his family's damn name?

He hadn't asked for any of it. Small-town life had been stifling enough to a rambunctious kid without the added pressure of trying to live up to what his parents wanted from him. It had been presumed he'd be groomed to take over the helm of the family vineyard. Everyone in town—except his father—had seen his future like it had already come to pass.

Griffin knew Dave Stone would never have allowed him to take over the business. Griffin hadn't been able to please his demanding father, and by the time he'd hit his troubled teen years, he'd stopped trying. Let Trevor be lauded as the family's favored child. Griffin had always been more suited to the role of black sheep.

He watched as Trevor smiled and inclined his head as the older woman patted his shoulder, playing the part of the brokenhearted groom to a T. If he hadn't been set on becoming the family scion, Trevor could have had a career in Hollywood. This little performance showed he was a consummate actor, although Griffin didn't believe a moment of it.

People turned as he stalked up the aisle, but his full attention was on Trevor. He hadn't seen his brother since their father's funeral four years ago. Trevor was a couple of inches shorter than Griffin, his hair a shade lighter, making him look even more the golden son.

"Griffin." Trevor's deep voice boomed through the nearly empty sanctuary. He opened his arms, preparing to greet the prodigal brother with a hug. As if that would ever happen. "Good to see you, man. Sorry you came all this way for—"

Griffin slammed his fist into Trevor's face without a second thought, the sharp pain in his knuckles a welcome outlet for his frustration.

Trevor muttered a curse as he stumbled back a few steps, covering his left eye with one hand. "What the hell was that for?"

"You tell me." Griffin shook out his hand, then

turned to meet the shocked gazes of the people still standing in the back of the church. "If you folks will excuse us, my brother and I need to speak in private."

"Maggie left him," said the older woman, whom Griffin finally recognized as his high school health teacher. "She walked out just as the ceremony was starting. It wasn't his fault. Trevor's the victim here. His poor face."

"Victim," Griffin repeated. "I don't think so."

"You don't know anything," Trevor said, the skin around his eye already turning a satisfying shade of purple.

"Really?" Griffin crossed his arms and arched a brow, letting Trevor know without words that he wasn't fooled by the jilted-groom act. "Do you want to have this conversation here or in private? Think long and hard about your answer, Trev."

Griffin was bluffing. Maggie had told him nothing, but he couldn't shake his suspicion that she'd had more of a reason for playing the runaway bride than she'd let on. Walking away wasn't in her character, and he didn't buy his self-important brother as the jilted groom for one minute.

Trevor stared at him for a moment, his eyes unreadable. Then a muscle ticked in his jaw, and Griffin wanted to punch him again. He recognized Trevor's tell from when they were kids, and Griffin knew without a doubt his brother was guilty of something.

"I'm not going to bore these nice people with our family drama," Trevor said, his tone smooth like Harvest Vineyards' flagship pinot.

"It's not boring," the health teacher—Mrs. Davis if Trevor remembered correctly—said enthusiastically.

Trevor flashed the most charming smile he could with his swollen eye. "You're a sweetheart, Mrs. D, and I'd appreciate a few of your famous oatmeal scotchies the next time you bake a batch. Right now, I'm going to take a minute with my brother." He glanced around the church, as pious as a choirboy. "This isn't the place for violence."

Immediately, Griffin regretted letting his temper get the best of him. Or at least he regretted hitting Trevor in a church. His mother would have a fit when she heard about it, and he'd already caused Jana Stone enough trouble to last a lifetime.

"I'll talk to you all soon," Trevor called to the rest of the onlookers. "Thanks for the support today."

Griffin looked over his shoulder as he followed Trevor toward the vestry. The few people who'd witnessed his outburst were whispering among themselves and met his gaze with a round of angry glares. Only an hour back in Stonecreek and he was bristling to escape again.

He didn't bother closing the door as Trevor walked to a small refrigerator positioned in the corner of the room and pulled a bottle of water from it.

"Did you talk to Maggie?" he asked, wincing as he pressed the water bottle to his eye.

"Yes. I was late for the ceremony and saw her walking down the sidewalk."

"I'm surprised you recognized her."

"She was wearing a damn bridal gown."

Trevor sighed. "I told her she could take my car when she left."

"A gentleman to the end," Griffin muttered, pacing to one side of the room and running a hand along the edge of the bookshelf lined with hymnals.

"What did she tell you?"

Griffin forced himself not to stiffen. "I want to hear it from you."

"Maggie promised she wouldn't talk. She said she understood." Trevor blew out a frustrated breath. "Neither one of us meant for it to happen. I tried to cut things off. Hell, she was here with Tommy. He was one of my groomsmen. I introduced them four months ago. You remember him, right?"

"The fool who accidentally set himself on fire at homecoming your freshman year?"

"The bonfire after the football game got out of hand," Trevor said almost reluctantly. "He's grown up a lot since then. Sort of."

"So you set your mistress up with an idiot? Nice backup plan."

"I chose Maggie," Trevor insisted. "But if she won't forgive—"

"She didn't tell me anything," he said through clenched teeth.

Trevor's mouth fell open. "Then how did you—"

"I didn't," Griffin interrupted. "Not until this moment. Maggie's version was that she realized the two of you were better as friends and she couldn't go through with the marriage."

"It's the truth," Trevor said, dropping into a chair positioned next to a rack of black robes.

This cramped room wasn't quite the pulpit, but Griffin still felt a stab of guilt for his violent thoughts under the church roof. "Not the whole truth."

"Hell, Grif, I tried. We both did. This wedding meant more to the families—more to the town—than to either of us."

"What a lame excuse for cheating."

Trevor's mouth tightened into a thin line. "I wasn't cheating today. Not really."

"Then what did Maggie see?"

"Julia and I were kissing. A farewell kiss."

"In the church before your wedding ceremony?" Griffin laughed without humor. "You're going to act holier-than-thou because I punched you in the sanctuary? The angels were probably cheering me on."

"What do you care?" Trevor demanded. "You told me you weren't even going to be here today. Suddenly you feel the need to come to Maggie's defense? You never liked her when we were younger. You have no relationship with her. I don't get it."

Griffin turned away toward the window overlooking the glen behind the church. The towering maple trees provided a lush green canopy, and tulips in a variety of colors lined the cobblestone path. Lilac bushes bloomed with lavender flowers, a short burst of color that would be gone by summer.

He'd spent most of the past decade in war-torn countries across the Middle East. Places baked by the sun, where it was as common to breathe in sand as air. There'd been moments where he'd felt like his throat would always be coated with the stuff, and he'd closed his eyes late at night and imagined himself back in this verdant valley.

He'd foregone college and joined the army against his parents' wishes. Life in Stonecreek had felt like it was choking him after a stupid mistake fractured any possible relationship with his father. It wasn't until he'd traveled halfway around the world that he'd realized how much home meant to him.

He hadn't wanted to come back here. Too many demons from his past lurked in the shadows. It seemed like he'd never be able to shrug off the disappointment and failure that were part of who he was in this town.

Trevor was the living embodiment of that. Three years younger, his brother had a knack for causing trouble but not being caught up in it. It was like Trevor wore a coat of armor preventing people from seeing anything but the best in him. The polar opposite of Griffin.

He might not have a relationship with Maggie, but the connection he felt had been immediate and almost palpable. He'd seen her walking down the street in that fancy gown, and his heart stuttered. How had the annoying, gangly girl he'd grown up with morphed into such a beautiful—and achingly melancholy—woman?

Every one of his boyhood transgressions had been magnified by the insinuation that he made his family look bad in front of the upstanding Spencers. Maggie had been their goody-two-shoes princess. The fact that she and Trevor had been friends despite the animosity between the two families hadn't surprised Griffin. They'd both been textbook perfect. But today she'd seemed truly alone. Griffin had always been a sucker for another loner.

"She doesn't mean anything to me," he lied. "I felt sorry for her, and obviously with good reason."

"You don't need to feel sorry for Maggie. She's tougher than she looks."

"That doesn't make it right."

"It wasn't my fault."

It never is, Griffin thought to himself.

"Do you love this Julia?" he asked.

Trevor pressed his fingers to his eyelids as if the

question gave him a headache. "Not exactly, but I can tell you I never felt anything like it with Maggie."

Griffin snorted. "Two years ago I ate some bad scallops in Dubai, and I've never felt anything like what came next."

"Shut up, Grif."

"You can't let Maggie take the fall for—"

"You're back!"

Both men turned as Jana Stone raced into the room. She spread her arms wide and Griffin walked into his mother's embrace, his heart swelling as she pulled him close. At five feet two inches tall, his mother barely grazed his chest, but a hug from her made him feel like he was a kid again.

He'd lost count of the times he'd been sent to his room by his father for one transgression or another. His mother had always sneaked upstairs to give him a hug and reassure him of his father's love.

He'd even spent one full Christmas dinner alone, sulking on his bed, after he'd accidentally knocked over the tree while he and Trevor were wrestling. The fight had started when Trevor purposely broke a radio-controlled robot Griffin had unwrapped earlier, but it didn't matter to his dad.

Griffin was the older brother who should have known better, so he'd been the one punished. When his mom couldn't convince Dave Stone to give him a break because of the holiday, she'd boycotted the family meal, making up two plates and joining him in his room.

They'd eaten cross-legged on the floor, taking turns choosing Christmas carols to sing. It had been one of the best Christmases Griffin could remember, free of the tension and awkward silences that accompanied regular family dinners at the vineyard.

"Why didn't you tell me you were coming?" she asked, giving him another squeeze before pulling away. She sucked in a breath as she glanced toward Trevor. "Oh, my gosh. What happened to your eye?"

Trevor helpfully pointed at Griffin, who yelped as his mother pinched him hard on the back of the arm.

"You hit your brother? What were you thinking?" She placed a hand on her chest. "Tell me you didn't fight with your brother in church."

"Can't do that, Mom. Sorry."

"You should be sorry, Griffin John Stone. After all Trevor has been through today. I swear I wouldn't put it past Vivian Spencer to have orchestrated this whole fiasco just to embarrass our family."

"I highly doubt it," Griffin muttered.

"Maggie had to follow her heart," Trevor said, sounding like the benevolent son his mother knew him to be. "No one is to blame."

"*She* is to blame," their mother countered. "You're the vice president of marketing for Harvest Vineyards. You're a public figure, Trevor. We did a special blend for the occasion." She threw up her hands. "With personalized labels. Press releases went out. This could hurt the brand."

"Mom." Griffin shook his head. "This was supposed to be a wedding, not a publicity event."

He glanced at his brother, who lifted his brows as if to say *I told you so.*

"You've been away from Stonecreek too long, Griffin. Social media has blurred the lines between our private lives and public branding for the company. There's too much competition these days to think otherwise."

She moved toward Trevor, gently touching the swelling around his eye. "We certainly have no time for nonsense between the two of you. I guarantee the Spencers are already doing damage control. What do you think this will do to Maggie's prospects for reelection in the fall?"

"Nothing," Trevor said immediately. "She's done a great job as mayor this first term so there's no reason to think she won't win again."

Jana tsk-tsked softly. "She won the first time because we endorsed her—she had the support of the whole town." She straightened and turned to Griffin. "Your second cousin is running against her. He's been giving me the 'blood is thicker' line for months. Everyone has seen that Mary Margaret Spencer can't follow through on a commitment of the most important kind. How can they trust her running Stonecreek? Especially given the Spencer single-mindedness in promoting a civic agenda benefiting her family's business interests."

Griffin rubbed the back of his neck. He'd returned because his mother had asked him to, but he didn't want any part of this small-town drama. "Hasn't the animosity between the two families gone on long enough?"

"We thought so," Jana admitted. "I know Jim wants peace between us. I do, too." She worried the pad of her thumb back and forth over the ring finger on her left hand, where she'd worn her wedding band for over two decades until her husband's death. "Today changed everything."

"Do you have something to add to this conversation?" Griffin asked Trevor.

His brother only shook his head and whispered, "Not now."

"Fine. I'll do it." Griffin turned toward his mother. "There are things about today you don't understand. Like the reason I hit Trevor."

The bejeweled purse hanging at her side began to buzz incessantly. "It's your grandmother," Jana said, pulling out the phone. "I'm late to pick her up. She's going to help me take the flowers from the reception site. We need to get to them before Vivian does. They'll work for a tasting event at the vineyard tomorrow night, but you can bet Vivian Spencer will use them for the inn if given half a chance."

"Mom, we need to talk."

"Later tonight," Jana promised, already heading for the door. "Family dinner at the house." She glanced toward Griffin. "Did you drop your stuff there already?"

"Not yet."

"I cleared out the caretaker's apartment above the garage like you asked, although I don't know why you won't move back into your old room. It's far more convenient." She blew each of them a kiss. "No fighting, you two. I mean it."

"Moving back?" Trevor asked as soon as she was gone. "To Stonecreek?"

"It's only for a few months," Griffin said, examining a scratch on one knuckle. "While I build the new tasting room."

"Wait a minute." Trevor stood and held up a hand. "You're the contractor Mom hired?"

Griffin nodded. "I asked her not to mention it to you."

"No way. You don't get to waltz back in here and start taking over. I've dedicated the past five years to the family business."

"I'm not a threat to you," Griffin said quietly. "I know my place."

"Since when?"

Griffin ignored the verbal jab. "I also know my way around a construction site and have a sense of the history of the vineyard. Mom wants it to be right, and I owe it to her."

"I'm the vice president—"

"Of marketing," Griffin interrupted.

Trevor narrowed his eyes. It was no secret his dream in life was to run Harvest Vineyards. Both of them had grown up working the land and learning the ins and outs of the wine-making process. As Griffin grew older, the animosity between him and his father had grown until the two hundred acres they owned felt like a cage, the home he'd lived in since he was born, a prison.

"Dad wouldn't have wanted this," Trevor said harshly. "After what you did…"

"Not his decision to make any longer."

Their father had died four years ago when the private plane he'd chartered crashed just after takeoff. The accident had been a shock to them all, and a huge blow to their mother. But Jana took her role as president of the board as seriously as if she'd been born into the family.

Griffin had come back for the funeral and stayed for the family meeting his mother insisted on presiding over the morning after the service. He knew Trevor had expected to be named CEO but instead Jana had offered the position to their longtime employee, Marcus Sanchez.

"I still should have been told."

"And you still need to tell Mom about why Maggie walked away," Griffin countered, unwilling to debate his worthiness to return to the vineyard with his younger brother.

Trevor studied him for a long moment, then flashed a sanctimonious grin. "You won't stick, Grif. You never do."

Fists tightly clenched, Griffin watched his brother walk out of the room. How could he argue when the desire to climb into his SUV and drive away made his skin itch like a junkie looking for his next fix?

He wasn't meant for Stonecreek. He'd been a different person here, a punk kid he didn't like very much. But he also had no idea how to be anyone else when faced with his past.

So where did that leave him?

He sure as hell wished he knew.

Chapter Three

"Do you hate me?"

Maggie paused in the act of folding the last of the tablecloths that would have been used at her reception. It was nearly eleven at night, and the Miriam Inn's ballroom was dark other than one dim bulb glowing in the entry, where Brenna Apria stood, her arms wrapped tightly around herself.

"Does it matter?" Maggie asked, then placed the tablecloth on top of the pile with more force than necessary. Nancy Schulman, who managed events at the inn, had called her earlier to report that Trevor's mom and grandma had descended on the venue and were scooping up the vases of flowers that Maggie and her bridesmaids had arranged and placed around the room the previous day.

The Spencers owned the inn and event center, and

Maggie had recommended Nancy for the manager position after a nasty divorce nine months ago. Maggie appreciated that the woman still felt some loyalty, when Grammy had made it clear in a barrage of texts and voice mails throughout the day that everyone else thought Maggie was either crazy or downright cruel to have left poor, sweet, upstanding Trevor Stone at the altar.

Maggie hated to admit how much it hurt that people who'd known her since she was in diapers could turn on her so quickly, but she wouldn't let it show. That was something she'd learned from her mother, who'd put on a brave front even when ovarian cancer ravaged her, metastasizing throughout her body.

She'd told Nancy to let the Stone women take whatever they wanted and that she'd clean up the rest after. Then she'd called the florist, the DJ and the photographer to personally apologize and assure them she'd pay each of their bills in full.

Even knowing they were getting their money, none of the vendors had been happy. Working the Spencer-Stone wedding was more than a regular job. The two families were practically royalty in the growing town, and Harvest Vineyards was quickly gaining a national reputation for its wine.

But the loss of visibility and free marketing couldn't be helped. At least not by Maggie. It was rapidly dawning on her exactly what she'd done with her promise to Trevor about keeping the real reason she'd walked away a secret.

Now the woman she'd considered her best friend, who'd known about Trevor's cheating, was standing here looking for what? Forgiveness? Absolution?

Maggie was fresh out of both.

"It matters. You're my best friend." Brenna walked forward, in and out of shadows, but Maggie could see how miserable she looked. Her dark eyes were red, her high cheekbones stained with the tracks of dried tears. Maggie didn't care. Her own face was puffy from crying and even now, when she thought she had no more tears to shed, she could feel moisture prick the corners of her eyes.

She bit down on the inside of her cheek until she tasted blood. "How long have you known?"

"Trevor promised he'd change," Brenna insisted instead of answering the question, then broke off at the glare Maggie sent her. "That it was a onetime lapse in judgment. I wanted to believe him, and I didn't want you to be hurt."

"That backfired," Maggie muttered.

"You have no idea how sorry I am."

"You're supposed to be my best friend."

"I am," Brenna whispered.

Maggie grabbed the tablecloths and shoved them into a cardboard box. "You were aware my fiancé was cheating and didn't tell me. I caught him swapping spit with another woman minutes before the wedding, and you weren't even shocked. Did you know about Julia?"

Brenna's full lips pressed into a thin line. "I thought it had ended, but they were flirty at your engagement party. I asked Trevor about it, and he said I was overreacting. He told me I'd ruin both of your lives if I said anything."

"Don't you think it would have been worse if I'd ended up married to a cheater?"

"He told me—"

"You must know you have terrible judgment when it comes to men," Maggie said through clenched teeth, unable to stop herself, even though she knew the comment was hurtful.

Brenna grimaced. "I know." She picked up a stack of napkins and thrust them toward Maggie. "You can hit me if you want, like Griffin did with Trevor. I deserve it as much as him."

Maggie stilled as unease snaked along her spine. She hadn't admitted anything to Griffin, so it was difficult to imagine him defending her to his brother. And yet... "What do you mean Griffin hit Trevor?"

"Decked him in front of the pulpit. Mrs. Davis was standing just a few feet away. She said Griffin looked like he wanted to kill Trevor but only threw one punch. Apparently, Trevor has a nasty shiner."

"Have you seen him?"

Brenna shook her head. "I also didn't realize Griffin was back in town. I thought he said he wasn't coming to the wedding."

"He had a change of plans," Maggie told her.

"You talked to him?" Brenna's brows shot up.

"As I was leaving the church," Maggie said with a nod. "He ended up giving me a ride home."

Brenna's sharp intake of breath was audible in the quiet space. "What does he know?"

Maggie bristled at the implied accusation in her friend's—former friend's—tone. "Nothing he heard from me. Trevor was the one who betrayed me, Brenna. I understand that, but it doesn't change how hurt I am that you didn't tell me what you knew."

She walked to the far side of the reception hall, where they'd set up a table for the buffet line. Thankfully, after a few hours off her feet with an HGTV-watching marathon, her ankle felt almost normal again so she wouldn't have to recount her embarrassing fall to Brenna. At one end of the long table stood a framed photo of Maggie and Trevor—their official engagement photo.

It had been taken just after Christmas, the two of them standing together on the bridge that spanned the creek snaking through the park in the middle of town. Snow covered the trees and their cheeks were rosy from the cold air. They looked happy. She'd *been* happy, or so she thought.

"I don't know why I agreed to take the blame for canceling the wedding in the first place." She lifted the picture off the table, gripping the frame so tight her knuckles went white. "How is it better this way?"

"It shows people that you were in control," Brenna suggested weakly.

"They hate me."

"No one could ever hate you," Brenna countered but they both knew that wasn't true.

"Why, Brenna?" Maggie hated the catch in her voice. "Why not talk to me? If I'd known, I would have broken up with him months ago."

Brenna put up her hands, palms out, defending herself from Maggie's simple line of questions. "I believe he loved you, and you deserve happiness more than anyone I know. I'd never do anything to hurt you. At least tell me you believe that."

"I do," Maggie agreed reluctantly. She and Brenna had met soon after Maggie returned to town when they'd taken a yoga class together. It was an unlikely friendship—Maggie had just been elected mayor and

Brenna had just filed a restraining order against her latest ex-boyfriend. "Can I ask you a question?"

Brenna nodded. "Of course."

Maggie appreciated both the other woman's commitment to making her life better and the fact that she didn't seem to care about Maggie's angelic reputation or who her family was in town. Brenna had been the first person since Maggie graduated college and returned to Stonecreek who liked Maggie for herself.

Brenna had a six-year-old daughter, Ellie, whom Maggie adored, and the two women had become fast friends. So much that when Jana Stone needed to hire a new assistant to work in the family's office and manage the vineyard's tiny tasting room, Maggie had recommended Brenna for the job.

She hadn't had a moment's doubt about her fiancé and where Brenna's loyalty would lie if it came to that. On paper, Maggie and Trevor were perfect, and she'd been willing to ignore the rather flat chemistry and lack of spark in favor of all the practical things they had in common. She'd assumed he felt the same. What an idiot she'd been.

"Do you think…" She paused, looking for the right words. When none came she simply blurted, "Was Trevor that desperate to not marry me?"

"Maggie, don't go there." Brenna wrung her hands in front of her waist. She'd changed from her bridesmaid's dress into a pair of black yoga pants and a baggy sweatshirt but other than her blotchy face, she was still a knockout. A few inches taller than Maggie's five-foot-six-inch frame, Brenna had curves for days. Combined with her olive skin and thick caramel-colored hair, men noticed her wherever she went.

"I need to know. Was he using the affair to force me to walk away so he didn't have to?"

"I believe so."

The simple statement was a physical blow. It was bad enough to believe that Trevor had betrayed her because he'd found his soul mate in another woman, but hearing that he just couldn't stand the thought of marrying Maggie? It was too much.

"You don't think they're in love?"

Brenna shook her head, a strand of shiny hair escaping the elastic band at the back of her hair.

"He should have told me he didn't want to go through with it." Maggie pressed her fingers to her temples. If she really examined the last couple of months, she could see the cracks in her relationship with Trevor turning into gaping chasms. They hadn't been intimate since…well, far too long. He'd shown no interest in wedding plans, which she'd attributed to him being a man and nothing more.

"I'm sorry I didn't say anything," Brenna repeated, and her voice cracked. "I don't want to lose you."

Maggie sighed. She didn't want to end the friendship, despite Brenna's dishonesty. Trevor was the one to blame in all this. She'd never admit it out loud, but the more she thought about a life without him at her side, the more relief spilled through her.

Had she really gotten so caught up in planning a wedding that she ignored the fact she didn't want to marry the man whose ring she wore? What did that say about her and how much she'd allowed her life to be dictated by what her family and the town expected of her?

"I'll call you next week," she offered, because the breach of trust still stung.

"Okay," Brenna agreed, swiping at her cheeks. "If you need anything…"

"Time," Maggie said quietly. "I need time."

"You deserve better than him," Brenna whispered, then turned and left Maggie alone in the empty reception hall once again.

"You're also too nice," a deep voice said from the back of the hall. "I remember that now."

She turned to see Griffin emerging from the door that led to the kitchen area.

Annoyance pricked Maggie's spine at the subtle condemnation in his words. As if being nice was a bad thing. "She apologized, and your brother's the one who cheated. What would you have me do?"

"Tell her she's a sorry excuse for a friend," Griffin suggested. "Yell and scream at her for not having your back."

Maggie grabbed another pile of napkins and shoved them into the box. "Or give her a black eye like you did to Trevor?"

One side of Griffin's mouth hitched up as he examined the knuckles on one hand. "It felt good."

"I told you I don't need you to defend me. Walking away from the wedding was my choice." She stalked forward, maneuvering around tables until she stood toe-to-toe with him. "What are you doing here anyway? Do you have some new sixth sense for predicting my lowest moments so you can watch and gloat?" She couldn't conceal the anger in her tone. Maggie always kept a tight hold on her emotions, but with Griffin she seemed unable to hide anything.

"Mom sent me over to pick up the cases of wine."

She stilled as he reached out a finger and traced it along the curve of her cheek. The touch was feather-light, and she resisted the urge to lean into it. Maggie had lived every day of her life surrounded by family, friends and the town she loved…until today. Now she was alone, and the solitude chafed at her in a way that made her feel weak. She hated being weak. "Brenna was right about one thing," Griffin told her. "My brother doesn't deserve you, and he sure as hell doesn't deserve your tears."

"It's *my* canceled wedding," Maggie said, making her voice light. "And I'll cry if I want to."

Griffin's green eyes softened, but he dropped his hand as if he realized the moment was too intimate. "What next?"

"Back to life." Maggie stepped away. "We weren't scheduled to leave on the honeymoon for a few weeks, so Monday it's business as usual at city hall."

"Right." Griffin gave a slight nod. "You're Stone-creek's incumbent mayor."

The thought of facing everyone at work and the members of the town council made a sick pit open in Maggie's gut. "When do you take off?"

Griffin didn't answer, so Maggie turned back to him, holding the cardboard box in front of her like a shield. He watched her, his gaze unreadable. "What?"

One broad shoulder lifted and lowered. "I may not be leaving for a while."

She concentrated on breathing, feeling like a thousand-pound weight sat on her chest. "How long is a while?"

Another shrug. "My mom wants me to build the

new tasting room at the vineyard, and I've tentatively agreed. I owe her since the fire in the original building was my fault."

"It was a stupid accident. Everyone knew that."

A muscle ticked in his jaw. "I think Dad never rebuilt because he wanted the reminder of how badly I'd failed him. Mom claims it's important someone in the family oversees the project. We still need to work out the particulars, but I might be around a few months."

"Oh." Her lips formed the word as her brain scrambled for purchase. Griffin Stone back in town. It shouldn't matter. It shouldn't affect her, not after everything that had happened today. But it did, and her reaction to him made all the other chaos in her life lose focus.

The only thing she could see was the tall, handsome man who'd come to her defense—even when she'd told him not to—standing in front of her.

"I'm going to start loading the wine," he said, still studying her. "See you around, Maggie."

She gave a small wave, then continued packing up boxes, telling herself Griffin didn't matter to her.

Too bad her heart refused to be convinced.

Chapter Four

Monday morning Griffin stood on the hilltop that overlooked the estate vineyard, emotion pinching his chest as he breathed in the musky scent of earth. The rows of vines spread across the property, neat and orderly like soldiers in a procession.

As a kid he'd spent hours running through the fields, measuring the progress of the seasons by the height of the vines and the colors of the grapes. The vineyard below him was called Inception, the first Dave Stone planted when he'd converted the farm, which had been marginally successful at best, to a vineyard.

Griffin had loved everything about the land until it became clear that his father didn't think him worthy to be involved in the family business. It had never made sense to Griffin. He was the older son, and he felt a connection to the vines in his heart, unlike Trevor, who'd been more interested in the flashy side of wine making only—the marketing and brand positioning.

But his dad had ever only found fault with the innovations and ideas Griffin suggested. Even the way Griffin hand harvested the grapes was never right. Eventually he'd stopped trying, at least when his father was around. He'd watch the workers during the harvest, pretending he was too interested in his own life to care about the vineyard.

It had always been a lie.

"Jana told me she'd convinced you to return," a voice said from behind him. "I wasn't sure I believed her."

Griffin turned as Marcus Sanchez, Harvest Vineyards' current CEO, walked up from the direction of the main office.

He held out a hand and Marcus shook it with a surprising amount of enthusiasm. "It's good to have you back."

"Only temporarily," Griffin clarified.

Marcus inclined his head. He was nearing fifty but still had the build of a younger man, with broad shoulders and a thick crop of dark hair. "You've been away from home too long, Grif. You belong on this land."

Griffin swallowed and kicked at a patch of dirt. Strange how much those words meant to him after all this time. Marcus had worked at Harvest for almost fifteen years, so he'd had a front-row seat to Griffin's teenage battles with Dave Stone.

Although he worked for Dave, Marcus had always been kind to Griffin, unlike many of the employees who seemed to feel like part of their loyalty to Dave included shunning Griffin. "Mom says she'd be lost without you around here. Thanks for taking care of her."

Marcus flashed a grin. "Your mother can take care of herself, and we both know it."

"I'm surprised she was able to lure you away from the grapes." He inclined his head toward Marcus's pressed jeans and dress shirt. "You clean up nice."

"Jana is a difficult woman to refuse." Marcus adjusted his collar with tentative fingers as if he was still unused to having his shirts starched. He'd come to work as a picker and quickly risen through the ranks until being promoted to vineyard manager a decade earlier.

"Tell me about it." Along with most everyone associated with Harvest, Griffin had expected Trevor to be made CEO after their father's death. Instead, Jana convinced Marcus to move from the fields into the corner office.

"Have you visited the winery yet?" Marcus asked.

Griffin shook his head. "I walked the fields but haven't made it inside yet. The expansion looks great."

"We took cuttings from the original vines to plant the newest vineyard. Your mother named it Promise." Marcus nodded. "The entire operation is certified sustainable now, and we've started bottling with eco-friendly glass and managed to eliminate some of the high-risk chemicals that were originally used for fertilization and in the pesticides."

"How's that going?" Griffin felt himself clench his hands into fists.

"It's making Harvest more responsible and adding to the efficiency of the operation. Just like you told your dad years ago."

Griffin blew out a breath. "I'm sure the technology has come a long way since then."

"It was still your idea," Marcus said softly. "And a good one."

"Thanks." The tension coiling through Griffin eased slightly. The argument about protecting the long-term health of the land had been one of the last he'd had with his father before their final, irrevocable falling-out.

Griffin had been a senior in high school and planning to go to college to study viticulture. Back then he'd still believed if he could prove to his father that he could offer value to the business that Dave Stone would find a place for him. But his dad had brushed aside the suggestions, asserting that it was too soon to worry about the future when they were still trying to establish the brand.

"There's more to be done," Marcus suggested quietly.

"You mean besides rebuilding the tasting room?" Griffin massaged a hand against the back of his neck. "Mom told me about her plans for a restaurant and guest cottages on the property."

Marcus shook his head. "I'm talking about additional sustainability measures. Making Harvest Vineyards not just a steward of the land but a true innovator in the industry. You could help."

"Not me. I'm here for the construction project and nothing more."

"You know this land and you have a sense of the business."

"Maybe I did back in the day, but not anymore. I work with my hands."

"That's what wine making is." Marcus held out his weathered hands, turning them over to expose the calluses on his palms.

Griffin chuckled. "You haven't gone soft yet."

"I spend time in the fields whenever I can." Marcus lifted a heavy brow. "I could do more if I had someone to take over the business end."

"You have Trevor."

"I'm not talking about designing labels and schmoozing distributors."

"You can't deny it's part of the industry."

"Your brother is immensely talented, but he doesn't see the big picture of the legacy of what your dad started here. He never did, Grif."

"But Dad wanted him, not me." Griffin pressed his lips together, hating the bitterness in his tone. He was a grown man. You'd think he'd be over not being his daddy's favorite by now. But it was more than that.

Marcus bent forward, plucked a blade of grass from the hillside and twirled it between his fingers. "You're a lot like your father."

"You don't have to say that." Griffin shook his head. "Hell, I don't want to be anything like him...except..."

He didn't need to finish the thought. Marcus knew. In a moment of weakness when Griffin was seventeen, after a blowout with his dad, he'd escaped to the fields and found Marcus carefully pruning a row of vines. He'd admitted out loud his biggest fear in life—that Dave Stone was not his biological father.

Neither of his parents had ever given him any indication that was the truth, although it would explain so much about his tense relationship with his dad. Griffin knew his parents' courtship had been a whirlwind and although he'd never had the guts to ask his mom outright, he'd often wondered if there had been someone else before his dad.

"He was your father," Marcus said. "Don't doubt it. You got all your bullheadedness from him."

"It doesn't matter now," Griffin said, even though they both knew it did. "You've done a great job around here. You don't need my help." He turned to survey the area where the new building was set to be constructed. "I've gone over the plans from the architect. There are a few things I'd like to tweak, but it's a solid design."

"We still need to get approval from the town council's development committee."

Griffin nodded. He'd worked with enough building departments over the past couple of years to understand what hoops they'd need to jump through.

"Everyone knows the fire was an accident." Marcus opened his fingers and the blade of grass fluttered to the ground. The words were a direct echo of what Maggie had told him.

"Dad didn't," Griffin muttered, repeating his stock answer. "I still can't believe he never rebuilt the tasting room. Using the lobby of the office for all these years makes Harvest Vineyards look like an amateur operation. Visitors expect an experience when they tour a winery, not being shoved into a cramped room."

Marcus sighed. "Your dad was too stubborn for his own good. We can thank Trevor for pushing the idea of building a new tasting room. It's part of his overall branding strategy."

"My brother's not stupid," Griffin said. Then he added, "At least when it comes to the business. His personal life is another story."

"I thought Maggie called off the wedding?"

"Let's just say she had more reason than just cold feet."

Marcus groaned. "Then Trevor's a fool. He isn't going to find a better woman than Maggie Spencer."

"Agreed." Griffin pressed three fingers to his chest where it tightened at the thought of seeing Maggie again. He had no business with her, and it was stupid to go anywhere near her for a dozen reasons, not the least of which was the canceled wedding. But erring on the side of caution was never his strong suit.

"I've got a conference call in a few minutes with one of our distributors." Marcus glanced at his watch. "Let me know if there's anything you need to move things along with construction. And when you're ready for more, my office is open to you."

Griffin huffed out a laugh. "You're like a dog with a bone," he muttered.

Marcus smiled. "Whatever it takes."

Brenna practically jumped out of her chair when the door to the main office opened. She breathed a sigh of relief as Marcus Sanchez walked through. Marcus was not quite six feet tall, with the lean frame of a man who'd spent most of his life working the fields.

She knew he missed the vines now that he was in the office most days. He favored pressed jeans or khakis with tailored shirts but had extras hanging in the hall closet since he often returned to the office after lunch with dirt stains on his shirts.

Whether clean or rumpled, Marcus had the air of a man who tolerated nothing less than perfection, which made him all the more intimidating to Brenna. She knew she was outwardly pretty but her inside was a jumble of insecurity and downright fear. Fear that she'd disappoint her daughter. Fear that she'd mess up her life more than she already had. Fear that she'd never find the happiness she so desperately craved.

"Are you okay?" His gentle brown eyes searched her face like he could read her innermost thoughts.

Terrified at the idea, Brenna pasted on a bright smile and tapped a finger on the edge of the computer monitor. "You startled me, that's all. I'm working on the schedule for the rest of the month. Trevor sent an email adding a few events." She pressed her lips together, forcing herself to stop babbling to Marcus.

The vineyard's serious CEO didn't need Brenna blathering on about her duties. But she was so worried about a possible confrontation with Trevor that adrenaline spiked through her, making her stomach jittery and her nerves strung tight.

Marcus gave her a warm smile. "How much coffee have you had this morning?"

"Oh, my gosh." Brenna popped out of her chair, banging her knee on the corner of the desk in the process. "I'm sorry. I forgot to make a fresh pot," she said, turning and hurrying down the hall toward the small kitchenette that was the company's break room.

She made coffee every morning, often pairing it with homemade muffins or sweet bread. Her official title was office assistant, but for the past six months she'd also managed the makeshift tasting room set up on one side of the Harvest Vineyards lobby.

Trevor had been the one to promote her into that position, and she was grateful for the additional responsibility and bump in pay. They didn't get a ton of tourist traffic like some of the larger vineyards, although the plan was for that to change with the opening of the new tasting room. But Brenna made sure the visitors who did find them got not only samples of their best vintages but also a warm welcome to the area.

Most of her work was with Trevor or the winery's operations manager. Although he was the CEO, Marcus liked to schedule meetings and handle personal correspondence himself. She tried not to take it personally but secretly wondered if he didn't ask for her assistance because he didn't trust her to do a good job.

Now she wished she had the tall, handsome leader in her corner. She hadn't spoken to Trevor since Maggie had walked out of the church. But he must know Brenna had been the one to confirm that the kiss was more than a onetime lapse in judgment. Why hadn't she told Maggie about his cheating before?

She'd betrayed her best friend and herself. Brenna had made plenty of mistakes, but she'd promised herself to be stronger in character when she moved to Stonecreek. Her six-year-old daughter, Ellie, was depending on her. It was the reason Brenna hadn't gone on one date since the move. She wanted to be a role model for her girl, not a cautionary tale like her own mother had been. Somehow, she'd still managed to mess things up.

She yanked the empty coffeepot off the counter and turned on the tap to refill it, startling again when a hand touched her shoulder.

"Something's wrong, Brenna," Marcus said quietly.

She wanted to scream. Or cry. Or run away. Maybe all three at the same time would do the trick. Other than superficial office pleasantries, she and Marcus had barely spoken in the year she'd worked at Harvest. She wasn't even sure he knew her name until this moment. Okay, Harvest employed fewer than a couple dozen people full-time, so of course Marcus knew her name. He saw her every day of the workweek.

He'd just never said it before. Hearing it and the sincerity in his tone almost undid her. She felt dirty and cheap in a way she hadn't even when her last boyfriend had put his hands on her in violence. She'd thought Trevor was her friend and had trusted him when he'd told her he loved Maggie.

Trusting the wrong people had always been her downfall. If only she'd had a Marcus in her life—someone constant and caring. Someone who might see her as something more than a pretty face.

"I'm a horrible person," she blurted, pouring the water into the coffee maker with shaking fingers. Anything to keep moving so she wouldn't break down completely.

"You're not," he countered.

She shoved the pot under the dispenser, flipped a lever and then whirled on him, unable to accept kindness she most definitely didn't deserve.

"Trevor was cheating on Maggie, and I knew it." She crossed her arms over her chest like she could ward off the judgment she was sure to see in Marcus's dark eyes. "I caught him with a woman months ago, but I never said anything to Maggie. She's my best friend and I didn't tell her."

Marcus's gaze was unreadable, his features a mask that was almost as disconcerting as outright condemnation. "Why?"

She opened her mouth, then shut it again. "Does it matter?"

"To me it does."

"He told me he loved her and was sorry," she whispered. "I wanted to believe him, and maybe he meant it. But Maggie is the best friend I've ever had. I betrayed her by not saying anything." She threw up her hands. "She even got me the interview with Jana for this job."

"I know."

"I love this job."

One side of his mouth quirked. "I know."

"I thought Trevor was a good guy. I thought he was my friend."

A muscle ticked in his jaw. "The two of you were certainly friendly—huddled around the computer or laughing together serving wine to guests."

She shook her head automatically. "No. It wasn't like that. I didn't mean for it to be taken that way. I'm flirty with men. It's my thing." She pointed a finger at him. "I hope you aren't insinuating that I did anything inappropriate with Trevor. I'm sure he's angry that I confirmed with Maggie that I knew he'd cheated. I could lose my job because of it, but I won't let you slut-shame me."

He took a step back, held up his hands, palms up, color rising to his cheeks. "Whoa there. I don't think you're a slut and I'm not shaming you for anything. You don't flirt with me," he added. "I'm a man."

"You're different."

"How?"

"You're the boss."

He let out a huff of a laugh. "Really?"

"I respect you," she said after a moment. "I want you to take me seriously."

"I do respect you," he told her. "You aren't going to lose your job because of this."

"If Trevor—"

He hitched a thumb at his chest. "Remember—I'm the boss."

"What about Jana?"

"She can deal with her son and his actions. I'll keep you safe, Brenna."

The air whooshed out of her lungs at the simple statement. That was the thing missing from any relationship she'd ever had with a man—the feeling of safety. She had a self-destructive streak a mile long. Marcus's words felt like a promise, and she tucked them into her heart.

He only said it because he was a nice guy. It didn't mean anything. She couldn't let it mean anything. She'd been fooled too many times to let her heart open to a man like Marcus Sanchez. He was way out of her league.

"I won't mess up like that again." She smoothed a hand over the floral-patterned dress she wore, fingering one of the delicate buttons. "This job is too important."

He gave a slight nod and moved forward. For a moment she thought he was going to reach for her. And in that moment, she wanted it. Wanted to be held by a man who valued her, to know what that felt like for once in her life.

"I'll make the coffee today," he said, his voice gruffer than normal. As if on cue, she heard the distant sound of the chime over the office's main entrance. "You'd better go see who's here."

"Thank you," she whispered and hurried out of the room. She might not be the sharpest knife in the drawer, but Brenna knew enough to accept a second chance.

Chapter Five

"You can't avoid the world forever. It's cowardly and not how a Spencer behaves."

Maggie stifled a groan as her grandmother barged into her office on the third floor of the historic building that housed Stonecreek's courthouse, city hall and police department.

"I'm working, Grammy." She stood, coming around the edge of the desk to give Vivian the requisite hug and kiss on her cheek. "The Pioneer Day Festival is next weekend. I've been updating the website and putting together last-minute posts for social media."

Maggie was Stonecreek's only full-time administrative staff member, so she took on most of the responsibilities for promoting the town—as well as dealing with city council, permits and contracts, plus anything else the community needed from her.

"You should be out in the community," Grammy

insisted, wagging a finger in Maggie's direction, "not hiding behind your computer."

"This is part of my job, too," Maggie argued. "It's not hiding."

Grammy tsk-tsked, then gripped Maggie's arms. "You have to show them you're not embarrassed by your horrible mistake and total lack of judgment."

"When you put it like that…"

"People are angry, Mary Margaret, and rightfully so. Your wedding was supposed to be the event of the year."

A sick pit opened in the center of Maggie's stomach. "Do you want to see the summer calendar? We have a half dozen great events scheduled. One of them can take the place of my wedding."

"They pale in comparison to your wedding," Vivian countered. "You're royalty in this town. The Spencers have always represented what's best about Stonecreek. Then Dave Stone had to open his winery and slowly that family has been chipping away at our status with their fancy wines. The Stones were nothing but a bunch of dirt-poor farmers before Harvest Vineyards."

"Grammy," Maggie said with a sigh, "we've talked about this before. The vineyard is good for the town. It brings in more tourism dollars. People come for the wine but they stay to discover everything else we have to offer."

"But the vineyard is the lure now. That isn't how it used to be. It isn't how we *want* it to be." Vivian stepped away, her lips pursed. "We want them here for the antiques and the tearoom. We need them to stay at our inn, Maggie, not stop through as part of a

valley wine tour. We're losing control, and that's un-
acceptable."

Maggie hated to see her grandmother so upset. The
Spencers had owned the majority of the businesses in
downtown Stonecreek for most of the town's history.
There was the Miriam Inn and Tearoom, named for
Maggie's great-great-grandmother, and the Stonecreek
Antiques Market across the street.

Her family also owned the market on the corner,
which had been managed by a neighbor for the past
twenty years. Maggie's uncle Frank ran the Stonecreek
Realty and Property Management Company, making
him the landlord for most of the other businesses in
downtown. A small faction of residents, led by members of the Stone family, lamented the fact that the
Spencers held a bit of a monopoly in town.

Truth be told, Harvest Vineyards leveled the playing
field and tilted the balance of power in a way that Maggie's family had never before seen. Secretly, she thought
it was about time but she'd never admit that out loud.
To do so would be tantamount to a betrayal of her family's legacy.

"We can still work with the Stones," she said, trying
another tack. "Trevor and I breaking up doesn't change
that we all want what's best for Stonecreek. I'm going
to put together a proposal for Jana Stone and Marcus
Sanchez to detail some ideas I have for cross promo-
tions that will benefit both the town *and* Harvest."

"It isn't the same as being connected by marriage,"
Grammy insisted, although her tone had gentled
slightly. "They have no reason for loyalty to us now.
Dave Stone carried a chip on his shoulder for most of

his life that the Spencers were more successful than his family."

"Jana isn't Dave. Neither is Trevor."

"She's a mother whose son was humiliated in front of her friends and family. If you don't think Jana and Trevor are going to want to exact some kind of revenge, you're being naive."

Maggie bristled at her grandmother's words. If anyone had a right to feel humiliated, it was her. Trevor was a genius at marketing, his work propelling Harvest wines to the national spotlight, critical acclaim and an ever-growing client base.

She couldn't help but think the timing of the kiss with Julia hadn't been an accident on his part, especially after talking to Brenna. Her friend thought Trevor had used the other woman to get out of the marriage. How did Trevor really feel at this point?

"I'll make things right with the Stones," Maggie promised. "Trevor and I were friends long before anything romantic happened between us. He'll make sure his mom knows that in the end it was for the best."

"And you'll stop hiding?" Vivian prompted.

Maggie nodded, although her throat went dry at the thought of venturing outside the safety of her office. "I was about to break for lunch," she said brightly. "Care to join me?" If Vivian came, Maggie could use her grandmother like a shield. No one would dare mess with her if her petite but stalwart Grammy was at her side.

"No, thank you, dear." Vivian approached Maggie again and patted her cheek. "Go to The Kitchen. It's the best place to be seen on a weekday afternoon."

"Because Irma Cole is the biggest gossip around," Maggie muttered.

"Play nice, Mary Margaret. I'm depending on you. Summer will pass quickly, and Election Day will be here before you know it. We can't let Jason Stone gain any traction."

After dropping a quick kiss on the tip of Maggie's nose, Vivian turned and walked out of the office, leaving a trail of White Diamonds–scented air in her wake.

Hands numb and palms sweating, Maggie went back to her computer and saved the graphic for the Pioneer Day Festival. Stupid to think she could go back to normal without facing the events of last weekend. Maybe it wouldn't be so bad, she told herself as she grabbed her purse, then left her office.

She slipped into the hall and gave a little wave to Megan Roe, the young woman who served as the secretary for Maggie, as well as police dispatcher and administrative support for the fire department. Megan, who was as eternally optimistic as her boss, smiled brightly and put her thumb in the air. "You've got this," she said with a nod.

Maggie had relied on Megan over the past couple of days to bring in food and coffee while Maggie was holed up in her office. She'd gotten to work before daybreak and stayed until the town was dark, skulking through the sidewalks like she had something to hide.

She didn't, but no one else knew that and she hadn't been ready to face censure from a community that believed she'd failed it.

Maggie got out of the building without seeing anyone else—maybe because she'd hurried to the back staircase and out the door that opened to the alley behind city hall. Heart hammering in her chest, she made her way through the shadowed walkway between two buildings. She stopped before reaching the main sidewalk and forced a few deep breaths.

This was the plight of being a good girl, Maggie thought to herself. Twenty-seven years old and she didn't know how to deal with disappointing the people around her. She'd been the kid who did chores without being asked and made her bed each morning. She'd been the teacher's pet in every grade, even more so in high school after her mother died. The structure and routine of school was the only thing that kept her sane when her father was falling apart in the months after cancer claimed his wife's life.

Her grandmother had stepped in, but with her dad so out of it and her mom no longer around to run interference, Maggie had been on the receiving end of the brunt of Vivian's attention.

Maggie wanted to make sure Morgan and Ben had normal childhoods—or as normal as kids could have without a mother. So she'd feigned interest in the lectures her grandmother constantly spouted on Spencer pride and expectations.

Maybe it was an inevitable osmosis, but eventually Maggie had gained a deep appreciation for her family's identity in town and taken up the mantle of the Spencer legacy. It had given her a purpose she'd desperately needed at that point.

Now that purpose was coming back to bite her in the butt. She paused at the corner of the building as her eye caught on a sign stuck into the soft ground at the edge of the park across from city hall.

There were two signs, actually. One advertised the

upcoming pancake breakfast, an annual fund-raiser held to raise money for the parks committee that she oversaw as part of her mayoral duties. Beneath that was another, hand-painted poster with the words Meet Candidate Jason Stone. Loyal. Dependable. He Won't Waffle.

She lifted her hand to the cool brick to steady herself. It was starting already. The repercussions of her decision on Saturday. Grammy had warned her people would use it against her. One mistake that wasn't even really a mistake, but she was still going to pay a price.

"Pancakes and waffles. He's going with a breakfast slogan." Maggie startled as Griffin moved into the shadows between the two buildings, the heat of his body making the air in the cool shade rise several degrees. "I prefer eggs and bacon, if you were wondering."

"It's not fair," she whispered, her gaze straying back to the sign.

"Don't tell me you're one of those 'I skip meals because I'm on a diet' women," he said, shaking his head. "Or worse, that you only have smoothies in the morning."

She blinked, turned to face the man at her side. He wore an olive green T-shirt, frayed at the collar, and faded jeans with a baseball cap on his head. "What are you talking about?"

"Breakfast." He said the word like it was obvious. "I told you my penchant for protein and you answered, 'It's not fair.'"

She scrunched up her nose, trying to follow his meandering train of thought. "I wasn't talking about food." She pointed to the sign across the street. "I meant it's not fair that Jason can use the fact that I canceled the wedding as part of his campaign."

Griffin tapped his chin as if he was just catching on to her meaning. "The waffling thing?"

"Yes," she said through clenched teeth. "The waffling thing."

"That guy has rocks for brains, obviously. It's been that way since we were kids. My nana barely acknowledged his part of the family, but Trevor and I used to have a great time baiting him at random family functions when we were together. We could tell him anything and he'd believe it. He's got the IQ of a caveman."

"Once again," Maggie said, holding up a hand, "I'm going to ask. What are you talking about?"

"Waffling," Griffin explained. "Not the breakfast food this time. He's not using the word right. To waffle you would have to walk away from Trevor, then change your mind and try to get back together with him. *To waffle* is to not be able to make up your mind. That wasn't what happened." One thick brow rose. "Unless you're thinking of reuniting?"

"Of course not."

"Then there's no waffling." He leaned in closer and she could smell the clean scent of shampoo and soap. Her stomach dipped. "Have you ever done it before?"

"I-it?" she stammered, her mind racing in a thousand inappropriate directions.

His lips curved like he knew exactly what she was thinking. "Walked away from a wedding," he clarified.

"No."

"Then you can't even be considered a serial runaway bride." He flashed a wide grin. "Get it? *Serial* versus *cereal*. I'm sticking with the breakfast analogies."

Maggie groaned but her chest no longer felt like an anvil was weighing it down. "Enough," she said, stifling a laugh. "What are you doing here?"

He glanced around the shadowed walkway. "I was heading to the hardware store and saw you in a dark alley. I thought you might need rescuing from a pickpocket or potential mayor-napper or something along those lines."

Maggie frowned.

"*Rescuing* is the wrong word." He held up his hands. "Backup. I thought you could use backup."

Once again Griffin had found her in a moment of need and was managing to make her feel better. His hair curled around the edges of his ball cap, and there was a layer of stubble shadowing his jaw like he hadn't bothered to shave this morning. Trevor had always been immaculately smooth shaven, to the point where Maggie wondered if he was one of those guys who drove around with an electric razor in his glove compartment.

Not Griffin. Griffin probably didn't care what anyone thought of him. Or what anyone thought of her, for that matter.

"I was going to get lunch," she said. Then she added on in a rush of breath, "Want to come?"

He studied her for a moment, scratching his jaw. How could that sound be so sexy? Then he leaned out from the shadows, glancing toward the front of city hall. "Why are you sneaking out the back door?" he asked, his gaze returning to her. "Did you need to stow your cape in the alley before hitting the light of day?"

She snorted. "I'm the antihero around here these days."

"You shouldn't be relegated to shadows, Maggie May. You've done nothing wrong."

The knot around her heart began to tighten again, and she raised fingers to her chest like she could manage her breathing that way. "Last Saturday was this town's version of a royal wedding, and I ruined it."

"Trevor—"

"I'm not heartbroken," she interrupted. "I'm embarrassed and angry but not heartbroken. People are going to see it in my face. I'm not even sure I really wanted to marry your brother, and part of me is relieved I had an excuse to walk away. That makes me the biggest coward on the planet." She threw out a hand toward the park across the street. "I'm worse than a waffler or a serial heartbreaker. I'm a big fat chicken."

"That's not breakfast," he said with a smile, "but you can serve it with waffles, so I'll let it slide."

She huffed out another laugh. "Do you take anything seriously?"

"Too much," he admitted quietly and while she couldn't name the emotion that darkened his green eyes for a fleeting moment, she felt it all the way to her toes. "Let's go have lunch, Maggie. If this town wants something to talk about, we'll give it to them."

She bit down on her lip and nodded, unable to form words at the moment without breaking down completely. With Griffin at her side, she stepped out into the bright sunshine of the perfect June afternoon.

Chapter Six

Griffin and Maggie were on the receiving end of several nasty stares as they walked a block to the restaurant. The Kitchen was obviously as popular now as it had been when he was a kid, based on the crowd milling about on the sidewalk.

A gaggle of women openly pointed and whispered until Maggie lifted a jaunty hand and called out a greeting. He was so damn proud of her in that moment, even though he could see her fingers shaking as she lowered her arm and clutched it to her side.

"Is my brother that popular in town these days? I can't figure out why everyone cares about your wedding."

The tip of her tongue darted out to wet her upper lip, sending a shocking jolt of awareness through him. This was the third version of Maggie he'd seen since return-

ing to Stonecreek, this one different than either the perfectly coiffed runaway bride or the dejected, deflated
woman cleaning up at the reception hall late at night.

Today she wore what he imagined amounted to her
version of a power suit—a tailored skirt and matching
jacket in a pale shade of blue with a white scoop-neck
T-shirt underneath. Her hair was pulled back into an
understated ponytail. Her makeup—if she wore any—
was subtle. Maybe a coat of mascara highlighting her
gray eyes and a bit of lip gloss, but he could see the
freckles that dotted her nose and cheeks. He liked her
better like this than fancy as she'd been on her wedding day. She even smelled different, more like fresh
shampoo and less like expensive perfume.

She was more the Maggie he remembered but still
changed from the girl he'd once known. Her gaze was
unsure and her shoulders hunched ever so slightly.

His gut had twisted when he'd seen her cowering
in the shadowed alley. All the color drained from her
face as she stared at the campaign sign his idiot relative had strategically placed across the street from city
hall. Jason wasn't book smart, but he clearly still had
a mean streak a mile long.

Griffin should have walked away, turned around and
gotten back in the Land Cruiser. He'd come into town
to talk to Kurt Meyer, who owned the town's hardware
store and lumber supply company. There was a big-box
store about forty minutes up the road, but Griffin was
determined to use local vendors as much as he could
for the project at the vineyard. Instead, he'd walked
right past the hardware store and crossed the street to
town hall, inserting himself into business that didn't
concern him in the least.

"It's not exactly about Trevor," she said, turning to him just before they got to the restaurant. "It's bigger than that. You know what our two families mean to this town."

"The nonwedding doesn't change anything."

"Are you sure?" Her throat moved as she swallowed. "The truce between the Spencers and the Stones has been tenuous at best. A lot of people around here remember a time when the families' fighting spelled disaster for the rest of the town."

"That was the past. Nothing like that would happen now."

Maggie picked an invisible piece of lint from her sleeve. "The wedding cost the vineyard both publicity and wine—all those bottles specially labeled for the occasion. You've been gone a long time. Things have changed. Stonecreek relies on support from the vineyard. Your family backs the hospital foundation, the school district, and a grant from Harvest almost single-handedly paid for the renovation of the arts center. But the money is only pledged."

"You think my mother will take it away?"

"I hope not."

Irritation bubbled up in Griffin, both at the insinuation that his mother would be so catty and the knowledge that Jana Stone might revel in a bit of behind-the-scenes vengeance. "I'll talk to her."

"You don't need to get involved."

They reached The Kitchen, leaning closer as Maggie entered the bustling restaurant. "Too late for that, sweetheart."

His aim had been to distract her. Her anxiety was

a palpable force, and he didn't want her to face the crowd in the restaurant showing any kind of weakness.

As soon as he followed her through the door, Griffin realized his mistake. Who was he kidding? As waitstaff and customers at the scuffed Formica tables turned to gawk, he wanted to whisk Maggie away from there to someplace quiet and safe.

He wasn't pretending to be involved to distract her. He cared. A few moments of vulnerability peppered with some spunky attitude and this woman had him wrapped around her little finger.

He was passing through Stonecreek, here to make right his past mistakes. He couldn't afford to care. Not about Maggie Spencer or how she fared in the town. Not about his duplicitous brother or running interference on any possible retribution his mom might try to concoct.

Griffin had made a life for himself away from the quirks of small-town life. First in the army and then as a contractor for various companies around the Pacific Northwest. But the one constant in his life was that he didn't set down roots. Ever.

Maggie was as established in Stonecreek as those hundred-year-old oak trees that bordered the town square. The two of them were oil and water, and it was only going to hurt them both if he didn't cut things off right now.

Then she turned to him, pushing her hair behind her ears and giving him a wisp of a smile filled with gratitude and hope and just the tiniest amount of steel.

Hell, she slayed him.

"We don't have your usual table available," the waitress behind the counter announced, her voice so cold it could freeze water.

"That's okay, Ginnie," Maggie said brightly. "Griffin and I will sit at the counter."

The woman, unfamiliar to Griffin, gave him a long stare. "Are you Griffin Stone?"

"Yep," he said. "I don't believe we've had the pleasure of meeting before. You must be new to Stonecreek."

"Been here five years," the woman said with a sniff. She had blond hair that had been colored blue at the ends, wore heavy black eyeliner and bright red lipstick. Her uniform was a The Kitchen T-shirt and a pair of multicolored leggings under a black miniskirt. She glanced at Maggie, then back to Griffin. "I'm a friend of your brother's. I hope he's doing okay after what happened. Tell him Ginnie sends her love."

Griffin felt Maggie stiffen next to him. He placed a hand on her back, gently guiding her to two empty seats at the counter. "He's fine."

"Wish I could say the same," an older man said from the table behind him.

Griffin glanced over, then did a double take. "Hey, Grady. How's business?"

Grady Wilson had owned the gas station in Stonecreek for as long as Griffin could remember. He used to love to go with his dad for a fill-up because Grady always gave him a piece of licorice from behind the counter. "They opened one of those fancy convenience stores just outside of town. It has a dozen gas pumps and a hundred ways to flavor a soda. I've tried to modernize things, but it's been a struggle." He inclined his head toward Maggie, who sat straight in her chair, pretending to study her menu. "Would have helped me if the town council had refused their application for a lease."

Maggie's lips pursed. "That land was in the next county so not under our domain," she said quietly. "He knows that."

"But that's not as bad as my Gloria's heartbreak after this weekend."

"Mrs. Wilson still teaching?" Griffin asked, not liking where the conversation was headed. Gloria Wilson had been his third-grade teacher and one of the few in his not-so-illustrious academic career to think he had any potential.

Grady shook his head. "Retired last year. Her arthritis got too bad to stand for long periods. Doesn't get out much, but she'd been looking forward to the wedding for months. Your mother was kind enough to invite us."

"*I* invited them," Maggie muttered under her breath.

"She about cried her eyes out Saturday afternoon. I haven't seen her that upset since Ross and Rachel broke up."

"Ross and Rachel got back together," Ginnie added, sliding two waters onto the counter in front of Maggie and Griffin. "I suppose there's always hope."

Griffin watched Maggie draw in a shaky breath, then square her shoulders. She looked directly at Ginnie. "I'll have a grilled-chicken sandwich and a diet soda, please," she said with a forced smile. "And there's no hope for Trevor and me."

"A cheeseburger and fries for me," Griffin said. "Along with a sweet tea."

Maggie turned in her seat. "Please tell Mrs. Wilson

I'm sorry she was upset. I didn't mean to disappoint anyone, but Trevor and I—"

"I heard Trevor was as surprised as the rest of us," a heavyset man called from the pass-through between the diner and the kitchen.

"The two of us made the decision together," Maggie insisted, but there was no fight in her voice.

"Gloria worried this would happen," Grady said, shaking his head. "When those two first got together, she told me it would divide the town when things went south."

Griffin massaged a hand along the back of his neck. "It hasn't divided the town."

"Because everyone around here's on Team Trevor," Ginnie said, leaning over the counter toward him. She smiled as she handed him a glass of tea, then flicked a glance toward Maggie. "No offense."

Maggie nodded, not daring to mention her diet soda. She turned back around in her seat. "None taken, I guess."

"I take offense." Griffin spun on his stool to address the entire restaurant. "And I'm speaking for my entire family. No one is angry with Maggie."

Grady laughed and leaned back in his chair, nudging the man who sat at the table next to him. "Less than a week back in town, and the black sheep is now the family spokesman."

"This was a terrible idea," Maggie said under her breath.

"No." Griffin pointed a finger toward Grady. "I'm not the spokesman, but I've talked to my brother. He doesn't blame Maggie." He pressed his lips together so the words *because the breakup was his fault* wouldn't fall from them. "Would I be here with her if there was bad blood between our families?"

"Why *are* you here with her?" Ginnie asked, folding her arms over her chest.

"We ran into each other on the street," Maggie said quickly, "and were both headed to lunch. It was a coincidence."

"We're friends," Griffin said simply. Despite how hard she was trying to keep it together, it was obvious Maggie needed a friend right now.

"Your brother is okay with that?" Ginnie raised a heavily penciled brow.

"There's no bad blood," Griffin repeated. He shifted, held out his hands to encompass all of the restaurant patrons. "Everyone hear the news? Spread it around. The Stones and the Spencers are still friends."

"Other than Jason," a voice called from one of the far tables.

"Jason doesn't count," Griffin shot back. "You know that."

Hushed laughter rippled through the room and the tension eased. He turned back around and picked up a french fry from the plate Ginnie had just set before him, popping it into his mouth.

He chewed for a few seconds before turning to Maggie. "This town is too small for its own good."

She gave a tiny nod, her eyes guarded as she stared at him. "Thank you. This time you really did play the hero."

"Don't get used to it," he said and dipped a fry into the ranch dressing drowning the sad pieces of lettuce the cook had seen fit to bestow upon her. "It was a one-time deal. I'm not the tights-wearing type."

Her mouth quirked at the edges. "I'll remember that, although back in high school you had the butt to pull off tights."

"I was a jerk back in high school."

"No argument from me," she said, taking a bite of her sandwich.

"I'm sorry I was a jerk," he said softly and was rewarded with a blush that colored her cheeks the most adorable soft pink hue.

"I'm not sure I forgive you," she said with a small smile, "but I shockingly like the man you've become."

Griffin's heart flipped, and he rubbed a hand against his chest, wholly unused to any activity from that part of his anatomy. It was simple praise, and maybe a little backhanded, but he felt proud to have earned it.

"It's not shocking," he said casually. "I'm irresistible. Everyone knows it. Ask Ginnie. She'll tell you."

Maggie's grin widened as she looked over to the young waitress, who was busy staring at Griffin and not so busy paying attention to her customers.

"I think she's available," Maggie said with a laugh.

"I'm not interested in her," Griffin answered, letting his gaze lower to Maggie's full mouth, then sighing as it pressed into a thin line.

"I should go," she said, her fork dropping to the plate with a clatter. "Now that I've outed myself in town, there are some businesses I need to check in with before the garden center open house this weekend." She pulled out her wallet and grabbed a wad of bills.

"Lunch is my treat," Griffin said, adjusting his ball cap and regretting his inherent need to flirt with this woman. He'd spooked her, which made her ten times smarter than him. The strange connection between them could go nowhere. They both knew it. But Griffin had a lot of experience ignoring things that he should do in favor of things he wanted to do. Apparently, Maggie Spencer was no exception.

"I insist on paying." She slapped some money onto the counter and took a step away. "It's the least I can do since I forced you to have lunch with me."

He laughed. "No one forces me to do anything I don't want to."

Her teeth tugged at her bottom lip. "Okay, then. Be sure to tell your mom that everything is copacetic with our families. I'll work on Grammy."

"Right." Griffin muttered a curse under his breath. He didn't want their families to be involved. He didn't want to admit most of the restaurant was staring at the two of them, and tongues would be wagging throughout town that Maggie had been spotted with the other Stone brother. The black sheep, as Grady had so helpfully pointed out. Griffin didn't want any of this.

Except Maggie. Despite everything else, he wanted Maggie more with each moment they spent together.

"I'll see you around. Thanks, Ginnie," she called, then turned to Grady. "Tell Gloria I'll save her seats in the first row for the benefit concert the high school a cappella group is doing at the garden center this weekend. I know she loves hearing the kids sing." She stepped forward, placed a hand on the man's meaty hand. "I'm really sorry I disappointed her. Sorry about everything."

Grady nodded. "You're still a good girl, Maggie, even if you messed up real bad."

As Griffin watched her walk out of the restaurant, he tamped down the urge to pound his fist into something. Trevor would be fitting. He hated that Maggie was the town good girl, a label she wore like a hair shirt. He hated seeing her apologize for something that wasn't her fault.

Most of all he hated how much he cared. That was a fast track to disaster for everyone.

Maggie plucked the game controller out of her brother's hand a few nights later.

"Give it back," Ben shouted, jumping up from the chair. "I'm going to…" He groaned as a bleating stream of beeps and buzzes came from the television screen. "I died."

"Great," Maggie said with an eye roll. "Now you have time to take out the trash."

Her brother groaned again. "Who died and made you boss?" he asked. He tapped an angry foot on the carpet as an awkward silence filled the air between them. She wasn't the boss, but their mother's death eleven years ago had thrust her into the role of care-giver, for both of her younger siblings. Their father was never much for rules or routines, so Maggie had become the one to keep order in the household.

"You can't spend the entire summer break playing video games."

"Dad doesn't care," Ben shot back.

"He does," Maggie argued. "But he's got the commissioned piece to finish in the next few weeks. He's distracted."

"He's always distracted." Ben grabbed the remote control from the coffee table and turned off the TV. "You just don't see it because you're too busy living your own life."

"I'm here now." Maggie had moved back into her father's house two days ago when she couldn't convince the couple who'd rented her house to find another place. Her stuff had already been in boxes, ready to be moved into Trevor's house on the edge of downtown.

She'd insisted they not move in together until after the wedding, and although Trevor had argued, now she was glad she'd followed her instinct. Her new tenants had rented her house furnished, so she'd only needed to move her personal belongings. It was strange and vaguely depressing to be an adult living in her girlhood room again. Of course, her father hadn't done anything to update the decor, so she had a canopy bed with pink ruffles on the edge of the comforter, random posters of boy band heartthrobs on the walls and her collection of snow globes standing sentry on her old dresser. She needed to change things but couldn't quite find the motivation.

"Nothing will change," Ben grumbled. "You'll get sick of us, and Dad will ignore everything outside his studio. Morgan will be a senior next year so then she'll go to college and I'll be alone."

"You're not alone." Maggie reached forward and brushed Ben's overlong bangs out of his eyes. "I'll take you for a haircut tomorrow."

"What does it matter?" Ben took the controller from her hand and tossed it on the recliner. "My hair, whether I brush my teeth, how many hours of video games I play. It doesn't really matter."

"You brush your teeth, right?" Maggie couldn't help but ask, earning another put-upon groan.

"I'll deal with the trash."

"Take Sadie for a walk, too." Hearing her name,

the springer spaniel lifted her head from her dog bed, yawned, then scratched an ear with her hind leg.

"Fine." He said the word with as much enthusiasm as if she'd asked him to scoop the dog's poop with his bare hands. He whistled, and Sadie hopped up and followed him toward the door.

"Hey, Ben."

He glanced over his shoulder.

"You matter," she said, gratified when he flashed a smile instead of rolling his eyes.

Maggie started toward the kitchen, then gave a yelp of surprise as Morgan stepped out of the laundry at the back of the house.

"He brushes his teeth," her sister reported, picking chipped polish off a fingernail. "But only because he has a crush on some girl in his Spanish class."

"Have you been standing there the whole time?"

"Long enough." Morgan shrugged. "I was separating whites and darks, but hearing you chew out Ben was more interesting."

"I wasn't chewing him out," Maggie sighed. Had she been chewing him out?

"We're doing fine. Ben and I aren't babies anymore. You check in plenty, and when it's important Dad pulls his head out of his—"

"Morgan."

"Dad pulls it together when we need him," her sister amended with a hint of a smile.

Tears pricked at the backs of Maggie's eyes. Was that enough? She'd been so preoccupied with town business and planning the wedding that she'd let her presence in her father's home slip over the past few months. Or years. Had it been years?

She glanced around the kitchen and suppressed another sigh. From the scuffed hardwood floors to the butcher-block counters to the stove with one burner that didn't light, nothing had changed since she went away to college almost a decade earlier. It was the same throughout the rest of the house, decor suspended in time. Her father didn't notice or care, but Maggie thought it was past time he should.

It was obvious he'd been spending more and more time in the studio he'd built behind the house six months before her mother's death. It had taken some lean years, but Jim Spencer was now recognized as one of the foremost bronze sculptors in this part of the country. The piece he was working on now for a private client in San Francisco would pay the mortgage on this place for over a year. His work was his passion, and although he loved his children, he'd never been a particularly attentive father.

"Can't get his head out of the clouds" was how her grammy described it, and Maggie wondered if the absentmindedness was an unconscious defense mechanism. Jim had never paid much attention to the family legacy, a fact that continually niggled at Vivian.

She hadn't stopped encouraging her son to do something "real" with his life until it became clear that Maggie could fill the void and uphold their standing in Stonecreek.

"Grab a box of pasta while I heat the water," Maggie told her sister. "I like your hair."

Morgan touched her hand to the blue strands like she was surprised to find them on her head. "Grammy wanted me go back to my boring natural color for the wedding."

"I didn't know that," Maggie said apologetically. "I think she means well."

"Because you're her favorite," Morgan said as she emerged from the pantry. "The rest of us are constant disappointments. Especially me."

Jim Spencer walked into the kitchen, wiping his hands on a towel. "You're not a disappointment to anyone. I'll talk to your grandmother." He dropped a kiss on the top of Morgan's blue-hued head. "You're perfect, Mo-mo."

Maggie breathed a sigh of relief. Her father might be scatterbrained and bordering on negligent, but he had his moments.

"I'm sick of people calling me that stupid nickname."

"I can call you whatever I like. How about Princess Morgana of the Butterfly Fairy Convention?"

Maggie smiled. Of the three Spencer kids, Morgan was the most like their father in terms of imagination. She'd spent hours as a child playing dress up and insisting on being referred to by her chosen identity of the week.

"Even worse," Morgan said with a groan. She handed Maggie the box of pasta.

"Are you making dinner tonight?" Jim asked Maggie. "You don't have to do that. I had a plan."

"Quesadillas?" Maggie asked, and Morgan hid her smile.

"What's wrong with cheese and tortillas?" Jim put his hands on his hips.

"Just changing things up a bit," Maggie answered. "I appreciate you letting me stay here, Dad."

"It's your home."

Emotion welled in Maggie's chest. "Grammy came to visit me at the office earlier."

"She mentioned that when she stopped by here," Jim said, looking sheepish when Maggie gasped.

"She talked to you about me?"

"Your grandmother loves you," he said by way of explanation.

Morgan snorted.

"She loves all of you," Jim amended, pulling a bottle of wine off the wrought iron baker's rack in the corner.

"She has to love me," Ben said, entering the room with Sadie trotting along at his ankles. "I'm the only one who can carry on the Spencer name."

"Don't be a Neanderthal." Morgan popped the top on a can of soda and took a long drink.

"Shouldn't you be having milk?" Maggie asked automatically.

Morgan held up the can in mock salute. "I liked you better when you were worried about Ben's teeth."

Their father paused in the act of pouring a glass of wine. "What's wrong with Ben's teeth?"

"Why am I a Neanderthal?" Ben swiped the soda can from Morgan, gulped it down, then burped loudly.

"He needs to brush regularly," Maggie told her father.

"I could have a baby on my own," Morgan said, swatting Ben on the back of the head. "My kid would have the Spencer name that way."

Jim jabbed a finger at Morgan. "No babies," he said, then sipped his wine. "Brush your teeth," he told his son.

"I told you he shows up when we need him," Morgan said to Maggie.

Jim narrowed his eyes. "Did you doubt it?"

Maggie's gaze hitched on the wine label. "Is that my wedding wine?"

"Don't want it to go to waste," her father said. "May I pour you a glass?"

"I had lunch at The Kitchen," Maggie said instead of answering. The thought of even a sip of the wine that had been bottled to celebrate her wedding made her stomach ache. But her father meant well so she didn't want to refuse outright.

"You definitely need a drink," he said and pulled out a second glass.

"Ben stole my soda and it was the last one," Morgan complained. "I should probably have wine, too."

"Only in church on Sundays," Jim countered.

Morgan scrunched up her nose. "We don't go to church."

"Then no wine. Listen to your sister and have some milk."

Maggie felt her shoulders begin to tremble and tears prick her eyes. She pressed three fingers to her mouth to prevent a full-blown sob from escaping, then dragged in a shaky breath and swiped at her cheeks.

Silence filled the room as the three members of her immediate family turned to stare at her.

"I love you guys," she whispered, squeezing shut her eyes. She needed to hold it together, but the stress of the past few days was too much. She might not be heartbroken, but she was humiliated, and the normalcy of her family's silly banter reminded her she wasn't going through this alone.

"It's going to be okay," her father said, wrapping his big body around her. He smelled like the clay he used to make the original sculptures that would then be cast into bronze. The earthy, musty scent would always remind her of home.

Morgan and Ben hugged her, too. "We love you, too," her sister said, adding the scent of patchouli to the mix.

"I could shank Trevor," Ben offered, "for whatever he did to make you into a runaway bride." Maggie smiled through her tears as she felt her brother wipe his nose on the sleeve of her shirt. Teenage boys were truly disgusting.

"No babies, wine or shanking," Jim said. "I might not run the tightest ship, but even I have lines you can't cross."

"The water's boiling over," Maggie said as she heard a sizzle from the stove. She pulled away from the family hug. "Dinner will be ready in about ten minutes."

"I'll make a salad," Morgan offered.

"I'll set the table," Ben added, playfully bumping Morgan out of the way as he moved toward the cabinets that held the plates and bowls.

Another wave of love swelling through her, Maggie dumped the pasta into the water and adjusted the burner's heat. Her father handed her a glass of wine when she turned to him.

"Don't say he didn't deserve me." She shook her head as she touched the glass to her lips. The pinot noir was fruity and light, with just the right amount of depth at the end. "I've heard that line too many times already."

"You deserve someone who can make you truly happy," Jim said instead, clinking his glass to hers.

"To your happiness, Maggie May, no matter how long it takes you to find it."

Maggie smiled and tried not to burst into tears again. "Thanks, Dad."

Chapter Seven

Brenna crossed her arms over her chest. "Are you trying to get in my pants?"

Marcus Sanchez paused in the act of pulling wrapped sandwiches from the brown paper bag he'd set on the tasting room counter.

"It's a turkey sandwich," he said, studying the bundle in his hands. "I'll admit the aioli is a nice touch, but it's not exactly seduction-worthy."

She kept her gaze focused on the sandwich and not Marcus's dark eyes and kind face. "You're being nice to me."

When he didn't respond, she eventually glanced up. One side of his mouth curved. "I like you."

Three words but they packed the wallop of a punch to her emotions, washing through her and wearing down most of her razor-sharp defenses. For the past four days Marcus had singled her out with some small act of kindness. First, it had been a vase of flowers on her desk, then yesterday he'd arrived at the office with a cup of her standing drink order from Espresso's Coffee Shop in town and now he'd brought lunch from her favorite deli.

Brenna was starving. Fridays in the summer were always busy at the vineyard, and she had almost a dozen reservations for the tasting room. She tried her best to make the space welcoming with twinkling lights and fresh flowers but it was difficult to ignore that her desk was just on the other side of the temporary partition that separated the room. She'd be scrambling until the planned renovations were complete.

Marcus handed her a sandwich, and she blushed as her stomach growled. "This doesn't have to be complicated," he told her. "I know you don't stop for lunch when things are swamped around here." He gestured to the empty seats at the counter in front of her. "You have a break so let's eat."

But it *was* complicated because Brenna had learned over and over that nothing good in life came without a price. From her mother's stingy, selfish love to the way Ellie's father had walked out as soon as Brenna told him she was pregnant. She'd thought Trevor was telling her the truth about his devotion to Maggie, and that had turned out disastrously.

Her interactions with him this week had been coolly awkward. He'd actually called her into his office on Monday afternoon to tell her he didn't blame her for telling Maggie the whole truth and assured her the scene at the church wouldn't affect her position at Harvest.

But she still blamed herself for being a fool and a terrible friend to Maggie. She wanted nothing to do with Trevor Stone, but Marcus was another story entirely. It was strange after a year of having him ignore her that suddenly he wanted to be her friend.

"I don't trust this," she murmured.

"The sandwich or the chips that go with it?"

She shook her head. "You have no reason to be nice to me."

He laughed softly. "I didn't realize I needed one."

"You know what I mean." She turned and busied herself with rearranging wineglasses on the shelf behind her.

"Brenna."

"I don't deserve anyone being nice to me right now."

He stepped around the counter, placed a gentle hand over hers to still her movements. "I can tell that last weekend is tearing you up inside."

She gave a jerky nod. "I should have told her."

"You made a mistake."

"A bad one."

"We all make mistakes."

She turned to him, bile rising in her throat at the thought of all the stupid choices she'd made over the years. "You're a good person, Marcus. Everyone knows it."

His hand was warm and comforting on hers, and she closed her eyes when he squeezed her fingers. "I was married once," he said quietly.

He still gripped her hand but when she glanced toward him he was staring at the shelf of wineglasses like he couldn't stand to meet her gaze.

"For how long?"

"Five years. I was working at a vineyard in Sonoma at the time. She worked in town as a waitress. She'd come from a big family and wanted lots of kids."

"You didn't?"

He shrugged. "The vines were my babies, so I didn't think much about it. But I wanted her to be happy."

"Of course you did." Brenna tugged at her hand, but Marcus held tight.

"It took eighteen months of trying for her to get pregnant, and she miscarried at nine weeks."

"I'm sorry," Brenna whispered.

He turned to her then, and his eyes were filled with a mix of regret and sorrow. "It broke her, and I couldn't deal with it. I left the hospital, drove to a bar, got drunk on the cheapest liquor I could find, then went home with a woman I met that night." His features were granite as if he couldn't afford to let any vulnerability show. But his eyes gave away everything, and Brenna's heart broke for him.

"A big mistake."

He swallowed, his throat bobbing. "She left me, and once I pulled myself together I moved to Oregon. Took a job at Harvest a few months later. She remarried and the last I heard they have three little ones." His lips pressed into a thin line. "And I still have the vines."

"Oh, Marcus." Brenna turned her hand over in his and linked their fingers.

"Don't think for a minute you have the market cornered on regret." He reached out and lifted a strand of her hair, watching it trail across his skin like it was the most fascinating thing he'd ever seen. "Let me be nice to you, Brenna. Not because I have an ulterior motive. Not because I'm in any position to pass judgment."

He took a step back when a car door slammed outside the office door, untangling their fingers and shoving his hands into his pockets. "I like you, and I like having some-one to be nice to again."

She bit down on her lip, so much she wanted to say to him but the words wouldn't form.

The chimes above the front door opened and two couples walked in, laughing and talking among them-selves. Her next reservation.

"Take the sandwich, okay?" Marcus gave her a pleading look.

She nodded, then turned to the foursome. "Welcome to Harvest Vineyards. Have a seat, everyone."

Marcus backed away, but she stepped closer to him, ignoring the customers for a moment. "Would you like to have dinner tonight?"

His brows rose and he glanced behind him like there might be someone else she was inviting.

"Yes, I'm talking to you." She flashed a smile. "It will be me and Ellie so nothing fancy. You're welcome to join us if you don't have plans."

"Is this a pity invite?" he asked, those dark eyes narrowing. "Because I told you about my awful mistake?"

She let her smile gentle. "It's an invite because I like you."

He seemed to relax at that. "What time?"

"Six," she said sheepishly. "Ellie still goes to bed early."

"Text me your address, and I'll be there."

"Okay." She clutched her hands in front of her stom-ach and watched him disappear around the partition. Then she stashed the sandwich and brown bag behind the counter.

"Let's start the weekend with our signature pinot

noir," she announced to the two couples. "It's going to be a great Friday here at Harvest."

Trevor stalked into his mother's kitchen the following Saturday morning.

"Where's Mom?" Trevor threw out the question, then veered toward the refrigerator in the family home that housed every generation of Stones since Stonecreek's founding.

Griffin returned his attention to the set of plans spread out in front of him on the dining room table. "She went to town to check in with the staff running the Pioneer Day booth."

"Did you drink the last of the coffee?" Trevor held up the stainless steel pot like he wanted to brain Griffin with it. "Mom always saves me a cup on Saturdays."

Griffin lifted a shoulder. "You should have gotten here earlier. I supplied coffee to the guys who showed up to help with pruning this morning."

"I'm off the clock on the weekend." Trevor set the coffeepot in the sink with a clatter.

"It's a vineyard. We're never off the clock."

"That's rich," Trevor shot back, "coming from the man who was gone for the better part of a decade." He moved closer and stared at the teenage boy standing just behind Griffin. "Who are you?"

"Cole Maren," the boy answered.

"What are you doing here?"

Cole adjusted the bill of his ball cap. "I work here."

"In my mother's house?"

Griffin pushed back from the table and stood. "What's with the interrogation, Trev? You can see the kid is here with me. He's going to run into town and pick up some supplies I need for excavation. The machinery arrives on Monday."

"Why do you want his help?" Trevor demanded.

"Is there a problem?"

"You know who his dad is, right?"

"Dude," Cole muttered, moving to put on his sweatshirt. "I don't need this."

"Don't go anywhere." Griffin placed a hand on Cole's shoulder. "I need your help.

"The office," he said to Trevor, nudging his brother out of the way as he moved past.

As soon as Trevor shut the door to the home office that had been their father's sanctuary, Griffin rounded on him. "What the hell was that about?"

"Toby Maren is the town drunk," Trevor said like that explained everything.

Griffin snorted. "You mean in all these years we still only have one?"

"The family is bad news. I heard Cole's brother is doing time over in Elbert County for assault and robbery. I don't think the mom is in the picture. So he's grown up with an alcoholic and a criminal." Trevor threw up his hands. "Where does that leave him?"

"In need of a decent role model?"

"You sound like Marcus," Trevor said with a derisive sniff. "Neither one of you has a sense of what's right. We have an image to protect at Harvest—our brand means quality. That means we need to employ quality people."

"You don't know Cole enough to say that he's not."

"I know he's trouble. Why can't you trust me on this? You don't have a clue what goes on in this town anymore. You can't just waltz back in here after a decade and act like you're going to take over."

Color flooded Trevor's face as he paced from one end of the wood-paneled office to the other. He and his brother had never been close, but Trevor had a point when he said that he'd stayed while Griffin had left the family business behind. Griffin wanted to show some respect for the years Trevor had put into building Harvest's market share. A great wine wasn't worth its grapes if no one discovered it.

"I'm not a threat to you," he said. "Mom wants me to build the tasting room, and I'm going to do that for her. Then I'll be gone."

"You had lunch with Maggie last week," Trevor said, his tone accusing.

Griffin's spine stiffened. "So what?"

"Why?" Trevor asked with a glare.

"I ran into her in town. We were both hungry."

"Give me a break." A muscle ticked in Trevor's jaw. "First you play her knight in shining armor after the wedding and now you're going on lunch dates? Are you suddenly interested in my girl?"

Anger bubbled up in Griffin along with an overwhelming sense of possession. "She isn't yours," he said through clenched teeth.

"Well, she sure as hell isn't going to go for someone like you." Trevor's eyes narrowed. "Maggie cares about her image and her family's reputation too much to start a scandal."

"That fact worked to your benefit after you cheated on her," Griffin said quietly.

"It's over," Trevor insisted. "Turns out there's nothing between Julia and me." He rubbed a hand over his jaw. "It was a mistake but also a blessing. Maggie wouldn't have made me happy."

"What would, Trev? You're mad that I'm working at the vineyard. You can't stand that I'm giving a kid a chance." Griffin lifted his hand, ticking off the list of grievances his brother seemed to have against him. "You don't like that I had lunch with Maggie. From the outside, you've got it pretty good. A great job, a breakup where you came out smelling like roses, even though the whole thing was your fault. Life is handing you pitchers of lemonade and you're pining for lemons. What exactly would make you happy?"

Trevor opened his mouth, then snapped it shut again. "Keep an eye on Cole Maren. I have a bad feeling about him." He stalked past Griffin and out of the room.

Griffin returned to the kitchen, his temper practically boiling over, then blew out a breath when Cole shoved a piece of paper in front of his face.

"I took your notes and made a list of the lumber and supplies we'll need to get started on the project. My dad used to work for the garbage company, so I called and arranged for them to drop off a Dumpster on Monday." He gave a small smile that looked more like a grimace. "If you don't think we need it, I can use one of the vineyard's trucks to haul away the waste."

"A Dumpster will make things faster." Griffin scanned the list. "You've done a good job here."

"Mr. Stone is wrong about me," Cole said, his words steely. "But he's right about my dad and brother."

Griffin raised a brow.

"Yeah, I eavesdropped," the boy admitted. "Only because I wanted to hear what he'd say so I'd know how to convince you to let me keep this job."

"You don't need to convince me." Griffin folded the piece of paper in half and handed it back to him. "I was a teenager once, and you can't help your family."

"I couldn't believe when Mr. Sanchez hired me for the summer. I'd applied for jobs all over town." He shook his head. "Then you picked me to help you with the construction."

"You practically threw yourself at me," Griffin said with a chuckle. He was planning on handling most of the work himself but needed a few laborers to do the heavy lifting. When he'd asked the field manager if he had any workers to spare, Cole had tripped all over himself to volunteer.

"I like building things," Cole said simply but there was an underlying meaning to the words. This was a kid who'd seen plenty of things in his life torn apart. He was tall, almost six feet with gangly arms, long legs and hair that was badly in need of a cut. He favored black metal band T-shirts and ripped jeans. Overall, he looked like another punk kid with a surly attitude. Much like Griffin had when he was that age. Maybe that was why he saw something more in Cole. Potential. Hope. Determination. Characteristics he recognized and respected even if Trevor couldn't.

"Take the truck and pick up this stuff from Kurt's. The vineyard has an account."

Cole nodded. "Then what?"

"It's Saturday." Griffin smiled. "Don't you have some lucky girl to take out for the night?"

The teen rolled his bright blue eyes. "The girls who run in my crowd are skanks."

"Hey." Griffin reached out and cuffed the back of

the boy's head. "Treat women with respect. Talk about them with respect."

"But they don't—"

"You should know better than most that what you do matters more than what the people around you do. Be the man you want others to see you as. Maybe you'll find a girl who wants to be with the best version of who you are."

Cole rolled his eyes. "Dr. Phil much?"

"That was some of my best stuff," Griffin countered with a laugh. "I have wisdom to impart, young apprentice."

"How's that advice working for *you*?"

Irritation scratched just under Griffin's skin, mainly because the question made too many of his own doubts crawl out of their dark caves yearning for the light. Returning to Stonecreek had turned his life upside down. He was back in his family home, trying hard not to become invested in the vineyard even as his fingers itched to work the vines.

He lusted after Maggie Spencer, a woman all wrong for him and not just because a week ago she'd been in a wedding gown ready to marry his brother. "This isn't about me," he mumbled.

"I know Morgan Spencer." Cole stared at a spot over Griffin's shoulder. "She's not like her sister—doesn't care about the Spencer name and all that."

Griffin rubbed the back of his neck, grateful for any change in topic, no matter how minuscule. "Are you friends?"

"Sort of. Maybe. Not really. She thinks she's some kind of rebel, but she's better than she pretends to be. Better than most of the guys in this town deserve."

"She has that in common with her sister," Griffin said, thinking of himself and Maggie.

"Yeah?" Cole asked and his young eyes held an understanding far beyond his years.

Griffin sighed. "Yeah."

Chapter Eight

Maggie felt like her cheeks might break if she held her tight smile for one more second.

She excused herself from the group she'd joined a few minutes earlier, and moved toward the one quiet corner of the town square. She lowered herself onto a park bench and leaned back, watching as folks streamed toward the strands of lights that marked the festival's midway.

The Pioneer Day Festival was in full force, and Maggie had been making the rounds for the past three hours. Before that she'd spent most of the morning helping to set up booths and unload food and supplies from the backs of trucks. Normally, she loved the start of festival season in Stonecreek. The town could find a reason to celebrate almost anything, and the summer calendar was crowded with weekends of barbecue, pies, flowers and art.

Even before Maggie had become mayor she'd volunteered for setup and teardown at almost every event. But today the camaraderie felt forced, her conversations with old friends stilted. Jason Stone had been holding court at the morning's pancake breakfast, which kicked off the festival, like he was already the front-runner in the election.

Maggie had found herself on the periphery of her beloved community. Ever since she'd ventured out to lunch with Griffin, people had been friendly but still standoffish, as if she had some sort of "tarnished bride" germs that might rub off on them if they got too close. Apparently, she'd taken for granted her position as "Stonecreek's sweetheart" and how one mistake could push her off that platform like a disgraced pirate shuffling along the plank.

"Shouldn't you be shaking hands or kissing babies?"

She turned as Griffin approached from the far side of the park, hands jammed into the pockets of his jeans. As always, he looked effortlessly handsome in a gray chambray shirt and dark jeans.

"I've already left lipstick marks on all the talcum powder–scented heads. My work here tonight is done."

"Then my timing is excellent."

Shivers of awareness spiking through her, she patted the bench. "Have a seat," she said, hoping she sounded casual as opposed to as nervous as a schoolgirl.

Griffin had always had that effect on her, even when they were younger and he'd made it his mission in life to ignore her. It didn't matter where she'd been as a teenager or how many people were surrounding her; as soon as Griffin had appeared her body had hummed liked a high-voltage power line.

"Do things ever change around here?" he asked as he dropped down next to her. "Pioneer Day looks the same as it did when we were kids."

Maggie smiled. That was one of the things she loved about festival season—the tradition of it. "Two years ago," she said solemnly, "the cooks at The Kitchen used a new batter recipe for their funnel cakes. They came out of the fryers as gelatinous grease blobs. Caused quite a stir and was the lead story in the community newspaper the next week."

"Lesson learned, I hope."

"Oh, yes." Maggie nodded and worked to keep her expression serious. "Back to the original batter the following year and they offered half-price funnel cakes on opening night to make it up to everyone."

Griffin laughed softly. "No wonder people around here are obsessed with your nonwedding. Nothing else has happened in years."

"Maybe I could orchestrate a minor zombie outbreak. That would take the attention off me."

"It's worth a shot."

She breathed in the cool air of evening, tinged with the scents of fried food and cotton candy. Griffin had the gift of helping her not take herself or the town too seriously. Through his perspective she was able to see how trivial some of her worries were in the bigger picture.

She turned her head to look at him. "What brings you into town if you weren't planning on attending the festival?"

"You," he said, keeping his gaze forward. "I didn't have a plan, but I wanted to see you."

Joy rushed through her like an electric current, making her body heat from the inside out. "I'm glad."

He cleared his throat. "Do you want to walk through the festival?"

"Not one bit," she admitted, earning a wide grin.

"What a relief," he said, standing and taking her hand. "Let's go."

She felt only a moment's hesitation that she might be shirking her duty to the town as its mayor.

Wasn't she obligated to attend every minute of every event sponsored in Stonecreek? That was how she'd lived her life for the past two years and, honestly, it was difficult to remember a time before responsibility was her norm.

Glancing at her hand joined with Griffin's, Maggie realized she wanted something different than the norm. She wanted excitement, adventure. More than anything, she wanted Griffin Stone.

"Hurry," she whispered, giggling for the first time in forever. "I need to get out of here before someone sees me."

They ran down the sidewalk, hand in hand, and Maggie felt freer with every step. She knew they weren't doing anything crazy or rebellious, but in her structured world, it felt like a revolution and she reveled in the moment.

By the time they got to the Land Cruiser, parked several blocks away, adrenaline coursed through her veins. Griffin released her hand to open the passenger door and she climbed in, placing a hand over her chest like she could calm her racing heart.

"You're beautiful," Griffin told her, tucking a strand of hair behind her ear. He gave her the cocky half grin that had practically melted her panties in high school, and tonight it made her feel like she might spontaneously combust.

"Oh" was the only response she could manage.

"Oh, yeah," he murmured, his grin widening. He came around the front of the SUV and got behind the wheel, and then they were turning the corner that led to the highway out of town.

"So what's the plan?" she asked, proud her voice didn't tremble.

"Do we need a plan?" Griffin drummed his fingers casually on the console between them. His hands were large, his fingers long and surprisingly elegant even with several scratches and scars. She liked seeing the evidence of his labor on his body.

"I never do anything without a plan."

"There's always a first time."

"But you have a plan," she insisted.

He laughed and turned on the radio. "Yes, Maggie May. I have a plan." Glancing over at her, he cocked a brow. "But I'm going to leave you in suspense."

"I hate suspense."

He laughed again, then began to sing along with the song on the radio. It was a classic rock anthem from the late seventies, and Maggie closed her eyes as she listened to Griffin's rich baritone strike the perfect harmony with the lead singer. She joined in when the chorus started, letting the music and the moment sweep her away. At least until she realized that Griffin had gone silent.

"What?" she said when she turned and found him staring at her.

"Finally, something you're not good at," he said with a mischievous smile. "I was beginning to think you were too perfect, but, Maggie Spencer, you couldn't carry a tune out of a bucket."

She gasped and leaned forward to flip off the radio. "It's no wonder you don't have a girlfriend when you're dishing out that kind of charm."

Silence filled the vehicle's interior for only a few seconds before she heard the deep rumble of Griffin's laughter. As much as embarrassment heated her cheeks, Maggie felt a smile pull at the corners of her mouth. "That was so rude," she muttered.

"You're adorable," he said, reaching a hand over and patting her leg. She wore a fitted blouse and crisp knee-length skirt so the feel of his calloused fingers against her bare skin sent awareness racing through her. "I like that you aren't perfect."

"I'm not that terrible of a singer," she insisted. He didn't answer and after a moment she huffed out an irritated breath. "Okay, I'm awful but it's still bad manners for you to point it out."

She stared at the rolling hills and open farmland. They were heading west toward the coast, and the landscape was slowly moving from verdant valley with mountains looming in the distance to the rockier geography of the Oregon coast.

"You're real." He turned the radio on again, humming along with a popular country hit. "That's way more interesting than your Stonecreek image if you ask me. Sing at the top of your lungs. I could care less if it sounds like a herd of cats dying a slow death."

She burst out laughing. "It's a good thing you're so darn hot," she said when she could control her laughter enough to speak. "Otherwise, women would run the other way as soon as you opened your mouth."

"Are you going to run?" he asked, his tone suddenly serious.

"No," she said without hesitation. She hadn't felt this happy in a long time. "But I am going to subject you to my singing." She turned up the volume knob on the radio as a Carrie Underwood song started. "I love this song so much."

Griffin grimaced but she could tell he liked her answer. It was close to seven when he pulled off the highway onto a two-lane road that followed the coastline. She rolled down her window and breathed deeply of the ocean-scented air.

"I don't know this town," she said, gazing at the clapboard houses and faded shingled buildings. There were huge pots of trailing vines and flowers situated on every block, and a few couples and several families meandered along the sidewalks. It was quaint and quiet and exactly the kind of place Maggie was in the mood to discover.

He parked the car in front of a cozy-looking used bookstore. "Lychen is more a town for locals than tourists. It's a fishing village really, but the people here are great."

They got out of the Land Cruiser and Griffin scanned the street. "It's grown some since I came here in high school, but it still looks pretty sleepy."

"How did you discover it?" She held up a hand. "Wait. I bet it was a girl."

He smiled sheepishly. "There were plenty of girls, but not here." He put a hand on her back to direct her onto the sidewalk, then kept it there as they walked. The light contact reverberated through Maggie.

"My dad and I got in an argument one weekend,

which was not uncommon. By the time I was in high school, it seemed like all we did was fight. That time was different because I'd just gotten my license. I finally had the freedom to leave, so I did."

"And you came to Lychen?"

He nodded. "Not on purpose at first. I had that old Chevy—"

"I remember," she murmured.

"I started driving and this is where I ended up. It was different than Stonecreek. At home I was the kid with an attitude. Everyone had me pegged and I did plenty to live down to their low expectations. But here, no one knew me. I could be whoever I wanted to be. I liked it, you know?"

She glanced over at him, taking in his strong jaw and the tiny lines fanning out from the corners of his eyes. Griffin was different than the boy she'd known growing up. He'd changed in the years he was away from Stonecreek, matured in a way she still could barely grasp.

"Who were you in Lychen?"

"Anonymous," he answered immediately. "I wasn't part of the Stone family. Generations of history didn't weigh me down. I was just a kid with a truck from out of town."

She bit down on her lower lip. How could she and Griffin have grown up so similarly but end up with such opposite views of what the past meant? "I always liked the history," she admitted. "Knowing where I came from gave me a sense of who I was supposed to be."

Griffin's shoulder bumped hers and she felt the heat of his body. The air was cooler on the coast, and she wanted to move closer and wrap herself in his warmth. "I guess I needed to figure it out on my own," he said with a shrug.

They stopped outside a storefront, and he pointed to the sign above the door. Luigi's Italian Inn.

"An original name for a restaurant," she offered.

"I used to walk by this place back in the day and salivate over the smells drifting out, but I didn't have the money for a sit-down dinner back then."

"It smells wonderful."

"What do you think? Spaghetti dinner?"

As if on cue, her stomach growled. She nodded and followed him into the restaurant, breathing in the scent of tangy sauce and yeasty bread. The restaurant was long and narrow, with booths lining the length of one wall. A woman with dark hair and kind eyes greeted them at the hostess stand.

"Welcome to Luigi's. I'm Bianca, the owner, and I'm proud to say we've been serving my *nonna*'s Sicilian recipes here for over thirty years."

Maggie stifled a laugh. "We're all about family history."

Griffin held up two fingers. "A table, please?"

"Our most romantic," Bianca answered with a wink. "It's clear this is a special date." She pointed at Maggie. "You have that look about you."

"I don't have a look," Maggie said automatically. She crossed her arms over her chest, embarrassed to be called out by a stranger. "No look. None."

The woman only laughed and gestured for them to follow her.

"I like your look," Griffin whispered as they moved

through the restaurant, his breath tickling the back of her neck.

What was she doing here? They'd only driven an hour but this place seemed like a lifetime away from Stonecreek.

Maybe that was the gift of this night and this tiny town. Like Griffin had experienced as a teen, she could be whomever she wanted without worrying about what anyone else would think.

They were seated at an intimate booth near the back of the restaurant. A red-checked tablecloth covered the table, and a votive candle flickered from its center. Bianca handed them each a menu.

"Would you like to see the wine list?" she asked, prompting Maggie to raise a brow at Griffin.

"We'll take a bottle of your favorite pinot noir," he responded.

The woman nodded approvingly. "Right away."

"What if it's not from Harvest?" Maggie asked when they were alone.

He laughed softly. "I think I'll manage."

She sat back against the booth's cushion. "If Trevor and I ordered wine at a restaurant, he insisted that it be from Harvest. He wouldn't drink anything else."

One side of Griffin's full mouth quirked. "Then he's missing out and besides—"

He broke off as the owner returned, presenting a bottle to Griffin. "I have one of Harvest Vineyards' best vintages. The volcanic soil makes the grapes especially crisp. I don't know if you're familiar with Harvest…"

Griffin nodded. "Vaguely."

"They're a rising star in the Oregon wine industry and also family owned, which we appreciate."

"I think we can trust your judgment." Griffin looked to Maggie for approval. "Sound good to you?"

"Of course."

The woman uncorked the wine and Griffin went through the process of inspecting the cork, then swirled and sniffed his sample before taking a sip. Amusement danced in his green eyes. "Very nice. A bit of cherry and currant. The tannins and acid are well-balanced."

"You know your wine," the owner murmured approvingly, pouring a generous amount for Maggie and then filling Griffin's glass. "We have a special that would pair beautifully with it. It's a poached salmon with goat cheese and asparagus, plus a side of mushroom risotto."

"Maggie?" Griffin asked, and the fact that he so easily deferred to her made her knees go weak. Other parts of her body gathered strength, like lusty soldiers standing at attention.

"Sure." She nodded, pressing her lips together. The woman could have offered her monkey brains and she would have agreed to it. Her head was in a fog; the fact that Griffin had no problem letting her take the lead was as attractive as his handsome face and killer body.

Despite being a grown woman and mayor of Stonecreek, Maggie felt like she spent most of her time deferring to other people's wishes. From her grandmother's expectations to Trevor's strict ideas about how their relationship should progress, Maggie rarely got to choose something solely for herself. Even when she went out to dinner in town, she consciously made the rounds of local restaurants so she'd be seen supporting a variety of businesses.

"Would you like a salad to start?"

"Yes," she said with probably more force than necessary as Bianca took a small step back.

"A house salad would be great," Maggie said, softening her tone. "Balsamic dressing, please."

The owner nodded and looked toward Griffin. "I'll have the same thing," he told her.

When Bianca walked away again, Griffin inclined his head. "You feel passionate about salad."

"I guess," Maggie said, feeling color rise to her cheeks once again. She took a long sip of wine. "It's good. Did you know they carried Harvest here?"

"Not specifically, but most of the coastal towns do. Trevor is good at his job."

"He's driven," she agreed. "But I don't want to talk about anything to do with Stonecreek tonight. Tell me about your time in the army."

"A light topic," he murmured. "Nice."

She rolled her eyes. "I never really understood what made you join in the first place," she admitted. "I remember that you'd been accepted to Oregon State. I thought you were going into business and—"

He held up a hand. "Me, too. But Dad and I had that last fight after the fire. He told me there was no way he'd let me work at Harvest. I was angry and hurt, although I probably deserved it."

"The fire was an accident."

"A cigarette left to burn next to a pile of magazines. My stupid friends and I had gone in to grab a few bottles of wine."

"Not many teenagers get drunk on quality wine."

"Totally unable to appreciate it at that age." Griffin picked up his glass, twirled the stem in his fingers.

"Especially when most nights ended with someone puking in the bushes."

"You learned a hard lesson."

"Dad didn't see it that way." He frowned. "In his opinion, I'd done it to sabotage the vineyard. They were hosting the Northwest Winemakers conference the following week."

"Everyone knew it wasn't on purpose."

"It didn't matter what anyone else thought. I understood at that moment that even if he relented—and Mom was going to do her best to make sure he did—even if he deigned to find a place for me at the vineyard, I couldn't work for him. Our relationship was toxic."

"There's a huge jump between not wanting to work for the family business and skipping college to join the army."

Griffin took a long drink of wine. "Not so big when you're an angry teen wanting to stick it to your parents." He shrugged. "The army was actually the best thing that could have happened to me at that point. It gave me purpose and structure—two things I didn't realize I wanted in my life."

A waitress brought their salads, and Maggie forked up a bite of lettuce, then pointed it at Griffin. "See, structure and planning have their benefits."

He clinked his fork against hers. "Touché, Maggie May."

Her name on his lips felt like a caress, and Maggie wanted to lean into it. Away from Stonecreek, she felt light and free. She could do anything, even explore her attraction to a man who could never be right for her.

They talked more about his time in the army and all

the places he'd visited. Listening to Griffin, Maggie realized how narrow her life had been. She'd gone to school an hour from Stonecreek and, other than a senior trip to London with her grandmother, she'd barely traveled past the Oregon state line.

Griffin didn't seem bothered by her lack of worldliness. He asked questions about her family and her role as mayor, seeming genuinely interested in her ideas about the town's future.

Maggie didn't want the night to end.

Griffin couldn't remember the last time he'd felt so happy. Had Maggie been this amazing when they were younger? Probably... Although he'd been too stupid and self-centered to see it.

He took her hand as they stood overlooking the beach on the town pier, lacing his fingers with hers. He'd never touch her so casually in Stonecreek, where curious eyes were everywhere. But here it was the two of them, and he wanted to make the most of every minute.

"I should come to the coast more often," she said, her chest rising and falling as she breathed in the salty air. "The sound of the ocean is the best."

"Next time we'll walk the beach before we eat." They'd lingered over dinner, and it was dark when they'd exited the restaurant. But the moon was almost full, so they could still see the waves crashing against the sand.

"Next time," she repeated quietly, then turned to him. "What's going on here, Griffin?"

He ran a hand through his hair, keeping his gaze

straight ahead. "I'm on an amazing date with an amazing woman and—"

"This isn't a date," she interrupted, tugging her hand from his.

His gut tightened. Those weren't the words he'd wanted or expected to hear from her.

Now he shifted, looking down into her gray eyes. Strands of lights lined the pier, so he could see that her gaze was guarded…serious. Not at all the easygoing, playful woman who'd sat across from him at dinner.

"What would you call it?"

"I'm not sure," she admitted.

"But you're confident it's not a date?"

She shook her head. "I'm not confident of anything at the moment. You might remember my life turned completely upside down last week. But even if that wasn't a factor, I can't imagine you wanting to go on a date with me."

"I'm not the same guy I used to be."

She laughed softly. "Well, thank heavens for that."

"I'm sorry," he blurted. "For who I was back then."

"I get that you were an angry kid and the whole 'rebel without a cause' bit."

She did air quotes with her fingers, making light of his teenage angst, which he definitely deserved. The things he'd seen after leaving Stonecreek made him understand how good he'd had it growing up.

That perspective allowed him to return, made him want to make amends with his mother. Even had him wishing he could have another chance with his dad.

"What was it about me in particular that you hated?"

The question caught him off guard and he felt his mouth drop open. "I didn't hate you," he muttered.

"Really?" Her delicate brows furrowed, and a line formed between her eyes that he wanted to smooth away with his fingertip. "Because the way I remember it you relished being churlish to everyone but I was in a special category."

He rubbed a hand along the back of his neck. "I hated myself," he admitted softly. "And I was jealous of you. You were perfect. Everyone in town loved you. It was clear even back then that you were the golden girl of Stonecreek, which meant you represented everything I could never hope to be."

"But now I'm okay because my crown has been knocked off?"

"That's not it," he said, needing her to understand. He paced to the edge of the pier, then back to her. "I can't explain it but there's a connection between us, Maggie. I know you feel it."

She glanced out to the ocean in front of them. "I do."

"I think maybe I realized it back then. Except you were younger and friends with Trevor and so far out of my league." He chuckled. "That part hasn't changed. But I'm not the same person, and I want a chance with you."

"It's complicated," she said softly. "A week ago I was supposed to marry your brother. If people in town caught wind that I'd now turned my sights to you, imagine what that would do to my reputation."

The words were a punch to the gut. He might not care what anyone in Stonecreek thought about him, but it was stupid to think Maggie would feel the same way. She was the mayor after all and up for reelection in the fall. He stared at her profile for several long moments. Her hair had fallen forward so that all he could see was the tip of her nose. She didn't turn to him or offer any more of an explanation.

"I understand," he told her finally.

"I had a good time tonight," she whispered, "but us being together in Stonecreek is different."

"I get it." He made a show of checking his watch. "It's almost eleven. We should head back."

Her shoulders rose and fell with another deep breath. She turned to him and cupped his jaw in her cool fingers. "Thank you, Griffin. For tonight. I really like the man you've become." Before he could respond, she reached up and kissed his cheek.

He wanted to grab her and pull her close, prove that she couldn't ignore this spark between them. Instead, he nodded, tucked a loose strand of hair behind her ear and took his keys from the pocket of his jeans. "Do you have a curfew these days?" he asked, forcing a playful tone. He wouldn't let her see how much her tacit rejection hurt.

"I'm an adult." She gave a wry smile. "Although I texted my dad earlier to let him know I'd be late. It's strange living in the house again. Morgan and Ben were little kids when I went to college."

"It's not like you've been out of their lives for years." They made their way down the now-empty street of the quaint coastal town. "You're all close."

"True," she admitted, "but my dad has never been a real 'hands-on' parent, and I'm always busy with work. It seems like Morgan and Ben have raised themselves, and that's not the way it should be."

"Don't give yourself a hard time. I'm sure they're doing great."

"Morgan has blue hair."

He gave a mock shudder. "A harbinger of evil without a doubt."

"Point taken," she said, nudging his arm as they walked. "I'm probably overreacting. I'll chill out."

"Chill out." He chuckled. "I haven't heard anyone use that phrase for years. You're cute, Maggie May, even if you shot me down during the best nondate of my life."

He opened the SUV's door for her. "Maybe we can go on another nondate?" she suggested with a small smile as she buckled her seat belt.

Okay, not shot down entirely.

Griffin found himself smiling as he walked around the front of the Land Cruiser. He wasn't giving up on Maggie. She was right. He didn't care about her history with Trevor or what anyone in Stonecreek thought. He liked her, and it was more than physical attraction. He'd seen and done enough in life to know she was worth fighting for. Griffin was a fighter.

He hopped in the car and turned the key in the ignition. "Next time we should head up to Portland. I was there a couple of months ago, and they have some great new restaurants." When she didn't respond, he looked over. "Maggie, what's wrong?"

She was furiously tapping the screen of her phone, the scowl on her face lit by its glow. "Morgan's missing," she whispered, then lifted the phone to her ear.

Griffin pulled away from the curb, glancing in her direction every few seconds. "Since when?"

She held up a hand at the same time she said, "Hey, Dad…No, I'm on my way back. We're about an hour from town." There was a short pause. "It doesn't matter who. Tell me about Morgan…Maybe she's just late." Another pause. "Grounded for what?" She blew out a sigh. "I get it. When was the last time you checked on her?…After dinner. What time did you have dinner?" She glanced to the clock on the dashboard. "Three hours, then," she muttered. "You've called her friends? Where does she like to hang out?" Pause. "And you're sure Ben's at home?" Her free hand tapped a rapid beat against her leg. "Have him reach out to her friends. Don't call Tom yet. I'll be there as soon as I can. We'll find her, Dad."

She clicked off the phone and dropped it into her lap, her eyes squeezing shut.

"Your sister?"

"She failed Biology last semester so she's doing summer school. Dad grounded her tonight for a bad test grade."

"Maybe he's a little more clued in than you thought," Griffin suggested gently.

Maggie snorted. "Other than the fact that she went to her room after dinner and he just checked on her and she's gone."

"She sneaked out?" Griffin didn't try to hide the shock in his voice.

"Apparently." Maggie held the phone up to her ear again. "Morgan, if you get this message, call me. Call Dad. Let us know you're okay."

"She's okay." Griffin reached across the console to pat her leg.

"How do you know?"

"Didn't you used to sneak out at night?" He felt his eyes widen. "Wait. You never sneaked out?"

"Not once. Why would Morgan sneak out? She barely has rules as it is."

"Um, she was grounded for a test grade. That's something."

"One night," Maggie countered. "Couldn't she have stayed in for one night?"

"Who are her friends?"

"I don't know anymore." Maggie thumped the heel of her hand against her forehead. "My dad doesn't know. He doesn't remember names or ask questions." She sighed. "I have a feeling they're wild."

Griffin thought about that for a moment, then nodded. "I have an idea. We'll find her, Maggie. Don't worry."

She looked over at him, the lights from the highway casting her pale skin in and out of shadow. "You can drop me off downtown. My car's parked there. This isn't your problem."

"Haven't you heard?" he asked with a small half smile. "I'm working on my hero status now that I'm back in town."

Chapter Nine

Maggie clutched her hands together as Griffin headed down the dark road toward the address he'd been given over the phone. They were about thirty minutes east of Stonecreek, in a section of ranch land she rarely visited.

According to what Griffin had been able to discern from a friend's nephew, there was a big party happening in one of the fields out this way. If Morgan had been looking for trouble, this was the place for it.

"We'll find her," he said for what must have been the tenth time since they'd begun to search. Morgan still wasn't picking up her phone and she'd disabled the location service built into it.

If Griffin wanted the role of hero, Maggie had no problem seeing him like that. Although, it was still difficult for her to believe Griffin Stone would take time out of his night—even a minute—to help track down her wayward sister.

Suddenly, he hit the brake as a figure stepped out onto the road, waving frantically.

"It's Cole Maren, the kid who's been working with me on the tasting room." Griffin pulled onto the gravel shoulder, his headlights illuminating the beat-up Chevy and a smaller silhouette sitting in the back of the truck bed.

"Morgan," Maggie breathed, heart hammering in her chest. All the anonymous faces she'd ignored on the side of milk cartons and in the post office ran through her mind as relief bubbled up inside her. She sent out a silent prayer for every missing child to be found safe as Morgan shielded her eyes against the glare of the light.

Griffin threw the truck into Park and jumped out. "What the hell?" He stalked forward with Maggie following.

"Morgan, are you okay?" she called as she rushed toward her sister.

"Is that you, Maggie?"

"I trusted you. I gave you a chance." Griffin grabbed the lanky boy by the shirt, yanking him forward, then slamming him into the side of the truck. "What did you do to her?"

As shocked as she was by Griffin's treatment of Cole, Maggie's first concern was Morgan. She reached her sister, who brushed away her touch. "I'm fine, Mags. Tell me Dad doesn't know I'm gone."

"Let me go," Cole shouted. "I didn't do anything wrong."

"Hey, stop that." Morgan jumped off the back of the truck, stumbling once before righting herself. Maggie felt sick to her stomach. Clearly, her sister had been drinking or worse. "You're going to hurt him."

"That's right." Griffin glanced at Morgan, then back to Cole. "For every way you hurt her, I'm going to hurt you."

"He hasn't done anything," Morgan screamed when Griffin tightened his grip on the teenager, who looked defiant but wasn't fighting Griffin's hold.

"Griffin, it's okay." Maggie made her voice soothing. "Let him go."

"I gave you a chance," Griffin repeated, shoving away from the boy and walking toward the back of the truck. His fists were tightly clenched at his sides.

Morgan placed a hand on Cole's arm, but he shrugged away.

"Where have you been?" Maggie stepped between her sister and Cole. "Why haven't you answered any calls or texts?"

"Check your phone," Morgan said unapologetically. "There's no service out here."

"You were grounded."

"For failing a stupid summer school science test," Morgan whined. "Which is your fault anyway."

"How am I to blame for a bad grade in science?"

Morgan snorted. "It's your fault I'm grounded," she clarified. "Dad didn't pay attention to any of my grades until you gave him grief about needing to be more involved. Suddenly, he decides to check up on me the weekend of the most important party of the summer."

Cole let out a harsh laugh at that. "The party was stupid."

"Then why did you come out here?" Morgan asked, her tone accusing.

"I don't know," Cole shot back, throwing up his

hands, "but it sure wasn't to get in trouble for pulling you out of there. I should have just left you to it."

"You said they called the cops."

"I'm sure someone was going to. And you've been drinking."

"Morgan," Maggie gasped, unable to contain her disappointment even though she'd guessed as much.

Morgan ignored Maggie and stepped around her to point a finger at Cole. "You drink. I've seen you drink."

"Not tonight." He looked past Morgan toward Maggie. "I promise I'm not drinking and driving."

Maggie nodded. "Thanks for taking care of Morgan." She didn't know Cole, although everyone was familiar with Toby Maren's drunken antics. But she could see how upset the kid was by this situation and her sister's involvement in it.

"He didn't take care of me," Morgan insisted, whirling on Maggie. "I don't need anyone to take care of me. I'm fine on my own."

"Not hanging all over Zach Bryant," Cole said, crossing his arms over his chest. "He's a loser, Morgan."

"At least he *likes* me." Morgan patted an angry hand against her chest. "He thinks I'm hot. He said so."

Cole opened his mouth, snapped it shut again. Morgan let out a frustrated groan, and Maggie sighed.

"What happened to the truck?" Griffin asked, stepping forward.

The boy stared at Morgan for a long moment before turning his attention to Griffin. "It overheated. Stupid piece of junk. The fan belt broke."

Griffin gave a curt nod. "Get in the Land Cruiser.

I'll take everyone home, and then you and I can come back out here tomorrow and put in a new belt."

Cole snorted. "Are you going to slam me up against the truck again?"

"Not tonight," Griffin said, his mouth thinning. Maggie waited for him to say more or apologize for how he'd handled Cole, but he only turned and stalked to the SUV, calling, "Let's go," over his shoulder.

Morgan gave Maggie a look like she wanted to argue. "Now, Mo-mo," Maggie said. "As soon as you have cell service, call Dad."

"We'll be home in twenty minutes," Morgan complained.

"You'll call him first," Maggie insisted. "He's worried."

Morgan grabbed her purse from the back of Cole's truck and stalked toward the Land Cruiser. "Maybe if the town would pay for more cell phone towers, we would've been able to call for help."

"Maybe if you hadn't sneaked out in the first place, this wouldn't be an issue for any of us."

Maggie watched as Cole leaned into the driver's side and grabbed his phone and wallet. "Thank you again," she said, moving in step next to him. "She'll appreciate it someday."

He shrugged. "Apparently, I didn't do anything but make her mad."

"You were her friend."

"She's really smart at school," Cole said with a shrug, "so I don't know why she wants to hang out with the people I do. We're not good enough for her."

Maggie put a hand on the kid's arm, waiting until

he turned to look at her before speaking. "Don't say that about yourself," she told him.

Cole rolled his eyes. "You know who I am, right? My dad and brother and the fact that my mom took off years ago."

"All circumstances you can't control."

"Yeah," he agreed after a moment. "But I've done plenty of bad shi– " He broke off and gave a small shake of his head. "Your sister should not be hanging with us."

The utter conviction in his words broke Maggie's heart. Everything was so clear in her world—who she was and her place in the community. It embarrassed her to realize that even after two years serving as mayor she didn't have a clear understanding of how people might be falling through the cracks in her town.

"Are you two coming or what?" Griffin called from the SUV.

"I'm still grateful," Maggie told Cole as they started walking again.

She climbed in, and Griffin turned back the way they'd driven on the highway. No one spoke, and Maggie eventually flipped on the radio, hoping the noise would disguise the tension filling the vehicle.

A few miles outside of town, her phone began to ding, and she could hear Morgan's making the same kind of incessant chirping.

"Text Dad," she commanded, looking around her seat to make certain her sister complied.

"I've got twenty-four missed calls from him," Morgan murmured, and Maggie thought she detected a slight note of wonder in her sister's voice.

"He was worried." Maggie looked at Cole. "Is there anyone you need to call?"

The boy's lips formed an almost painful smile. He pulled his phone from his back pocket and held it up, the screen resolutely dark. "No one's worried about me."

"Oh," Maggie breathed. She turned toward the front again, glancing at the hard set of Griffin's features. "Thanks for helping me track her down."

He nodded. "Cole, you guys still out on Maple Lane?"

"Yeah, but you can let me off wherever. I'll walk."

Griffin made a noise that was somewhere between a snort and a sigh. "I'm taking you home."

He turned off the highway onto a dirt road, driving past ramshackle houses and a few trailers thrown into the mix. Maggie knew this part of town existed, but she wasn't familiar with it. Another strike against her as mayor, she supposed.

"Dad says I'm grounded for the whole summer," Morgan complained from the back seat. "Why did he have to start caring tonight?"

"He's always cared," Maggie told her, "but he gets distracted."

"It's not fair," her sister insisted. "I only wanted to—"

"This is it," Cole announced.

Maggie heard Morgan's tiny gasp and tried hard to hide her own reaction to the property in front of them. The house—if you could call it that—was little more than a dilapidated double-wide trailer with boards covering one of the windows and a tarp draped over half the roof. The yard was riddled with weeds and various broken lawn chairs strewed about. It was difficult to see how bad it truly was with only the headlights illuminating a narrow swath across the property as Griffin pulled into the gravel driveway. The Land Cruiser dipped as it hit a rut and Griffin steered toward the edge of the drive.

"I'll get out here," Cole said, his voice tight. "If the dogs start barking, my dad will wake up."

Griffin stopped and put the truck into Park. "You'll be okay?" he asked, eyes trained on the ramshackle house.

Cole laughed. "I'm fine." He opened the door to climb out, and Maggie reached behind her seat to slap her sister's knee.

"Thanks for your help tonight," Morgan mumbled.

"Seems like I did more harm than good," Cole said with another hollow laugh. "What's new?"

He slammed the door shut and started up the driveway, a dark silhouette in the glare of the headlights.

Griffin watched him for a moment, then thumped his closed fist on the steering wheel. A moment later he got out and jogged toward Cole.

"Griffin Stone's kind of intense," Morgan said, shifting forward and resting her chin on the back of Maggie's seat.

"How does he know Cole?" Maggie asked, wondering what they were talking about in the driveway.

"Cole works at Harvest." Morgan blew out a breath. "He hates me."

"He doesn't hate you." Maggie shifted so she could look at her sister. "He was trying to keep you safe tonight."

"He thinks I don't belong with his friends. Like I'm such a loser I can't fit in with the popular crowd."

"The way he said it to me," Maggie explained, "was that he believes you're too smart to lower yourself to the standards of kids who only care about the next party."

"No way." Morgan laughed. "Cole would never have strung so many words together in one sentence."

"More or less." Maggie raised a brow. "You get the gist."

"I can take care of myself," Morgan said through clenched teeth. "I'm not a baby."

"No one thinks you are." Maggie ran a fingertip across Morgan's forehead, along the baby-fine strands at her hairline. Morgan used to love for Maggie to play with her hair. They'd snuggle in Maggie's bed late at night in the months after their mom had died. Morgan was only five, infinitely too young for that kind of loss.

"Why were you with Griffin tonight?" Morgan asked, her voice gentler than it had been earlier. Curious but not accusatory.

"We drove down to the coast. I'd spent the whole morning at the Pioneer Day Festival and wanted to get away for a bit."

"You left a town event?" One side of Morgan's mouth curved. "First the wedding and now you're skipping out on official duties. Who's the real rebel around here?"

Maggie was saved from answering when Griffin returned to the car.

"Everything okay with Cole?"

"He didn't do anything wrong," Morgan offered

from the back seat. "You don't need to be so hard on him."

"He told me he wants to change his reputation," Griffin said, shifting the SUV into Reverse. "So he should stay away from parties where the cops are going to be called."

"He was only there for a few minutes," Morgan argued. "He came in, pulled me out and we left."

Griffin flicked a pointed look at Maggie. "He mentioned that."

"Morgan, no more sneaking out."

"Tell Dad not to ground me."

"I can't." Maggie sighed. "He's the parent, and he's trying. Give him a little credit."

"It was one stupid test and she didn't give us a decent study guide. I don't even know if I'm going to go to college."

Maggie sat forward so abruptly the seat belt cut into the skin at the base of her neck. "Excuse me?"

"Just because it was your path," Morgan said, derision dripping from her voice, "doesn't mean it's mine. Ask Grammy. She'll be happy to tell you all the ways I pale in comparison to you. I have to find my own way."

"Okay," Maggie said slowly, ignoring the way her stomach lurched. They reached her father's house, and Griffin pulled into the driveway. "We can talk about that later. Go deal with Dad."

"Fine." Morgan gave another put-upon sigh. "Are you coming in?"

"Give me a minute."

"Thanks for the ride," she said to Griffin.

"You're welcome."

She opened the door and started to climb out. Then

she scooted back over to the center of the back seat. "Tonight wasn't Cole's fault. For real. Don't…like… fire him or anything, okay?"

Griffin nodded. "He still has a job at Harvest."

When Morgan closed the door, Maggie dropped her head into her hands. "What happened to our perfect night?"

"Too much adulting," Griffin said, reaching out to massage his fingers against the back of her neck.

"She's out of control," Maggie whispered.

"Only by your standards. In normal teenager land, she's doing great."

Maggie snorted. "Not go to college? Are you joking?"

"I didn't make it to college," Griffin reminded her.

"You're different. Do you think Morgan is going to join the army with her current path?"

"She's got nothing on me as a teen," Griffin answered immediately. "Probably not on Cole Maren, either."

"You were hard on him." Maggie undid her seat belt, rested a hand on Griffin's arm. He stiffened under her touch. "Why?"

He didn't answer for a moment, only lifted his hands in front of him like the answers to all of life's questions could be found in the lines on his palms.

"I know he comes from a troubled family," she continued. "But he seems like a good kid."

"He reminds me of me at that age, and that's not saying much." Griffin squeezed his hands into fists. "Would you have dated me when we were younger?" He laughed. "Don't answer that. You won't date me now, so there's no way I would have stood a chance back then."

She felt her mouth drop open. "You wouldn't have wanted a chance when we were in high school. I was three years younger for one thing, and not at all your type for another. Now is different. It's not about you, Griffin. You don't understand how things are in this town."

"An excuse and we both know it."

Maggie reached for the door, then stopped. Was he right? Was she using her position as mayor as a reason not to take a chance with Griffin? What would be so bad if she and Griffin were dating? Everyone thought she was horrible for walking away from her wedding and Trevor. How much worse could her reputation get at this point?

She realized with sudden clarity that her reputation was not the issue. She'd learned a painfully abrupt lesson in the past week. People would judge her no matter what, and she was sick of caring about the opinion of everyone around her. But what she did care about was having her heart well and truly broken.

Walking away from Trevor and taking the blame for ruining the wedding had been humiliating—but also brought a strange kind of relief. Griffin would be different. He was a man who truly had the ability to hurt her if she gave him the chance.

Could she trust him?

"I'm scared," she whispered, then blew out a breath as he took her hand in his. "I haven't been truly terrified of something for years."

"I'm not going to hurt you," he said like he could read her mind.

She turned to him, gazed into his green eyes, lit by the dashboard lights. The mix of vulnerability and hope there made her heart hammer in her chest. Griffin didn't let people in easily, and the fact that he seemed ready to lower his walls for her made her want to be brave for him in return.

"What if *I* hurt *you*?" she asked, her voice breathless.

He lifted her hand to his mouth, pressed a gentle kiss on each of her knuckles. Her skin tingled where his lips touched her. She wanted more. So much more. "I'll risk it."

Risk. That was the key word. There was no good return without taking a risk.

Maggie licked her lips, then leaned over and kissed Griffin. His mouth was soft yet firm against hers. She breathed in the scent of him, clean and spicy, and realized that everything about this moment felt right. Despite the crazy circumstances that led them here, she couldn't imagine being with anyone else in the world right now.

Griffin tilted his head, and she opened for him as he deepened the kiss. A moan rose in her throat, or maybe the sound came from him. It was difficult to know where she left off and he began. Her body was on fire, and she tried to move closer, wanting the feel of his body against hers. Wanting everything he could give her.

But the blasted man was in no hurry. He seemed content to savor her, trailing kisses across her jaw and nipping on her sensitive earlobe. She gave a little cry in response, and desire pooled low in her belly. Her body was alive in a way she'd never experienced. Griffin's kiss was everything.

He cupped her face in his hands, kissed her once more, then pulled away.

She shook her head, twining her arms around his neck. "Not enough," she whispered.

"Not nearly enough," he agreed but pulled away farther, circling her wrists with his fingers. "But we're in the driveway of your father's house. Anyone could walk by and see us."

She rolled her eyes. "It's after midnight."

"Your dad could come out."

"We're adults, Griffin. I'm not the one who was grounded tonight."

"I want to be respectful."

"Words I never expected to hear coming from you," she said with a laugh.

He smoothed his thumbs over the pulse points on the insides of her wrists, the touch at once tender and erotic. "I told you I've changed."

"Thank you again for tonight, both the date—" she emphasized the word, needing to reassure herself it was real "—and your help with tracking down Morgan."

"You're welcome," he told her. He glanced past her toward the house, his mouth quirking on one side. "Your dad is headed this way."

Maggie tugged her arms out of his grasp and automatically smoothed a hand through her hair. She opened the SUV's door just as her father reached the car.

"Everything okay?" he asked, glancing from her to Griffin with a raised brow. "Hey, Grif."

"Jim."

"It's fine." Maggie climbed out of the car.

"You two were out to dinner tonight?" Her father rubbed a hand over his face in a gesture that must have been universal for exasperated dads everywhere.

"We drove over to Lychen," Maggie told him. "I needed to get out of town."

Her father looked shocked. "That's a first. I didn't realize the two of you were friends."

"Thanks again, Griffin," Maggie said and quickly shut the door before her father could ask any questions. They stood in silence as Griffin pulled away, the red taillights disappearing around the corner at the end of the street.

"So, Griffin Stone," her dad murmured. "Seems like I'm too out of touch with both my daughters."

"You're doing fine," Maggie said, linking her arm with his. "Is Morgan in bed?"

Jim sighed and let her lead him back toward the house. "I took away her phone, so now she really hates me."

"I think that's normal at her age."

He held the front door for her. "You were never like that," he said as she passed through.

"I wasn't normal," she admitted.

"You didn't get to be because of your mom," he said quietly. "I'm sorry for that."

She turned and hugged him. "You did the best you could."

"You're sweet but we both know that's not true. I'm trying to do better now."

"Good." She pulled away. "I'm going up to bed."

"Do you want to talk about you and Griffin kissing in the driveway?"

Heat colored her cheeks and she shook her head. "Nope."

"I'll admit," her dad said with a laugh, "that's a relief. But I'm here if you need me. I love you, Mags."

"You, too, Dad." She walked up the stairs, and although everything in her life was uncertain at the moment, she felt more at peace than she had in ages.

Chapter Ten

The following Wednesday morning Griffin looked up from the piece of trim he'd just cut to find Trevor glaring at him.

"Come to lend a hand?" he asked, gesturing to the men lifting load-bearing wall beams into place. Marcus had lent him several laborers to help with demolition earlier in the week, and Griffin had hired a framing crew to handle the main structure.

It was too soon to make real predictions, but if work continued at this pace they'd have the tasting room open for the busy fall tourist season. With the valley painted in Mother Nature's finest palette and the lingering warm daytime temperatures and crisp nights, Stonecreek was always a popular destination in late September and early October.

"What are you doing with Maggie?" Trevor demanded, his gaze laser focused on Griffin.

Griffin set down the circular saw he'd been using, peeled off his leather gloves and wiped a hand over the sweat beading at his temple. "I don't suppose none of your business would suffice as an answer?"

"Half a dozen people have called or texted me to say that they saw the two of you together the past week looking quite chummy."

"Um…" Griffin tapped a finger on his chin. "I don't think of Maggie as a 'chum,' but whatever works for you, Trev."

"Nothing about this works for me," Trevor shouted, then closed his eyes and took an audible breath as the men working on the other side of the room stopped to stare.

"Let's walk outside," Griffin offered, not wanting to have this conversation with an audience. He didn't particularly care about Trevor's temper, but there was no doubt the Stone brothers arguing over Maggie Spencer would be hot news. Griffin wanted to avoid anything that might upset her.

This worrying about someone else's feelings was a new thing for him. Sure he'd cared about his army buddies. He would have gladly taken a bullet for any of them. Since retiring from the service, he'd made friends on construction sites across the Pacific Northwest. But Maggie was different. He didn't want anything to give her a reason to end what was happening between them.

He'd seen her only twice since their trip to Lychen— once for a quick dinner at the pizza place in town and then a picnic and hiking at Strouds Run State Park last night. The picnic had been her idea, mostly due to the attention they'd received in town. They'd taken a long walk through the park's trail system, then spread a blanket in a grassy meadow for a romantic dinner. But it wasn't enough for Griffin.

He wanted to spend more time together—he could imagine sharing every little thing that happened in his day with her. Another new phenomenon since he'd always thought of himself as a loner. But they'd talked on the phone each night, and just hearing her voice made him happy.

The exact opposite of how he felt facing his brother now.

"I thought your lunch was a coincidence," Trevor said, hands on his hips.

"It was."

"What about this week?"

Griffin shrugged. "Not a coincidence."

"So you're taking on my sloppy seconds?"

The words were no sooner out of Trevor's mouth than Griffin reached out and grabbed his brother's shirtfront, yanking him closer. "Don't talk about her that way. You said she didn't make you happy. Why does it bother you if I'm dating her?"

"Dating." Trevor jerked out of Griffin's hold. "Why doesn't it bother you that I had her first? Unless you're seriously trying to imitate my life."

"I won't do this with you anymore," Griffin answered, even though he wanted to go after Trevor with every fiber of his being. This is how it had always started with the two of them. Trevor goading Griffin into a reaction, and Griffin taking the bait every time. Then he'd be the one to look like the hot-tempered jerk for arguing or fighting or doing something stupid.

"What if I'd married her?" Trevor straightened the

collar of his shirt, color creeping up his neck. "Would you be lusting after my wife?"

"You *didn't* marry her."

A muscle ticked in Trevor's jaw. "This is going to hurt her chances for reelection. This town is everything to the Spencers."

"It won't," Griffin insisted, even though he had a suspicion Trevor was right. Their cousin Jason had called yesterday to simultaneously warn him away from Maggie and thank him for helping to cast more of a shadow on her reputation.

As much as he wanted to believe her personal life wouldn't have an effect on the community supporting her in the election, he wasn't that naive. Emotions always played a part in politics, and those in Stonecreek were running high against Maggie.

"Whatever you're playing at with her can't last," Trevor said, his tone cool.

Griffin kept his features placid, even though he felt his brother's words like a sharp right to the jaw.

"It's none of your business," Griffin muttered, hating that it was the best he could come up with. He wasn't one for long relationships, hadn't had a girlfriend for more than a few months at a time his whole life.

Yes, Maggie was different, but had he really changed that much?

"You already realize it." Trevor's smile was smug. "I knew this was some stupid game to get back at me."

"For what?" Griffin demanded, letting anger seep into his tone. "I left Stonecreek. I have a life beyond the family business. I got out from under Dad's thumb. Why would I want to get back at you?"

The smile vanished from Trevor's face as quickly as it had appeared. "Because he loved me," he answered before turning and walking away. He climbed into his Porsche and raced down the driveway, disappearing in a cloud of dust.

Bile rose in Griffin's throat, razor sharp and rancid. He swallowed against it, then paced to the edge of the hillside. Since he'd returned home, the vineyard felt like a sanctuary. He walked the rows of vines in the early mornings, sometimes on his own or sometimes with Marcus, who kept the same presunrise hours as Griffin did.

He loved the scent of the earth and watching the grapes begin to flower, the young shoots like buttons on the tips of the vines. He and Marcus spoke about the growing cycle, the climate, pests and the season's progression to the fruit set and beyond to harvesting. It calmed Griffin in a way nothing had in years to reconnect with the land that way.

In the space of a few minutes Trevor made him question everything about his life here. Were he and Maggie doomed from the start? Was he only trying to prove that his dad had been wrong about him for so many years? Was all of this a mistake?

He turned back to the tasting room, watching as workers made their ways in and out of the front of the building. It had seemed so easy—returning and becoming part of the business again. Marcus sought him out each day, asking his opinion on various viticultural practices. It was what Griffin had wanted growing up—to become an integral part of Harvest. Trevor's words reminded him he was an outsider even now.

Then Maggie appeared from around the corner, her gaze taking in the busy construction site as she walked.

She wore a fitted dress that just grazed her knees with a wide belt encircling her waist. Her hair was pulled back in a low ponytail, and his fingers itched to pull out the elastic that held it in place and watch it cascade over her shoulders. What he wanted more was to see it pool across his pillow, but he was determined to take things slow. She was skittish and he didn't want his shocking need for her to ruin things before they started.

Griffin had never considered himself much of a gentleman, but for her he wanted to make everything perfect.

He held up a hand and waved when she looked in his direction, and the smile that lit her face made his heart stammer.

He wanted to be a man who always deserved that smile.

"Hi," she said, her grin turning shy as she approached him. "I hope you don't mind a surprise visit." She glanced around, then reached up and brushed a quick, nervous kiss across his lips.

He felt the touch all the way to his toes.

"I'm always happy to see you." He wrapped his arms around her waist and pulled her close, chuckling when a couple of wolf whistles came from the men taking a break for lunch. "But I didn't think you were comfortable coming out here."

"I'm not," she admitted, her cheek resting against his chest. "I parked at the office and walked over here so I could hide in the trees if I saw your mom or Trevor."

"You don't need to hide from anyone." He dropped a kiss on the top of her head. "Especially not my mom."

"Liar," she whispered. "But thank you for saying that."

There was a note of sadness in her voice that made pain slice across his chest. "What's wrong?"

"Nothing."

He cupped her face in his palms and tipped up her head until she met his gaze. Tears swam in her eyes. "Liar," he said softly, swiping his thumbs across her cheeks.

She sniffed and flashed him a watery smile. "Is there someplace we could go and talk?" She looked over her shoulder. "Somewhere a little more private?"

He took her hand and led her down the flagstone staircase toward the vineyard. Soon they were surrounded on all sides by vines, with only the fertile earth below them and the cloudless sky above. It was like a maze, although Griffin knew his way through the rows of grapes as well as he knew his own smile.

As much as he resented his dad for withholding love from him for so many years, he could still appreciate what Dave Stone had built.

In the fields, more than any other place on earth, Griffin understood the meaning of the word *legacy*. He glanced down at Maggie, smiled at the look on her face—pure wonder. It was a gift to share this with her, and he could tell she appreciated it. He wouldn't give her up without a fight.

"Tell me you're not breaking up with me," he said, skimming his fingers over the grape leaves as they walked. "We've only been on three official dates, and I don't think lunch counts. We haven't gotten to the good stuff yet." He stopped and turned to face her, bending his knees so they were at eye level. "I have a feeling that with us the good stuff is going to be great."

"My grammy came to see me today," she said, tugging her lower lip between her teeth.

Griffin straightened. "That's a mood dampener."

"No doubt," Maggie agreed.

"Trevor confronted me at the work site a few minutes before you arrived. I'm guessing they conveyed similar messages."

She sucked in a breath. "I'm glad I missed him," she admitted.

"Tell me about your grandma."

"She told me I'm tarnishing my reputation beyond repair by seeing you so quickly after..."

"Trevor gave me a similar version of the same message." Griffin turned, unable to look at her. Unwilling to know if she was walking away. He plucked a bud from a vine and rolled it between his fingers. In a couple of months, they'd be working all hours to ensure the harvest went off without a hitch. Would he still be in Stonecreek when autumn rolled around?

He couldn't imagine leaving Maggie, but it might be too difficult to stay if they weren't together.

"Why is it selfish for me to want to be happy?"

"It's not selfish, Maggie May. It's human."

He felt her at his back a moment later, the heat of her body as she encircled his waist with her arms. "I've made this town my life," she said against the fabric of his shirt. "I don't regret it, but I want more."

He held his breath, waiting for her to continue.

"I want us, Griffin. It doesn't make sense, and the timing is horrible." She laughed softly. "Honestly, up until that moment when you carried me into my house, I could have sworn I hated you."

"You and a lot of people around here."

"You're a different man now."

"Am I?" He'd thought that but every run-in with his brother left Griffin feeling like the same hothead he'd always been.

Maggie released her hold on him and he turned. "Or you're the same man," she suggested, "only better."

"I'm trying."

He reached for her and she twined her arms around his neck, their kiss lighting his body on fire.

"I want you," he whispered when he could finally stand to drag his mouth away from hers.

She made a noise of agreement, soft and sexy, and he felt it all the way to his toes.

"How sad is it," she whispered against his throat, "that we both live with our parents?"

He chuckled. "It's an issue, but we have options. I don't want to rush you or what's between us, Maggie. You're too important to me."

She tipped back her head and gazed up at the sky above them. "It feels like we're in our own little world out here. I could get used to this."

"Me, too. Unfortunately, I have to head back to the construction site. The architect is stopping by this afternoon to tweak the plans." He wished they could hide out like this forever. "I have an idea. Can you get away Saturday for the whole day?"

"There's a campaign event in the morning," she answered. "But after that I'm free."

"I'll pick you up at noon," he said, dropping a kiss

on the tip of her nose. He laced his fingers with hers again and they headed for the end of the row.

"Where are we going?"

"It's a surprise."

She groaned. "You can't keep surprising someone who's a type A control freak. I need to know what to wear."

"Something I can take off you easily," he said, squeezing her fingers.

"Oh." She giggled. "Well, that's straightforward."

He glanced down at her, inordinately proud to put a smile on her face after her mood when she'd shown up at the vineyard. "You type A people like straightforward, right?"

"I like you," she whispered and he couldn't stop himself from kissing her again.

They made it to the top of the hill and rounded the corner of the tasting room building. A line of men stood just outside the front door, a few on their phones while the rest talked among themselves. "Does everyone take lunch at the same time?" Maggie asked.

"Not usually." A man Griffin didn't recognize approached them. "Griffin Stone?"

Griffin nodded. "What can I do for you?"

The man held out a single sheet of paper. "I'm shutting you down."

"Are you joking?" Griffin took the paper, scanned it and muttered a curse. "This is totally bogus."

"The building department doesn't see it that way." The man shrugged. "You can file an appeal downtown. Have a good day."

Anger and frustration roared through Griffin. "Did

you know about this?" he demanded, waving the paper in front of Maggie.

She looked from him to the man climbing into the Prius parked at the edge of the construction site. "Know what? Who was that?"

Griffin swore again. "I got a cease and desist by order of the town council." He pushed the paper toward her. "More specifically, it comes from the office of the mayor."

Maggie skimmed the two-paragraph letter that stated the Stones couldn't rebuild on a designated historic site without approval from the Stonecreek Historical Society. She looked up at Griffin. "Did you get the permit?"

He threw up his hands. "What permit?"

"The one referenced here from the historical society."

"I pulled a construction permit," he said, working hard not to grit his teeth. "As one does for a construction project. All this historic site business is nonsense. It's my family's property." He narrowed his eyes. "Did you know?"

She shook her head. "No, and I apologize for that. But you have to suspend work until it's resolved."

"You can't be serious."

"The town has rules, Griffin. Even your family has to follow them."

"This isn't about my family." He plucked the paper out of her fingers. "Look at the list of names on the historical society letterhead. Your grandmother and her friends. She's got it in for us."

Maggie opened her mouth, then snapped it shut

again. "That's not what it's about," she insisted, but there was no fight in her tone.

He shook his head, amazed at how quickly his blissful bubble from minutes earlier had popped. "I need to make some calls. I've got subcontractors ready to go, and if this holds us up for any length of time, it's going to throw the whole schedule out of whack."

"I'm sorry, Griffin." Maggie's voice was quiet, defeated.

He took a breath, then reached out a finger and traced it down her cheek, as always marveling at the softness of her skin. "We say that to each other far too often."

She gave a barely perceptible nod.

"Can I walk you to your car?"

"I'm fine. Go deal with the letter."

"I'll talk to you soon, Maggie May."

He waited until she'd disappeared around the side of the building before pulling out his phone. No matter what Maggie said, this had something to do with his last name and Vivian Spencer's need to control everything that happened in Stonecreek.

But Griffin wasn't going to let anyone tell him what to do any longer. He'd find a way to fix this and keep construction on track, even if meant making enemies out of every person in this town.

Chapter Eleven

"I don't have time for this today, Morgan."

Maggie stalked away from the principal's office at the high school, hands clenched at her sides, shooting daggers at her sister out of the corner of her eye.

Instead of contrition, Morgan glared right back. "You didn't have to come."

"Mr. Peterson called me when he couldn't reach Dad. Was I supposed to ignore it?"

"Dad obviously did."

"He's working in the studio." Maggie threw up her hands. "You know he doesn't bring a phone out there."

Morgan snorted. "Trust me. I know. He barely remembers to change clothes when he's deep in a project. It used to be embarrassing when I'd have friends come over. Now I don't bother."

Maggie pushed open the metal door that opened to

the school's front staircase. Clouds billowed across the sky, a summer storm imminent. She closed her eyes and concentrated on breathing in and out, trying to calm her already-frayed nerves.

"Why, Mo-mo?" she asked, turning to face her sister. "Summer school's not even in session. Mr. Peterson just happened to be here. If he hadn't, the janitor who found you might have called the police."

"It was a dare," Morgan mumbled.

"A dare." Maggie shook her head. "Who would dare you to spray paint the first-floor lockers?"

"Friends."

"Who are these so-called friends?"

"You don't know them."

"With antics like that I don't want to." Maggie reached out and tugged on the end of her sister's blue braid. "Why do you hang around people like that?"

"They're fun," Morgan answered, although she didn't sound convinced at the moment.

"Then maybe they'll join you for the fun of scrubbing the girls' locker room."

"I sprayed one letter," Morgan said, a whine in her voice. "I should have to clean one locker in return."

"Nice try." Maggie headed down the steps toward her car, which was parked in front of the school. "You're grounded anyway. You weren't supposed to leave the house."

"Dad didn't notice."

"He's working," Maggie insisted. "You can't fault him for the time he spends on his sculptures."

"Whatever."

"Is this about Mom? Do you need to talk to someone?"

Morgan's eyes darkened, mimicking the charcoal sky above them. "She's been gone for eleven years. Why would this have anything to do with her?"

"Because it's still hard to lose your mom, Mo-mo. That doesn't change. I know because I miss her all the time."

"It's not her," Morgan mumbled, but Maggie didn't believe her. She loved her sister so much but had no idea how to break through the attitude she'd taken to wearing like armor. Unfortunately, she also had other issues to deal with today.

Maggie waited until Morgan had climbed into the Volkswagen Jetta and fastened her seat belt. "Well, you've earned yourself a visit with Grammy," she said, hitting the button on the door locks.

"No way," Morgan said automatically. "You're going to send me to Grammy for punishment?"

Maggie backed the car out of the parking space, then headed through the empty lot and onto the road that led to the Miriam Inn. "Lucky for you, this is my business with her. I need to stop in at the weekly historical society meeting."

"Going to polish each other's golden crowns?" Morgan asked with a snicker.

"Not exactly."

It was only five minutes to the far side of Main Street where the hotel was situated. Maggie had been almost there when she'd received the call from Principal Peterson. She'd returned to her office after leaving the vineyard, pulling up meeting records from the town's computer database. She wanted to believe the cease and desist order Griffin received hadn't been a personal vendetta, but she had a difficult time finding any precedence for the historical society inserting it-self into any past remodeling projects in town.

Mostly the group was concerned with paint colors and preserving the Victorian-style homes that made up the downtown area.

Interference like she'd witnessed at Harvest was something new, and it made her temper spike to think her grandmother might be purposely thwarting the project that meant so much to Griffin.

She understood why Dave Stone would have ap-plied for historic designation. He'd been in the process of renovating the old building that housed the tasting room, and the grants available for a historic building would have gone a long way to fund the project.

"Are you mad at Grammy?" Morgan demanded as Maggie pulled to the curb in front of the inn. "Or is this still about me?"

"What?"

"To quote Ben, you look like you're ready to 'shank' someone."

"When did this family become so bloodthirsty?" She turned off the car, then flipped down the visor to check her appearance. Pale skin, wide, uncertain eyes, a slight tremble of her lips. All as expected. "You can stay here if you want," she told Morgan. "I'll roll down the windows so you get some fresh air."

"I'm coming with you. You look like you need backup."

Maggie sucked in a shaky breath. "Thanks, Mo."

They entered the Miriam Inn, with its muted, taste-ful walls and thick Aubusson carpet. A few people in the lobby looked up and waved politely. Normally, Maggie received a warm welcome, and the change stung but she was getting oddly used to not being the town's golden girl. It was liberating to just be herself and not have to worry about constantly keeping her perfect mask in place.

"Mary Margaret," her grandmother called as Maggie and Morgan entered the conference room down the hall from the lobby. "How lovely of you to stop by. We were discussing the upcoming debate."

"Hey, Grammy, great to see you," Morgan muttered under her breath. "It's like I'm invisible to her."

"I see you, Morgan," Vivian said, her tone slightly sharper. "You're difficult to miss with that hair." She sniffed and turned to the other people at the table. "I don't understand trends these days."

Maggie placed a supportive hand on Morgan's arm. "Your hair is lovely."

Morgan leaned over and whispered, "I'm supposed to be giving you support."

"We're getting to that part," Maggie assured her. "I need to talk to you," she said to their grandmother, then let her gaze travel around the table. "All of you."

"Sit down, dear." Vivian patted the empty seat next to her. "Would you like tea or a brownie? We were just discussing Joellyn George's recent house project."

The man seated across the table made a dismissive sound. "She painted it a garish red, like it's some kind of brothel or whatnot."

"That's why we approved the town's official color palette last year," Vivian assured him. "Maggie signed off on it as mayor so we're well within our rights to require Joellyn to repaint the house."

"Can we talk about those awful streamers she has draped across the front porch?" Lucy Winters asked, wrinkling her nose. Lucy was a few years younger than Vivian, and liked to think of herself as edgy because her left earlobe was double pierced. Her husband was Stonecreek's leading family practice doctor, which gave her a certain amount of clout in the community. "We should demand she remove those."

Morgan rolled her eyes. "They're Tibetan prayer flags."

"They're tacky," Lucy said.

The more Maggie thought about the town and how they'd been running it in the same way since practically the beginning of time, she realized how out of touch and provincial she'd allowed things to become around here. Stonecreek wasn't Mayberry and they weren't living in the fifties. She needed to start leading based on what she knew would be right for everyone, not just the small group of civic leaders who had control fisted in their collective hand.

A group, unfortunately, led by her grandmother.

"The flags stay," Maggie said, gripping the back of the chair in front of her. "As long as Joellyn wants them hanging. What she does on her porch is none of our business."

Her grandmother raised a brow as the other members of the historical society shifted in their chairs or busied themselves with the paperwork in front of them. "This is *our* town," Vivian countered. "We have a duty to uphold the standards people expect from Stonecreek."

Maggie shook her head. "The town belongs to everyone who lives here. Diversity—even in decorating porches—is a good thing, Grammy. We want people to feel welcome here."

"The right people," Henry Simon added.

Maggie leveled a look at him and said slowly, "All people."

"Verbal shank," Morgan whispered behind her. "Nice one."

"What's this about, Maggie?"

"I'm up for reelection this year," Maggie answered. "I need to make sure I'm representing the voters to the best of my ability."

"You need to be certain," her grandma insisted, "that you aren't making additional enemies around town. I've been doing my best to shore up the holes in your reputation, dear, but you aren't making it easy."

"This isn't about my personal life."

Grammy smiled. "It's always personal."

"Which brings us to the point of my visit." Maggie inclined her head. "I heard that you delivered a cease and desist letter to Harvest Vineyards."

"I didn't deliver it personally," Grammy said sweetly.

"We had Roger from the building department take it over," Lucy offered. "Seemed more official that way."

"You have no jurisdiction over the Stones' property."

Henry raised a gnarled finger. "We do, actually. Dave Stone applied for historic status on several of the structures about a year before he died. He wanted the tax breaks and funding that the state offers."

"The tasting room was included in that," Lucy added.

"I've been out there," Maggie said. "Griffin's renovation is fixing the damage from the fire and improving the space. They'll be able to do more events and wine tours. It'll be good for the economy."

"Good for Harvest's bottom line, you mean." Vivian pulled out a three-ring binder from the stack of papers in front of her. "Jana Stone has been talking to people about hosting wedding receptions."

"So what?"

"That will directly impact the reception room here."

"There are plenty of weddings to go around," Maggie insisted.

"You don't know that. These tours and wine groups you're talking about bring revenue to Harvest, not the town."

"They use local caterers to provide food."

"Have you seen the plans for the second phase of construction at the vineyard?" Vivian opened the binder and flipped through several pages. "She wants to open a farm-to-table restaurant and a series of cottages."

"None of that is bad." Maggie turned to her sister. "Have you heard anything in this conversation that sounds dire for the town?"

Morgan made a show of pulling a stick of gum from her purse, unwrapping it and then popping it into her mouth. "It all sounds great to me."

"It will give them too much power," Vivian said, while the others at the table nodded. "Jana Stone will throw her money around like some sort of benevolent goddess but it will all be on *her* terms."

"Like the grant for the community center," Lucy said, nodding enthusiastically. "I heard she's going to rescind the money until after the election and then give it only if Jason wins."

Vivian sighed. "That's what I'm talking about. Maggie, in a town like Stonecreek and a public office like the one you hold, there is no such thing as a personal life. If the Stones want to giveth and taketh away their largesse, we need to show them there can be consequences on both sides."

"We aren't the Mayberry mafia." Maggie thumped her hand on the back of the chair, feeling like she'd entered some sort of alternate universe where her grammy was playing the part of a mafiosa. "Has anyone talked to Jana?"

The historical society members, even her grandmother, shook their heads. "Where did you hear about her rescinding the grant money?"

Lucy sat forward. "My daughter's best friend heard it from someone in her mommy-and-me group who goes to yoga class with Jason Stone's wife."

"That's like a bad game of telephone. I'll call Jana."

"You can't call Jana," Lucy said quickly. "If you call, then she'll know we've been talking about her and—"

"That will give her the upper hand," Vivian finished.

"Your logic is ridiculous," Maggie muttered.

Her grandmother pointed. "Watch your tone, young lady."

"Grammy, I'm sorry. This is silly. You need to tell Griffin he can go back to work on the tasting room."

"We have rules," Henry explained.

"You gave us this power," Vivian reminded her.

"Then I'll find a way to take it back. It's not right."

Lucy mumbled something under her breath.

"Oh, man," Morgan whispered.

Maggie leaned forward, zeroing her gaze on the petite woman. "What did you say?"

"I don't think any of this would be an issue if you'd

married Trevor." Lucy threw up her hands when Grammy groaned. "Don't act like that, Vivi. We all know it's true. Now she's cavorting with the other one and no one knows what to think."

"You don't have to *think* anything," Maggie said through clenched teeth. "It's my private life."

"The order has been delivered," her grandmother said, making it clear from her tone that this was the end of the conversation.

Maggie felt her mouth drop open. She was the mayor of Stonecreek yet here she was being dismissed like a child at the grown-up dinner table. She wanted to scream, but that wasn't done with her grandmother.

She owed Grammy respect and loved her more than words, but she wasn't going to be a puppet for anyone— even the woman who meant the most to her in the world.

"Is there something else you need from us, Maggie?"

"No," she said then turned and stalked away without another word.

That afternoon Brenna walked into the crowded coffee shop, scanning the tables until she found Maggie at one of the booths in the back.

With a deep breath, she moved forward, hands clasped tightly in front of her stomach. Maggie's text had been cryptic.

I need to see you. Cuppa Joe at 1.

Brenna hadn't hesitated. She'd left a note on her computer at the Harvest office saying she was taking a late lunch and driven toward downtown Stonecreek.

Although now she wasn't sure if meeting Maggie in such a public location was a good idea. She could have decided to publicly humiliate Brenna the way she'd been embarrassed at suddenly learning of Trevor's cheating.

Brenna shook her head. It didn't matter. As Marcus regularly reminded her, she'd made a mistake. That didn't make her a horrible person.

"Hey," she said, sliding into the booth.

"Did you order a cappuccino?" Maggie asked, scowling at Brenna's empty hands.

"I'm too nervous for caffeine," Brenna said with a shaky laugh. "I'll get something after."

"Nervous?"

"Your summons was kind of abrupt," Brenna admitted.

Maggie sighed and pressed two fingers to her temple. "I'm sorry. I'm upset, but it has nothing to do with you. I just needed a friend and…"

"You called me?" Brenna felt her mouth widen into a huge grin. "That's so great."

"That I'm upset?" Maggie asked with a wry smile.

"Stop. I'm so glad you called me. You never have to apologize for anything. After what I did—"

Maggie held up a hand. "I get that you regret not telling me, but I don't want to keep reliving that moment, okay? I feel like that day is going to haunt me for the rest of my life."

"I understand." Maybe Marcus was right and things would work out in the end. It was odd how quickly he'd become an integral part of her life. Between seeing him at the office, and the time he spent with her and Ellie, the soft-spoken vintner filled a hole in her heart she didn't even realize was there.

Now to have Maggie back… Well, Brenna couldn't remember a time she'd felt so happy. But she focused on her friend, noting Maggie's red-rimmed eyes and pasty complexion. "What's going on, sweetie?"

"Am I a pushover?" Maggie asked.

"No," Brenna answered automatically, mainly because she knew that was what her friend wanted to hear.

"Are you sure?"

Brenna thought about some of the late-night conversations she'd had with Marcus. He was always supportive when she talked about her worries and fears, but he never coddled her. Sometimes his straightforward opinion was tough to hear, but she appreciated the honesty.

"You can be," she admitted, then quickly added, "It's because you try to make everyone happy."

"Everyone but myself," Maggie said quietly. She thumped her head against the table. "How did I let this happen?"

"You haven't done anything wrong." Brenna reached out a hand to stroke the back of Maggie's head. "You're a good person. This town respects you."

"Do people think I'm a mouthpiece for my grandma or my family in general?" Maggie lifted her head, narrowing her eyes. "That the only thing I care about is advancing my family?"

"They know it's not the *only* thing you care about." Brenna broke off a corner of the scone on Maggie's plate and popped it into her mouth.

"Have the rest." Maggie pushed the plate forward. "I'm too sick of myself to eat."

"Where is this coming from? I don't think it's been a secret that you support your family. The Spencers are an institution around here. You're not a mouthpiece as much as a spokesperson."

Maggie shook her head. "I'm everyone's mayor. I'm supposed to represent *all* the town, not just my little slice of it."

"You do."

"What about the Stones?"

Brenna made a face. "That's more complicated." She plucked another bite of scone. "Is the rumor about you and Griffin true?"

"Where'd you hear it?"

"Come on. This is Stonecreek. Where haven't I heard it?"

"It's new and we've been keeping a low profile," Maggie said. "I didn't mean for it to happen."

"I know how that goes." She shook her head when Maggie blinked. "Forget I said anything. This is about you."

"Distract me. Make it about you instead."

Maggie split the remaining scone in half and took a big bite. Brenna didn't want to talk about Marcus, but Maggie seemed genuinely interested and at least she was eating.

"I've been hanging out with Marcus Sanchez a little." She raised her brows. "More like a lot."

Maggie's eyes widened, clearly in shock, before she schooled her features. "He's a great guy."

"You think he's too good for me." Brenna wiped

her hands on a napkin, the pastry sitting like a brick in her stomach.

"Not at all," Maggie said quickly, "but he's not exactly your type."

"We're friends. Nothing else has happened. We talk, and Ellie loves him."

"You've introduced him to Ellie?"

"Yes. Is that bad? I know I usually shield her from the men I'm dating...but I'm not really dating Marcus."

"But you want to," Maggie suggested.

"Like I said, he's too good for me."

"He's perfect." Maggie reached forward and took Brenna's hands. "You deserve someone like him in your life."

"You're a great mayor." Brenna squeezed her friend's fingers. "Not because of your grandma but because you're smart and hardworking and you care about this town. If you want to start doing things differently, that's your choice. No one else's."

"I've missed you," Maggie said quietly.

"Me, too."

Her phone buzzed and she quickly pulled it out of her purse. "It's Ellie's school."

"Go ahead," Maggie said, sitting back against the booth.

Brenna held the phone up to her ear and answered.

"Brenna," the voice on the other end of the line said, "it's Denise in the front office. Ellie got sick on the way to music class a few minutes ago. She's with the nurse and isn't feeling too good."

"I'll be right there," Brenna answered, already moving out of the booth. "Thanks for the call." She hit the end-call button. "I hate to cut this short but Ellie threw up at school."

"Oh, no. Poor thing. Puking at school is the worst." Maggie scooted out of the booth as well, and gave Brenna a quick hug. "I'll call you later to check on her."

"Don't doubt yourself," Brenna told her friend. "You've got this."

Maggie flashed a grateful smile. "We both do."

Brenna could only hope that was true.

Chapter Twelve

"Griffin's not here."

Maggie shielded her eyes against the afternoon sun as she approached the rustic farmhouse on the Harvest Vineyards property. The front of the home was cast in shadow, but she saw a figure rise from a chair on the far end of the porch.

"He went into town," Jana continued, "to meet with Roger at the building department and try to straighten out the mess your vindictive grandmother and her group of cronies left us in."

"I'm here to talk to *you*," Maggie said simply, deciding it best to ignore the comment about her grammy.

Jana walked to the top of the porch steps. "And which one of my sons do you want to talk about?" she asked, her tone crisp and a little tart, like the first bite of a fall apple.

"I'd like to speak to you regarding your grant for the community center."

"Ah. Of course." Jana sniffed as if she'd just taken a whiff of something unpleasant. "Priorities and all that."

Claws out, Maggie thought. Good to know going in. She and her former mother-in-law-to-be had never been particularly close. Maggie had gotten the impression Jana didn't approve of her, although she couldn't have been certain of the reason. Trevor told her she was being paranoid, and while Jana was never outright rude, she kept her distance no matter how much Maggie tried to connect with her.

Clearly, Jana no longer felt the need to keep up the pretense of civility. So be it. Maggie knew now she could deal with much worse.

"Do you have a few minutes?"

Jana inclined her head and leveled Maggie with a stare that weeks ago would have made her knees knock. Lately she'd become rather skilled at tolerating glares.

"If now doesn't work, we could set up a time next week. Either here or at my office."

"Now is fine."

Maggie followed Jana to the cozy seating area at the far end of the porch. A wrought iron love seat with thick cushions was arranged next to two wicker chairs and an iron table in the middle.

"Would you like a glass of iced tea?" Jana asked, polite but cool.

"No, thanks." Maggie lowered herself into one of the chairs as Jana took a seat on the love seat. She took a deep breath and said, "First, I wanted to apologize to you for the trouble you went through with the wine for the wedding. I'm sure you were upset that—"

"The wine is nothing," Jana interrupted with a wave of her hand, "compared to how I felt about my son being left at the altar."

"Of course," Maggie agreed automatically. Her decision to take the blame for calling off the wedding was destined to haunt her for all eternity. "I'm sorry for that, too."

"Trevor insists it wasn't your fault. Griffin is even more adamant."

Maggie kept her features schooled. "Trevor and I made the decision together."

"It's like there's something both my boys know but aren't telling me."

"I'm sorry," Maggie said slowly, trying to figure out how to avoid revealing too much, "for any pain and embarrassment this caused you. It wasn't my intention."

"Truly?" Jana asked almost absently. "Part of me wondered if the last-minute cancellation had been some overarching scheme to humiliate my family."

"No," Maggie breathed.

"I wouldn't put it past your grandmother." Jana's tone was scathing.

Maggie opened her mouth to argue, then snapped it shut again. She thought for a moment about how to answer. "I look like a heartless witch in all this. Grammy is probably as angry with me as you are."

"I doubt it," Jana said but laughed softly. "I want my son to be happy. Both of my sons."

Maggie nodded. "You're a good mother. They're lucky to have you."

"Thank you," Jana said, her tone gentler. "How are Morgan and Ben?"

"I thought they were fine," Maggie admitted with a

sigh. "Turns out raising teenagers is harder than I remember from when I was one."

"You were different, even before your mom died, but especially after. An old soul."

"I've heard that before." Maggie smiled. "I think it's another way of saying a boring fuddy-duddy."

"Not at all." Jana picked at a loose string on one of the cushions. "Your father's doing well? I don't see him around town often."

"He's working a lot lately. He gets pretty focused when he's sculpting."

"I remember," Jana agreed, and something flashed in her eyes, a mix of affection and understanding that had Maggie's brow furrowing. She didn't realize Jana Stone knew her father well enough to understand his idiosyncrasies.

"Were you and my dad friends growing up?"

"Of a sort," Jana said. "My family moved here when I was in high school. Jim was one of the first people I met." She closed her eyes for a moment, and when she opened them again all the emotion Maggie had seen moments earlier was gone. "So you'd like to talk about the money for the community center?"

Maggie swallowed. Apparently, the small talk portion of the visit had ended. "Is it true that you're thinking of rescinding the donation?"

"I wouldn't call it rescinding when I've yet to write a check."

"You made a verbal commitment."

Jana held up one finger. "Actually, Trevor suggested I make the donation. I never officially agreed."

"We had an understanding," Maggie insisted.

"Yes, you did," Jana agreed, and Maggie imagined

if the smooth, cool, slithery feel of a snake could be translated into a tone of voice, it would sound just like Jana Stone at the moment.

"So this is personal?" She worked to keep her voice neutral.

"Everything's personal, Maggie." Jana sounded a lot like her grandmother. "The truth is I was never convinced about the need for my money based on how it was going to be used. You know it's only been recently our family has had the financial resources to make a significant contribution to this community?"

Maggie nodded.

"I realize my support is a bit of a hot commodity now, but refurbishing a building that's only ten years old seems frivolous when there are services that could be enhanced. Trevor believed it was an important goodwill gesture—an olive branch between the Stones and the Spencers." She quirked a brow. "Although I'm not sure why it was ever my responsibility in the first place. I'm not trying to be difficult, but I don't think it's a good use of the funds."

"I agree," Maggie said quietly.

"You do?" Jana asked, clearly not believing the words.

"Yes," Maggie continued. "I've thought more about the project." She paused, then added, "I've been thinking about a lot of things recently that have been ignored for too long. Stonecreek has needs, but a decorating project isn't one of them. I'm mayor of the town, not a specific cross section of our residents. Did you know that over seventy percent of Stonecreek Elementary students are home alone after school?"

Jana shook her head.

"I'd like to do something real and meaningful to help our kids. A program that would bring people together, no matter their background or age or socio-economic status."

"What did you have in mind?" Jana leaned forward, uncrossing her legs.

"A youth development program. I was thinking we could utilize the community center as a central location to provide mentoring, arts and athletic activities. Open to anyone but with an emphasis on recruiting kids who'd be without supervision otherwise."

"That isn't what your grandma had in mind."

"She's not the one who was voted mayor," Maggie countered.

Jana studied her for another moment. "True."

"I don't have the resources to do this on my own," Maggie admitted. "Either financially or in manpower. I was hoping if it appealed to you, that you'd be willing to head up a youth development committee."

"You want me in charge of it?" Jana looked incredulous.

"If you have time." Maggie nodded. "And you're interested."

"I'm interested," Jana said. "But I'm not going to jump through a bunch of bogus hoops because of my last name."

"You won't have to," Maggie promised.

"I won't be able to get started until Griffin straightens things out on the tasting room. That project needs to stay on track."

"I'll do my best to make sure it does."

They both looked up at the sound of a vehicle pulling up the driveway. Butterflies fluttered across Maggie's stomach as Griffin's Land Cruiser came into view.

"He's been happy since he came back to Stonecreek," Jana said, rising from the love seat. "Different than he was before, more at peace."

"Um, that's good." Maggie stood as well, smoothing a hand over the front of her dress.

"I think you have something to do with the change in him."

Maggie turned toward Jana. "Really?" She wasn't sure whether she was more shocked to hear the words or the fact that they were coming out of Jana's mouth.

"I don't think it comes as a surprise that I never approved of you and Trevor together."

Maggie gave a soft chuckle. "He told me I was imagining it."

"I love both my boys." Jana fingered the delicate gold chain around her neck. "I try to let them make their own decisions, even when I believe they're making a mistake."

"It would have been a mistake for Trevor and me to marry," Maggie murmured. She'd known it for some time but somehow knowing Jana agreed gave her a sense of comfort.

"You're tied to this town in a way he isn't. In a way I don't believe he wants to be, even if he doesn't see it yet. Griffin is different." She held up a hand to wave as Griffin parked and climbed out of the SUV.

Maggie mimicked the gesture, smiling at the shocked look on his face as he took in the two of them together.

"Griffin hasn't lived in Stonecreek for almost a decade," Maggie pointed out gently.

"But it's still his home." Jana placed a hand on Maggie's arm. "It always will be. He belongs here, but he needs us to help him understand that."

Maggie nodded, trying not to look as shocked as she felt. "I'll try."

"How did it go in town?" Jana asked Griffin as he walked up the porch steps.

"I spoke with the guys down at the building department." He gave his mother a quick hug, then glanced over at Maggie. "What are you doing here?"

Not exactly a warm and fuzzy greeting, but Maggie smiled anyway. "I came to see your mother."

One thick brow rose.

"We had a lovely talk," Jana said, patting his shoulder. "I have a few phone calls to make now. Email me some of your initial thoughts on the youth program, Maggie."

"I will," Maggie promised. "Thank you."

The front door clicked shut behind Jana, and Maggie met Griffin's questioning gaze with a shrug. "I'm not going to apologize again, because we say those words too often. But I will do everything I can to make sure the historical society approves your permit."

"Roger told me you'd already talked to him about how to push it through."

She nodded. "I wish I could just make it disappear but—"

"It's okay." Griffin stepped forward, laced his fingers with hers and drew her closer. "And hopefully this will be the last time I say the words for a long time, but I'm sorry, Maggie. I should have known you didn't know about the order. This isn't your fault. I'm a big boy, and I'll manage through whatever roadblocks your grandma and her geriatric posse want to throw in the way."

"You shouldn't have to," she insisted with a sigh. "I'm the mayor. This is my town now, and I have to start managing things like I believe that's true." She reached up and kissed the side of his jaw. "You're helping me do that, and I'm grateful, Griffin."

"How grateful?" He nuzzled the side of her neck, sending sparks racing along her skin.

"Grateful enough that I need to change our plans for this weekend."

He stilled. "I'm having trouble following that train of thought, and it's not because I'm distracted by how good you smell."

"It's a surprise," she told him, her voice breathless as he made a show of sniffing her neck. "But pack an overnight bag."

He pulled back, his gaze filled with banked desire as he stared down at her. "I really like the sound of that."

When the doorbell buzzed for a third time, Brenna finally managed to drag herself off the couch to answer it. She wouldn't have been able to manage moving if she hadn't been worried the sound would wake Ellie.

After a day and a half, her daughter was on the mend from her stomach bug. Ellie had eaten some soup and dry toast earlier, although Brenna couldn't say the same for herself.

She'd woken up at 2:00 a.m. last night with the same violently upset stomach that had plagued Ellie. She'd thought there was nothing worse than her daughter being sick, but the two of them feeling awful at the same time had upped the ante tenfold.

She wiped the back of her hand across her mouth as she pulled open the door.

"Brenna?"

"Oh, Lord, no," she whispered as another wave of nausea turned in her belly.

"Are you okay?" Marcus stood on the small stoop in front of her duplex, a bouquet of flowers in one hand. "I know you called in sick today, but I got worried when you didn't answer my calls or texts and—"

"I'm going to puke," she told him, then turned and rushed toward the bathroom. After the nausea subsided, she emerged, shocked to see Marcus in her kitchen, quietly unloading the dishwasher.

"You look like death warmed over," he told her, and she didn't even bat an eye. She felt worse than death at the moment. "Go to bed. I've got things under control."

"You can't be here." She tugged on the hem of her faded sweatshirt. "We're sick."

"I see that," he agreed. "Ellie told me she's feeling better. I'm going to heat up soup for her when I'm finished here."

Tears pricked the backs of Brenna's eyes, a mix of gratitude and embarrassment. She never let anyone see her unless she was showered, with her hair fixed and makeup applied.

"I'm a mom," she said weakly. "I don't need to rest."

"Go rest anyway." He moved toward her, but she backed away when he would have touched her.

"You can't see me like this." She smoothed a hand over her stringy hair, then cringed.

"Too late." His smile was tender. "Rest, Brenna. Let me help you."

She wanted to argue, to tell him that she could

handle her own life, even with a raging stomach bug. She'd learned not to depend on anyone but herself. Men like Marcus didn't want to play nursemaid. Yes, they'd gotten to know each other recently, but Brenna had made sure the house was clean, Ellie on her best behavior and everything else easy and smooth whenever he'd visited.

She didn't want to scare him off by making him think she was too much trouble. Tossing her cookies every twenty minutes would definitely fall under the category of too much trouble.

Yet Marcus didn't look scared right now. He only seemed concerned and determined to make sure she got to bed. Too tired to put up any sort of real argument, she turned and headed down the hall toward her bedroom. She stopped at Ellie's door and peeked her head in the room.

Her daughter was on the floor with her favorite coloring book.

"Sweetie, I'm going to rest for just a few minutes," Brenna said. "Is it okay if Marcus is here with you?"

Ellie nodded but didn't look up from her coloring. "We're going to play Candy Land after I have soup."

"Marcus is doing Mommy a big favor while my tummy hurts. If he needs to work or just wants to watch television, you and I can play a game later, okay?"

"He said he wants to play," Ellie answered simply.

Brenna pressed two fingers to her temple and sighed. Oh, to be young and unaware that she wasn't everyone's top priority. Had Brenna ever felt that way? She'd always had the uncomfortable awareness of being a burden to her single mother. She was proud of herself for always putting Ellie first, but she also knew it could be a heartbreaking lesson to realize not everyone felt that way.

"I know, baby," she said, keeping her voice quiet. She certainly didn't want Marcus guilted into an evening of board games. "But grown-ups sometimes have to work even when they don't want to."

Ellie paused and looked up. "Feel better, Mommy," she said, and Brenna would have laughed at being summarily dismissed if she wasn't so looking forward to collapsing in her bed.

She crawled under the sheets in the darkened room, knowing she'd only get a few minutes of rest before the next round of nausea hit.

But when she opened her eyes, light slanted through the blinds over her windows and she felt weak but no longer ill.

Yelping as she glanced at the clock on the nightstand, she stumbled from the bed and down the hall, following the scent of something sweet baking in the kitchen.

"Ellie?"

"We made muffins, Mommy," her daughter announced. "Do you want one or are you still pukey?"

"I'm so sorry," Brenna said to Marcus, who was now loading dishes from the sink into the dishwasher. Seriously, what kind of superhuman man would both load and unload the dishwasher without being asked? "Why didn't you wake me?"

He shrugged, looking almost embarrassed. "I thought you needed some rest. How are you feeling?"

"Do you want a muffin?" Ellie asked again.

"Maybe later, sweetie." Brenna bent and kissed the top of her daughter's head.

"You stayed here all night," Brenna told Marcus as if he didn't realize it.

"The couch isn't bad." His mouth curved into a half smile. "Would you like toast or soup? A glass of water?" He frowned as his gaze focused on a section of her hair. "A shower?"

"I have dried vomit on me," she muttered without raising her fingers to her head. Mortification heated her cheeks.

"A little," he confirmed. "But you look like you're feeling better."

She crossed her arms over her chest. "Less like death warmed over?"

"You were beautiful even then."

She laughed. "How are you this perfect and still single?"

He inclined his head, the sudden intensity of his dark gaze making her knees go weak. "Maybe I was waiting for you to notice me."

She swallowed, her throat raw. "I'm going to shower now," she whispered. "Probably a cold one for good measure."

He grinned like her response made him happy. Like she made him happy, even with dark circles under her eyes and puke in her hair. The thought of someone—a man—caring about her no matter what made her ridiculously happy. She wondered if she could be brave enough to trust that happiness.

Griffin slung the duffel bag over his shoulder and headed out the door of the caretaker's apartment over the barn on the Harvest property when he heard the car door slam late Saturday morning.

He wasn't sure what Maggie had planned, but he couldn't wait to spend the day, and particularly the night, with her. The rest of the week had brought a mix of frustration and promise for Griffin. The meeting with the historical society had been moved to Monday, so he'd get an answer on going forward with the tasting room project at that time.

He'd filled out paperwork and submitted an addendum to his plans detailing how the renovation fitted within the society's guidelines. Roger at the building department assured him the vote was just a formality. Maggie told him the same thing, but Griffin still didn't trust that the members of the committee, led by her grandmother, wouldn't try to stick it to him just because of his last name. No matter. Griffin was a fighter, and this was one battle he didn't plan to lose.

He'd coordinated his subcontractors and gotten them to agree to an accelerated timeline so that even with almost a week delay, he could still finish the project on time and under budget.

When he hadn't been refining his construction plans, he'd spent the past few days with Marcus Sanchez, getting caught up on the current business model and the plans for grafting a few of their most popular vines to create a new vintage. But now he was looking forward to thinking of nothing but Maggie for a while.

Instead of finding her waiting to greet him, he found Trevor leaning against his shiny black Porsche convertible, hands shoved in pockets, staring at the front of the old barn.

"Remember when Dad tried to be a goat farmer?"

The question surprised a chuckle out of Griffin. "Yeah. He bought a pair," he answered. "But Grandpa still had this place and wouldn't let him keep the goats here so Dad brought them home."

Trevor straightened, stretching his arms overhead. "I thought Mom was going to kill us when they got in through the back door."

"That you left open," Griffin reminded him. "Even though I got blamed."

"You're the one who poured them a big bowl of Frosted Flakes."

"Whatever," Griffin muttered but laughed again. "You were a suck-up."

"A skill you evidently never learned," Trevor said. "Vivian Spencer is going to fight you on the permit."

"I imagine that makes you giddy. If I can't get approval for the original building with its historic status, you get to start on your new shiny monstrosity."

"It's called progress," Trevor said.

"Why do we have to compete?" Griffin asked. "I've been talking to Marcus the past couple of days. Harvest is carving out a niche as a leader in sustainable wine making. If we grow too big too fast, we'll lose some of the control we have over best practices."

Trevor thumped a palm on his forehead. "You sound just like him. This isn't what Dad wanted, Grif. He had a vision of making Harvest the biggest player in the Pacific Northwest."

"Did he?" Griffin walked a few paces to the edge of the hillside, where he could see the original estate vineyard below, the rows neat and green in the hazy sunlight of late morning. "I know I haven't been around for a while, but the way I remember it, Dad was all about his legacy and reputation, not how many barrels we produced each year."

"It's one and the same," Trevor argued.

"We both know that's not true."

"You don't know." Trevor stalked forward until he was standing shoulder to shoulder with Griffin. "You say you don't want control, but everything has to be your way."

"I'm listening to what Marcus tells me. He's the CEO, Trevor."

Trevor snorted. "A mistake on Mom's part."

"Did you stop by to gloat about my troubles with the historical society?" Griffin asked casually. "Or was there something else?"

At that moment another car came up the gravel drive that led to the barn. Trevor's eyes narrowed at the sight of Maggie's compact Volkswagen.

He let out a harsh breath. "Believe it or not, I stopped by to see if you wanted to head out on a bike ride for the day. My gear is at Mom's, but I see you have plans."

Unfamiliar guilt ripped through Griffin. Long mountain bike rides on the nearby trails had been one of the few ways he and Trevor had bonded when they were teens. He hadn't returned to Stonecreek to make an enemy of his brother.

Trevor had hurt Maggie, but if he'd been a better man… Griffin didn't want to think about that. "How about next weekend?" he suggested.

Trevor nodded. "Yeah, next weekend."

He moved toward the Porsche just as Maggie stepped out of her car. "Hi, Trevor," she said, and Griffin heard the slight tremble in her voice. "How are you?"

"Great," Trevor answered coolly. "Never better. You?"

She shrugged. "It's been a rough couple of weeks.

I guess people only appreciate a runaway bride when Julia Roberts is playing the part."

Griffin watched emotions play across his brother's features—anger, resentment and then finally guilt. As if for a few moments Trevor had forgotten the reason Maggie walked away—the reason no one else knew and the fact that Trevor was to blame for it.

"I know it's not fair," Trevor offered.

"They'll get over it eventually," she told him, her hands gripping her keys so hard her knuckles had gone white. "I hope things won't be weird between us forever. We've been friends a long time, you know?"

"You're dating my brother," Trevor said as if that explained everything.

"You kissed another woman the morning of our wedding." Although Maggie's voice was calm, it was clear from Trevor's reaction that the words hit their mark.

"I'm sorry," he whispered, and the flash of pain in Maggie's gaze made an answering ache rise in Griffin's chest.

"I wish you would have just told me you didn't want to go through with it."

"I didn't want to disappoint you."

One side of Maggie's mouth curved. "I'm not spending time with Griffin to hurt you, Trev. We've made our choices and there are consequences for both of us."

Trevor turned so his back was fully to Griffin. "I hate seeing the two of you together," he said to Maggie. Although spoken softly, the words carried through the quiet morning.

Griffin's gut twisted as she nodded. "I know, but you'll get over it. We need you to be okay with this so that everyone else accepts it. You'll do that for me. Right?"

Trevor didn't answer for several moments and Griffin would have given anything to read his brother's expression. "Yeah, I'll get over it. We're friends, Mags. No matter what."

"I hope you two aren't going to hug it out," Griffin called, unable to stay silent any longer.

Trevor looked back over his shoulder. "It's tempting just to see your reaction."

"No, it's not," Maggie said, giving Trevor a playful slap on the arm.

"Have a good time today," Trevor told Maggie, then inclined his head toward Griffin. "Both of you."

He got in his car and backed down the driveway. Maggie waited until the Porsche disappeared down the hill before approaching Griffin. "I'm glad I had a chance to talk to him."

"That was horrible." Griffin ran a hand through his hair. "I'm sick of him playing the victim. I'd like to kick his—"

"No more about your brother." Maggie lifted onto her toes and kissed him lightly. Griffin felt the tension knotted in his shoulders release as a result. "Are you ready for the best date of your life?"

"You're confident," he murmured. "I like it."

She scrunched up her nose. "Fake it until you make it," she admitted. "I'm actually nervous that you'll be bored out of your mind."

"Never with the two of us," he assured her. There was more he wanted to say. His heart pounded against his ribs as he thought of how much Maggie had come to mean to him in such a short time. He'd never expected to feel this happy and content in Stonecreek, like he really belonged here.

So much of that had to do with the woman in front of him. She made everything better. But he couldn't reveal the depth of his emotions so soon, especially when the dust had barely settled on his brother's exit from the picture. He'd scare her off, and that was the last thing he wanted to do.

Her brows lowered as she gazed up at him. "Are you sure?" she asked quietly. "You seem different right now."

"I'm good." He picked up his duffel bag and slung it over his shoulder. "And once it's just the two of us, I'll be even better."

Chapter Thirteen

The longer Maggie drove, the more her nerves took over. A few days ago the idea to surprise Griffin with a night away had seemed perfect, but now she worried that he'd find her plan boring and stupid.

"I forgot how gorgeous this part of the state is." Griffin leaned forward to look out the front window at the old-growth forest, with branches forming an archway over the two-lane road they'd turned on about twenty minutes earlier. "But I'm curious as to what we're doing out here."

They'd driven south from Stonecreek to the Ore Creek Wilderness area, which was made up of dense forests, wide canyons and quirky spires of native rock formations.

She slowed as a mailbox came into view and she turned up a winding driveway. "We don't have to stay down here," she offered. "If you'd rather head to the city and do something more adventurous, that's fine, too."

"More adventurous than what?" he asked with a soft laugh. "Remember, I don't know where we're headed."

"Here." Maggie pointed to the rustic cabin situated in a clearing ahead of them. She pulled to a stop in the gravel driveway but left the car running. "The property belongs to the family of one of my college roommates. We used to come down here on weekends to chill. I called and asked her if I could use it for the night." She gave him a hopeful smile. "I thought we could both use some time away."

"Is that a lake in the back?"

Maggie nodded. "There's a dock with canoes and hiking trails. They have twenty acres so the nearest neighbor is on the other side of the water. But there's no internet or cell service. They don't even have a TV, unless something's changed from the last time I was here. Clearly, I was a loser even in college, because while other people were at frat parties or the bars, we'd come here and play Scrabble all weekend. You probably expected something exciting like skydiving or—"

"I love Scrabble," Griffin said.

Maggie felt her smile widen. "No way. You're saying that to make me feel better."

"I once won with the word *umiak*." He spelled out the letters for her and she laughed.

"That's not a real word."

"Look it up." He arched a brow, looking wholly self-satisfied. "It's an Eskimo canoe."

"The former bad boy of Stonecreek is now a word

nerd?" Delight rushed through her as pink tinged his cheeks. "You're blushing."

"I'm not blushing." Griffin scoffed. "I don't blush."

"But—"

He pressed one finger to her lips, the touch warm and gentle. "We had an unofficial Scrabble club at one of the bases. So I'm a manly man who happens to appreciate Scrabble strategy." He leaned over the console and replaced his finger with his mouth, the kiss long and sweet like he had all the time in the world to savor her. Maybe not all the time, but all day and night, which, to Maggie, was a wonderful thing.

"It's okay that my big surprise is a quiet night at a remote cabin?"

"Sweetheart," he whispered against her lips, "the only person I want to see is you so this is perfect."

She gave a little squeal of happiness. Now that she knew he was on board with her plan, Maggie couldn't wait to show him around the property.

"What should we do first?" she asked, pulling the keys out of the ignition. "We could hike or take out the canoes. They keep fishing poles in the shed out back and there used to be a hammock between two fir trees overlooking the water." She clapped her hands. "What are you most interested in?"

"You," Griffin said, his voice a low rumble.

Her hands stilled as awareness tingled through her. "I'm still a loser even as a grown woman," she said and sighed. "This is a romantic night away. I should be more interested in getting down and dirty than going fishing. I'm sorry."

"No apologies," he reminded her. "I want to do

whatever makes you happy, although I'll admit I'm plenty interested in down and dirty."

"Me, too," she said in a squeak of breath.

He raised a brow. "More important, I want to spend time with you. And I really want to watch you bait a hook."

"I picked up a container of night crawlers." She climbed out and gave him an exaggerated wink over the hood when he got out, too. "How's that for down and dirty?"

"It's about the sexiest fishing talk I've ever heard."

"Then fishing is first on the agenda."

They unloaded the back of her car, and she showed him around the cozy cabin, unchanged from the last time she'd visited.

The walls were paneled with rough pine, and the artwork consisted of photos of the nearby waterfalls or drawings of wildlife. She'd loved this place when she and her college roommate had stayed here, and her appreciation of it hadn't waned.

"I never really took you for an outdoors woman," Griffin said as he set down his duffel bag and her backpack onto the overstuffed couch.

"I wasn't until I came here," she told him. "That's part of what makes it so special to me. My girlfriend lives in Bend now with a husband and two kids, and her parents have retired to Arizona but they still keep the place. She doesn't make it here often, but she likes it to be in use." She shrugged. "Everyone knows me in Stonecreek, so when I want to get away, I come here."

"Did you bring Trevor?" he asked.

"No," she admitted. "He was more a 'getaway to

the Four Seasons' type of guy. No one knows about this place but you."

"Not even your family?"

She shook her head. "It was easier to tell them I was going to visit my girlfriend and her family on the weekends I came here. They wouldn't understand that I needed time alone."

"I do."

She smiled. "I know, but I'm happy to not be alone this weekend. I need to unpack the groceries before we head out. Will you grab the fishing poles from the shed and I'll meet you down by the lake?"

Griffin studied her for several long moments. "Thank you for sharing this with me."

"Thanks for being the kind of guy who can appreciate it."

He grinned, then headed out the back. Maggie watched him walk toward the shed, the warm summer sun glinting off the glassy water of the lake. How had Griffin Stone become such an important part of her life so quickly? It was difficult to fathom, but there was no denying the hold he had on her heart.

It still worried her that she was headed toward heartbreak. Griffin hadn't mentioned his plans beyond the completion of the tasting room. For all Maggie knew he'd finish the work and be on his way again. Her chest tightened at the thought, but she wasn't ready to ask him outright.

Not today anyway. This was about a perfect getaway, and she was going to enjoy every second of it. She quickly unpacked the supplies, grabbed the box of worms and then followed the flagstone path that led to the lake.

Griffin met her there, a fishing pole in each hand, and for the next hour they fished and talked and enjoyed a beautiful summer day surrounded by nature.

"I give up," he said after Maggie reeled in her eighth fish. "You can outfish me and you look a helluva lot sexier doing it."

Maggie laughed as she tossed the cutthroat trout back into the water. The fish was immobile for a few seconds, then twisted and swam off to join his buddies in the depths of the lake. She wiped her hands on her jeans and made a face at Griffin. "There's nothing sexy about fishing."

"From where I'm standing there most certainly is," he said, leaning his rod against a nearby tree. She handed him her pole, then he laced his fingers with hers and tugged her closer.

"I have fish guts on me." Her words faded into a sigh as he claimed her mouth.

A few moments of kissing, and she was lost in a haze of desire. Griffin nuzzled her neck, and she bit back a moan. His arms twined around her waist, and one hand skimmed along her hip, lighting her skin on fire as it moved.

"Canoeing's next on the list," she said breathlessly, tugging away from his embrace. If he kept touching her like that she was going to rip off his T-shirt and shorts and have her merry way with him on the spot.

His chest rose and fell in uneven breaths, and it made her girlie parts want to break into a tap dance to think that he was as affected by her as she was by him.

"You're definitely focused." He scrubbed a hand along his jaw. "No wonder they elected you mayor. If you do your job with as much efficiency as you spend your downtime…"

She inclined her head, suddenly feeling far too serious. "I was elected because my grandmother told people to vote for me."

"I don't believe that for a minute," Griffin said with a frown. "I've seen you in action, Maggie. I know how much you care about the community."

"I was twenty-five during my first campaign. I had history in the town, but not much in the way of leadership experience. Grammy was determined that I'd be her successor. I didn't even want to run at first. She convinced me I could do it because I'd have her to mentor me along the way."

"Maybe that's how it started…" Griffin took a step closer.

"Nepotism," Maggie muttered. "It started as nepotism."

"You got the votes and you've earned your place in the community. This next election is all you."

She turned and looked out over the clear water. She didn't want reality to intrude on their time in this magical place. It would be waiting for her when she returned to Stonecreek whether she liked it or not.

"I saw the canoe hanging in the shed," Griffin said as if he understood she couldn't talk any more about the election or real life.

They carried the canoe and two paddles to the water's edge. Maggie took off her shoes and rolled up the cuffs of her jeans to her knees, then gasped as she waded into the cold water to climb into the front.

Griffin followed, and they paddled toward the center of the lake, the warm breeze blowing her hair as the water rippled around them.

"I love it here," she whispered but caught herself before she added *I love you* out loud. She couldn't love Griffin Stone. It was too soon. Heck, she and Trevor hadn't said those words to each other until the night he'd asked her to marry him.

She hadn't even realized she felt it until he'd slipped the ring onto her finger. Looking back now, the way she'd felt might have had more to do with expectations than emotions.

"Did you ever consider not returning to Stonecreek?" Griffin asked, and Maggie paused with her paddle dipped into the water.

She glanced over her shoulder at him, then out to the thick forest surrounding the lake. "No," she answered. "It's my home."

"You can make a home wherever you are in the world," he suggested gently. "Places where the past doesn't weigh so heavily on your shoulders."

"I suppose," she agreed, "but I can't imagine living anywhere else. Don't you feel it now that you're back? There's something special about the town. It's home."

"You're the thing that's special to me," Griffin offered.

Suddenly, a fish jumped out of the water, just in front of the boat. Maggie yelped as she released her paddle, watching as it floated just out of reach. "I wasn't expecting that," she said, leaning over the side to grab it.

"Wait," Griffin warned. "You'll tip us."

"We're fine," she assured him. "The canoe is stable."

"Maggie."

"See." Her fingers curved around the paddle's handle, and she rested a hand on the canoe's side as she lifted. She straightened and turned to Griffin, working to keep her feet balanced on either side of the floor of the boat. "You said it yourself—I'm outdoorsy. I'll add more. I'm brave and strong and have no doubts about my ability to lead the town or…" She broke off as the canoe tipped precariously, then bent her knees and managed to maintain her balance.

"Sit down," Griffin said with a grin. "Tell me more about how great you are back on dry land."

"You're not the boss of me." She dipped her paddle in the water and flipped a spray of water at him. "I'm the boss of me," she called out into the clear afternoon, laughing as the truth of the words spilled over her. She raised the paddle over her head and shouted, "I'm queen of my own world."

"You're brave and strong," Griffin shouted back, "and soon to be soaking wet if you don't sit down."

Maggie stuck her tongue out at him, then turned to lower herself back to her seat. At that very moment her footing slipped and she went tumbling into the cold water with a splash.

She surfaced with a small scream, panting to regain the breath stolen from her when she hit the cold water. Swiping her soaking hair away from her face, she met Griffin's amused gaze.

"Don't say *I told you so*," she called to him, swimming toward the paddle that floated a few feet from her.

"I wouldn't dare." She watched as he tugged his T-shirt over his head, and her mouth went dry at the sight of the hard planes of his chest. "I thought you were going to capsize us, not go for a swim." He stood, then immediately dived in, his head emerging from the water a moment later. "You forgot to invite me."

"You're invited," she whispered, mesmerized by the water beading on his chiseled jaw. "But I should have warned you it's freezing here."

He swam closer, encircling her waist with one arm. "All the more reason to head to shore so we can find a creative way to warm up." He kissed her, their legs tangling under water, and as cold as her body felt, heat infused her belly.

She pressed closer, craving more, then laughed as they both began to sink. "I should concentrate on treading water," she said, pulling away reluctantly. "Maybe you should have stayed in the canoe so we wouldn't be stranded in the middle of the lake." She lifted her chin to glance toward the shore. "Are you up for a swim?"

"No need," he answered and, with another kiss, turned and swam toward the canoe. It had drifted several yards away but Griffin reached it in a few long strokes.

Muscles bulged as he expertly lifted himself up and over the side, and Maggie felt her eyes grow wide. She was pretty sure she'd look like a beached whale trying that same maneuver.

He grabbed the paddle and steered toward her. "Take my hand," he told her and a moment later he'd pulled her up and over the side. As she suspected, she landed on her belly in the middle of the canoe, then quickly righted herself. He'd already retrieved her paddle, grinning as he handed it to her.

"You planning to stay seated this time?"

She gathered her hair in her hands and wrung the

water out of it into the boat. "I think so," she said, teeth beginning to chatter.

They paddled to the shore in silence, and as grateful as Maggie was for the bright sunshine, she couldn't wait for a hot shower to truly warm her.

She hopped out as soon as they'd beached the canoe and they carried it up into the grass.

Griffin grabbed his discarded shirt and shrugged it over his head, mischief dancing in his eyes as he took in the sight of her staring at him.

"Would you rather I keep it off?"

"Yes," she blurted, then shook her head. "No. I can't exactly think with all of that—" she waved her hand toward him "—staring me in the face."

He immediately pulled the shirt back over his head. "I don't want you thinking about anything but—" he gestured to his body with a wink "—all of this."

"Good to see that a decade out in the world hasn't changed your opinion of yourself," she told him with a laugh, and he took her hand as they walked toward the house. "But right now we both need a shower."

She led him down the hall toward the bathroom, but he tugged on her fingers until she turned to face him in the narrow space. "You can go first," he told her, releasing her hand.

"I thought this was a together kind of moment," she said, confused by his sudden reluctance.

"I wasn't joking when I said I'm happy just to be hanging out with you. You don't owe me anything."

Maggie appreciated his willingness to be a gentleman, but she was long past the point of wanting that from him. "Don't tell me you're getting cold feet." She moved her hand up his body, running her fingers along the rippled muscles of his abdomen. "We're just getting to the real adventure portion of the weekend."

He sucked in a breath, his eyes darkening. "Every second with you is an adventure, Maggie May." He scooped her up, fusing his mouth to hers, and she twined her legs around his lean hips.

They continued kissing as he maneuvered them into the bathroom and turned on the shower. As steam filled the small space, she took off her shirt, then undid the button at the top of her jeans.

Griffin was already shoving down his shorts and boxers and her whole body stilled as he straightened again. She knew he had a great body but seeing him in his full glory was another thing entirely.

"Wow," she whispered and was rewarded with a slow, sexy smile from him.

"Back at you," he said and hooked one finger under the strap of her bra, tugging it over her shoulder. He moved closer, reaching around her to undo the clasp, and she was unable to do anything but try to catch her breath as the lacy fabric fell from her body.

"Wow, indeed." He dropped to his knees in front of her, and she swallowed, then let out a little moan as he pressed a kiss low on her belly, dragging her jeans and panties down over her hips as he did.

Goose bumps erupted across her skin as his calloused palms skimmed the tops of her thighs.

"You're cold," he said, straightening. He opened the glass shower door, steam billowing out, then stepped in, crooking a finger for her to follow.

Maggie wasn't even sure her legs would hold her at the moment but she managed to squeeze into the tight space behind him.

He shifted so that the water sprayed directly onto her overly sensitive skin, and she closed her eyes, letting sensation wash over her. Griffin ran the bar of soap along her body, taking his time as layers of need built with his touch, and the spray of the water rinsed her. A moment later he knelt and nudged her legs apart. She opened for him, gasping at the first touch of his mouth against her center.

"You don't mess around," she choked out and he gave a wicked chuckle that reverberated along her nerve endings.

He kissed and sucked, nipped and licked until she thought she would lose her mind. Then she did lose her mind, crying out his name as pleasure roared through her, like fireworks erupting inside her body.

Boneless with satisfaction, she pressed against the cool tile wall to keep from sinking to the floor. Griffin took his time trailing kisses up her body until he tenderly took her face in his hands.

"Warmer now?" he asked, and the intensity of his gaze made her feel bold. She reached her hand between them, cupped his hard length and raised her brows.

"Not quite," she answered and felt him grow more rigid in her hand.

With a groan, he pressed his forehead to hers. "Then let's remedy that." He skimmed his hand along her arm, encircling her wrist and tugging it away from him. "But don't make me embarrass myself by losing control too soon."

She kissed the side of his jaw. "I make you lose control?"

"Hell, yeah."

He turned off the water, stepped out of the shower

and pulled two towels from the linen closet, wrapping one around his waist and enveloping her in the second. She looked down at her pink skin peeking out the top and reveled in how amazing this day had already been.

She led him down the hall to the bedroom, cringing a little as she took in the simple quilt covering the bed and outdated furnishings. "It's not exactly five-star accommodations."

"We'll make our own stars."

"You're a romantic at heart, Griffin Stone." She dropped the towel on the braided rug as she slipped between the sheets.

"Hold that thought," he told her and disappeared down the hall. A few seconds later he reappeared, holding a condom wrapper between two fingers.

"Romantic and practical all in one." She grinned. "My type A personality loves it."

"I had a feeling," he said, letting the towel fall from his waist as he opened the wrapper and sheathed himself. She lifted the sheet so he could join her, and her heart sang as he covered her body with his.

He kissed her long and deep and she arched off the bed with pleasure when he finally entered her. They moved together, and Maggie never imagined it could be so good. It was as if their bodies had been made for each other. She let herself be lost in the moment, and when stars rained down on her minutes later, Maggie knew she'd never be the same.

Chapter Fourteen

"Work can wait until Monday."

Brenna shook her head. "Fridays at the office are the hardest to miss. If I pick up my reservation binder and the mail that's come in, I can get caught up tomorrow so I won't be behind on Monday." She flashed a smile. "Feel free to report my dedication to the boss."

"Duly noted," Marcus said with a laugh as he steered his Range Rover down the winding highway that led to Harvest Vineyards Saturday night.

He'd gone to his house to shower and change, then returned to Brenna's apartment, insisting on driving her to Harvest when he hadn't been able to convince her to rest longer. She'd bounced back from her stomach bug quickly, and Ellie was feeling much like her normal self. Brenna's neighbor was at the apartment now, staying in case Ellie woke while they were gone.

Sirens sounded in the distance, and Marcus pulled

onto the shoulder as the noise got louder and lights flashed behind the SUV.

"I wonder what's going on," Brenna murmured when a fire truck and two police cars raced by.

Marcus's brows furrowed as the red and blue lights disappeared around a bend. "Not much out this way other than farms and the vineyard."

"You don't think they were heading to Harvest?" She gripped the side door handle as Marcus accelerated, speeding along the quiet highway.

He made the turn into Harvest, and Brenna gasped as they made their way up the long gravel drive. In the distance she could clearly see the bright glow of flames through the trees that bordered the vineyard's main buildings.

"It's the tasting room building," he whispered and she could hear the dread and disbelief in his voice.

Fear spiked through her, sharp and deep, like a blade driven into her heart. If the fire reached the vines, it would be catastrophic for Harvest.

"What could have caused it?"

Marcus shook his head. "I don't know." He slammed on the brakes, parking at the edge of the clearing. "Stay here."

Before she could respond, he was out of the car and rushing toward the burning building. Brenna lost sight of him for several seconds in the smoke, then let out a sharp cry as bright flames licked the night air.

She got out of the car, coughing when the wind shifted and smoke filled her lungs. "Marcus!" she screamed, then felt an arm wrap around her waist.

"He knows what he's doing," Jana Stone yelled into

Brenna's ear. "Marcus worked as a volunteer firefighter when he first came to Stonecreek. He can help."

Brenna nodded even though she wanted to argue. She didn't care if he'd been fire chief of the world. The thought of Marcus anywhere near that burning building made her blood run cold.

Then she looked at Jana, stark fear etched into her delicate features. Brenna hugged the older woman's shoulders. "They'll contain it. We'll rebuild."

"Again," Jana said with a strangled sob.

It seemed like a lifetime of watching the firefighters battle the blaze, but within an hour the flames subsided.

Relief poured through Brenna as Marcus, along with Trevor, walked toward them, both of their faces covered with soot and sweat.

"Did you get a hold of Griffin?" Trevor asked his mother as she broke away from Brenna to hug him.

"I've texted and left messages. He'll call when he can. Thank heavens no one was hurt." She glanced toward Marcus. "It's like déjà vu."

Marcus shook his head. "It's not a total loss. The back corner is in bad shape, but most of the building is still intact."

"Someone needs to talk to the fire chief," Trevor told Jana and Marcus. "It would be best if we were all there."

"Give me a minute," Marcus murmured.

"Of course," Jana whispered. Before leaving with Trevor, she reached out a hand to squeeze Marcus's arm. "Thank you for everything you did tonight."

"Of course." As Jana and Trevor walked away, he turned to Brenna. "Did you call the sitter and tell her we're delayed? I don't want her to worry when—"

Brenna launched herself at him, wrapping her arms tight around his neck as she kissed him. She felt him stumble back a step before he gained his footing. Then he lifted her into his arms. "I'm a mess, Brenna."

"My mess," she whispered, breathing in the smoky scent that clung to him. "Don't ever scare me like that again."

They held on to each other for several minutes. Brenna couldn't speak with all the emotions swirling through her.

Finally, Marcus set her on the ground, taking her hand between his palms. "I'm fine," he assured her. "You don't have to worry."

"I have every right to worry, stupid man." She swiped at the tears clinging to her lashes. "I'm in love with you."

His strong jaw went slack. "Say that again."

She laughed. "You heard me."

"Yes, but I want to hear you say it again."

"I love you," she whispered and leaned in to brush her lips over his.

"Is it possible I've been waiting my whole life for this moment?" he asked, smoothing a hand over her hair. "I love you, Brenna. I've loved you for so long, sweetheart. If I'd known all it would take to win you was running into a burning building, I would have found one months ago."

She gently swatted his shoulder. "It's not the burning building, and no more of that kind of talk. It's you, Marcus. You're the strongest, kindest man I've ever met and I feel like the luckiest woman on the planet that you chose me."

"I'll choose you a million times over," he whispered.

She laced her fingers with his. "Let's go home," she told him, knowing that as long as they were together she'd found her place in the world.

Griffin watched the light slanting through the window turn from gray to pink as the next morning dawned.

Maggie lay snuggled against him, one arm draped over his chest and her knee pressing into his thigh. As conventional as she was in her waking life, Maggie slept like a crazy woman, constantly tossing and turning with limbs flung in every direction. She even talked in her sleep, mumbling bits of incoherent nonsense throughout the night.

Griffin must have it really bad for this woman because he found even her wild sleeping habits utterly charming. After their first time together yesterday afternoon, they'd made lunch, then played a cutthroat round of Scrabble.

She'd been horrified when he beat her, claiming that a true gentleman would have let her win. He'd countered that a real man knew she had enough brains to beat him without needing to be given the win. So with a gleam in her eye that was exactly what she'd done two more times.

Then he'd carried her up to the bedroom and showed her the exact meaning of her winning word, amorous. They'd spent the evening on the back porch, watching the sun set over the lake as they shared a bottle of wine. He'd told her the ideas he had for the vineyard after talking to Marcus.

Griffin still couldn't quite believe how much he wanted to be involved in Harvest, especially given his determination never to return after that last fight with his father. He wondered what his dad would think of the man he'd become and knew part of what motivated him to stay in Stonecreek was that he still had something to prove.

Too many people remembered the disappointment he'd been to his dad, and he wanted to change that. He wanted to be recognized for how far he'd come in life.

But it was more than that. He'd always loved the land, and there was something satisfying in marking the passage of time by the seasons of the vines.

Maggie was also a big factor in his desire to make their town his permanent home. He smiled as she snuffled, then burrowed more closely against him. He'd told her initially that he wasn't a long-term bet, and she'd still taken him on. Doubt niggled inside his chest, worry that the exact reason she wanted to be with him was because they could have this relationship with no real strings attached.

Now he wanted strings and complications and everything that went with it. He wanted to show her he was there for the long haul. He placed a soft kiss on the top of her head and gingerly got out of bed so as not to wake her.

They weren't expected back in town until tonight, and Griffin was already looking forward to another perfect day with just the two of them.

With the coffee brewing and a pan of bacon sizzling on the stovetop, he walked out onto the back deck, breathing deeply the sultry air of the late-June morning. If only they could stay this way forever, with no issues of family or work to invade this blissful bubble.

A fish jumped in the center of the lake, making him

smile as he thought about Maggie's warrior yell from the previous afternoon. She was so different from the broken, humiliated woman he'd found on the sidewalk that first day back.

He wanted her to always feel as confident as she had in the canoe. The thought that he'd helped her regain her footing filled his chest with a quiet, satisfying pride.

As if he'd summoned her with his thoughts, Maggie appeared at the back door in a white T-shirt and denim shorts. Griffin took one look at her face and a sick pit opened in his stomach.

"What's wrong?"

"We have to go back now," she said, pressing a hand to her chest like she couldn't get a breath.

"Why? What is it?"

"I used the landline to call home this morning to check on Morgan and Ben."

He took a step closer. "Did something—"

"There was a fire," she whispered. "Last night in the tasting room."

Griffin's head swam as he tried to process her words. His world, which minutes earlier had seemed so steady and sure, tilted on its axis, then plummeted to the ground, splintering into a million tiny shards.

"No."

"I'm sorry, Griffin."

The words came to him through a tunnel of denial, hollow and tinny. He was so damn sick of apologies.

"You can use the phone in the living room to call your mom. My dad didn't know how serious the damage was. He heard from—"

"Stop." He held up a hand. How could he call from

here when there was nothing he could do to make it better? He had to see it with his own two eyes. "I need to get back there. Now."

To her credit, Maggie didn't argue or offer platitudes. "I'll grab my keys."

He followed her into the house, only pausing to turn off the stove and unplug the coffeepot before heading toward her car parked out front.

"I'll drive," he told her, and she only hesitated a moment before tossing the keys to him.

The idyllic cabin grew smaller in the rearview mirror, and Griffin had a vile suspicion that his happiness was fading away at the same time.

As soon as they hit the main highway, his phone began to buzz and vibrate, a flurry of missed texts and voice mails coming through.

"We have service," Maggie said, pulling her phone from her purse. "Do you want me to—"

"No." He tightened his grip on the steering wheel. "I want to get home."

Out of the corner of his eye he could see her watching him, fingers squeezed tight around her cell phone. Of course she wanted to find out what had happened at the tasting room, and he knew he sounded crazy. So much anxiety could be alleviated with one quick phone call.

But this unknowing, the teeth-clenching worry, was part of his penance. Whatever caused the fire had happened when he was away. He'd come home for one purpose only—to prove that his dad had been wrong about him. Griffin wanted to make amends for the pain he'd caused his mom all those years ago. To show that he was worthy of being a part of Harvest Vineyards' legacy. Now history was repeating itself, and he hadn't even been there to deal with the disaster.

Had the fire started from a faulty electric wire or something else to do with his work? If he'd been at the barn last night, he might have seen a plume of smoke rise from the tasting room. He might have saved the building the way he hadn't been able to as a teenager.

But he'd been with Maggie, blissfully unaware of anything except his own desires. His father had called him selfish and irresponsible, and maybe those words had been truer than Griffin could stand to admit.

The minutes ticked by as the landscape outside the car went from forest to farmland, the only sound the intermittent chirping from both of their phones. Finally, he pulled into the long, winding drive that led to Harvest.

Heart hammering in his chest and breath coming out in unsteady puffs, he steered the car up the hill toward the tasting room. He felt the weight of Maggie's hand on his arm, but his skin was numb to her touch.

The building came into view, and it was like looking at history come to life all over again. One side of the building remained intact but the southeast corner of the structure was nothing more than blackened boards and a pile of wet ash on the ground.

Several cars were parked in front of the building, and he could see his mother, Marcus and Trevor standing to one side.

He parked and got out of Maggie's car, swallowing back the bile that rose in his throat.

"Was anyone hurt?" he called and felt relief hit him like a tidal wave when his mother shook her head.

"The fire department got it contained within an hour," she reported as he approached.

"Hope you had a great getaway," Trevor said drily. "Once again leaving the rest of us to clean up your mess."

Jana raised a hand before Griffin could respond. "Don't do that, Trevor. This isn't Griffin's mess. The fire would have happened whether he'd been here or not."

Trevor didn't look convinced, and Griffin couldn't blame him. "What caused it?"

Marcus stepped forward so that he was standing between Griffin and Trevor. "They think it was a candle that got knocked over."

"We don't have candles in there," Griffin said. "It's a construction site."

"Someone was trespassing last night," Trevor reported, and Griffin frowned as his brother shifted to look at Maggie. "One of the neighbors saw a red Jeep racing away from the property when he let his dog out before bed. Mom saw the flames just after eleven."

"You think Morgan had something to do with this?" Maggie's voice was high and tight. "That's a bold accusation, Trevor."

"She was here yesterday." Jana wrapped her arms tight around her middle. "I'm sorry, Maggie, but I heard her fighting with the Maren boy when I was taking my evening walk."

"Cole wanted some extra hours so I knew he was here." Griffin moved closer to the fire-ravaged building, reached out to run his fingers over the charred wood.

He glanced back to see his mother nodding. "They

were out here. I didn't think much of it until Fred mentioned the Jeep."

"Morgan didn't cause the fire," Maggie said, stalking forward. "You can't accuse her of this without proof."

"No one's accusing your sister," Marcus said gently.

"But it's suspicious," Trevor added.

"Why would she do this?" Maggie demanded. Griffin turned as she jabbed a finger at Trevor. "You don't want this tasting room to open. I know you want to see your new grand fancy building take its place. Maybe you're trying to frame Morgan."

"You think I want to start a fire on this property?" Trevor threw up his hands. "I'm going to have enough of a PR nightmare dealing with questions about smoke taint after this. What if the fire had spread to the vines? It would have been devastating." He leveled a look at Maggie. "But not to your family."

"Trevor." Marcus's voice was firm. "This isn't helping. Placing blame prematurely isn't going to do any good."

"Whatever." Trevor shook his head. "I've got phone calls to return. We all know who in this community benefits most by hurting Harvest."

He stalked off down the sloping hill toward the main office on the other side of the open courtyard.

Griffin wanted to yell or hit something or walk away. *Run away.* Life had been easier when he wasn't emotionally involved. Right now he couldn't figure out what to feel. Anger…regret…guilt. He'd spent years trying to convince himself he wanted nothing to do with the family business after his father kicked him out. Now he was back but his second chance seemed doomed, much like the happiness he thought he'd found.

Maggie stood in stunned silence as she watched Trevor walk away. Marcus gave her an apologetic smile while Jana seemed to deliberately avoid eye contact.

They couldn't truly believe Morgan had anything to do with the fire? And certainly not that it was some sort of larger scheme to undermine their family business.

Griffin would never stand for that.

Would he?

"We'll rebuild," Jana said gently, putting a hand on Griffin's broad shoulder. He didn't move or react; he just continued to stare at the fire-ravaged building in front of him.

Jana gave him a short hug, then turned and joined Marcus at the edge of the gravel drive. It was clear they were giving Maggie and Griffin a bit of privacy. Maggie only wished she knew how to make this better.

She remembered the first fire at the tasting room. She'd driven her grandmother out here to survey the damage. Harvest had been a fledgling business at that point, and Dave Stone had looked as shell-shocked as Griffin did now when he'd met them on this very same hill.

That was the moment she'd learned that Griffin had left town. It had been a shock, and Dave's voice sounded hollow as he spoke of his careless, reckless son and the damage he'd caused.

Maggie knew how much it meant to Griffin to rebuild this part of his family's property. She walked toward him, aching to offer whatever comfort she could.

"You should go," he said, stepping away as if he couldn't stand to have her too close.

"I want to help," Maggie said, "both as the mayor and as your friend. I know everyone is upset and angry, but you can't possibly believe my family had anything to do with this."

"This isn't about you," he said, his tone biting.

She swallowed, shocked at the insinuation of his words. "I know, Griffin. But it's not about Morgan, either."

"Your sister is a spoiled, self-centered kid." He turned, and the anger in the depths of his eyes felt like poison seeping through her veins—destroying her from the inside out. "I should know because I was one."

"That doesn't mean—"

"You Spencers like to believe you're above everyone else in this town, that you hold some sort of exalted status because of your last name."

"You're not being fair," Maggie insisted. Where was the man who had held her so tenderly through the night? Who laughed at her silly jokes and made her feel like she could accomplish anything? "If Morgan was involved, we'll make it right."

"You can't," he said quietly, then turned and walked away.

Maggie stood there for several moments, too stunned to move. Everything she'd thought they meant to each other was gone. She realized her dreams were castles built from sand, easily toppled by the smallest wave.

"Give him time," Marcus said from behind her.

"Why?" she asked, a tremble in her voice.

"The fire is messing with his head. It puts him back

to where he was ten years ago, and that was a bad time for the whole family. Even if Morgan had something to do with that candle, we all know it was an accident."

"Griffin doesn't seem to," she muttered. "The things he said…that he believes about us."

"He's angry and emotional."

"It's not an excuse." She took a deep breath and squared her shoulders. "I need to talk to my sister. Would you call Cole to get his side of the story?"

Marcus nodded. "We'll figure it out, Maggie."

She swallowed back the tears rising in her throat and walked to her car, wondering if her life would ever feel normal again.

Chapter Fifteen

"They're going to hate me forever," Morgan said from the back seat of their father's Volvo station wagon later that evening.

"They won't hate you," Maggie said, although her stomach knotted in anticipation of the meeting with the Stones.

She'd returned home earlier, numb from the barrage of Griffin's words to find Morgan concerned about the fire at the winery but unaware she'd had any part in it.

Maggie had sat down with Morgan and their dad, explaining what she knew about the circumstances of the blaze. Her sister's face immediately lost all of its color as she began to hyperventilate, realizing that her careless actions had caused the blaze.

When Maggie finally got Morgan calm enough to speak coherently, the girl explained that she had a crush on Cole and had gone to the winery knowing he was working late that evening. She'd set up a romantic tableau in the empty building, complete with candles, a blanket and a bottle of wine she'd stolen from the rack in the kitchen.

It had taken a bit of coaxing to keep Jim Spencer from getting totally sidetracked by the idea that his teenage daughter had wanted to seduce a boy. Maggie managed to pull from Morgan that Cole had rebuffed her advances, leading to a huge argument. Morgan claimed she'd thrown everything she'd brought into her backpack and driven away, but admitted that she might have left behind a candle in her hurry to get away.

Maggie had been unable to reach Jana or Griffin to explain the situation, so they were driving out to the vineyard so Morgan could apologize in person and Jim could work out the details of making restitution for the damages.

If they handled this privately, Maggie hoped they could avoid getting law enforcement involved. But based on Griffin's anger earlier, she wasn't sure what might happen.

Her father parked in front of Jana's house and Maggie put an arm around Morgan's waist as they walked up the front porch steps as somber as a funeral procession.

Jim knocked and a minute later Jana appeared at the door.

"Jim," she whispered like she'd just seen a ghost.

"Hello, Jana." Maggie glanced sharply at her father, something in his tone making her think there was more to his greeting than the two simple words.

He ran a hand over his clean-shaven jaw. "I know

this is a difficult time," he said slowly, "and we wouldn't be here if it wasn't important."

She looked from him to Maggie and then Morgan, the corners of her mouth dipping slightly. "Come in."

Maggie had been in the Stone family home countless times, but today she took in the expensive furnishings, the framed black-and-white photos, everything neat as a pin and so different from her cozy, cluttered family home.

"Have a seat," Jana offered, gesturing to the damask-covered sofa and two coordinating side chairs arranged in the living room.

Maggie's father took a seat on the far side of the couch, and Maggie ushered Morgan next to him before sitting. She tugged on her sister's hand when Morgan continued to stand, but the girl ignored her.

Jana clasped her hands in front of her stomach, looking as formal as the decor. "May I get anyone a glass of wat—"

"I'm so sorry," Morgan blurted, then covered her mouth with a hand as her shoulders shook uncontrollably. "It was an accident. The candle... I didn't mean..."

"It's all right, dear," Jana said gently, tension slipping from her petite frame. She came forward and reached a hand out to pat Morgan's arm. "Cole explained everything. We know what he did."

Maggie straightened as her sister went perfectly still. "Cole didn't do anything," Morgan whispered.

"What did he tell you, Jana?" Maggie asked.

Jana closed her eyes, dragged in what looked to be a calming breath, then opened her eyes again. "He said he invited you to the property and when you weren't receptive to his advances, he got angry. I believe he didn't realize he'd knocked over the candle after your argument." She flashed a wistful smile. "I was young once so I remember how emotions can sometimes get the best of us."

"That isn't how it happened." Morgan looked between Maggie and their father, who stood and paced to the window, massaging a hand over the back of his neck. "I came out here on my own."

"Are you protecting him, Morgan?" Jim demanded, turning around and gripping the back of the tufted side chair. "Did that boy try to take advantage of you?"

"No," Morgan insisted. "Maggie, you know Cole. He isn't like that."

"Don't worry," Jana assured them. "We're not going to press charges. Griffin…" Her voice trailed off and she sighed and then continued, "Griffin appreciates his honesty. Obviously, this isn't the first time teenage emotions have had devastating repercussions on our vineyard."

"I left the candle burning," Morgan said, her voice rising. "I got mad and stormed off and forgot it. Cole didn't do anything."

"He's going to work to pay off the cost of the repairs," Jana continued as if Morgan hadn't spoken. "It might take a while, but Griffin had no reservations about giving him a second chance."

"Maggie." Morgan turned, disbelief and guilt warring in her eyes. "You can't let him take the blame for this."

Dumbfounded at the boy's sacrifice, Maggie turned to Jana, who held up a hand. "He warned us Morgan would defend him this way." Her smile was gentle. "You've raised a good girl, Jim. You should be proud."

"No," Morgan whispered. "Dad, no."

"I'll pay for the reconstruction," Maggie's father said, stepping around the chair, closer to Jana. "I don't know what happened here last night, but that boy shouldn't have to bear the responsibility of it."

Jana's eyes widened. "But he said—"

"I know what Cole told you, and I know what Morgan explained to us. But only the two of them know the truth."

"Dad," Morgan said, her voice a low whine. "I'm not lying. I promise."

"Teenage promises," he murmured, never taking his eyes off Jana. "You and I both know how well those can be trusted."

Maggie frowned as Jana drew in a sharp breath. What did she not understand about her father's history with Griffin's mother?

"I'll have Griffin contact you once he has figures on what it will take to fix the damage. I can't guarantee Cole will appreciate your generosity…"

"He doesn't need to. They both have some responsibility in this. I'll talk to Griffin about how Morgan can do her part."

"Fine."

They stared at each other for several seconds, and Maggie wished she could see her father's face. When he finally turned, his gaze was unreadable.

"Let's go," he said and Maggie wondered where her absentminded father had gone. In his place stood a man who looked ready to go to war for or against his younger daughter. Maggie couldn't quite decide which.

Morgan looked like she wanted to argue, but Maggie took her hand and led her from the room.

As soon as they were out of the house, Morgan wrenched away from her grasp. "This isn't fair."

"No more from you," Jim said. "You *will* turn this around, Morgan. You've been given a chance here."

"What about Cole?"

Their father narrowed his eyes. "That boy is not my responsibility."

"Dad," Maggie and Morgan said at once.

Jim blew out a long breath. "Fine. I'll make sure Griffin understands that Cole is trying to take the blame for something he didn't do. I won't let anything bad happen to him."

With a soft cry, Morgan threw her arms around their father's waist and burrowed into his chest. "Thanks, Daddy," she whispered.

Maggie met his gaze and nodded, her nerves settling at the knowledge that one section of her life was slowly getting back on track.

It was nearly midnight before she made it back down to the cabin to pack up from earlier. Her father had suggested she wait until the following day, but Maggie knew she wouldn't sleep tonight and so welcomed the distraction.

Her heart stuttered as her headlights picked up the outline of Griffin's Land Cruiser already parked in the driveway.

The lights were on in the cabin, and she could see him in the kitchen, moving back and forth from the refrigerator to the counter. She hadn't bothered to lock the door when they'd rushed out this morning.

She wanted to put the car into Reverse, to speed away and avoid the confrontation she knew was inevitable. But this was her mess to clean up as much as his, so she parked and walked up the steps to the front door, trying to keep her heartbeat steady.

He glanced up as she entered the kitchen.

"I can take care of this," she said, wishing he would leave without speaking.

"I made you hurry out this morning." He picked up a pan from the drainer next to the sink and began to wipe it dry. "It's the least I can do."

She crossed her arms over her chest, hating the implication of his words. "You didn't make me do anything."

One side of his mouth curved. "Good to know."

"I'm sorry about the tasting room," she said quietly, moving forward to put the rest of the supplies into the cardboard box he'd set on the counter.

"We'll rebuild."

"My dad and I brought Morgan over to talk to your mom today." Maggie shouldn't have brought her sister into the conversation. There was enough tension between Griffin and her without adding more. But she had to address it.

He inclined his head. "Your dad left me a message."

She waited for him to say more.

"It wasn't Cole's fault," she whispered when he remained silent.

"I know."

"But Morgan isn't all of the things you accused her of being. My family doesn't have it out for yours that way."

He shrugged. "If you say so."

"Do you really believe that?"

"I don't know what to believe at this point," he admitted.

"Me, neither," she agreed. "It's all so complicated."

"Complicated isn't really my thing."

"I understand."

"Do you?"

"No, but I get what you're telling me. You can't be with me."

"I want to."

"Sure." It felt like a boot was stomping across her chest.

"I'm sorry," he whispered and then closed his eyes. "Damn, I hate apologies."

"I need you to leave," she said.

"Maggie."

"Please, Griffin." She hated that her voice broke on his name. "Please," she repeated, looking down at the floor, unable to watch him walk away.

Listening to his footsteps and then the front door opening and closing was bad enough. She gripped the edge of the counter, willing herself to stay standing as tears poured down her cheeks. This moment would not break her. She'd been through too much to be felled by an aching heart now.

But she wouldn't force back the tears. She needed to feel everything if she had any chance of moving forward. She walked through the cabin, packing her belongings and loading them into her car. Griffin had packed his stuff and done most of the cleaning before she arrived, so once her bags were in the trunk, she turned off the lights, locked the front door and headed back home.

As she entered her father's darkened house, a light flipped on in the living room, revealing her dad in the big leather recliner that had been his official chair since she was a girl.

"You doing okay?" he asked gently.

"No." She dropped her backpack to the hardwood floor. "Griffin was at the cabin."

"Things didn't go well, I take it?"

She leaned against the door frame. "Spencers and Stones aren't meant to mix."

"I could have told you that," he said with a quiet chuckle.

"Why didn't you?"

He gave an apologetic shake of his head. "I never thought you needed my advice. You were always so sure of yourself, Maggie. You and your grandmother never seemed to have doubts about anything."

"I have plenty of doubts," she admitted, "and Grammy is at the heart of most of them."

"I'm a lousy father," Jim said with a sigh.

"You did good today."

"Thanks, girl. But I want to do good for you, too."

"Was I elected mayor only because of Grammy?" she asked.

Her father smiled. "No, despite what your grandmother would have you believe."

"I want to lead this town, all of it."

"You can," he assured her.

"But if I go against Grammy, will it cost me the election?"

"I hope not. I guarantee you've got my vote."

"Thanks, Dad," she whispered and smiled. One way